"I've decided to take you up on your offer.

"But before I say yes, I want you to know that I was engaged once before. My fiancé left town the night before our wedding and broke my heart. I can't take that type of heartbreak again, so know this...I most likely will never love you. At least not the way a wife should love her husband." She breathed out heavily. "There, I've said it. So if you don't want to marry me after hearing this, I understand."

Josiah's heart went out to Anna Mae for her loss. But still it felt as if a huge weight had been lifted off his shoulders. She didn't want a real marriage, either. This was perfect. He laughed.

"You're happy I won't ever love you?"

"Yes. I want to be friends with you, but I can never love you the way I did my first wife."

"Oh, I see." Anna Mae nodded. "But I'd rather no one else knows that this is a marriage of convenience."

He nodded in turn. Anna Mae laughed. "Good, then we can get married whenever you're ready."

Was it his imagination or did her laugh sound forced?

Rhonda Gibson
and
Sherri Shackelford

A Convenient
Christmas Bride
&
The Rancher's
Christmas Proposal

LOVE INSPIRED
INSPIRATIONAL ROMANCE

Recycling programs
for this product may
not exist in your area.

LOVE INSPIRED®
INSPIRATIONAL ROMANCE

ISBN-13: 978-1-335-45675-5

A Convenient Christmas Bride and The Rancher's Christmas Proposal

Copyright © 2021 by Harlequin Books S.A.

A Convenient Christmas Bride
First published in 2015. This edition published in 2021.
Copyright © 2015 by Rhonda Gibson

The Rancher's Christmas Proposal
First published in 2015. This edition published in 2021.
Copyright © 2015 by Sherri Shackelford

This edition published by arrangement with Harlequin Books S.A.

For questions and comments about the quality of this book, please contact us at CustomerService@Harlequin.com.

Love Inspired
22 Adelaide St. West, 40th Floor
Toronto, Ontario M5H 4E3, Canada
www.LoveInspired.com

Printed in U.S.A.

CONTENTS

Rhonda Gibson lives in New Mexico with her husband, James. She has two children and three beautiful grandchildren. Reading is something she has enjoyed her whole life, and writing stemmed from that love. When she isn't writing or reading, she enjoys gardening, beading and playing with her dog, Sheba. You can visit her at rhondagibson.net. Rhonda hopes her writing will entertain, encourage and bring others closer to God.

Books by Rhonda Gibson

Love Inspired Historical

The Marshal's Promise
Groom by Arrangement
Taming the Texas Rancher
His Chosen Bride
A Pony Express Christmas
The Texan's Twin Blessings
A Convenient Christmas Bride
Baby on Her Doorstep

Saddles and Spurs

Pony Express Courtship
Pony Express Hero
Pony Express Christmas Bride
Pony Express Mail-Order Bride
Pony Express Special Delivery

Visit the Author Profile page
at LoveInspired.com for more titles.

A CONVENIENT CHRISTMAS BRIDE

Rhonda Gibson

Humble yourselves therefore under the mighty hand of God, that he may exalt you in due time: Casting all your care upon him; for he careth for you.
—*1 Peter 5:6–7*

To God be the glory and to James,
who continues to believe in me.

Chapter One

Granite, Texas
October 1887

Sheriff Josiah Miller peered out his cabin window into the darkness, searching for a plausible explanation for the uneasiness shivering down his spine. What had set off the warning bells in his body?

His twin daughters snuggled deeply under their covers, sleeping soundly on this cold winter's night, and for that he was thankful. No worries on that front because he'd just checked on them. So what accounted for the dull disquiet that had him pacing the floor, looking out the window every few seconds?

They were in the midst of a fierce snowstorm and it was only October. Maybe that's what had him skittish as an unbroken mare. Signs pointed to a harsh winter. He dreaded it. Lonely nights out in the cold could work on a man's mind. He shrugged his shoulders in mock resignation.

Dratted snow! He blamed the white stuff for his dismal thoughts.

Josiah stopped pacing midstride and slowly turned back to the window. Snow swirled about, creating almost zero visibility. In spite of the fire that burned in the fireplace, he shivered, not only from the cold pressing against the glass but from the banshee-like wails of the wind.

On nights like this he missed Mary the most. If she were alive, Mary would be humming and the aroma of fresh baked bread would draw him to the kitchen. How often he'd slipped up behind her, slid his arms around her waist, kissing her, tickling her, till she cut him a slice. She'd scold him for his impatience, but always with a twinkle in her eyes that belied her words. She knew how to make a home cozy and warm; a place where he longed to be. Now, when it was too late, Josiah realized how much he missed her and the home they'd shared.

Perhaps he should begin looking for a wife so that his twin daughters wouldn't have to grow up motherless. Raising them alone was hard. Finding a babysitter even harder. They needed a mother's love and he needed help.

Shadowy movement beside the barn caught his attention. Josiah focused intently on the area. There. Right at the front edge by the door something moved again. His eyes weren't deceiving him. What in the world could that be?

He cupped his hands around his face and pressed his nose against the cold windowpane. His breath fogged up the glass. Josiah wiped away the condensation. Could it be an animal? Had his horse gotten out of the barn into the snow and cold? Josiah grunted, tempted to leave the beast to his own devices, but he wasn't a coldhearted man and knew it was a disgruntled thought he'd never act upon. A lawman's horse was as important to him as his right arm.

At the door, he eased his warm feet out of his slippers and into heavy boots. He pulled his fur jacket off the coatrack, thrust his arms inside and then put on gloves. Pulling his hat down tight on his head and wrapping a long woolen scarf around his face, Josiah stepped out into the freezing, swirling snowstorm.

Gripping the rope he'd tied from the rail of the porch to the barn door, Josiah gave a little tug. It held fast. That was reassuring. Some men got lost in a storm like this and died feet away from their barn or house. Josiah had no intentions of dying like that.

After he'd inched away from the house, he glanced over his shoulder. He could barely see the light from his front window. His chest bumped into something and he turned back around. "Well, I'll be."

A small mule waited patiently, head down, nose almost touching the snow. "So it was you instead of my faithful horse that I saw out here." Josiah reached out and touched her nose. Warm air filled his glove. "Poor thing, must be half frozen," he muttered.

A soft thud sounded beside the animal as its rider fell into the snow. Josiah eased around the mule to see who it had been carrying. Yards of dark fabric covered the woman's legs. A scarf much like his own covered her face. He reached down and lifted her out of the snow.

The woman sagged against his chest. In a weak voice

that sounded low and scratchy she moaned, "Please, take care of my mule."

He couldn't make out her face, but her voice sounded familiar. Her wet dress, slightly frozen in places, pressed against his coat and he felt no warmth from her whatsoever. Big brown eyes beseeched him, glazed with what he could only assume was a fever. "Now don't you go fretting, ma'am. I'm not one to leave an animal out in this storm."

Josiah looked to the mule. He could take care of only one of them at a time. "Sorry, lil' feller. I'll be back as soon as I get your mistress settled." He weighed his options for a few moments, then decided there was nothing for it but to place the woman over his shoulder like a sack of potatoes. He had to have a hand free to hold on to the line and be guided back to the house. Expecting a fight, he immediately knew her condition to be serious when she only groaned slightly. He grabbed the rope in his gloved hand and headed back to the house.

His thoughts bumped together as he worked to get there. What a night for being out in this weather. Where had she been going? And why couldn't it have waited until after the storm. The woman slumped limply against him as she lost consciousness.

Out of breath from his battle through the snowdrifts, bearing the slight weight of the woman, Josiah gave a sigh of relief to find the bottom step of the porch. He pulled her closer to his chest and carried her the rest of the way to the front door.

Wet clothes added weight to her body. In the light from his window he could see that her hood had fallen back and brown hair spilled out over the fabric. Deep brown eyes fluttered open for a brief moment, causing Josiah to gasp as recognition gripped him.

"Anna Mae?"

"Josiah." His name whispered across her lips as she slipped back into unconsciousness.

His name, spoken in a weak and tremulous whisper, was the sweetest sound he'd heard in a long time. As long as she could speak, he had a chance to save her. His heart leaped in his chest with fear as her breathing became raspy. Josiah pushed the door open and carried her to the couch. He laid her down gently. Now what was he going to do?

"I suppose I should get that wet cloak off of you. I'm sure you'll feel much better once that is removed." Whiskers scratched his palm as he rubbed his jaw.

Carefully, he shifted Anna Mae up and about until he was able to remove the heavy, wet cloak. He lowered her. Brown hair that he'd only seen up in a bun now cascaded about her shoulders in a soft curtain of silk.

Anna Mae Leland was the town's schoolteacher and a good friend of his sister-in-law, Emily Jane Barns. What had she been doing out in this weather? He'd known her only a few months but Josiah believed her to be a sensible woman. So why was she traveling in a blizzard? And where had she been going?

He walked to the door and looked out at the shadow of the mule. His gaze moved back to Anna Mae. Both of them needed immediate care, both needed warmth.

Josiah tossed more wood on the fire and then went into the bedroom where his girls slept. He pulled blankets from the chest at the foot of the bed and carried them back to her. Should he try to make her more comfortable by getting her into dry clothes? Or leave her in the wet dress? The thought came that she needed another woman, not him. He tucked her tightly within the blankets.

Unsure what to do for her next, Josiah decided to take care of the mule. He opened the door and stepped out into the raging blizzard. He'd been in enough storms in his lifetime to know that this one was going to be long and hard.

His gaze moved back to the window, which offered light and comfort. What on earth was he going to do about the woman resting on his couch?

For the first time since her arrival at the farm, Anna Mae sat at the kitchen table with the Miller family. It had been all she could do to walk the short distance from the bedroom where she'd been for over a week.

The day before, her fever had finally broken, and she'd awakened and explained to the sheriff that she'd been lured out into the storm by Bart, her ten-year-old student. She'd told him it was probably just a prank but still hoped he'd check on the boy. Josiah assured her that the boy was probably home before the storm ever hit. She latched on to that small ray of hope, trying hard to be very thankful.

But now she had other problems. She traced the outline of a knot in the wooden table. "What am I going to do? As soon as word gets out that I've been here throughout the entire storm, the school board will fire me for sure." She rested her arms on the tabletop and dropped her head on them. Weakness overwhelmed her. Her throat still hurt, but not like it had.

"Here, drink this." Josiah placed a hot cup in front of her.

She raised her head. Rose and Ruby, the sheriff's two-year-old twins, sat on their side of the table motionless, watching the adults. Each held a handful of eggs and a piece of bread.

Josiah dished scrambled eggs onto a plate and set it before her. "I don't see what the fuss is about, Annie. We'll just explain what happened and everything will be fine." He returned to the stove.

"Eat?" Rose asked hopefully.

"Not yet. Let me get my plate and we'll be ready," Josiah answered, pouring coffee into another mug and bringing it and his plate to the table.

Anna Mae tried to think of the children as chaperones, but didn't believe the school board would go for that. No, she was doomed.

"Please don't call me Annie, Sheriff Miller. And I really don't think they are going to care what my excuse is. They aren't going to approve of my staying here with you for so long." Anna Mae sighed. She'd asked him not to call her Annie before but it didn't do much good. He seemed to enjoy teasing her.

The big sheriff shrugged his shoulders and sat down at the table, his plate heaped with eggs, bacon and bread. "I believe you are wrong. All they have to do is take one look at you and know you've been sick."

Did she look that bad? Anna Mae tucked a stringy hank of hair behind her ear. Sadly, he was right. She knew without looking into a mirror that she was a sight.

"Now don't go fussin'. All I meant was that you've lost weight and the luster in your eyes hasn't quite come back. If you add that to your scratchy sounding voice, well there's no mistaken you've been under the weather."

"Eat now?" Rose pleaded, looking from one adult to the other.

Josiah's gaze moved to the girls. They sat poised at the table just as they'd been moments ago. "We best pray before these two get tired of waiting and start throwing those eggs at us to get our attention." A wide grin spread over his face just before he bowed his head to pray.

Anna Mae couldn't concentrate on his prayer. Just like before, she was out of a job and it wasn't even her fault. If Bart hadn't lured her out into the storm, she would be home in her room at the boardinghouse.

As soon as he said amen, Anna Mae asked, "Did you go check on Bart?"

Josiah laid his fork down. "Haven't had a chance to but I'm sure the boy is fine. If he weren't they would have sent out a search party for him, and I'd have been the first one they came to for help. Why don't you tell me how that happened again?"

Anna Mae sighed. "I was at the school grading papers when Bart came running inside. He asked me to go with him into the woods. He said Miles Carter, one of the smaller boys in my class, was hurt and I was the closest adult who could help him." She took a sip of her coffee.

"Go on." Josiah helped the girls with their meals and ate his breakfast at the same time. Her heart went out to him. She would have been dead now if he hadn't helped her. He already had so much to do and he'd stayed with her during the worst of her illness. His eyes were surrounded by dark circles, showing his lack of sleep since her arrival.

She focused on her story. "He'd already brought the little mule to the front of the school so we left almost immediately. At first I believed him, but the deeper we went into the woods the more I began to doubt his story. I knew Bart was still sore that he had to stay in at lunch and sweep up the school, but I really hadn't thought he'd do spite work."

"Spite work?" The sheriff turned quizzical eyes on her.

"That he'd leave me alone." A deep sigh slipped from between her lips. "I was wrong." Anna Mae set her cup down and reached for her fork.

He looked up and smiled. "Well, no matter what brought you here, it's nice to see you up and sitting at my table, Annie." A wicked twinkle entered his eyes.

She almost corrected him again, but he'd saved her life so she decided he could call her whatever he wanted to. "It's nice to be here, Sheriff Miller."

He bent over to pick up the bread Rose had dropped. When he straightened he asked, "Then what happened?"

"Bart distracted me by saying he thought Miles was directly in front of us. While I focused on the spot where he pointed, Bart took off, leaving me alone in the woods. I never even saw him go." Anna Mae felt foolish, but continued on. "The sky had become overcast and I couldn't get my bearings. I think I wandered around at least an hour before it started to rain, and then the rain quickly turned to snow. It got so bad I couldn't see two feet in front of me, so I decided to give the mule her lead, praying she'd take me back to the schoolhouse."

Anna Mae shivered. "I was so cold and wet." Just the memory of the sharp pain in her chest as she breathed in the icy air sent another shiver down her spine.

"It's a good thing your mule found my place. I hate to think what would have become of you," Josiah stated, before dishing more food into his mouth.

"Thank you for saving my life."

He held her gaze as he swallowed and then said, "That mule out there saved your life. All I did was keep the fever down and get a little water in ya. Now eat up." He waved his fork toward the plate in front of her. "You tell the school board what you just told me and I'm sure everything will be fine."

The eggs scratched as they went down, and Anna Mae turned her head to cough. The cough seemed to come and go, but at least her chest no longer burned from the pain of it.

Once the coughing subsided, she asked, "Do you think it's safe to go to town today?"

He shook his head, gently wiping eggs off the side of Ruby's mouth. "Not with a wagon. That rainstorm we got right before the snow turned into a layer of ice. Besides, it's best to stay out of the cold air and let that cough heal."

"But the longer I stay here…" She left the words hanging in the air.

"Nothin' to do for it. I can't have you and the girls out in this weather." He sipped his coffee.

He was right. If it were just her safety, Anna Mae felt sure she'd risk going out. But it wasn't just hers, it was the twins', too. She sighed.

"If you need something, I can take Roy and go out."

"Roy?"

A grin split the sheriff's face. "Yeah, my horse."

"You named him Roy?" Anna Mae felt a chuckle rise in her sore throat. The big black gelding Josiah rode looked like anything but a Roy. Her papa had a business associate named Roy who was old, bent over at the waist, and sported a bald spot right in the center of his hair. Other than their names, there were no similarities between the fine-looking horse and the balding old man.

"Now don't go makin' fun of Roy, he's seen me through some rough weather. I believe he could get me to town without too many mishaps."

The thought of Josiah out on ice and snow with his horse slipping and possibly breaking a leg didn't appeal to her at all. She shook her head. "No, I don't need anything. Just wanted to get back before the school board missed me." She spooned another bite of egg into her mouth, worry making the food flavorless. She brushed crumbs from her lap. If the board were to see her wearing Josiah's shirt and long johns, she'd be in more than a heap of trouble. She'd be run out of town on a rail.

Thankfully, his shirt covered her to right below the knees, but still her cheeks flushed every time she remembered struggling into the clothes that belonged to the sheriff.

Shortly after she'd arrived, Josiah had insisted she put on dry clothes. She'd been shaking so badly from the cold and the fever that consumed her body that it had taken much longer than normal for her to change. Concerned, he'd threatened to come in and help her. She'd managed to get them on before he'd made good on his threat, but was so exhausted she'd fallen into a deep sleep. Hopefully, she'd be able to change back into her own dress right after breakfast.

Josiah pushed away from the table, taking his and the twins' plates with him. The little girls were covered in egg and wet crumbs. "Maybe, if the sun comes out full force, we'll be able to get to town in a couple of days." He raked the scraps into the slop bucket and carried it to the back porch to be thrown out later.

Anna Mae offered, "I can help you with that." She pushed away from the table and immediately felt the weakness in her limbs.

"Nope, you are just recovering." He walked over to her and placed a hand under her arm. "I'll help you to the couch and you can rest there until you need to return to bed. I don't want you to come down with another fever."

Tears filled her eyes as he walked beside her into the sitting room. Josiah had been so nice to her. He'd saved her life and then tried to make her comfortable during the worst of her sickness. Anna Mae vowed that during the time she had to stay here, she'd offer her help and make herself useful.

"Why don't you bring the girls in here and I'll read to them," she said, hoping he'd at least let her help out in that way.

"Now that's a right nice idea. Give me a minute to get them cleaned up and I'll put them in the corral." He waited until she seated herself on the sofa, then handed her a small quilt before he returned to the kitchen.

Anna Mae stared into the fire, disturbing thoughts troubling her. Would she have a job when this was all over? If not, where would she go? Would this town be as hard on her as her hometown had been? Fears and past hurts ran deep within her. How she hated this feeling of uncertainty. She'd just lately felt secure enough to put down roots. As if she finally belonged. Now her very livelihood could be decided by others known for judging harshly.

Without warning, Anna Mae remembered the shame she'd felt when her ex-fiancé, Mark Peters, had left her standing at the altar. She'd given up her teaching job to marry him. She'd thought he loved her, but he'd left the night before their wedding and had a note delivered at the hour of the marriage ceremony. Fresh tears filled her eyes, for just thinking of it shattered her. Not because she'd loved Mark to the point of distraction, but because he'd made a laughingstock of her. The whole town had shaken their heads and secretly called her a fool. With her teaching job no longer available, Anna Mae had done the only thing she felt she could do. She'd answered Levi Westland's ad for a mail-order bride.

But thankfully, God knew that Levi wasn't the man for her, and had sent Millie Hamilton to be his new bride. Anna Mae had breathed a sigh of relief the day Levi announced his intention to marry Millie, confirming in Anna Mae's heart that she was meant to be a schoolteacher and a spinster.

"I wish you'd stop worrying about the school board. Whatever comes, we'll face it together and I'll make sure that they understand." Josiah placed the girls into what he'd called the corral, made of boards and fabric, and stood to smile at her.

Lost in thoughts of the past, Anna Mae needed a

moment to reorient herself. She longed to trust in Josiah's assurances, but she was reluctant to place her faith with a man again.

Chapter Two

Josiah stood in the kitchen and listened to Anna Mae's soft voice as she read to the girls from the book of Genesis. He knew the girls didn't understand the story of Adam and Eve, but they looked up at Anna Mae with sincere interest. He dried the last dish and laid the towel to the side.

His boots made a soft clomping sound as he walked across the floor. He knelt down beside her chair and touched her hand. It felt soft under his rough fingers. She turned her big brown eyes upon him. "Would you mind terribly if I go check on Roy and the mule?"

A soft smile graced her chapped lips, reminding him that she needed to drink more water. "Not at all. I'm sure they would enjoy breakfast and a little attention."

He nodded and stood. Josiah reached for Ruby and touched the soft black curls on her head. He glanced between her and Rose. "You girls be good for Annie, ya hear?"

"Go," Ruby said as she worked to stand up.

"Not this time, little one. It's too cold out there for little girls." He leaned over and kissed her soft cheek.

Rose scrambled for him. She smacked her lips, wanting her kisses, too. "Tisses!" she demanded.

He laughed and scooped both girls up into his arms. Kissing them both all over their faces sent them into squeals of delight. Josiah's love for the girls grew stronger every day. They were changing so much as they got older.

Anna Mae's soft laughter joined in. He looked over at her and saw that her face looked a little pale. Had she overdone it this morning? Possibly. Maybe now wasn't a good time to leave her alone with the twins. He stood to his full height and looked down on her.

As if she could read his mind, Anna Mae said, "You better hurry and take care of the animals. We'll be fine until you return."

Josiah nodded and quickly set the girls back into the corral. He pulled on his coat and scarf. Cold air blasted into the house as he hurried out the door.

Snow glistened on the ground and the early morning sun rays added to the brightness. He shielded his eyes and exhaled, his breath forming a cloudy vapor. Thankfully, the snow had stopped falling. He followed the trail to the barn, the cold air stinging his face.

When he opened the door, warmth greeted him along with the scent of hay and dust. Roy snorted from his corner of the barn and the little mule hailed him with a loud bray. "I hear ya, you ornery beasts."

Josiah hurried to give the animals water, grain and hay. As quickly as he could, he mucked out their stalls and laid fresh hay. A glance at his pocket watch told him he'd been out of the house for close to two hours. Giving the horse and mule a final pat, Josiah started the trek back to the house. He glanced up at the sky. In another hour or so the sun would sit directly over the house. That would help heat the place up a bit.

Lord willing, in the spring he could add another fireplace; or maybe he'd just buy one of those new-fangled stoves he'd seen advertised down at the dry goods store. He figured Anna Mae would like that. He reined in his thoughts immediately. What in the world was he thinking? She wouldn't be here in the spring. A woman like Anna Mae was looking for a love relationship, and he wasn't. He didn't want love. It hurt too much when the one you loved died.

For all he knew, he might not be here, either. He'd thought about getting a house in town but didn't want to seem ungrateful to William, his brother-in-law. After all, he'd been the one to buy the orchard. William might not like the idea of him moving to town and leaving it vacant. When he got to the front porch, Josiah stomped as much snow from his boots as possible before entering the house.

His gaze roved around the room and he saw the twins napping in their corral and Anna Mae asleep on the couch. He walked over and gently, so as not to wake her, covered her with a quilt.

Josiah reached out and touched Anna Mae's forehead. Cool. He stared down into her lovely face. Dark lashes rested against her pale cheeks. Her dark hair feathered about the pillow. Anna Mae Leland truly was beautiful.

He grinned as he remembered the first time he'd

called her Annie. She'd flared up like a hissing cat. That little bit of spitfire seemed to rouse her to get stronger. Truth be told, he preferred Annie over Anna Mae. The name seemed softer. It suited her better, so he'd continued to tease her with the name. Now it just felt natural.

Josiah made a mental note not to call her Annie once their lives returned to normal. It was a little too informal for the schoolteacher position that she held. Would the school board fire her? He took a deep breath. He'd only wanted to help her, keep her safe, and he may have ruined this sweet woman's life. It couldn't be helped. There was no way that he would have turned her away, sick and in the middle of a blizzard.

Josiah caressed her cheek with the back of his hand. He cared about her. How could he not? For the past week, he'd worried over her health and at times her life. Did Anna Mae realize how close she'd come to death?

He shook off the worry he felt for her even now and, with a sigh, turned to the kitchen for a hot cup of coffee.

If he could save her job and reputation, he would. If not, well, he'd cross that bridge when he got there.

Anna Mae woke to childish giggles and the smell of frying ham. She pushed herself up and looked about. Josiah stood at the stove and the girls played in their corral.

How long had she slept? Her gaze went to the window. The sun still shone through the glass, and she sighed, thankful she hadn't slept the whole day away.

"I see you are awake." Josiah cradled a cup of coffee in his hands and rested a hip against the sturdy kitchen table. "Did you have a good nap?"

Her throat felt so dry, Anna Mae couldn't speak. She tried to swallow but found she couldn't do that, either. She nodded.

He must have sensed her need because Josiah walked to the stove and poured her a cup of coffee. He held it out to her. "Take small sips. It might burn a little going down."

She took the cup and did as he instructed. The warm liquid both felt good and hurt. It was just what she needed to be able to speak. "Thank you." The two words sounded scratchy as she forced them out of her tight throat.

"You're welcome." He sat down beside her on the couch.

"It's kind of early for dinner, isn't it?" she asked. "Or are you making a late lunch?"

Josiah laughed. "Trying to get a head start on dinner tomorrow night. My wife used to make the best ham and beans. I thought I'd try my hand at it, but I think I'm doing something wrong." He sighed dramatically. "Mine never tastes like hers."

"Is that why you're frying ham now?" Anna Mae asked, looking toward the stove.

He nodded. "But for the life of me, I can't seem to get it right."

She grinned. "That's because you don't fry the ham first. Do you have a ham hock that hasn't been cooked?" she asked.

"I'm sure there is one in the root cellar. Why?"

Anna Mae swung her legs off the couch. "Because that's what you should put into your beans." She croaked hoarsely as she spoke.

"Now, Annie, don't go thinking I wanted you to get up and cook." He stood also. "Because that wasn't my plan."

She smiled over her shoulder. "Go get the ham hock and we can have boiled beans and fresh bread for dinner tomorrow." Anna Mae watched him slip into his coat and scarf, then head out the back door.

In the bedroom she hurried out of his clothes and into her dress. It felt good to be back in her own clothes, and Anna Mae realized that if she must stay with the Millers, she needed to give Josiah his bedroom back.

She eased her feet into her stockings, thankful for their warmth. As she made the bed Anna Mae made a decision. No one she'd ever known liked feeling beholden to someone, and neither did she. If she could pull her weight around here it would benefit them both. She'd look for other ways to help and right now she needed to get the beans on.

She returned to the kitchen, pausing to check on the twins, stealing a kiss from each one. Worn-out from everything she'd done, Anna Mae sat at the kitchen table and began sorting the dry beans, making sure not one black rock remained in the mix. She could almost taste tomorrow's meal.

She heard Josiah before she saw him. He stomped the snow from his feet, then entered the house, triumphantly waving a ham hock in his hand. "I found it, took a while, but we now have meat." He seemed undecided what to do with it and she stifled a giggle. "Boy, it's cold out there. Brrr."

Anna Mae laughed. "Set the ham hock in that bowl

to thaw. I'll put the beans on to soak on the stove as soon as I finish sorting them."

If he noticed she'd changed clothes, Josiah didn't say anything about it. Instead he asked, "Would you mind having fried eggs and ham for dinner tonight?"

"Not at all." Anna Mae set a rock off to the side of her bowl.

"Good. Eggs, bacon, ham and beans are about all I know how to make. Mary was the cook, not me." He pulled a chair out and sat down. "And when I'm on the trail of bad guys, I don't have to cook much." He grinned.

Anna Mae focused on the job at hand. She wondered about his wife, but didn't want to be nosy. She knew that Mary had been killed during a bank robbery and that she was William Barns's sister, but that was all anyone seemed to know about her. "Back when we lived together, Emily Jane did all our cooking, before she married William. I'd gotten used to her fixing all my meals, and now that I'm staying at the boardinghouse and Beth provides my meals, well, I'm a little rusty at cooking myself. But together I think we'll do just fine."

"Well, we won't starve to death, that's for sure. Emily Jane helped me stock the pantry before the storm hit, and the root cellar is full of meats and vegetables." He leaned back and studied her. "But I don't want you to overdo it today."

She smiled. It was nice having someone care about her. Since Emily Jane married, Anna Mae had felt alone. A feeling she was very familiar with, since she'd felt that way most of her life. She couldn't deny that of all the things she longed for in her life, belonging to someone, being important to at least one person, ranked right at the top of her list.

The flames crackled in the fireplace, drawing her back to the present. There was nothing like a fire to give the house a cozy feeling. She raised her eyes to find the sheriff watching her, a glint of concern in his analyzing gaze.

"I won't overdo, I promise." She dumped the clean beans in the pot beside her. "It just feels so good to actually be up and moving about. To be doing something of importance. I am not fond of idleness at all."

Josiah picked up the pot of beans and moved to the counter. He rinsed the beans well before setting the pot on the back of the stove. When he returned to the table Anna Mae asked him, "What do you normally do while the girls have their afternoon nap?"

Josiah shrugged. "Read or clean my guns."

Anna Mae pushed away from the table. "I don't want you to change your routine because of me." She walked back to the couch and sat down.

Josiah followed. He dropped into the rocker beside the fireplace. "All right. What do you normally do midafternoon?" he asked, setting the rocker into motion.

"Well, if I'm at the school I teach math, but if I'm at home I sew, read or create lessons for the next day." She pulled her legs up onto the couch and slipped them under the quilt she'd left there earlier.

"What made you want to be a teacher?" Josiah asked as he put a cloth ball back into the corral with the girls, who had awakened when the adults started talking.

Her gaze moved to Rose and Ruby. "I loved to read as a child and my teacher had all kinds of books he'd loan me. He told me I was smart enough that I could teach, if I wanted to. So when I got old enough to do so, I did." She paused, watching the twins play together. They rolled the ball back and forth between them and giggled as if each time something new happened. Their enjoyment of such a simple task reminded Anna Mae of her calling.

"Watching children learn new things and the excitement on their faces when they realize they've figured out a math problem, or understand a new word they just read, gives me a thrill that I can't explain." Anna Mae looked up to see Josiah studying her face.

"What made you want to become a farmer?" she asked, feeling a little self-conscious.

He laughed. "I never wanted to be a farmer. William bought this place, and while I'm happy for the home, I never figured to be a farmer." He shook his head as if to shake away funny memories.

"So was your dream to become a sheriff?"

Josiah set the rocker into motion again with his foot. "I'm not sure I'd call it a dream. When I was a boy, I was accused of stealing my neighbor's puppy." He chuckled. "I didn't take the pup, but since it was the doctor's dog and his son was pitching a fit, the sheriff came to 'talk' to me about it. Well, I tried to convince him I hadn't taken the puppy, but he didn't believe me. So after he left our house, I set out to find out where the little dog had gone." He closed his eyes and rocked.

When it became apparent he wasn't going to continue, Anna Mae leaned forward and asked, "Did you find the puppy?"

His eyes flittered open. "Sure did. It was at the meat

market, trapped under the boardwalk with a bone too big to get out." Josiah chuckled. "I enjoyed looking for that pup and proving to the sheriff that I hadn't stolen it. It was then that I decided I wanted to be a lawman when I grew up." He glanced at the girls, who continued to crawl about the corral like playful puppies.

"I imagine it's an exciting job." Anna Mae sat back against the cushions.

"It can be, but it's also dangerous and stressful when you have a family to consider."

Her gaze moved to the girls once more and narrowed speculatively. "Have you ever considered a different line of work?"

"Yes and no." He sighed. "Right after Mary died, while I searched for the bank robbers who shot her, I thought a lot about quitting. But what can a seasoned lawman do besides upkeep the law?"

Anna Mae grinned at him. "Farm?"

He chuckled. "I know little to nothing about farming."

She tucked the thin quilt closer around her legs. Even covered as she was, she felt the chill in the air. "So I take it you grew up in town?"

Again he nodded. "Yep, I was known as a street rat. My mother had died when I was a baby and my father… he hadn't taken her death well. So to my way of thinking, when the doctor's kid accused me of stealing his puppy, he did me a great favor."

"Gave you a direction to follow?"

"You could say that. I went to Sheriff Grady and told him I wanted to work for him. He took a twelve-year-old boy under his wing and helped me grow to manhood." For a moment Josiah seemed to travel back in time.

Anna Mae could barely stifle a yawn. "I'm glad. We were both fortunate to have someone mentor us." She covered her mouth to conceal another yawn.

"You look like a woman who needs more rest. Why don't you go on back to bed for a little while? I will call you for dinner."

She shook her head. "No, it's time I started sleeping out here and let you have your room back."

"Now, Annie. You aren't fully well yet and I can't allow you to do that." He stood and pulled the rifle down from over the fireplace.

"I appreciate all the help you've given me, Sheriff Miller, but I am well enough now to take care of myself." It was a weak protest that came from a still scratchy throat.

He grinned at her and said. "Sheriff Grady used to say, 'Young man, as long as you live under my roof, you'll abide by my rules.' I think I'll use those words on you. So no more protesting, go get some rest." Josiah set the gun down and reached for her hand.

Anna Mae wanted to argue but didn't have the strength. She took his hand and allowed him to pull her up. "All right, but as soon as I'm feeling better, I will be moving to the couch."

He laughed at her weak words. "We'll see."

Anna Mae went into the bedroom and shut the door. If truth were told, she liked him being in charge. But Anna Mae refused to allow herself the luxury of depending on a man. The last man she'd depended on to keep his word had failed miserably. No, she wasn't going to get close enough to Josiah or his girls to depend on them for happiness or anything else.

A few days later, Josiah inhaled the hearty fragrance of fresh, hot bread mingled with a pork stew cooking on the stove. His gaze moved to the woman who sat reading with his girls.

She was amazing.

Over the past few days, she'd managed to clean the house and at the same time keep the girls happy. He'd helped her with a lot of the cleaning, but still she seemed to be able to spot just what needed to be done. She'd also allowed the girls more freedom from the corral. They'd wobbled about the house and seemed happy just to explore and play.

Unfortunately, the storm had picked up once more, and as the snow fell, Anna Mae became quieter and quieter. Josiah assumed she worried over what the school board would say once she did make it back to town. He noticed little Rose releasing a mighty big yawn.

"Looks like these two are ready for a nap," Josiah said, taking Rose from Anna Mae's lap.

"Yes, it is that time," she answered, swinging her legs off the couch.

"You stay put. I'll come back for Ruby," he instructed as he carried the little girl into the bedroom he shared with the two children. He glanced over his shoulder.

"No nap," Ruby muttered, tucking her head under Anna Mae's chin. Her chubby little thumb found her mouth and her eyes began to close.

Josiah slipped Rose into her crib and then returned for Ruby.

Anna Mae yawned, too, as she met him halfway to the bedroom. She offered him a gentle smile as he took Ruby from her arms.

"Go lie down. You could use some rest, too, after all you've done this morning." He turned to the bedroom before she could protest.

Ruby was already asleep as he tucked her little blanket about her small shoulders. His gaze moved to her twin, who also breathed in a steady, slow manner. His girls were freshly bathed, wore clean dresses and smelled of talc powder. If only they had a mother to keep them smelling and looking like sweet little girls.

Josiah walked back to the sitting room. Anna Mae rested on the couch with the quilt over her. Her steady breathing told him that she, too, had settled in for a nap. Had she overdone it? He'd noticed she grew tired after each task, but would take a short break and then start back to cleaning or doing something with the girls. Maybe he should have made her relax more.

She'd been at the cabin now well over a week. It was time she had her own bedroom. When he and the girls had first moved into the house, he'd started using the extra two rooms as storage rooms. Now his guest needed one of them.

As he cleaned and straightened it up, his thoughts turned to Anna Mae's future. Would the school board fire her for being at his place for so long? Josiah sighed. Even he knew that they weren't going to approve of her extended stay.

Maybe Levi Westland would be able to help her. Levi was the reason Anna Mae was in Granite in the first place. He'd invited her to their small town as a mail-order bride. Then when he'd chosen to marry Millie Hamilton, Levi had made sure that Anna Mae got the teacher's position when it became available.

But if Levi couldn't persuade the school board, what in the world was Josiah going to do about her? He had no idea what would become of Anna Mae should she lose her job. Would he be able to help her? And if so, how?

Chapter Three

There days later, the sun came out and melted most of the snow and ice, making it possible for Anna Mae to return to town. Mud squished under Josiah's boots as he hitched his horse to the wagon. He'd decided to leave the mule in the barn. It would be hard enough driving the wagon through the mud without trying to pull a cankerous mule behind it. Josiah had assured Anna Mae he'd bring it back to town as soon as the ground hardened up a bit.

Anna Mae remained inside, preparing the kids for the trip. Her illness had taken its toll on her body and she appeared much slimmer than she'd been when she'd arrived two weeks earlier. He wasn't sure if the weight loss was due to her being sick or from worrying about her job. She'd lost her appetite but had kept up her good nature.

He watched as Anna Mae stepped out onto the porch, holding a child in each arm. What he could see of her dress looked clean and pressed. She also wore her green cloak and gloves. She'd drawn her hair into a tight knot at the nape of her neck, giving her pale face a pinched look.

Josiah guided the horse up to the porch and reached for Rose.

"Thank you, Sheriff Miller." She passed the child to him and waited as he placed Rose upon the seat and then handed the child a small rope attached to the bench for her to hold on to. Next, he took Ruby from Anna Mae's arms and did the same. The twins looked at each other and grinned happily as they clung to the rope. The word *go* was about the only recognizable thing they said to each other. The rest of the sounds they made were not real words, but the twins seemed to have no problem understanding each other as they nodded and smiled.

Anna Mae turned back to the open door and retrieved a picnic basket. "I packed a lunch for you and the girls' return trip." She offered him the hamper.

"That was very nice of you, Annie." He took the basket and placed it in the bed of the wagon. He checked that the girls were comfortable and covered with a thick blanket before turning to assist Anna Mae.

"Please, Sheriff Miller, don't call me Annie while we are in town." Anna Mae twisted her hands in the folds of her dress.

He gave her a gentle smile. "I'll be on my best behavior."

Anna Mae gave him a doubtful look, then took his hand while she pulled herself up onto the seat beside the girls. "See that you are."

"I promise." Josiah planned on being the perfect gentleman once they entered town. He had to admit, though, that he felt a sense of loss already with her leaving. He shook his head regretfully. He sure was going to miss Anna Mae.

When he seated himself on the other side of the twins, she asked, "Is it very far to the Bradshaws' place?"

"No, just across the pasture." Widow Bradshaw lived a little too close for his comfort. True, she supplied him with fresh bread each week, but her constant hinting that she'd make a good mother for the girls was becoming a nuisance.

"Good. I know you think I'm being silly, but I want to make sure that Bart is doing all right," Anna Mae said, smoothing the wrinkles from her skirts.

Josiah raised the reins and was about to gently slap them over the horse's back when he heard another wagon pulling onto his property. He looked behind him and saw Mrs. Bradshaw and Bart. "It looks like Bart made it home," he said matter-of-factly.

Anna Mae nodded. "Yes, it would appear so."

The widow called out as their wagon drew closer. "Yoo-hoo! Sheriff Miller! I see you are able to get out today, too. I've been so worried about you and the girls."

Josiah put a smile on his face, praying that it looked sincere. "Yes, ma'am, we were just heading to town."

The wagon stopped beside them and Mrs. Bradshaw's smile faded away. "Why, Miss Leland, what are you doing out here?"

"Uh…"

The widow's face slowly began to turn red. Whether she was angry or embarrassed, Josiah wasn't sure. "We were just headed to your house, Mrs. Bradshaw.

It seems that Bart thought it funny to strand Miss Leland out in the snowstorm last week."

She looked to her son. "Bart, darling, what is he talking about?"

The boy glanced down at his feet. "It was just a joke."

"A joke that could have cost your teacher her life," Josiah answered in a firm voice.

"What was just a joke?" Bart's mother demanded.

Bart sank deeper onto the wagon seat and refused to answer. His brown hair was tousled. And his deep brown eyes focused on his feet.

Mrs. Bradshaw turned her attention back to Josiah. "I don't understand."

He nodded toward the boy. "Bart told his teacher that one of the younger boys was hurt, and led her into the woods right before the storm. Then he disappeared, leaving her lost. When the freezing rain and snow hit, Miss Leland almost froze to death before she arrived here at my farm."

The boy looked up as if shocked by his words. Had Bart not realized the danger he'd put his teacher in? Probably not. Josiah held Bart's gaze with his own.

The widow looked to Anna Mae. "Are you saying she's been here for over two weeks?" When no one answered, she crossed her arms and huffed. "She doesn't look injured to me."

Josiah cleared his throat and then said with quiet emphasis, "Regardless of how she looks now, Miss Leland has been very sick due to your son's deceitfulness. The facts are, he lured her into the woods, then left her in the middle of a fierce storm." Josiah so badly wanted to add that all of the above were offenses against the law.

"I don't believe it." Mrs. Bradshaw glared at Anna Mae.

Still sounding a little hoarse, Anna Mae answered, "I'm afraid it's true, Mrs. Bradshaw. Isn't it, Bart?" Her gaze moved to the little boy.

"Yes, ma'am," he answered, before ducking his head once more. "I didn't think about you getting caught in the storm," Bart admitted.

"I believe you owe your teacher an apology. She's been very worried about you and whether or not you made it home safely," Josiah told him.

Bart looked up. "I'm sorry, Miss Leland." His young voice sounded hopeful as he asked, "Were you really worried about me?"

A tender smile touched Anna Mae's lips. "Of course I was."

His young cheeks turned a bright pink and once more he looked away.

Mrs. Bradshaw's voice sounded colder than the icicles that had been hanging from the roof a few days ago. "Well, it's done and over and the boy has apologized. Since you've had a woman to cook and bake for you, I don't suppose you need fresh bread."

"No, we don't, but thank you for offering," Josiah answered, still looking at the boy. Bart had been doing lots of mischievous things over the last few weeks. Josiah wondered if the boy simply craved attention. "Now, back to Bart." He let his words hang between the two wagons.

"What about him?" his mother demanded.

"I think the boy needs to be punished for leaving his teacher out in the woods to freeze. Don't you?" Josiah asked, fearing what she'd say.

"No, I don't." She sputtered. "I think you are—"

Bart's young voice interrupted her. "He's right, Ma." The boy turned to look at him. "I could chop your wood for you, Sheriff, if you think that would be a good punishment," he offered.

"What do you think, Miss Leland?" Josiah asked.

Anna Mae nodded. "I think that would be good for the boy. Plus, he could cut some for the school, as well."

Mrs. Bradshaw sat on the wagon bench with her mouth hanging open. "You are seriously going to punish my boy for a childish trick?" She shook her head.

Bart looked to his mother. "I shouldn't have deceived her and then left her in the woods, Ma." He turned his attention back to Josiah and lifted his chin. "I'll cut the wood."

Mrs. Bradshaw slapped the reins over her horse's back. "Good day to the both of you," she said, turning the horse back in the direction of town. Josiah watched her leave, utterly mystified.

Anna Mae leaned back and sighed. Her fears had been realized, and they hadn't even left the Miller property. Mrs. Bradshaw would be knocking on the door of every school board member as soon as she got to town. It was as plain as the nose on her face that the other woman was interested in the sheriff and that she'd assumed the worst when she'd learned that Anna Mae had been staying with him.

She turned to look at the little girls, who up to this

point had sat quietly listening to the adults talk. Rose pulled at her left ear and puckered her little face into a frown. Was she coming down with an ear infection? Anna Mae reached across and touched her forehead.

"Something wrong?" Josiah asked.

"I'm not sure. You might have Doc look at the girls' ears when we get to town. Rose acts as if hers might be hurting." Anna Mae turned back around on the hard seat.

Josiah nodded. "I'll do that as soon as I drop you off at the boardinghouse." He snapped the reins over the horse's back and the wheels made a sucking noise as they pulled free of the mud.

Anna Mae wanted to bring up Mrs. Bradshaw, but didn't know how to go about it. She couldn't come right out and say that the other woman hadn't been happy to see her with Josiah. Did he realize that the widow was sweet on him?

That didn't matter. What did concern Anna Mae was that the widow would tell the whole town that she'd been out at the Miller farm for over two weeks. She feared the other women in town would think ill of her. Anna Mae chewed the inside of her cheek as she worried about what would be waiting for her in Granite.

Would the school board demand her resignation? Or simply fire her on the spot? Would the women avoid her? Would she ever be able to look anyone in the eyes again?

She'd gone through this before, but at least when her fiancé had left her at the altar, the women knew that she'd done no wrong. He simply hadn't loved her enough to keep his word or take her with him when he left town. This would be different. The women would talk. Everyone would talk. She was sure to be fired from her job and looked upon as a wayward woman.

As they pulled up in front of the boardinghouse Josiah said, "It looks like the good widow has gotten here before us."

Anna Mae saw three of the board members' buggies already parked in front of the boardinghouse. She offered a wobbly smile. "Well, she did have a head start." Anna Mae climbed down from the wagon and took Ruby from Josiah.

Levi Westland stood on the porch waiting for them as they walked up to the front door, hands shoved in his pockets, shoulders hunched forward. He tipped his hat to Anna Mae and nodded to Josiah. "Glad to see you are safe, Miss Leland." His voice was calm, his gaze steady. Icy fingers of fear seeped into every pore of her being.

"Thank you, Mr. Westland," she answered, her voice shakier than she would have liked, fully aware that he was a member of the school board.

His mouth spread into a thin-lipped smile. "So the rumor is true."

"Rumor?" Josiah repeated the word, but Anna Mae watched him tighten his hold on Rose. His vexation was evident.

The talk had already begun. Anna Mae hugged Ruby to her and inhaled the baby smell. It had a calming effect on her and she looked to Levi. With a slight smile of defiance, she responded, "If the rumor is that I've been out at the Miller farm waiting out the storm, then yes, the rumor is true." She pulled her shoulders back and raised her head. Anna Mae knew she had nothing to be ashamed of, but if Levi's manner and tone of questioning mirrored the rest of the town, then she didn't stand a chance.

Levi sighed in resignation. "I hoped it wasn't. We've been worried about you, but with the weather the way it was, none of us could come looking for you. We searched the school and about town, but weren't sure where to look from there." His handsome face twisted in regret. "I'd intended to come out and get Josiah to help round up a search party, but Mrs. Bradshaw just arrived in town and said there was no need." He paused, the silence stretching between them as the severity of the situation became clearer. Finally Levi offered her a sad smile. "I truly am glad you are safe."

Josiah placed his hand at the small of her back and gently urged her toward the door. "Let's go inside and talk where it's warmer."

Levi nodded and held the door open for them.

Anna Mae slipped inside. Her heart raced in her chest. She felt her face flush with humiliation. She didn't want to lose her job or reputation, but deep down felt as if she probably had already lost both. Anna Mae just couldn't accept the dull ache of foreboding. And once again in her young life, she experienced the nauseating, sinking feeling of despair.

A terrible sense of bitterness threatened to overwhelm her. She glanced at Josiah and found his expression grim as he watched her. He'd said he'd stand beside her, but what good would that do? Would his being there only make things worse?

Tears filled her eyes, but she refused to release them as the questions roared through her mind, one more insistent than the others. What was she going to do now?

Chapter Four

$\backsim$

As Anna Mae had expected, within minutes of her arrival the last remaining two board members miraculously showed up at Beth's Boardinghouse.

They whispered among themselves, argued a bit, then called her into the sitting room and invited her to sit. Mrs. Anderson, the bank president's wife and head of the school board, pointed to a chair placed in the center of the room, and it was not lost on Anna Mae that her back was to the door. The board was in full intimidation mode and wanted no interruptions or distractions. She sat in the chair, her fingers tensed in her lap.

Josiah slipped into the room and sat off to her right, with his cowboy hat resting on his knee. Anna Mae could only assume that he'd left his girls with Emily Jane. Having him there made her feel somewhat better, but not much.

Mr. Holiday, the newly elected town mayor, leaned forward and lowered his voice as if the charges against her were too vile to speak out loud. In a soft, yet firm tone he said, "Miss Leland, it has come to our attention that you were out past dark on the night the storm hit. That you ended up at the Miller farm, where you have resided for over two weeks. Would you say that these statements are true?"

He was a large man, with a walrus-type body and face. His mustache twitched when he spoke and his normal voice came out loud and robust. But not today. Now his dark eyes searched her face as he waited for an answer.

"Yes, that is true but—"

Mrs. Thelma Anderson, the bank president's wife, interrupted with a sharp tone. "There are no excuses for such conduct. It is very plain in your contract that we will not tolerate this type of behavior."

Anna Mae's breath caught in her throat, her heart pounded, and her eyes widened in astonishment. The suddenness of the attack took her breath away. Surely they would give her a fair hearing before pronouncing her guilty and firing her. "If you will just let me explain," she pleaded. She couldn't accept the dull ache of foreboding.

Levi Westland nodded. "Yes, I believe we should allow her to explain."

"I don't see the point. The evidence is here for all to view. Miss Leland admits she spent many nights at the Miller farm." The bank president's wife spoke with a contempt that forbade any further argument.

"Now, dear, let her speak." Mr. Anderson patted his wife's hand.

The woman looked ready to argue further, then took a deep breath and sighed. "I don't see the point, but if she must."

"I believe she must." Josiah's low voice reminded Anna Mae of his presence. She hated that he was here to witness her shame.

Mr. Anderson waved his hand in her direction. "Go ahead, Miss Leland. Tell us what happened."

Anna Mae remembered Josiah's words, *"Just tell them what you told me."* She took a deep, calming breath and did just that. Her hands shook in her lap as Mrs. Anderson studied her with impassive coldness. The woman's mouth twisted wryly as Anna Mae recounted how she'd followed Bart out into the woods.

Levi nodded his head as if agreeing with her choice to go search for the little boy, as did a couple of the other men.

She assured them of the innocence of her stay and that she'd been very ill. Anna Mae finished by explaining that she and Mr. Miller had returned to town the moment it was safe to travel with the girls.

Josiah stood. His hands worked the rim of his hat while he spoke. "I can vouch for Miss Leland. Everything she has told you is the truth. When she arrived at the farm, Miss Leland was very ill. It wasn't until the last few days that she's felt well enough to get up and eat."

Mrs. Anderson gasped, but he pressed on. "I'd like to add that Miss Leland behaved like a perfect lady, watching over the girls as best she could, being sick and all, while I handled the care of the horse and mule. She has done nothing wrong and I request that you allow her to keep her teaching position."

Anna Mae knew that in his own way Josiah thought to help her, but she feared his words caused more damage than good. He must have felt so, too, as the tensing of his jaw betrayed his deep frustration. Her heart warmed at the thought that at least he'd tried to help her. She watched the play of emotions on his face and realized he felt the same hopelessness that tore through her.

For a moment she allowed bitterness to slip in. He would walk away with no repercussions. His job wasn't threatened. He would suffer no embarrassment, no aftermaths, yet she stood to lose everything. Where was the fairness in that?

Then she realized how unfair her thoughts were. He'd been nothing but kind to her. Even in front of these people, Josiah had tried to help her. They'd become friends during her stay with him. If truth be known, it was a friendship she wouldn't have minded cultivating, if the circumstances were different.

She imposed an iron control on herself, stifling any warmth she felt toward the sheriff. Josiah simply felt guilty for her predicament. It wasn't his fault, but she knew he felt as if part of it were. Either way, Anna Mae refused to allow herself to soften toward him. She couldn't afford to let another man break her heart. Besides, by the way things looked, after today she wouldn't be staying in Granite.

She raised her eyes to find the board members watching her, gauging her reaction to Josiah's words. Her gaze shifted from one person to the other, the majority of them staring back in accusation. Thoughtfully, she searched each man and woman's face. Several of the men looked at her with what appeared to be sympathy, while Mrs. Anderson's features showed nothing but scorn. Levi Westland held her gaze as if to say he was on her side.

Mrs. Anderson spoke once more. "As honorable as Miss Leland's tale sounds, she still broke several of the rules of her contract. Gentlemen, I realize you think she did the right thing by going out for the boy, but that doesn't take away from the fact that she signed a contract. What good is the contract if we do not hold our schoolteachers to it?"

When no one answered, Anna Mae was assailed by a terrible sense of bitterness. She knit her fingers together and rested them in her lap. Her throat ached with defeat. *Lord, why?* In desperation her heart cried out to her creator. *Have You forgotten me? Is there a purpose in allowing this to happen a second time? Did I not learn the lesson You wanted me to through the humiliation of being stranded at the altar? Must I be humiliated again through no fault of my own?* Bitter tears burned the backs of her eyes. She lowered her head so that they couldn't see them.

The woman's voice droned on. "I move that we dismiss Miss Leland as our schoolteacher. She broke the contract when she left town with Bart Bradshaw and stayed out after dark. As for what happened at the Miller farm, that is between Sheriff Miller, Miss Leland and the good Lord."

Anna Mae raised her head and boldly looked Mrs. Anderson straight in the eyes. She might stand accused, but she most definitely was not guilty, and she refused to cower in front of them as if she were. God knew that she had done no wrong and therefore had nothing to be ashamed of.

Mr. Anderson spoke up. "I second the motion."

Mrs. Anderson continued with the ruling. "All in favor raise your right hands."

Three of the men raised their hands. Levi Westland sat staring at them with hard eyes.

"All opposed." Mrs. Anderson continued as if daring Levi to raise his hand.

He did so and said, "This is wrong, Thelma Anderson, and you know it."

She ignored him as if he hadn't spoken. "Miss Leland, you are hereby removed as the schoolteacher of Granite, Texas, for your unladylike conduct."

"Now hold on just a moment." Josiah's voice boomed about the room. "Miss Leland never once misbehaved as a lady. And if I hear such words bantered about town, I may just lock you up for slander."

Anna Mae stood. "Sheriff Miller. Thank you for your kind words, but the school board has spoken." She smoothed out her skirt and walked to the door. Just before exiting, she added, "I'm sure Mrs. Anderson is too much of a Christian to go speaking falsehoods about me. Now, if you all will excuse me, I will be retiring to my room." Her chin quivered but she managed to hold her head high as she exited the room.

Josiah looked at each of the school board members. He ought to arrest every one of them. They'd just delivered a verdict without any evidence. A court of law would have thrown them out of the courthouse. He could think of any number of things to charge them with. Slander, destruction of character and illegal firing from a job. And the unfairness of it—now that cut the cake. All in the name of moral correctness.

"Well, now, what will we do for a schoolteacher?" he asked, noting that none of them would meet his eyes.

Mrs. Anderson raised her head and sighed dramatically. "I suppose I shall have to fill in until another teacher can be found. I suggest we advertise for a male teacher this time."

He looked at the older woman, her actions finally making sense. "Ah…" He deliberately drew the word out. "I see." Everyone knew the bank president's wife was bored, but Josiah wouldn't have thought she'd fire Anna Mae to give herself a job to do.

She glared at him, but a telling flush crept into her cheeks and deepened to crimson.

Josiah shook his head, distaste curling the edges of his mouth into a grimace, which he allowed the board members to see. To their credit a few of them had the grace to look ashamed, and dropped their heads. He slapped his hat back on his head and left.

He made his way to Emily Jane, who sat with the twins just outside the door. "Thank you for watching the girls," he said in greeting.

"It didn't go well for Anna Mae, did it?"

"I'm afraid not." Josiah took Rose from Emily Jane and looked about for Ruby.

The little girl sat at the foot of the stairs, looking up. Ruby held a soft spot for the young schoolteacher. She pulled herself up on the bottom step and began to climb.

"Oh, no, you don't, little lady." Josiah scooped her into his free arm and held her tight. His gaze moved up the stairs, where he knew Anna Mae had fled.

Poor woman. She'd lost her job and her reputation today. When word got out that the school board was looking for a new teacher, everyone would want to know why, and even though he'd threatened to toss Mrs. Anderson in jail if she bad-mouthed Anna Mae, he knew the older woman would tell everyone what had happened. And if she didn't, Mrs. Bradshaw would. He sighed heavily.

"I think I'll go up and see if I can make her feel any better." His sister-in-law pushed herself up from the bench.

Josiah nodded. "Thank you again for taking care of the girls."

"You're welcome. They were good." She walked past him and headed up the stairs, then stopped and said, "I hope you and the girls can come into town for Sunday lunch. I'll fry up a chicken if you do."

He grinned at her. "If the weather stays clear, we'll be there."

She nodded and then continued up the stairs.

Josiah carried the girls out to his wagon and put them onto the seat. He handed them the rope to hold on to and then tucked several blankets around them. The wagon tipped slightly as he pulled himself up and sat down beside Rose. As long as he was in town with the wagon he might as well go to the general store for supplies.

Mentally he ticked off what he needed—coffee, salt and beans. Thanks to Anna Mae, he now knew how to cook ham and beans that didn't taste plain and hard. He guided the horse to the store.

Once inside, he sat the girls down and took each one

by the hand. They were old enough now to toddle along with him. Carolyn Moore came out of the back room.

"Josiah, how good to see you. Did you get a lot of snow out at your place?" she asked, coming around and kneeling in front of the girls.

"We got our share, that's for sure." He laughed as he watched Carolyn give both twins a big hug.

"You girls don't look too frostbitten," she teased.

They giggled and tucked their faces into his legs.

It always amazed him that the girls could turn shy in an instant. He stroked their curls and grinned like the proud papa he was.

"What can I help you with today?" Carolyn asked. She wiped at a thin layer of flour on her apron, reminding him that he should get some more of that, too.

"It seems I'm in need of coffee, beans, flour and something else." For the life of him Josiah couldn't remember the other item. Anna Mae would know what he needed at the house.

Would she be all right? Now that she'd lost her teaching job, what would she do? Maybe instead of denying that the school board would release her, he should have helped Annie plan a new future.

"I'll gather the coffee, beans and flour for you. As for the something else, as soon as you remember what it is, let me know and I'll add it to your pile." Carolyn went to measure out his requests.

A heaviness centered in his chest and there was a sour feeling in the pit of his stomach that caused him to rub the affected area. He should have stood up for her better. But what more could he have said to help her keep her job? As it was, he thought he might have made the situation worse. He could still see the look of tiredness that had passed over her features, and hear the strained tone of her voice.

"Have you remembered what the other something was that you needed?" Carolyn asked as she placed a brown paper bag full of beans onto the counter.

Josiah looked about the store. His gaze landed where the spices were and he remembered. "Salt."

Rose and Ruby pulled at his hands. He didn't understand their babble, but looked toward where they were straining. They seemed to have spotted a section of toys and wanted to get closer to them. "When did you start carrying toys?" he asked, as he allowed the girls to pull him forward.

Carolyn grinned. "We got a shipment in right before the storm hit. Wilson thought it would be good to carry toys, since Christmas is right around the corner."

"If these girls are any indication, I believe your husband was right," Josiah said, releasing their little hands so that the girls could get to the toys. It wouldn't hurt to see what they might be interested in. As Carolyn had said, Christmas was right around the corner. He watched as Ruby grabbed a stuffed brown horse with a white mane and white spots, and Rose pulled at an ugly gray toy elephant.

What would Anna Mae do about the upcoming holidays? With no job and no income, she certainly wouldn't have much of a Christmas. He sighed and let his gaze move about the store. A dress hung in the dry goods area. The pretty fabric would look nice on the schoolteacher.

Josiah shook his head. His thoughts refused to stop

bringing Anna Mae to mind. He felt responsible for her. Hadn't he said that no matter what happened he'd stand beside her?

"Is there anything else I can get you, Sheriff?" Carolyn asked, placing the salt into a box for him.

"Do you think the twins will remember the toys they're playing with now, if I buy and hide them until Christmas morning?" he asked, picking up each of the girls, who held tightly to the toys. Josiah carried them to the counter.

"I doubt it. They are still pretty young," Carolyn said, tickling Rose and taking the toy from her at the same time.

"Then go ahead and wrap them up for me, if you will."

"Be my pleasure to do so." Carolyn handed Rose a peppermint stick to replace the toy.

Josiah grinned at the ease with which the shopkeeper distracted the girls with candy. She took Ruby's toy also and replaced it likewise. The twins smiled and smacked their lips as they sucked on the candy. They were so, oh what was that word Anna Mae described them with? Oh yes, adorable. They had a double dose of it.

"You do have a way with children," he said.

Carolyn wrapped the toys in brown paper and placed them in the box. "I've had lots of experience." She smiled at him and then added the cost of the toys to the list she'd been tallying for him.

Josiah paid for his supplies and the toys and then carried them out to the wagon, while Carolyn watched the girls. As he placed the box in the back, he froze, his hand clenched on the sideboard. Suddenly, with crystal clarity, he knew what he had to do to make things right with Anna Mae.

The girls needed a mother and Anna Mae needed a home and her reputation restored. And he needed someone he could trust to take care of his girls while he worked. His sister-in-law could no longer watch his girls and run a bakery with a newborn to take care of as well.

With courage and determination settling like a rock inside him, he girded himself with resolve. He would marry her.

His mind went through a thorough deliberation process before he allowed himself to act. Would this benefit them both or were his motives selfish? If she agreed to this harebrained scheme, what would her motives be? Would a marriage between them benefit them each?

He already knew that marriage would solve both their problems. She would have a home and the girls would have a mother. But would it produce positive results like he pictured in his mind, or bring regrets further down the road?

Josiah stood still and listened to his gut. In the few years he'd been sheriff, it had never steered him wrong. He turned his head sideways to hear better. Not a word; not even a growl.

He fell back on the evidence. She cooked better than he did. She'd been sick the entire time she was with him, yet his house looked cleaner. The most persuasive piece of evidence won the case. She loved his girls and she tolerated him pretty well.

Now all he had to do was convince her that marrying him would solve both their problems. He'd have to be up front with her and tell her that he could never offer her a husband's love, but that he would happily and freely supply her basic needs for the rest of her life. Surely she'd understand that he'd already lost the love of his life and that he couldn't risk losing another person that he loved that deeply.

Would Anna Mae agree to such a proposition? The future looked so vague and shadowy. Why, he didn't know what would take place in his own life, so how could he expect her to join up with him? He had a farm, yet wasn't a farmer; he was a sheriff.

But could he keep being a sheriff and possibly leave his daughters without a daddy? If he married Anna Mae, and something did happen to him, he knew she'd take care of the girls. Yes, the girls needed a mother. A stable woman they could depend on to take care of them. They needed Anna Mae.

Chapter Five

"How could I have been so stupid?" Anna Mae folded another dress and placed it in her satchel. She might as well get this over with; there was no way she could survive another smirch against her character. If she left before the entire town knew, which should be in about an hour, give or take a few minutes, she'd avoid the pitying glances and censuring looks.

She plopped down on the bed, a green shawl clutched in her hands. How could this keep happening to her? It would be different if she engaged in bad behavior. But she didn't; never had, never planned to.

All her loneliness and confusion welded together in one upsurge of yearning, and she bent over, her hands clutched against her stomach, a groan pushing through her gritted teeth. Would she ever belong? She thought she'd found a place to call home, but now she'd have to move on.

Without warning, Emily Jane rushed through her door and knelt in front of her. "Oh, Anna Mae, I'm so sorry. Please don't cry."

Anna Mae collapsed into her friend's arms, yielding to the compulsive sobs that shook her. She wept aloud, as Emily Jane rocked her back and forth.

Little by little Anna Mae gained control of her emotions, and with a hiccup or two accepted a hanky from Emily Jane. She mopped up her face, but the compassionate, caring look in her friend's eyes almost undid her all over again.

"Why are you packing, Anna Mae?" Emily Jane spoke in an odd, yet gentle voice, as if she were afraid she'd cause the waterworks to start again. "We're not letting you leave. Why, where would you go?" Emily Jane's eyes grew large and liquid. "I couldn't bear it if you weren't around to talk to. We've lived together since we both arrived here." She took one of the dresses from the valise and hung it back on the hanger. "Plus, I need you around so my baby will have an aunt to spoil it rotten and let it do things that as its mother I can't." She rubbed her rounded belly and offered a genuine smile.

"How can I stay, Emily Jane? Everyone thinks the worst of me." Anna Mae shivered, uncertain if it was from the fear taking root in her heart or from the cold that crept through the window.

Emily Jane lifted the shawl off the bed where it had fallen during their embrace, and wrapped it around Anna Mae's shoulders. "Come. Let's get out of this cold room and go sit in the dining room." She turned her toward the door with a slight nudge.

Moments later, a sigh shuddered through Anna Mae as she took a deep drink of her cream-and-sugar-laden hot coffee. "I can't believe I acted so stupidly and placed my employment in jeopardy."

"It wasn't stupid to want to help one of your students," Emily Jane said, patting her hand in comfort.

Anna Mae looked about the room. Thankfully, the noon lunch rush hadn't begun and she and Emily Jane were the only occupants. "Thank you, Emily Jane, but I knew better than to believe a student as mischievous as Bart."

"Then why did you go with him?"

Anna Mae's breath caught in her throat and tears filled her eyes again. Did Emily Jane realize her voice sounded accusatory?

"No, no. Don't look at me like that. I meant, was there a reason beyond what you've said so far? Did he act scared or was he crying?"

Anna Mae thought back to the day Bart had lured her into the woods with his lie. Maybe she had still wanted to help him, to win him over. She didn't know. Her stomach growled and she wished suddenly she'd taken Emily Jane up on her offer of cake. It was probably for the best. Anna Mae didn't think she'd be able to get food down her tight throat, anyway.

"Anna Mae?" Emily Jane's voice was infinitely compassionate, but probing, snatching Anna Mae back to reality. She realized she'd been quiet for too long.

"Oh, I'm sorry. I went because he seemed so upset and he rushed me so that I didn't take the time to think it through. If I had, I would have realized that he was lying." She took another sip of coffee, the sweet taste mingling with the sourness in her stomach. "Well, it can't be helped now."

"What are you going to do?" Emily Jane nibbled on the applesauce cake she'd ordered.

Anna Mae set her cup down. "There's nothing else for it, Emily Jane. I'll have to leave town."

"But why?" Her friend dropped her fork, creating a clatter that sounded loudly in the room. "I don't understand that way of thinking. Why would you leave town?" She scrambled to retrieve her fork.

"I have no job, and as soon as word gets out that I spent two weeks out at the Miller farm, my reputation will be ruined." Fresh sorrow filled her at the truth of her words. "I have to leave." Her sense of loss was beyond tears. Everything had been going well. She'd had a job, a home and friends.

Emily Jane shook her head. She lowered her voice so that the few people who had filtered into the dining room wouldn't hear her. "The only ones who will think ill of you are the ladies who are jealous of you, like Mrs. Bradshaw. Why don't you give it a few days and see what happens? I'll check with William and see if I have enough money to hire you to work at the bakery. I'm sure I'll need the extra help with the arrival of our new baby." She rested her hands protectively around her rounded tummy with a small grin.

"Thank you, dear friend, but I can't ask you to create a job for me. I love you for wanting to, but I can't accept it."

A pair of boot tips appeared in her line of vision and then a man cleared his throat. Anna Mae looked up to find Josiah standing beside the table. She took a quick sharp breath. What was he doing back at the boardinghouse? Had he come to tell her what the doctor had said about Rose's ear?

"Ladies, mind if I join you?" He twisted his hat in his hands as he waited for an answer.

Emily Jane responded first. "Of course, please do." She indicated he should take the seat between them.

Beth Winters hurried over to take his order. "What would you like, Sheriff?"

He pulled the chair out and sat down. "Coffee and a piece of whatever kind of cake my sister-in-law is having."

She nodded and hurried off to get them.

Anna Mae nervously fingered the handle of her cup. Where were the twins? Didn't he know it would add fuel to the fodder if they were seen together?

"Where are the girls?" Emily Jane asked.

He hung his hat on the back of his chair. "I left them with Carolyn Moore for a few minutes."

"Did you take Rose to the doctor?" Anna Mae asked, drawing his attention back to her.

"Yep. He said her ear is a little red and to put a few drops of oil in it this evening before putting her down for the night." He grinned at Anna Mae.

As their eyes met the tenderness in his expression amazed her. But there was something more. She couldn't put her finger on it, but he almost seemed pleased with himself; as if he'd just confirmed something that had been on his mind. Good for him, she thought sarcastically, irked by his easy manner.

Beth returned with his coffee and cake. "Here you go, Sheriff, it's on the house."

"That's right nice of you, Mrs. Winters." He tipped his head in her direction.

A soft pink filled Beth's cheeks as she turned to go.

Was Beth sweet on him? Anna Mae realized that first Mrs. Bradshaw and now Beth seemed to be interested in the sheriff. She crossed her arms protectively across her chest and studied him thoroughly.

He was handsome, with wavy black hair that touched the back of his collar, and deep blue eyes. His nose was a little crooked, as if it had been broken at one time or another. When he smiled his eyes seemed to hold an inner light that drew a person, much like a bee to a honeycomb, but was that any reason to fall over one-self around him?

Josiah glanced up from his dessert to catch her staring at him. He measured her with a cool, appraising look. "I've been worried about you, Annie."

She peered about to see if anyone had heard him use his pet name for her. Assured that no other diners sat close by, she returned her attention to him. "I'm fine, Sheriff Miller." She stressed his last name, reminding him they were no longer at his cabin and not to call her by her given name.

"Anna Mae just told me she's thinking about leaving town," Emily Jane interjected, taking a big bite of her cake and carefully observing both of them.

Anna Mae felt more than saw Josiah's posture stiffen. She would have liked to be the one to tell him that she was leaving. Not that it mattered, but she wanted him to know that it wasn't his fault. He couldn't help it that Bart had led her into the woods on a stormy night, or that her mule had chosen Josiah's farm to take her to. Anna Mae hadn't decided when or how she would tell him, but she had hoped to do so herself.

"So you're thinking about leaving?"

She nodded. "I planned to tell you before I left." She became aware of Emily Jane watching them with acute interest. "Because I wanted to thank you for all that you did for me when I was sick."

Josiah looked to his sister-in-law. As if he'd silently asked her to leave, Emily Jane picked up her purse and said, "Well, I hate to eat and run, but I need to get back to the bakery and start tomorrow's bread."

She hugged Anna Mae and whispered in her ear, "Don't make any rash decisions today." Then she waved, leaving the two of them sitting silently.

Without Emily Jane's presence, Josiah suddenly felt tongue-tied. How did one propose a marriage of convenience? He didn't want Anna Mae leaving Granite. She seemed to sincerely care about his daughters and they needed a mother. Josiah knew deep down, though, that she'd never capture his heart the way Mary had. It was impossible that any woman would truly take her place. Because he felt so sure of this, Anna Mae would never be a true wife to him. However, for the girls' sake, and to save Anna Mae's reputation, he had to ask her to marry him. He might as well jump in with both feet. As casually as he could, he said, "You don't have to leave, you know."

She looked at him over her coffee cup. Clear brown eyes rimmed with pink puffiness regarded him curiously. He could tell she'd been crying earlier, and an emotion he hadn't felt in a long time swept through him. He wanted to take away all her pain and embarrassment.

Her sigh tore at him. "Yes, I do. I don't want my

friends feeling sorry for me, and I can't face the shame of having to impose on them for my livelihood."

Josiah knew that feeling. Maybe not for his means of support, but didn't he have to impose on others to watch his children so he could work? It felt like the same thing. Maybe he could convince her that he knew the feeling, and that if she'd permit it he'd make certain neither of them would feel that way again. But even a small-town sheriff like himself knew this was a delicate situation and should be handled with care.

He reconsidered that tack. One wrong word or move and he could push her in the opposite direction. "Maybe you don't have to impose on your friends for your livelihood." He said the words tentatively, as if testing the idea.

"I know I don't. And I won't. That's why I'm leaving. My room is paid here until the first of November. Emily Jane asked me not to make any rash decisions, so I suppose I'll stay until then. Hopefully, by the first I will know where I'm going and what I must do when I get there. I'll simply have to endure the gossip until I leave." She set her cup on the table and squared her shoulders. Determination tightened her jawline.

He admired her fortitude. It would serve her well in the days ahead. But right now he didn't need her stubborn and unwilling; he wanted to be her knight in shining armor and rescue her from distress. He breathed a plea heavenward. *Lord, a little help here, please. Can You make her receptive and sensible?*

Half in anticipation, half in dread, Josiah pushed his plate back and reached for her hands. "What I mean, sweet Annie, is that maybe we can help each other."

Her fingers shook against his palm so he tightened his grip. "How?" Confusion laced her pretty features as she held his gaze.

"You could marry me," he blurted, scarcely aware of his own voice.

Anna Mae snatched her hands back and shook her head. "What did you say?" She pushed stray tendrils of hair away from her cheek.

Josiah felt a curious, swooping pull inside him, surprising him to stillness. Why had he never noticed how incredibly beautiful Annie was? Her features were dainty, her wrists small and her waist curving and regal.

He forced himself to focus on the statement he'd just made. All right, it probably wasn't the best proposal she'd ever heard. She must think him an insensitive clod. Josiah cleared his throat and tried again. "We could get married. I need someone to take care of the girls, and you wouldn't have to find another job or leave." To his annoyance he felt heat climb up his neck and into his face. His aggravation increased when he noticed his hands were shaking. What was wrong with him? This was how a man in love acted; and he certainly wasn't in love. He made a gesture with his right hand. "This is not how I rehearsed this in my head on the way over here."

She leaned closer and whispered, "You want to marry me so you'll have a babysitter for the girls?"

He ran a hand behind his neck and rubbed. "Well, yes, but it would benefit you, too."

Anna Mae crossed her arms over her chest once more. "Explain to me how that would work exactly?"

At his puzzled look, she pressed on. "How marrying you and taking care of the girls will help me?"

"You wouldn't have to leave your friends."

She laughed bitterly and wagged the tip of her finger at him. "Believe it or not, I am capable of making new friends, Sheriff."

He dropped his head and stared at the checkered tablecloth. "I'm sorry. This isn't coming out right." Josiah sighed heavily, and without looking up at her, he continued. "All I'm proposing is a marriage of convenience. It wouldn't be a real marriage." He lowered his voice as she had done. "I don't expect us to share a bedroom, only the responsibilities of the children, the farm and the house."

How could he explain to her that he only wanted to help? He'd been partially responsible for her job loss and the town thinking they'd been intimate. He just wanted to make up for that. Maybe this had been a bad idea. She was right. How would marrying him help her face the women in town who were probably gossiping over their luncheons right now? Still, he gave an impatient shrug. The idea had merit and he'd be foolish not to realize how much it would benefit him. *Lord, if You're of a mind to, I could use that help right about now.*

Her soft hand covered his and he looked up quickly, so surprised his mouth dropped open. He merely stared, tongue-tied. Tears filled the beautiful milk-chocolate orbs regarding him with tenderness. Her voice, when she spoke, still held a touch of hoarseness. "I know you're trying to help me, and what you said is right; the girls do need someone to take care of them. In a real sense, it's a lovely suggestion. As my grandmother used to say, it would kill two birds with one stone."

Josiah watched as she fought some inner battle before speaking again. What an honorable woman she was. Even in distress, she managed to consider the feelings of others. She was three times a lady compared to her accusers.

"I can't give you my answer right now, Josiah, but I'll pray about it." She lifted her hand from his and stood up. She touched his shoulder briefly. "Thank you."

She walked away with stiff dignity, the long skirt of her dress swaying gently. She paused just inside the door and looked back at him. For a moment she studied him intently and then she was gone.

She'd said thank you? What on earth did that mean? He hadn't done anything that she had to be thankful for. Had she been referring to him nursing her while she was sick? For proposing marriage to her? What? He gritted his teeth and barely suppressed a groan of frustration.

If he lived to be a hundred, he'd never understand women. *And why, Lord, didn't You give me a more elegant way of speaking and expressing myself?* One thing was for certain; Josiah hadn't the foggiest idea what Anna Mae's answer would be, nor when she'd tell him.

Chapter Six

Anna Mae took one more look at her reflection in the mirror, then gathered her Bible and shawl in preparation for church. Today, sink, swim or drown, she'd face the gossipmongers and learn if her friends were true or not.

Almost a week had passed since Josiah's proposal. She'd cowered in her room as much as possible, coming down for meals only after everyone else had left.

Miserable without the twins, she'd worried over Rose. Had Josiah remembered to administer the sweet oil twice a day? Were the girls wondering where she was? Did they cry for her at night? She'd shared their bedroom, many nights placing them in bed with her if they seemed distressed after she diapered them. Their mother had died when they were just babies, then their uncle and Emily Jane had cared for them. Finally their daddy had shown up and taken them. At least with Anna Mae at the farm they'd had the sense of stability of a mother for a brief few days.

Needless to say, the twins needed her, and she needed them. They filled a void she hadn't recognized she had.

That still small voice she'd grown to recognize as the Lord's asked if she could just walk away from them.

Her friends, Emily Jane and Susanna had visited her. She'd shared Josiah's proposal with them, purposefully leaving out the marriage-of-convenience part. They'd both been thrilled that he'd offered marriage and that she would be staying if she accepted his proposal.

When she finally wrapped her mind around that Josiah was offering "a marriage of convenience only," she found it lacking to say the least. Josiah was another man who didn't see her as a true wife. What was wrong with her? Did men see something she didn't? Why couldn't someone love her?

She arrived late at the church but still beat Josiah and the girls there by mere seconds. Josiah pulled the wagon to a stop at the boardwalk. The twins spotted her and both scrambled to get out of the box in the back. Anna Mae could no more stop herself from reaching for them than she could stop breathing. They fell over the side into her arms, causing her Bible to fall to the ground. Both chattered a mile a minute, though most of their words were unintelligible.

"Girls, girls. Calm down," Josiah chided, but his eyes were lit with laughter and he seemed as pleased to see her as the twins. He recovered her Bible and reached for Rose. She fussed but finally released her hold on Anna Mae.

"Shall we go in?" he asked.

A wave of anxiety swept through her. "Maybe you should go first and I will sit near the back." She started to hand Ruby over, but two little hands pressed against Anna Mae's cheeks and Ruby's lips quivered. "Ruby go you." The little head shook up and down positively, a question in the depths of her eyes.

Anna Mae placed her forehead against the little girl's. To turn this baby away could possibly relay that she wasn't loved enough, that she somehow lacked the ability to be loved. Anna Mae knew all about those feelings. No way would she ever make this child feel unloved or unimportant. "We'll all go together." Bolstering her courage, she shifted Ruby to her side and walked up the church steps.

Josiah rushed ahead and pulled the door open. Anna Mae was happy to see that no one else waited on the steps or in the entryway as they entered. She slipped into the back pew and made room for Josiah and Rose. The piano began playing the moment they were seated. She breathed a sigh of relief, realizing that no one would be able to speak openly to her or about her until after the service.

When it was finished, Anna Mae hurriedly gathered her things. *Please, Lord, don't let anyone speak to me. Just this once, please, can I be selfish and make it out of here without embarrassment? Please, Lord? Just this once?*

It seemed as if the Lord had too many people at that moment to listen to because Mrs. Harvey, a sweet older woman, immediately turned in her seat. "Anna Mae, I am so glad to see you this morning. I'd heard you were sick. Are you feeling better now?"

Anna Mae smiled at her. "Much better, thank you."

The woman motioned for her to sit back down. She did and then Mrs. Harvey leaned against the pew and whispered, "You won't have any more trouble from

Thelma. I told her that if she breathed one word as to why you chose to quit teaching, I'd tell some of her secrets." The sweet woman chuckled. "Don't expect to hear her ever speak of it again." She patted Anna Mae's hand.

Could it be true? Had Mrs. Harvey really stood up to the bank president's wife? Anna Mae lifted her hands in utter disbelief before exhaling loudly. "How can I ever thank you, Mrs. Harvey?"

Ruby tugged at her. Anna Mae pulled the little girl into her lap, her mind searching frantically for words to express her relief. She came up empty. She simply didn't know what else to say to Mrs. Harvey. Such kindness seemed to render her speechless.

"Nonsense, no one hurts one of my kids and gets away with it. Not even my best friend." Mrs. Harvey stood slowly. "Well, I best be getting back to the house. I understand we're having meat loaf for lunch." She looked down and winked at Anna Mae. "It's my favorite, you know."

As the older woman walked away, Anna Mae felt blessed. She hadn't realized how much she'd meant to Mrs. Harvey.

In the spring, when they'd all lost their homes to a tornado, Mrs. Harvey had become a dear friend. When William had left the girls in Emily Jane's care while he worked, Anna Mae became close to them as she assisted with some of their daily care. Mrs. Harvey had helped them with the girls and had been there to support everyone after the tornado. The older woman called Anna Mae one of her kids. It felt good.

Thank You, Lord, for answering my prayer. It's not

exactly what I expected but You do work in mysterious ways, don't You? She smiled secretly, knowing the Lord had heard her and answered in His own way.

"Anna Mae? Would you join us for lunch? I've fried a chicken and made potato salad."

She turned to find Emily Jane and William standing beside Josiah and Rose. Still a little befuddled by Mrs. Harvey's kindness, Anna Mae nodded.

"Ruby go you, too."

Anna Mae grinned at the little girl in her arms. She'd missed her so much.

"You're coming, too." Emily Jane tickled Ruby's tummy, sending childish squeals throughout the church.

Several women and men stopped to shake hands with them and wish Anna Mae well. She had thought they'd all turn on her. How foolish she felt now. Her true friends stood faithfully beside her.

Anna Mae looked at Josiah; a dark figure of a man, big and powerful, yet the blue eyes intent upon her brimmed with tenderness. She felt weak in the knees. She thought again of his proposal. Did he still want to marry her? Or had he changed his mind?

"I do believe that's the best fried chicken I've had in a long time," Josiah said, wiping potato salad out of Rose's hair.

Emily Jane picked up his empty plate and carried it to the kitchen. "Thank you, Josiah. I'm glad you enjoyed it."

Anna Mae had been quiet during lunch. She'd hardly eaten anything and her brown eyes seemed glued to her plate. Was she nervous around him and the girls?

Or did she fear he'd ask what she'd decided regarding his proposal?

Her sweet voice filled his ears. "Yes, I think you out-did yourself this time, Emily Jane."

"If you think that was good, just wait until you taste her fruitcake. She's been working on this recipe for weeks and has finally perfected it." William rubbed his tummy and licked his lips.

Josiah shook his head. His brother-in-law had always been a ham, but since he'd married Emily Jane he seemed to have gotten worse at overacting.

"If you haven't noticed, Anna Mae, I think my husband's saying he's tired of eating fruitcake." Emily Jane carried what looked like more of a fruit loaf than a fruit-cake into the dining area.

William put on his shocked face. "I didn't say that."

"No, you implied it. No cake for you." Emily Jane handed each of the girls a cookie and then sliced the moist cake. She passed a piece to Josiah.

Josiah laughed. "Serves him right." He took the dish and passed it to Anna Mae.

"It looks wonderful, Emily Jane." Anna Mae set the dessert down and stood. "Who would like a cup of fresh coffee?"

Both Josiah and William answered, "I would."

Her blue skirt swished about her ankles as she walked. Today her hair wasn't up in its normal teacher-style bun but hung in long graceful curves over her shoulders. She carried herself confidently. Josiah's admiration grew. Anna Mae had a strength and stamina at odds with the slenderness of her body.

He watched her fill everyone's cup and return the

pot to the stove. She sat back down and lifted the fork to her lips. He noticed that Emily Jane closely watched for Anna Mae's reaction. What did his sister-in-law expect? He held his own fork midair, preparing to taste the cake, but decided to see what Anna Mae thought first.

Josiah sat mesmerized as she took a bite, chewed slowly and then sighed. Anna Mae took a sip of coffee before saying, "I believe William is right. This is the best fruitcake I've ever tasted. You will have to give me your recipe." Her brown eyes met his as if she realized that he was staring.

He quickly lowered his gaze.

"I'll give it to you, but you have to promise not to share with any of the other ladies. I'm going to start serving it in the bakery and then take orders for Thanksgiving and Christmas." Emily Jane sat down and smiled at Anna Mae. "I've missed having meals with you," she said before digging into her own slice of cake. "You were a great sampler."

Anna Mae teased. "I miss you, too, as well as a couple of pounds." She smoothed her hands over her waist. "I could never turn down your desserts."

Women were so strange. Men never gushed over each other like they did. Josiah felt relieved that his brother-in-law's wife liked Anna Mae, since he'd asked her to marry him. A question she hadn't yet given him an answer to.

He ate his dessert in silence. Josiah didn't really care for fruitcake, but Emily Jane's was probably the best he'd tasted. He didn't tell her of his dislike for fruitcake in general, not wanting to appear ungrateful.

His gaze moved to his silent daughters. They each

held part of a cookie in their chubby hands, but were fast asleep, leaning into each other like kittens in a basket. He'd missed Anna Mae over the past few days. *Lord, for the girls' sake, please let her say yes to my proposal.*

As if Emily Jane had heard his prayer, she said, "William, why don't you and I take our nieces to the bedroom and lay them down for a nap? I believe Anna Mae and Josiah would like to catch up."

"Catch up?" William looked from one to the other. "Catch up on what?"

Emily Jane laughed. "You'll find out soon enough." She gently lifted Rose into her arms and carried her to the bedroom.

With one last look at both of them, William carefully scooped Ruby from her chair and followed his wife. He patted the fussing little girl's back as he left.

Josiah reached out and took Anna Mae's hand in his. "The girls missed you, Annie."

Her big brown eyes looked overly large in her pale face. "They did?"

He stroked the back of her hand with his thumb. "Of course they did."

"I missed you and the girls, too," she quietly replied.

Josiah released her hand. He didn't want her to miss him, just the girls. The last thing he needed was for her to have deeper feelings for him than friendship. He rubbed the back of his neck and cleared his throat. "Have you given any thought to the question I asked you?"

She nodded. "Yes, and I've decided to take you up on your offer. But…" Anna Mae paused. Her big brown eyes searched his intently.

What was she going to say? That she'd decided she wanted a real marriage? That she expected him to fall in love with her? He held his breath and waited. After several long moments he couldn't stand it any longer and asked, "But what?"

"Before I say yes, I want you to know that I was engaged once before I came here. My fiancé left town the night before our wedding and broke my heart. I can't take that type of heartbreak again, so know this... I most likely will never love you. At least not the way a wife should love her husband." She breathed out heavily. "There. I've said it, so if you don't want to marry me after hearing this, I understand."

Josiah's heart went out to Anna Mae for her loss. But still it felt as if a huge weight had been lifted off his shoulders. She didn't want a real marriage, either. This was perfect. He felt laughter bubble up in his stomach and exit his lips.

Anna Mae sat looking at him as if he'd grown horns. He was sure she wondered what had overcome him. "You're happy I won't ever love you?"

He forced himself to stop smiling. "Yes. I want to be friends with you, but I can never love you the way I did my first wife, Mary."

"Oh, I see." Anna Mae nodded. "But I'd rather no one else knows that this is a marriage of convenience."

He turned up his smile a notch and nodded in turn. Anna Mae laughed. "Good, then we can get married whenever you're ready."

Was it his imagination or did her laugh sound forced? He searched her face but saw no sorrow in it. Was it possible they were making a mistake they both would regret in the near future? Should they allow a bunch of townspeople to dictate to them how they should behave? What they should do?

Chapter Seven

When Josiah had said he didn't think he could ever love her as he did Mary, something inside Anna Mae felt crushed. She continued to smile and forced herself to laugh with him, but actually, she wanted to cry. Deep down she had hoped to find love someday.

"Do I hear laughter in here? Does that mean what I think it does?" Emily Jane asked, pulling William behind her.

Josiah stood up and smiled. "I've asked Anna Mae to marry me and she's agreed."

"Marry you?"

William looked as if someone had gut punched him. Anna Mae should have seen this coming; after all, Mary had been William's sister. He sank into one of the chairs.

Josiah nodded, "Yes."

Anna Mae watched realization of the impact this would have on his brother-in-law cross Josiah's features. His expression turned somber. "I'm sorry, William. I didn't consider how you would feel about it. I just assumed you'd be happy for me. For us." He reached down and took Anna Mae's hand, pulling her to her feet.

"I didn't figure you'd get married so soon." William shook his head as if to clear it. "But of course you'd want to get married. You have the girls to consider." He stood and then walked over and slapped a hand on Josiah's shoulder. "I'm sure Mary would understand, too."

Anna Mae watched the two men, surprised that William chose to believe that his brother-in-law was marrying her only for the girls' sake. Josiah's confirming nod bore witness that sadly, it was true.

Seemingly unaware of the truth, Emily Jane ran over and hugged Anna Mae. "I can't wait to tell Susanna. You know she's going to want to make your dress, like she did mine. Oh, you are going to have the most beautiful wedding. I think you should make it a Christmas wedding. Think how pretty the church will look." It was as if the woman couldn't contain her joy. "And I will make your cake. Oh, I am so excited for you!" She clapped her hands happily.

"Emily Jane, we aren't having a big wedding. I want a simple ceremony. And I think the sooner the better, don't you agree, Josiah?" She prayed he'd give the correct answer.

As if they were a loving couple, Josiah lifted her hand and kissed the backs of her fingers. "Anything you want, Annie."

"See?" Emily Jane pressed. "He doesn't mind waiting until Christmas."

Anna Mae pulled her hand from his. Her skin tingled where his warm lips had touched. She stood. Her voice came out as electrified as her hand felt. "Well, I don't want to wait until Christmas. That's almost two full months away. I'm ready to get married now."

The room grew silent as all three adults stared at her, various degrees of questioning in each expression. Josiah seemed pleased as punch and William looked as if he'd suffered another punch. Emily Jane appeared ready to hit someone if she didn't get her way. Anna Mae stifled a giggle, then sobered.

They each had their own thoughts, but she was the one who had to prepare for the worst. The worst being that Mrs. Bradshaw still might spread rumors. Mrs. Harvey had put a stop to Mrs. Anderson's meddling, but that might not stop Mrs. Bradshaw.

Anna Mae knew her friends would ignore the widow's lies, but what if Josiah started thinking she wasn't good enough to be a stand-in mother for his girls? Then what? She would be left stranded again.

Until she said her vows, Anna Mae knew she had to be on her toes, ready for anything. So to her way of thinking, the sooner the better.

"She's right." Josiah placed his strong arm around her waist. "We don't want to take the chance of being separated should another storm arrive, with me and the girls stranded at the farm and Annie here in town."

His arm about her waist gave her a sense of protection, a feeling that they would stand together against anything or any person that came between them. She leaned lightly into him, tilting her face up to his, wishing there was a way to express how she felt about their united stance.

She felt rather than saw his shocked reaction. Had he thought she wanted to kiss him? She stepped out of the circle of his arm, her face flushed with humiliation and anger at herself. She'd only wanted his protection.

Just when she started to put distance between them, he caught her elbow, gently turning her to face him. "So how soon will you do me the honor of becoming my bride?

Anna Mae couldn't believe she was married. The last three days had felt like a Texas twister. She was blown about preparing for the big day that just didn't seem real.

As Emily Jane had predicted, Susanna created a dress just for her wedding. It was a soft peach with lace ruffles around the long sleeves and neck. Her friend had fussed that it wasn't enough, but Anna Mae thought it was perfect.

Emily Jane baked a two-tiered cake much too large for the handful of friends and family who were present at the church. It seemed extravagant for a marriage of convenience, but then again, her friends didn't know it was just that.

Josiah stood with the minister in a black suit, black boots, and his black hat in his hands as she'd walked down the aisle. They hadn't spent much time together since having Sunday lunch at William and Emily Jane's house. Anna Mae had questioned her decision several times, but when she saw him standing there, a pillar of strength and security, she felt the Lord's peace wash over her and knew she was doing the right thing.

The twins had walked in front of her, throwing colorful ribbon bows onto the hardwood floor and giggling. Their little legs were slow moving and it had seemed like an eternity before she'd arrived at Josiah's side.

They'd said their vows, he'd kissed her lightly on the cheek and the minister had pronounced them husband and wife. What had taken three days to prepare for was over in less than five minutes.

Josiah helped her up into the wagon and then turned to take Rose and Ruby from Emily Jane and William. As he reached for Rose, his sister-in-law said, "We could keep the girls tonight, Josiah. They wouldn't be any trouble."

"Thank you, but those clouds look like they might contain snow and I'd just as soon have the twins with us if we get another storm." He handed Rose up to Anna Mae.

She released the breath she'd unintentionally held, relieved that he'd declined to leave the girls. Even though they were now married, Anna Mae wasn't prepared to spend an entire evening alone with her husband. She set her new daughter into the wooden box that Josiah used to keep them safe when it was just him and the twins riding in the wagon. She knew the crowd of well-wishers would expect her to sit beside her new husband.

William gave Ruby to Josiah, who handed the second little girl up to her. Then he hurried around to pull himself up beside Anna Mae.

She set Ruby beside Rose and then turned to wave at the small crowd of people as he pulled away from the church. She turned back around in her seat to find them heading toward the farm. Now her home.

When they were far enough away from the church so that no one would hear him, Josiah said, "That went well." He smiled over at her. "Did I tell you how pretty you look?"

She eased farther across the seat from him and smoothed out the wrinkles in her dress. "No, I believe you were too busy getting married," she teased.

"True, but you do look very pretty. I like the way you're wearing your hair." He clicked his tongue, causing his horse to pick up the pace.

"Thank you." Anna Mae reached up and touched the silky strands and ringlets that Mrs. Harvey had declared was her gift to Anna Mae. The older woman had insisted that she leave it down, flowing sleekly over her shoulders with wisps curled in ringlets about her face. It had taken a long time to get the curls to hold. They would be out by tomorrow morning and Anna Mae's hair would be back to its old mousy-looking style.

She turned to check on the girls, who had grown quiet and found they had slumped down in the box and fallen asleep against each other. Their little faces shone with sweet dreams. Anna Mae tucked a thick blanket around them and then took another and placed it over the top of the box to help lock in their warmth.

Knowing they were safe, she turned back on the seat just as large fluffy snowflakes began to fall. She pulled her cloak tighter around her body and looked up at the sky. If the truth were truly to be known, aside from worrying about her job and the reaction of the townspeople, she had enjoyed being snowed in at the farm. It had seemed as if they were alone in their own little world, snug, cozy and warm. Now it looked as if it would happen again. Her silent prayers of thanks winged up to the Lord, for the small addition of snow on her wedding day and especially for her new family.

She and Josiah may not have married for love, but

Anna Mae felt she'd done the right thing by marrying him. She felt an inner peace, as if she finally belonged somewhere. Josiah might not need her, but his girls did, and she planned to be the best mother she could be.

They rode for several minutes before he glanced her way again. "Why so quiet? Do you regret marrying me?"

"No." She grinned. "But I am glad the service is over. I'm not a fan of being in front of everybody."

His brows drew together. "Really? I figured it wouldn't bother you, since you stand in front of a classroom full of children every day." Josiah lifted one hand and lightly slapped the reins against the horse's back to speed him up a bit. The blowing snow came against their faces in a cold, wet kiss.

"They're children. Not adults. Besides, kids really don't pay attention to the way I'm dressed or the way I walk and talk. Today I felt like an ugly ink blot on a fresh piece of paper."

Josiah pulled the wagon to a halt.

Why had he stopped? She looked about but didn't see anything amiss. The snow wasn't falling at an alarming rate, so there was no reason for him to stop and turn them around. When she looked at him to inquire, Anna Mae found him turned in the seat, studying her face. "You really do feel that way, don't you?"

She nodded. "Yes. But it's no reason to concern yourself. I've always felt like that." Anna Mae offered him what she hoped was a cheery smile. She hadn't been looking for sympathy, just stating how she felt. How she'd always felt.

He picked up her hands. "You are far from ugly.

Next to my Mary, you're the most beautiful woman I've ever seen. Your hair looks silky soft, and your brown eyes have a mysterious, captivating glint in them. Your smile…well, it warms a person right up, and the shape of your face is beautiful."

She didn't know what to say. His gloved hands holding hers made her feel as if he truly meant every word. "Thank you. I believe that's the nicest thing anyone has ever said to me." Her face flushed right to the tips of her burning ears.

Josiah nodded and then released her hands. He quickly got the horse moving toward home once more. "You're welcome. I hope you never believe such negative things about yourself again."

Anna Mae didn't answer him. She'd been told all her life that she was plain. It was sweet of him to tell her differently, but she knew the truth. Once the wedding day came to an end, Josiah would see her for who she truly was—simple, plain Anna Mae.

Half an hour later he pulled up to the front of the house and stopped. Josiah jumped from the wagon and hurried to her side to help her down.

"The girls are still napping. I'll bring them in as soon as I get the horse taken care of." He smiled down at her.

"Are you sure they will be all right? It's pretty cold out here." She gnawed at her lower lip.

He gently touched her cheek. "Thank you for worrying about them, but this is the way we have done it the last few months." He dropped his hand and climbed back onto the wagon. "As long as they are covered up in that box, they are toasty warm."

Anna Mae nodded, missing his touch. He was right,

and she could get a few things done in the house before they woke up. "Are you hungry? I could fix us something to eat while you are out in the barn."

He grinned. "I'm starving. That bite of cake wasn't nearly enough."

Torn by conflicting emotions, Anna Mae watched him drive the wagon to the barn. She was married to a virtual stranger. What did the future hold for her now? What did the Lord expect her to do from here on out? Would she be a good wife and mother? Girding herself with resolve, Anna Mae forced her lips to part in a curved, stiff smile. She vowed right then that Josiah, Ruby and Rose would never have reason to complain.

Chapter Eight

Josiah wiped his feet before entering the house. Mud and straw caked on the bottom of his boots. He set down the box that held the sleeping girls. They were getting heavier and soon wouldn't be able to sleep in the box or be carried into the house like that.

He took a few minutes to pull the footwear off. Mary had always hated when he'd come home and mucked up her floors. What would she think if she could see him now with a new bride? He set his boots beside the closed door and carried the girls to the sitting room.

Josiah checked that the twins still slept and then made his way into the kitchen. He inhaled deeply. Was that fried chicken he smelled? Anna Mae didn't have time to fry up a hen. Well, that didn't make no never mind; he smelled fried chicken, so if she did cook it, she was the most amazing wife a man could ask for.

Anna Mae stepped out of the bedroom. She had taken off her wedding dress and now wore a light pink housedress. A big white apron covered the front of it. "Emily Jane left us a wedding present," she said, motioning toward the kitchen stove, where several covered dishes sat.

"Fried chicken?"

"Yes, with a note that says she wanted to make sure I didn't cook on my wedding day. Wasn't that sweet?"

When had Emily Jane had time to do that? He remembered William being late for the service and now knew why. "My sister-in-law never ceases to amaze me," he said, realizing that Anna Mae still waited for some form of answer from him.

She pulled fried chicken, baked beans and big fluffy biscuits from the back of the stove. "It's still warm, too."

"Good, I'm starving." He met her at the table. She'd already set it with four plates, silverware and glasses.

"What about the girls?" she asked, looking toward the box that sat beside the fireplace.

Josiah grinned. "Let them sleep. We can enjoy a rare meal without them demanding to be fed first."

Anna Mae smiled and motioned for him to sit down. "Emily Jane also left us warm apple cider, or you can have coffee if you'd prefer." She paused for him to answer.

"Coffee for me, please." Josiah waited for her to return and sit down. They needed to talk about their marriage, what it would be and what it wouldn't be, but first he'd enjoy their wedding present.

Once she was seated, Josiah said a quick prayer over the food and then dug in. He wasn't sure what to say to his new bride, so they ate in silence. She obviously felt as unsure of him as he did her. It seemed a little awkward, but not intensely so.

After several minutes Anna Mae laid her fork down and sighed. "The service was beautiful, wasn't it?"

"I believe so." Josiah set his fork down also and wiped his mouth. "The women did a fine job."

"Yes, I really do have wonderful friends here. I couldn't have done it without them." She picked up her plate and carried it to the scrap bucket.

"Or without me." Josiah laughed out loud at the shocked expression on her face. "Well, do you think you could have gotten married without a groom?" he teased.

Josiah saw in her face that he'd hit a nerve. She didn't look angry, just hurt. "I'm sorry, Annie. I was only teasing."

She offered a wobbly smile. "You didn't say anything wrong. You're right, a woman can't get married without a groom. No one knows that better than me."

He hurried around the table and hugged her. "Annie, for a moment I forgot about that clod of dirt who left you. It was insensitive of me to say what I did. I really am sorry." Josiah gently squeezed her. The sweet scent of lavender teased his nose. He leaned forward and sniffed her hair.

Anna Mae returned the hug and then stepped out of his embrace. "Really, Josiah. It's all right." She walked to the table and collected the rest of the dirty dishes.

With her back to him she said, "We need to talk about our marriage."

Josiah sat down at the table. He missed the warmth of her in his arms. "Yes, I've been meaning to talk to you, too."

She poured water into a large pan and set it on the back of the stove. "Do you want to go first?"

"No, you go ahead." He decided the polite thing to do was let her get out whatever she had on her mind.

Anna Mae cleared her throat. "Well, I was thinking that I would like to stay in the room I used last time I was here. If that's all right with you?" The question in her voice made him smile.

"No, I want you with the girls. There will be lots of nights when I won't be home. I'd rather you be close to them. You can have my room and I'll take the smaller room."

"Oh, I hadn't thought of that." She glanced toward the fireplace, where the twins slept peacefully. "But don't you think they are old enough now for their own room?"

Josiah looked at his girls, too. Rose and Ruby would always be his babies. He couldn't imagine them having a room of their own, and yet knew that they were almost old enough now to do so.

"I suppose so," he admitted grudgingly. Then another thought sent his pulse spinning. Maybe Anna Mae didn't want the girls with her. Was that why she'd made that comment? His head swirled with doubts. How well did he actually know her? He'd known plenty of women who acted a certain way until they had a man all hogtied, then their true colors showed up.

He regarded her thoughtfully for a moment. She lifted the pan of water from the stove to the counter and filled it with the dirty dishes. She moved quickly from one task to the other, wiping off the table, covering the food, refilling their coffee cups. The apron tied behind her back accentuated her slender waist. There was both delicacy and strength in her face, but did he know much about her character?

He had to find out. He couldn't just sit quietly and let his girls suffer from his poor judgment. He stood and with heavy steps walked to Anna Mae's side. He put his hand on her shoulder and turned her so he could see into her face.

She looked up at him, brows raised with what seemed to be genuine concern. "What is it, Josiah?"

"The statement you made a few minutes ago. Do you not want the girls in the same room with you?"

Her shiny brown eyes widened in surprise. He heard her quick intake of breath, before she placed a hand against his chest. She spoke in a broken whisper. "How can you even ask me that?" Anna Mae dropped her hand.

Didn't she realize they truly were practically strangers? What did she know of him? That he was William's brother-in-law. The father of Rose and Ruby. And that was all. She didn't know what his character was, so how could she expect him to know hers?

"But you must have doubts or you wouldn't have had to ask that. Please—" Anna Mae motioned to the table "—let's sit down and talk a bit more."

When they were seated opposite each other, she reached out and laced her fingers in his. "I know that we don't actually know each other that well, and I guess I assumed you could tell my character by the company I keep. But you can rest assured in this one thing." Raising fine arched brows, she spoke firmly. "I love Rose and Ruby. I loved them even before you showed up in town. Emily Jane and I took turns watching them while

William worked at the store. It was easy to fall in love with them."

Anna Mae's eyes clung to his as she analyzed his reaction. He had no idea what she saw in his expression, but her voice gentled and she squeezed his hands. "Over the last couple of weeks, when I was sick, the twins wound up in bed with me more often than not. I love sleeping with their little bodies cuddled up next to me. But they are getting bigger, and giving them space of their own is the next step. And that is all I meant by the comment."

Josiah felt an indefinable feeling of rightness. He believed her. He stretched out an arm and touched her cheek. "Thank you for not being mad at me. I learned too late in my first marriage that communication was seventy-five percent of what made a partnership work. I hope we always talk things out, and with a marriage like we have, we both need assurances from each other on private subjects that most couples work out during their courting days." He joined their hands again. "Is there anything you would like to ask me? Something that might make you feel better?"

"Well, yes, actually there is." Amusement flickered in the eyes that met his. "Where is your gun?"

Laughter floated up from her throat as Anna Mae observed the changing expressions that crossed Josiah's face. Clear, observant eyes looked out from his suntanned face, regarding her speculatively before his mouth twitched with amusement. His voice, though quiet, held an ominous quality. Had she not seen the flash of humor, she would have felt like one of his prisoners being interrogated.

"Now why would a sweet little thing like you need a gun?"

"Oh, I didn't say a word about needing a gun."

Josiah untangled their hands, making her wonder if she'd pushed him too far in their teasing. He bent over and pulled a small hand gun out of his boot and laid it on the table. "There's this one. It's a Philadelphia Derringer." He pulled his coat aside and pulled a larger gun from behind his waist. "There is also one here; it's a Colt revolver. And of course when I'm not traveling, the rifle will always be over the fireplace."

He leaned back, sizing her up. "Where's yours?" he asked with an arched eyebrow.

He'd figured her concern was that the guns not be lying around where the twins, or anyone else for that matter, could get hold of them, causing Lord knows what kind of trouble. She gloried briefly in the shared moment. She tipped her cup to her lips and tried to force her expression into all seriousness. "Why, Sheriff, I thought you knew that schoolteachers are not allowed to carry weapons."

Laughter floated up from his throat. It was the first time Anna Mae had heard him sound so merry. The only problem being his happiness woke the girls.

Two twin heads popped out of the box. "Out," they echoed and then grinned at each other. "Eat," they called.

"Now look what you've done. The monster babies are awake." Josiah turned and collected the two girls.

Anna Mae shook her head. "I'm not the one that was

laughing, you were." She turned to the stove and collected the two plates that she'd prepared earlier.

Josiah got the twins seated and then handed each of them a spoon. She returned to the table with cups of warm apple cider. "I wouldn't give this to them until they've eaten their fill," she suggested, "otherwise you won't get them to eat another bite."

"It's that good, huh?"

"Emily Jane made it, what do you think?" she asked.

The two girls stared up at them. Each held a spoon and a piece of bread. Anna Mae realized that neither had taken a bite of their food.

"What are you two waiting for? Eat up," Josiah said, giving them permission to eat.

They shook their heads and closed their eyes before bowing their heads.

Puzzled, Josiah looked from the girls to Anna Mae. She giggled. "They are waiting for you to say grace."

Josiah bowed his head and said a quick prayer of thanks. Anna Mae's heart swelled when he thanked the Lord for bringing her into their lives one stormy night, and then closed by thanking Him for his thoughtful sister-in-law and the food the girls were about to consume. Anna Mae looked up and found it impossible not to return his disarming smile.

While the children ate, Josiah talked to them as he helped them. Anna Mae washed up the few dishes they had dirtied and poured herself a cup of the warm cider. Her life here was going to be pleasant. It didn't have to have the type of love a man and wife shared. She would be happy with the blessing of a family.

* * *

Three nights later, Anna Mae sat at the kitchen table and wrote to her parents. She wondered what her mother would think of her quick marriage. The last time she'd written, Anna Mae had bragged on how well school was going and how much she loved teaching. She'd assured her mother that she'd probably never marry. But now, less than a month later, she anxiously tried to figure out how to tell her that not only was she married, she also had two little girls.

The fire crackled and popped. Anna Mae's gaze moved to Josiah. The girls were already in bed sleeping, and he sat reading the Bible that was open in his lap. She had to admit that her feelings of friendship for him were growing. Anna Mae felt certain it wasn't love, because her heart didn't seem to be involved. The Lord knew her heart couldn't take another breaking. And she planned to guard against such things as love.

Anna Mae refocused on the letter.

Dear Mom and Dad,
A lot has happened since I last wrote to you. We have had some really bad weather here and…

Anna Mae chewed on the pencil. And what? And I got married? I was accused of breaking the rules of my contract and was fired as the Granite schoolteacher? Or guess what? You are the grandparents of two very precious girls? How did she tell her parents all the things that had happened over the last few weeks?

Her gaze moved to her kitchen. She'd done a lot of work, cleaning and reorganizing it to fit her style and mood. A new curtain hung at the window over her wash area. She loved the window being there. Come spring, she could look out at her garden in the backyard. She'd also scrubbed all the pots and pans, and Josiah agreed to help her hang them along the back wall. That job they planned to do tomorrow. He'd said something about large hooks packed somewhere in the barn attic.

Outside, the snow drifted down in glistening white flakes. She sighed. Would her mother be interested in hearing about that? Anna Mae wasn't sure. Mother lived in a big house with lots of servants. What would she think of her daughter's three-bedroom farmhouse? What would she think of her sheriff husband and twin daughters?

Did it matter what her mother thought? Not really, since it was already a done deal. Then why should she agonize over it? Anna Mae looked back down at her letter. She picked up where she'd left off.

And since my last letter, I have gotten married. Josiah Miller is a wonderful man and the sheriff of Granite. He has twin daughters that are almost two years old. They are adorable. Both are small because they are twins, but they talk more than any girls their age that I've ever met. Not that I've actually met that many others.

We live on a small farm that has a three-bedroom house and an orchard. I'm hoping to have a nice garden next summer. Maybe you can come visit then.

Well, it is getting late and I need to get some rest. I love you both, Anna Mae Miller.

She looked at her name. It was the first time since they'd gotten married that she'd written it out. She whispered, "Anna Mae Miller."

"It has a nice ring to it."

She jumped. When had Josiah come up behind her? Had he read her letter as she wrote? Anna Mae glanced over her shoulder at him. He smiled down on her. A cup of coffee filled his large hands.

"I think so, too," she admitted. "I was just writing my parents to tell them about our marriage." She folded the letter and tucked it inside a homemade envelope.

"I hope they approve of our marrying." He slipped into the chair beside her.

She smiled. Anna Mae hoped so, too, but if they didn't there was nothing they could do about it now. They'd thought Mark Peters was the catch of the season and look where that had gotten her.

Josiah Miller was a good man. She just prayed their marriage could stand the test of time. A flicker of apprehension coursed through her. What if it didn't? Where on earth would she go? Would she be forced to return to her parents' home? Anna Mae didn't think she could face her mother's disappointment in her again.

Chapter Nine

Josiah sipped his coffee. He'd read the letter over Anna Mae's shoulder. Not to be nosy but because he wanted to make sure she was happy. The letter hadn't indicated either sadness or unhappiness. She did seem a little awed when she'd said her married name aloud. He guessed all women had to get used to the name change and possibly enjoyed the sound of their married name. It seemed odd to him but what did he know?

She looked up from the envelope she held. "I'm sure my parents will approve of our marriage." Her hand shook slightly, leading him to believe that maybe she wasn't as sure as she sounded. "After all, what's not to like? You were the catch of the season. Never mind that I had to catch a few other things before I caught you, like pneumonia, high fever…" Her voice contained a strong suggestion of reproach, but her eyes flashed with humor and teasing.

He couldn't help himself as he burst out laughing. On almost every topic they'd discussed, Anna Mae had the best attitude of anyone he'd ever met. "I hope you think you wound up with the best deal of all that catching." He grinned.

"What about you? I noticed a few heads turning in your direction before I allowed you to catch me. One of them being Mrs. Bradshaw's," she teased back.

Josiah frowned. "I refuse to give the woman any more of my thoughts. As the sheriff, I am duty bound to protect her, but as a citizen I think I'll give her a wide berth."

Why had she brought up Mrs. Bradshaw? The woman left a sour taste in his mouth and stomach. He took his coffee to the sink. Or maybe it was the coffee. He might need to stop drinking the stuff for a while if it kept affecting his stomach. Josiah decided to change the subject. "I need to go to town early in the morning. I'll try to be back by midafternoon to help hang those pots and pans." He set the half-empty cup down.

Her gaze moved to the window. "What about the storm?" Was that concern he heard in her voice?

"I'll be fine. It's not supposed to be as bad as the last one, and besides, with my job I have to be out in all kinds of weather."

Anna Mae nodded. "I suppose you do. It will take some getting used to, being married to the town sheriff."

As if to deny his very words, the wind whipped fiercely about the farmhouse windows. Anna Mae noticed it, too, and caught her lower lip between her teeth. He sought for ways to distract her. He'd never asked her about her family. "What does your father do for a living?"

Josiah rinsed his coffee cup, refilled it with cider and walked back to the table. He enjoyed the feel of the warmth of the cup against his palms. Maybe he was addicted to having something occupy his hands more than actual coffee.

She set back in her chair. "Papa runs a shipping company."

"So I gather that doesn't require him to be away from home in the evenings?"

Her brown hair swayed with the shake of her head. "No, he keeps regular business hours."

"And your mother? Does she work outside the home?"

An amused laugh bubbled out of Anna Mae. "Hardly. She thought I was crazy for wanting to be a teacher. Said a woman's place is in the home."

"What do you think, Annie?" Josiah looked over at her and raised his eyebrows. Did she want to work outside the home or was she content to stay at the house and watch the girls? Perhaps he should have asked her those questions before they got married, Josiah mused.

"I loved being a teacher but I think I'll enjoy staying at home and taking care of things around here." She smiled at him. "Did Mary enjoy staying home or did she want to work?"

"You know, it never occurred to me to ask her." Josiah had just assumed when he'd married his first wife that she wanted to stay home and raise his children. As far as he knew, Mary had never worked.

"Do you have anything against women working?"

"No. Not that I've thought much on the matter. I guess as long as a woman's job didn't interfere with the running of the house or care of her husband and family, it's fine."

"And if it did interfere, how would you feel?"

He couldn't tell from Anna Mae's expression what she was getting at, so he thought carefully about his answer. "Again, to be fair, I don't know how I'd feel. I think the Bible is the final authority and it states that a woman's place is in the home. In other places in God's word, like Proverbs, it speaks of all the work that a woman does and a lot of it is outside the home. So like everything else the Bible teaches, I think moderation is the key."

In neat tight handwriting, Anna Mae wrote her mother's name and address on the envelope. Josiah wondered briefly why she didn't address the letter to both parents. The more he learned about his new wife, the more he realized Anna Mae thought carefully about the decisions she made, never acted flighty or careless, and observed the dictates of society on manners and charity. She made a perfect sheriff's wife. But he guessed correctly, it might take him a lifetime to find out the reasoning going on behind those beautiful eyes.

"Will you mail this for me tomorrow?" She ran a finger over the flap, sealing it tight.

"Be glad to. Do you have a list of things you might need from the dry goods store?"

"No, I haven't checked the larder, but Emily Jane told me there was food in the root cellar that the former owners left."

"Why, yes, there is. I'll bring some of it up tomorrow when I get home. I know there's a lot of beans in a sack down there. I'll get some salt pork from the store and milk from the Smiths' dairy."

Josiah made a mental note to bring other goodies to

make their next few weeks a little easier, because from the sound of the storm, they would be closed in for a little while.

"I know it may be a bit uncomfortable for you, but could you bring my book satchel from the school? It has my sight cards…" Her eyes grew round. "Oh, Josiah, those are my writing examples on the walls, and the two red readers are mine. Would it be wrong of me to want to keep them? I could use them to teach the girls when they're older, on snowy days when we can't get to the school. They mean a lot to me. I spent my first paycheck on them."

That was his Annie. She had an inherent kindness and sense of rightness that showed up in her thought processes. He, on the other hand, wouldn't leave anything in the school to help Mrs. Anderson. Let her buy her own books and supplies. *Yes, Lord, I know that's the wrong way to be. I'll try harder.*

"I'll get your things for you. And no, it isn't wrong. If you can think of anything else, let me know before I leave and I'll get it for you."

"Thanks, Josiah." Anna Mae propped the letter against the saltshaker, then stood. "Well, I'll say good-night. Will you be leaving early in the morning or some-time after breakfast?"

"I'll leave before daylight so no need to get up. I'll let the latch down behind me so you'll be locked in. If all goes as planned I should be back shortly after lunch."

"Be safe, Josiah. 'Night."

Josiah savored the feeling of satisfaction her words left with him. It had been a long time since anyone cared about his safety. It felt good.

"'Night, Annie."

* * *

The next morning, Anna Mae heard the latch fall into the slot and jumped from the bed as if it was on fire. She'd awakened at the first sound of Josiah moving in the next room. She'd lain perfectly still, aware that the walls were paper thin, and hoping and praying the twins wouldn't wake just yet. She'd like to get a start on the day while they still slept.

In less than fifteen minutes she'd finished her morning ablutions, dressed and tiptoed into the sitting room. She stood back a ways from the window, but watched as Josiah vanished into the gray dawn. Then she ran and stared, faced pressed against the pane, to see if she could spot him at any other site down the road. Thankfully, it had stopped precipitating, so she could see clearly across the snowy landscape. The road dipped and when he came back up the other side she could barely make him out, but this satisfied one of her many curiosities. If she watched for him at lunch, he wouldn't be able to sneak up on her; for some reason that was important right now.

After all, she planned to move some of his stuff around. Well, she had no idea if the things in the house were his or the former owners, but she knew she could make it look better than it did right now. To her way of thinking it was easier to ask forgiveness than permission. Still, she'd rather not get caught in the act. She was totally bewildered by her mixed emotions, but decided the job before her was more important than analyzing why she felt like a trespasser in her own home. Besides, it would be hers after she put her mark on it.

She looked around the sitting room. It was partially

open to the kitchen, but the entrance, which should have permitted one to see all of the kitchen except the pantry and back door, had been blocked off by crates, and Anna Mae could see a shovel and what looked like the girls' wagon that William had used to pull them about in a few months ago.

She quietly lifted the first crate from the top and carried it to the table. Stacks of wanted posters and official looking forms were tossed in haphazardly, so she set it against the wall in the kitchen.

Thirty minutes later, the wagon had been moved to the third bedroom, where Anna Mae nearly fainted. The room looked like the gardener's shed at her parents' estate. Everything from hoes to milk cans filled the space, and even the bed was covered with junk. She closed the door quickly so she wouldn't be tempted to drag everything out and rearrange. If she did that, she'd never be through by the time Josiah arrived home.

Finally, she had the opening cleared and the couch pulled out from the wall. She never had been one to cover windows, and furniture pushed up against one seemed out of place to her. She put a chair on either side of the fireplace and moved the couch in closer. If they sat on the sofa and read to the girls, they could stretch their toes toward the fire. Anna Mae could envision their happy family doing just that and felt deep satisfaction that her thoughts were for their well-being.

She heard the girls stirring, but decided not to rush them. She stepped out on the back porch and pulled bacon from the larder. She did a quick check of the other contents and found quite a bit of meat. There were several packages marked Rabbit and those she had no problem with, but the ones marked Squirrel gave her a moment's pause.

Anna Mae shivered from the cold air whipping at the bottom of her dress, and hurriedly reentered the house. She put bacon in the pan and set it on the stove. Next she whipped up three eggs with a little milk, salt and pepper, and dipped in it three slices of bread from last night's supper. She set another pan on the stove and put in the bread to fry.

The whines and calls from the bedroom had gotten louder and she could barely control her burst of laughter when she peeped around the door. Ruby, with one leg over the rail, could neither get herself over enough to fall to the floor, nor climb back in the crib. Considering she was only about a foot and a half off the floor, the fall would not have hurt her, but her diaper had caught on a decorative wooden knob and she pretty much hung suspended in the air. Rose sat staring at her as if to say, "I told you not to try it, but you wouldn't listen. Now what are we going to do?"

Anna Mae masked her humor and rushed to rescue Ruby. "You naughty girl. What are you doing?" She unhooked the little one and set her on the bed. Then she reached for Rose, who'd stood up with arms raised. Anna Mae could barely scold for laughing. "What if you had fallen and banged your head, Ruby?"

"Uby bad." Rose had no intention of taking her sister's side.

"No bad. Me no bad," Ruby insisted, as Anna Mae pulled off the soiled diaper and set her on the chamber pot.

By the time she freed Rose of her soiled diaper, Ruby

had used the potty and was running happily around the room in her gown, with her backside showing. Giggling as Anna Mae tried to catch her, she screamed with joy to be finally caught, tossed in the air, then pinned on the bed.

Minutes later, with both freshly diapered, Anna Mae carried a girl under each arm into the kitchen. She set them at their respective places and hurried to rescue the bacon and bread. She saw Rose shiver and realized she had let the fire get too low, which had been good for cooking breakfast and her cleaning spree, but bad because the house had gotten chilly.

As she stoked the fire, Anna Mae couldn't help but worry about Josiah's reaction to her rearranging his home. Would he like it? Or demand she put things back the way she'd found them?

Chapter Ten

The sound of a wagon coming down the dirt road drew Anna Mae's attention. Rose and Ruby were playing with their pull toys. She looked out the window and saw Mrs. Linker and her daughter draw up in the yard.

The Linkers were their closest neighbors. Josiah had said that they were the first to greet him and the girls when he'd moved in. It looked as if the two ladies were going to be the first to welcome her, too.

She stepped out on the porch to greet them. "Mrs. Linker, Margaret, come on in here and get warmed up."

"Thank you. We thought we'd bring a loaf of Margaret's favorite apple bake bread." Mrs. Linker was a tall woman with gray hair that she kept pulled into a bun on the top of her head. She wore a brown housedress with matching brown shoes and a bulky coat that came a little below her waist.

Margaret climbed down from the wagon. She was dressed much like her mother, only instead of a bun on her head, her hair hung to her waist in a long braid down her slim back. "I hope you like it as much as I do," Mrs. Linker said, hurrying up the icy steps.

"I'm sure I will." Anna Mae held the door open for them to pass. Her gaze swept the room, searching for the twins. Both girls stood beside the couch, eyeing their neighbors.

"Oh, Margaret." Mrs. Linker's voice held a strong suggestion of reproach. "I can't believe we forgot our wedding gifts in the wagon. Will you run out and get them, please?"

"Sure, Mama." The girl left quickly, without a backward glance.

"You didn't have to get us a wedding gift," Anna Mae protested as she took the bread. She inhaled the sweet smell of apple and cinnamon. "This is gift enough. I can't wait to try it."

"Nonsense. Though our gift really won't be much of one until spring."

Now what did that mean? Anna Mae frowned. "I don't understand." She set the bread on the table.

Margaret hurried back through the door carrying a large wooden box much like the one Josiah used in the wagon for the girls. It jostled against her as she hurried to set it down by the fireplace. "Here you go."

A weird yet familiar sound met Anna Mae's ears. Rose and Ruby hurriedly toddled to her, grabbing her skirt in their chubby little hands. Then it dawned on her what she was hearing. Her mouth dropped open. "You brought us chickens?" She turned to the women. Although Mrs. Linker quickly hid her smile, Anna Mae could see it in her eyes.

"Yep, all farms need a mess of chickens. 'Course, I

only brought you three, two hens and a rooster to get you started."

Anna Mae worried her lower lip with her teeth. "It's a lovely gift, but I don't have a place to keep them." She didn't want to offend the Linkers, and even though chickens scared her, the idea of having fresh eggs appealed to her. But where would they keep them?

"I'm sure our sheriff will be able to build a chicken coop in no time." Mrs. Linker rubbed her hands together to warm them up. "How about we make a hot pot of coffee to go with that bread and have a nice chat?" she suggested, looking longingly toward the kitchen.

"Of course." Anna Mae nodded, still worried about the chickens. What would Josiah say when he came home? Did he know how to build a chicken coop?

Margaret followed her mother to the kitchen table. "I told you we should have waited." Her gaze moved to Anna Mae, who continued to gnaw her bottom lip.

The older woman waved the statement away. "Nonsense."

Anna Mae dislodged the girls from her dress and Ruby immediately plopped to the floor. Anna Mae hurried to the stove and put on a fresh pot of coffee, while wondering what she should do with the chickens. "I don't suppose you'd want to hang on to them for me until we can get the coop made," she suggested, bringing a knife to cut the bread, and several dessert plates to the table.

"They'll be fine in that box for a couple of days." Mrs. Linker licked her lips in anticipation of eating the bread. "Be sure and tell the sheriff that we clipped their wings, so if he wants to put them in a bigger box until you get that coop done they won't fly off."

Anna Mae didn't even want to think what the inside of that box would look like in a couple days. And just who would take those chickens out in order to clean the coop. She couldn't. Simple as that. To say she was scared out of her wits at the thought of handling the chickens would be putting it mildly. She returned to the cupboard and took down three saucers and cups.

Rose pulled on her skirt. "Eat!" she demanded.

The Linkers had shaken her up so much she'd all but forgotten about the little girls. Her gaze darted about the room, searching for Ruby. She found her still sitting on the floor, staring at the chicken-filled box. Confusion laced her tiny features. Anna Mae felt the same way.

Again the thought rushed through her mind—what was Josiah going to think of the "gift"? And until the coop was built, where were they going to keep the chickens? Surely after a day the box would start to smell, and then what?

Mrs. Linker and Margaret enjoyed their coffee and apple bread. The twins smacked their lips as they ate their share.

"This is a mighty nice place ya got here." Mrs. Linker looked around with interest. Anna Mae felt pride in all she'd accomplished earlier in the day. All the things that didn't belong had been removed and the walls and floor had been scrubbed, swept and mopped. The smell of Dutch Glow furniture polish and the shine of the stone hearth in front of the fireplace caused her confidence to spiral upward.

"Thank you, Mrs. Linker. It's a very nice home for

sure." Anna Mae didn't know if it was proper for her to speak so about her own house, but it was the truth and surely one couldn't go wrong talking honestly. "There is still so much to be done. I'm sure there's laundry waiting somewhere, but I haven't found it yet." She laughed self-consciously.

"Oh!" Her neighbor clapped her hands. "Speaking of laundry…" She grabbed a flimsily wrapped present from the counter where Margaret had placed it earlier. "These are for you and Sheriff Miller."

"But I thought the chickens were our gift." Anna Mae unwrapped two striped dishcloths with the letter *M* cross-stitched in the lower right-hand corner. She ran a finger over the monogram. "These are lovely, Mrs. Linker. I don't think I'll ever use them. They're too pretty."

"Pish, now don't go getting no ideas they're special. Just plain cotton, but they make good dish towels. You use them, you hear? The best thanks you can give a person is to put their gifts to good use. Same as with them there chickens. You raise 'em and they will supply you with eggs and baby chicks and then you can have fried chicken for Sunday dinner."

So that's that, Anna Mae thought. *You got chickens as a wedding gift and you can't look a gift horse in the mouth.* "Thank you so much, Mrs. Linker and Margaret."

An hour later, she was no closer to a solution as to what to do with her new gifts. Mrs. Linker and Margaret waved goodbye and turned their wagon toward home. Anna Mae closed the door and scooped up the girls. "Nap time."

"No nap," they both protested with a yawn.

"Yes, nap. You need to rest and I need to think." She carried them into the bedroom and put them in their bed.

"Tisses!" Rose demanded.

Anna Mae laughed. "Okay, I'll give you kisses, but only if you promise to go right to sleep."

Both girls nodded.

She kissed them each on the cheek and they both lay down with cheeky grins on their faces. "Remember, you promised to go to sleep."

They closed their eyes and pretended to be asleep. Anna Mae returned to the sitting room. She left the door open so she could hear them and then sat down on the couch.

The chickens grumbled low in their throats. At least she thought it was a grumble. Again she shook her head. What was Josiah going to think of having three chickens in the house? She didn't want three chickens in the house. She knew what he'd think. Chickens belonged outside. At this rate he'd think her crazy for keeping them inside and there would go any chance of her finding love with him. Anna Mae sighed her prayer. *Lord, what am I going to do about this?*

The sun was setting when Josiah rode Roy into the yard. He looked to the house, expecting to see Anna Mae in the window or at the door. Disappointment hit him unexpectedly when she didn't appear in either. "Come on, Roy, let's get you settled in the nice warm barn."

He groomed the horse with an air of calm and self-confidence that belied his anxiety to rush in the house and check on things. All day he'd wondered what Anna Mae and the girls were doing. He'd worked in his office, sorting through the mail and new wanted posters. Then he'd checked with all the businesses to make sure everything was running smoothly. It was a habit he'd gotten into when he'd started as sheriff of the small town. Not only was it neighborly but it also assured him that no one had seen any shady characters about town. Then, Emily Jane had run into him and invited him to the bakery for lunch, which he'd gladly accepted. Still, he couldn't seem to get his mind to focus on the job or lunch. His thoughts continually strayed to Anna Mae and the twins.

He finished with Roy and then headed to the house. When he walked in Josiah was surprised to hear the clucking of chickens. He followed the sound and found Anna Mae in the spare bedroom, trying to herd two hens and a rooster into a corner, where she'd piled up furniture to create a pen of sorts. Feathers floated about the room as if the birds had been chased for quite a while. Anna Mae seemed unaware of him standing in the doorway watching her. Every curve of her body spoke defiance.

Her hands trembled as she eyed the chickens. Every time they moved, she jumped. Was she scared of them?

"I've about had it with you three. Either you get into this pen or so help me, you will be Sunday dinner for sure." She planted her hands on her hips and glared at the unruly animals. Did she really think they'd do what she said?

Her back was to him, but Josiah could see that half

her hair was up and the other half down. Feathers stuck out of the locks that hung against her neck, giving him the impression that one of the chickens had decided to make its nest there. A grin teased his lips. Anna Mae's sleeves were pushed up and she had scratches along both arms.

Still unaware of him, she mumbled, "I wonder how one goes about killing two hens and a rooster?"

The rooster squawked and entered the pen. The two hens hurried after him.

"Now that's more like it." She rushed to shut the makeshift door. "You guys aren't as tough as I thought you were."

The rooster changed his mind and ran out of the pen toward her. Anna Mae jumped back and looked as if she might run for the door. When she saw Josiah, she came to an abrupt stop. Her eyes were wide and her breathing quick.

He couldn't contain his merriment any longer. Josiah burst out laughing. He slapped his knees. "You're scared of them? And you let them loose in here?" he asked, still roaring with laughter.

"What was I supposed to do with them? They would have died in that box." Her lip trembled and tears welled in her eyes.

Josiah immediately sobered. He never could stomach a woman's tears. "Aw, Annie, why didn't you wait until I got home?" He walked across the room and dropped an arm around her shoulders.

"If I'm going to take care of them, I have to overcome my fear. You won't be here all the time," she stated, trying to look brave and failing miserably.

"Where did they come from?" They looked like Rhode Island Reds. The rooster strutted about his new home and the hens followed him dutifully.

"Mrs. Linker gave them to us as a wedding present." Anna Mae smiled up at him, a sheen of purpose in her observant eyes. "Can we keep them? She assured me that come spring the hens will start laying eggs. Just think, we wouldn't have to buy eggs and I might even get enough to be able to sell them at Carolyn's store. Wouldn't that be something?"

Where was the woman who moments before had been scared of the chickens? "You do realize you'll have to feed them? Water them? And collect those eggs, don't you?"

"Of course." She pulled out of his embrace.

She confused him. "But you're afraid of them," he pointed out.

"Well, yes, but I'll just have to overcome that." Determination laced her pretty brown eyes. "If I can face down a roomful of children, I can face three chickens." She looked back at them and shuddered.

"I'm sure you can," he chuckled.

Anna Mae offered him a sweet smile. "Would you like a slice of apple bread and a cup of coffee? Both are still warm."

"I'd love some." He started to follow her through the doorway.

She held her arm out and planted a palm on his chest. "No bread until those chickens are in the pen where they belong."

Josiah watched her turn and head to the kitchen. A grin spread over his face as he called, "Annie, I hate to tell you, but if you're going to sell eggs at the general store, you're going to need more than two chickens and a rooster."

After putting the chickens in her makeshift pen, Josiah entered the sitting room. He stopped. In his rush to discover the chickens, he'd not paid much attention to the rest of the house. She'd rearranged the furniture. The scent of lemon oil reached his nose. The whole house seemed so clean and fresh. Well, all except the spare bedroom where the chickens now resided.

He heard the soft rustle of her skirt as she approached him from behind. "Do you like it?" The uncertainty in her voice had him answering quickly.

"I do. It's different, but I'm sure I'll get used to it." Josiah glanced over his shoulder and offered her a smile. Where had she put the girls' corral?

"The twins are getting too big for that pen you had, so I moved it to the back porch for the moment."

Was she a mind reader? Josiah studied her serious face for a moment. "How will we keep them out of trouble?"

Anna Mae's tinkling laughter would have been endearing if it wasn't pointed at him. "There are two of us now to watch them, and they need to be able to explore and learn what they can and can't do."

Josiah doubted the wisdom of letting them run free, but since she was the one watching them most of the time, he'd let her make that decision. He nodded. "Fair enough."

"Are you hungry for something more hearty than apple bread?" she asked, returning to the kitchen.

He followed. "No. I had lunch with Emily Jane and

William. She asked if she could bring the rest of your stuff out and I told her sure. I hope you don't mind, but I also invited them out for dinner."

That smile he'd begun to love graced Anna Mae's face again. "Of course I don't mind. I started a stew earlier; it won't take long to whip up a pan of corn bread to go with it."

"You are amazing, did you know that?" The words came out of his mouth faster than his thoughts.

"For that, sir, you will receive a bigger helping of the apple bread." She sliced off an inch-thick slice, placed it on a small plate and handed it to him.

He teased, "So compliments mean more food?"

She turned to get his coffee. "That depends."

Josiah carried the bread to the table and slid into one of the chairs. "Depends on what?"

Anna Mae carried two cups to the table and set one in front of him. "On my mood." Her eyes twinkled with merriment.

Would he get used to a playful wife? Or would she become bitter at being stuck out on the farm with very few adults to talk to?

Mary had been more of the serious type. She wasn't bitter or playful, she was simply Mary, and he'd loved her. *Lord, don't let me forget how much I loved Mary. I can't allow Anna Mae into my heart. If I should lose her it would hurt even more if I truly loved her.*

Chapter Eleven

How did she do it? Josiah stood out in the cold, hammering boards together to make a chicken coop. Anna Mae had already talked him into hanging pots and pans, and now here he was freezing half to death, making a chicken coop with old boards from the barn. He shook his head.

Josiah heard wheels crunching into the front yard before he ever saw the wagon. He laid the hammer down and walked around the house. *Saved by the Barnses,* he thought happily.

William had just helped Emily Jane down from the wagon. Josiah hurried forward to help them carry Anna Mae's trunk and other things into the house.

"You take the pies in and we'll get the heavy stuff," William was saying as Josiah approached.

"Thank you." Emily Jane grasped two pie pans and turned toward the house.

Anna Mae opened the front door. She stood with a twin on each side of her. "Come on in here and warm up."

"Thanks, I believe I will." With a little giggle Emily Jane hurried up the porch steps.

Josiah noticed his brother-in-law never took his eyes away from his wife. "Be careful. Those steps might be slippery," William called after her.

"Yes, dear." Emily Jane's voice didn't sound as endearing as her words would lead one to believe.

William waited until she and Anna Mae had entered the house before saying, "I do believe that woman is getting tired of me mothering her."

Josiah laughed. "You reckon so?"

William playfully punched him in the shoulder. "I'll have none of that from you. I remember how you hovered about Mary when she was carrying the twins." He pulled a large box from the wagon and thrust it into Josiah's hands.

He had to admit he'd been more than worried about his wife when she carried the girls. Mary's middle had been impossible to ignore as she'd grown larger and larger. Toward the end she'd grown miserable and cranky.

But his girls had come and they were the most beautiful creations he'd ever seen. Briefly he allowed himself to feel sorrow that they would never know their mother.

William pulled another large box from the wagon, the same size as the one he'd given Josiah, and headed toward the house. "What are you waiting for, an invitation?"

Josiah shook his head and grinned. "Don't beat around the bush, tell me how you feel," he answered, following.

William chuckled. "We still have a big trunk to un-load and a boxful of books. So no sassing."

Josiah entered the house to find Emily Jane and Anna Mae sitting on the couch, each holding one of the girls and giggling. He heard Emily Jane say, "Se-riously, she gave you chickens and hand towels for a wedding gift?"

"Yes."

"But you're afraid of most animals."

He continued walking, but noticed Anna Mae glance his way and whisper, "Shh, I don't want Josiah to know."

Not know? He already knew she feared the chick-ens. Josiah continued on to the bedroom and set his box beside the one William had just put down. What other animals was Anna Mae afraid of?

"What do you think? Bring the trunk in next?" Wil-liam asked as they headed back to the sitting room.

Josiah nodded. He'd noticed the trunk and two smaller boxes still in the wagon. "Are both the other boxes Annie's, too?"

William raised his voice for the women to hear. "Yep, between the stuff you brought from the school and the stuff we picked up from the boardinghouse, your Annie has a lot of things to lug around." William pressed his hand playfully against his back as if he were in great pain.

Laughter from the ladies followed his antics. Anna Mae wiggled a finger at them. "As soon as you men get the wagon unloaded, we'll reward you with din-ner and pie."

Josiah hurried after William, who acted as if he'd gotten his strength back and part of a child's energy to continue on with what needed to be done. His brother-in-law was a ham, through and through.

As he hefted the trunk and felt the weight of what must be books, Josiah wondered again what other animals Anna Mae feared. Since they didn't have any, besides Roy and the mule, he really didn't have to worry about that, now did he?

Josiah found himself silently praying. *Lord, there is so much I don't know about my new wife. Please help her to overcome her fears. No man or woman should ever be fearful of one of Your creations. And Lord, help me to be a good helpmate to her.*

Anna Mae enjoyed having Emily Jane and William over, but as soon as they left she hurried to her boxes. She left her bedroom door open and listened while Josiah read to the girls from the Bible. She'd made the suggestion earlier, saying it would do the girls good to start putting the word of God in their hearts now, while they were still young enough to teach them how to do so. She explained that the earlier they began to learn about God and His word, the easier it would be for them to turn to Him when times were hard on them later in life. Josiah seemed to have liked the idea, and his reading to them now proved it.

It didn't take long to put her clothes away, but going through the books and things would take a little more time.

Anna Mae pulled out the books and stacked them neatly against the wall. Would Josiah be willing to build her a bookshelf? Or was there one in the room with the sleeping chickens? She'd look tomorrow.

Josiah had seemed tired this evening. Had she worked him too hard? He'd hung the pots and pans and then ventured out into the cold to make the chicken coop. She knew it wasn't finished and thought perhaps she would help him tomorrow. Those chickens had to get out of her house.

She heard Josiah say, "The end." And the sound of the Bible closing assured her he was finished reading to the girls for the night. For a few brief moments Rose and Ruby squealed with joy. Anna Mae wondered what Josiah was doing to bring them so much happiness.

With giggling and heavy footsteps, she heard him bringing them to the bedroom, and Anna Mae sighed. It would have been nice to find her journal before she had to put the girls to bed. One more night of not writing in her diary wouldn't kill her, she guessed. Anna Mae knew she'd find the book in the morning and would record all that had happened since her wedding.

"I think my playful kittens are about ready for bed," Josiah announced, coming into the room. He held a little girl's hand in each of his.

"No bed!" Ruby protested, pulling at his hand.

Rose watched her sister and her lips began to pucker.

He'd said the bed word. Anna Mae shook her head with a grin. It would have been easier to dress them and then put them to bed. "Now, girls, you know the routine. Anna Mae said, read a story and then off to bed." Josiah said, putting blame on her for their routine and newly applied rules.

Her joy quickly turned to sorrow. So that's how it was. If he didn't like her suggestions, he should have said so. They were his daughters. Maybe it was time to remind him of just that.

"Josiah, you know that was only a suggestion, right? I didn't mean to encroach on your rights as their father. They are your children and you must always do as you feel best." There, she'd said it.

His jaw clenched and his eyes narrowed slightly. "Well, that certainly puts a damper on my evening."

What was wrong? She'd only given him the option of setting his own rules. Anna Mae didn't understand and said so. "Why? What do you mean?"

He drew his lips in thoughtfully. "I must have gotten it all wrong, but I thought when you became my wife, you also became their mother." His fingers grasped a hand of each girl.

Anna Mae shook her head in dismay. "No! I mean, yes, I did."

He released their hands and studied her face as if she were an outlaw he hadn't expected to come upon. Josiah ran his hand across the back of his neck.

Anna Mae wanted to scream. This marriage thing was much tougher when you started out with a family, and without the love of your partner.

Josiah sighed heavily as if he were having the same thoughts.

She threw up her hands in surrender. "The way you told the girls it was bedtime made me feel I had taken away your rights to keep them up as long as you wanted. I feel as if I've crossed some invisible line." She swallowed hard, lifted her chin and boldly met his gaze. "Look, I only meant that I'm a schoolteacher and I'm used to dealing with children, but I would never override your decisions concerning the girls. That's all I wanted to say."

He came close, looking down at her intently. "I'm sorry, Annie. I jumped to the wrong conclusion, again." Josiah reached out and fingered a stray piece of hair that had come out of her ponytail near her cheek. "I'm very much aware of the burden I've placed on you, saddling you with a sheriff and two little girls. It's a huge task, to say the least. I thought perhaps today had proved to be too much and you had changed your mind."

Reaching up, Anna Mae covered his hand with her own. "No, Josiah. I could not love the girls more if they were my own flesh and blood. Still, I have no right—"

He placed a finger across her lips. "Don't say it, Annie girl. I gave you the right the day we got married, and I want you to always do what's best for our children. If you must argue your point with me, do so. That's what parents do. That's what real love is." He paused and then retracted his words. "I mean real love for the girls."

A raw, primitive grief overtook her. He'd just reminded her that she would never have his love or know the joy of bringing new life into the world. Not that Anna Mae would ever love him, either, but having it pressed home like that…well, it just wasn't something that she enjoyed. She dropped her lashes quickly to hide the hurt.

Concern laced his rich voice as he asked, "What is it, Annie? What did I say that was wrong?" He caressed her cheek.

Anna Mae took a step back, breaking his hold on her. "Nothing, Josiah," she hurried to assure him. "Just please have patience with me. I'm new at this, too, and will get it wrong more often than not, but I promise you this. I will give our girls the best care that I can and their health and happiness will always come first."

He didn't seem to want to accept her explanation at first, but thankfully, he let it go. Josiah looked down. "Speaking of our little girls, where did they get to?"

Both adults turned to the bedroom door, to find Rose and Ruby sitting on the floor examining their belly buttons, quietly pointing and touching, seemingly happy that they both had one in the exact same place. Once more laughter sprang from Josiah as he walked over, swept them both into his arms and deposited them in their beds.

Rose and Ruby shrieked and cried for "tisses."

Anna Mae tapped him on the shoulder, aware that he was making them squeal even louder. "Stop riling them up. I'll never get them to sleep if you keep on this way."

He stepped back. "Good night, girls." Josiah offered her a smile and then left the room.

Fifteen minutes later, Anna Mae turned down the covers of her bed and slid between the sheets. She'd wanted to join Josiah in the sitting room, but her emotions had been on a roller coaster all day and she needed time to absorb the things she hadn't understood, and meditate on ways to change or accept her new way of life.

One thing Josiah was dead right about…raising two little girls was a huge task, and with a heavy heart she wondered if she truly was up to it.

Chapter Twelve

Josiah arrived home the following evening, tired and confused. His thoughts had been on Anna Mae all day.

Last night, he'd waited for her to join him after putting the girls to bed, but that hadn't happened. Now that he examined their actions and words from the previous evening, he realized in surprise that they'd both been on the defensive. And why was that? Action and reaction. Interesting. But even more troubling was the look of pure hurt that had entered her eyes when he'd told her the girls were hers.

He felt certain he loved the twins. She'd shown that in more ways than one, so what caused the sadness? Had Anna Mae realized the time-consuming job she'd taken on, and even though she loved the girls, regretted giving up her own life to join his?

He rubbed the back of his neck wearily. What caused women to twist up a man's insides like this? Mary had done the same. It had gotten to where every time he left on sheriff business she'd become quiet and withdrawn. More and more she'd taken to spending time in the bedroom rather than in the sitting room with him. He'd thought maybe it was those woman emotions that took over after giving birth, but now Anna Mae acted the same way.

His communication skills hadn't improved at all. Looking back only brought more confusion and sadness; a feeling of failure.

Instead of going straight to the barn and putting Roy away, Josiah decided to go to the house first. He needed to make sure that Anna Mae was doing all right.

He opened the door slowly and the warm scent of fried potatoes greeted him. The house was unusually quiet. Josiah walked to Anna Mae's and the girls' bedroom. Everything was in its place, but they were nowhere to be found. He hurried to the guest room, where the chickens clucked in low undertones. Again, the room was empty. His heart skipped a beat.

Had she left and taken his girls with her? Where had she gone? And why? He hurried back outside. If Anna Mae had really left, she'd have to have used the mule and wagon.

Roy snorted as Josiah passed by. Josiah's boots squished in the mud and snow as he rushed to the barn. With more strength then he knew he possessed, he jerked the door open.

"Papa!" Rose hurried to him on her short little legs.

Seeing her twin sister and father, Ruby squealed and ran toward him, too.

Josiah's heart leaped with gladness. The girls were safe. His gaze swept the barn and he found Anna Mae kneeling in front of a wooden structure of some type.

She had a mouthful of nails and a hammer poised to do some damage.

Both girls grabbed him around the calves and hung on tightly. "Up!" they demanded.

He picked them both up and kissed their little cheeks. His gaze held Anna Mae's as she spit the nails into her hand.

"I wasn't expecting you back so early," she said, once her mouth was empty.

Josiah carried the girls to her. "I'm not early." His gaze moved to whatever it was she was trying so hard to make. "What is that supposed to be?"

"A bookshelf?" Anna Mae turned to look at the wood. With a heavy sigh she said, "Doesn't look much like a bookshelf, does it?"

He didn't want to hurt her feelings. "Well, I'm not a carpenter."

Her delicate laughter took him by surprise. "No, but you are a really sweet man." She looked up at him with joyful eyes. "Come on inside and we'll get everyone fed." She reached up and took Ruby from his arms.

He followed her from the barn. Roy snorted from the front porch. Josiah had completely forgotten about his dear friend.

"I was thinking, Josiah." Anna Mae paused as she reached the front door.

This couldn't be good for him. It seemed every time the woman said "I was thinking," it meant work for him. He started to ask her what she'd been thinking about, dreading what she'd say, when she continued.

"Why don't we put the chicken coop in the barn until spring. That way they would be warm, and all we'd have to do is set up a place for them to sleep." She opened the door and set Ruby down. The little girl immediately started taking off her coat and boots.

Josiah did the same with Rose. "I need to put Roy away for the night. I'll see if I can find space for the chickens."

"The last stall on the right should work well," Anna Mae suggested, as she helped Rose with her buttons.

He headed back to the horse, which nudged him with his nose as if to say "Forgot all about me, didn't you?"

Josiah rubbed his nose. "I didn't forget about you, ole man. It's just now I have a wife and kids to think about, too."

Roy bumped him in the shoulder. Josiah laughed, picked up his reins and led him toward the barn. As he entered the warm building, Josiah had to admit she might have a good idea about keeping the chickens there.

With Roy properly taken care of, he walked back to the stall Anna Mae had said would be good for the chickens. It needed a little repair. Several of the boards looked as if they were going to pop loose.

Josiah shook his head. He'd placed his horse and the mule in the better maintained stalls, thinking he had until spring to repair the rest that needed work. Josiah sighed. Women always wanted something done right away, and Anna Mae was no different.

He gave Roy a final pat on the nose and then headed back to the house. Anna Mae wanted bookshelves, the stall fixed and a nesting box for the chickens. Thankfully, he didn't have anything pressing going on in town and could stay home tomorrow and work on the chores.

When he entered the house Anna Mae had already taken care of getting the girls to the table, and the food smelled wonderful. Rose and Ruby smiled, their freshly scrubbed faces shining. His girls had never looked happier.

"What took so long?" Anna Mae asked, as she set plates before them.

"I checked out the stall you mentioned." He pulled his coat off, hung it on the rack beside the door, then stopped.

When had Anna Mae hung the rack? His gaze roved the house and he saw several other things she'd done to improve the function of his home. He'd been so busy working that he'd neglected noticing the small changes. She'd brought warmth to his home. Would his new wife soon expect him to make changes, too? Would she expect him to express his appreciation with love?

The next afternoon, Anna Mae hummed as she finished wiping down the counters, then hung the dishcloth on the drying rod. Josiah had been called away shortly after breakfast, so she'd found her yarn, and while she knitted two pot holders, the girls played with balls of bright colored yarn. Then she'd started dinner and fixed lunch all at the same time.

Now that the noon dishes were done, she thought about slipping out to the barn and working on the bookshelf while the girls napped. Anna Mae pulled on her gloves, cloak and finally her boots. She'd be out for only an hour and then she'd come back inside.

The sun shone brightly and felt warm on her cheeks. Anna Mae hurried to the barn and pulled the door open;

the warm scent of hay and dust filling her lungs. She loved the barn and couldn't wait for Josiah to get the nesting box built for the chickens.

Maybe she could help him do that. She was sick of cleaning up their mess, so something must be done. She walked to the stall and looked about.

From what she could see, all the stall needed was a few boards nailed back into place, and then she could bring the chickens out here and clean up the spare room. With that thought in mind, Anna Mae forgot all about making the bookshelf.

She grabbed the hammer and nails, then hung her cloak on a peg. It took her almost an hour to get the stall secure and in the shape that she thought it should be.

Her hands hurt from hammering and holding boards in place. She'd taken her gloves off and now regretted the action. Anna Mae looked at her swollen, throbbing thumb and sighed. She didn't dare glance at her palms, where she felt confident the blisters were rising.

After spreading fresh hay and sprinkling a few kernels of corn into it, she pulled her cloak back on and headed inside to check on the girls. The wind had picked up and felt colder than when she'd gone out. She opened the door and listened. No sounds came from the bedroom where the twins slept. The chickens were clucking softly in their room.

Anna Mae checked on Rose and Ruby. They were still sleeping. She smiled. Maybe she could get the chickens out to the barn before they woke.

It was one thing to think she could get them out there. It was another to actually do it. Anna Mae gazed at the birds. How was she going to get them back inside the box she'd taken them out of?

She stared at them and they stared back. Anna Mae didn't know how, but she could tell from their beady eyes that they knew she was up to something. The rooster raised his head, stretching his neck up toward the ceiling, and then strutted about as if daring her to try and catch him.

The hens looked more approachable. Anna Mae shut the bedroom door and then stepped into the pen she'd made. "You can do this, Anna Mae. They are just as afraid of you as you are of them."

She chased the chickens at a walking pace. Just as she reach down to grab one it would dart away. Soon she found herself running about the room, the hens jumping to escape her. They squawked in alarm and feathers flew.

Anna Mae would get ahold of one and it would flap its wings and try to peck her. She'd squeal and let it go. She didn't know how long she'd been trying to catch the hens or how many times she'd let them go when she heard the sound of laughter. She turned to find Josiah leaning against the door frame and laughing as if he couldn't catch his breath. His reaction both annoyed and pleased her.

"How long have you been standing there?" she demanded, out of breath and tired from her day's work.

He tried to compose his features, but failed miserably. "Long enough to see you are no chicken catcher."

"Do you think you can do any better?" she asked, leaning against a wooden chest.

"I didn't say that." He continued to laugh. "You should see yourself."

Anna Mae didn't doubt that she was a sight. Her hair hung about her shoulders and feathers covered her arms. She was sure they were in her hair, as well. "If it's all the same to you, I believe I'll avoid a mirror for a while."

He straightened. "What were you going to do once you caught one?"

"Put it in that box." Anna Mae pointed to the crate Mrs. Linker had brought them in.

He opened his mouth as if to ask another question, but one of the twins interrupted him by yelling from the other room. "Up!"

Anna Mae left the pen and walked toward Josiah. "I'm going to go get the girls up from their nap. If you think you can catch the chickens, by all means do so." She raised her chin and continued past him.

Once she was out the door, Anna Mae headed to the kitchen, where she quickly washed her hands, arms and face. The cool water both stung and felt good as she splashed it over her many scrapes and the broken blisters on her hands. All the while the girls continued to yell, "Up!"

"I'm coming," she called back to them. Anna Mae hurried to the bedroom and found Rose and Ruby clutching the rails and looking unhappy.

When they saw her, their sweet faces broke into smiles. Anna Mae hurried to get them up, and by the time she had them out of the bed and into dry clothes Josiah stood in the doorway waiting for her.

"They are in the box. Now what?" he asked, his eyes still dancing with merriment.

"Now you can take them to the barn," she answered, setting Rose down and watching as she ran to her papa.

He shook his head. "That stall needs to be repaired before we can put them inside."

Anna Mae ran her fingers through her hair, removing feathers, careful to avoid using her aching thumb and sore palms. "I already fixed it."

Disbelief filled his face. "You did?"

"Sure did." She heard the pride in her voice, but couldn't contain it. "I might not be able to catch chickens, but I can nail boards together." She hoped him seeing that she could get some things done about the place would endear her to him. Maybe what Josiah was looking for in a woman was someone strong who could work alongside him. Maybe he'd see that as a reason to love her. Maybe.

Chapter Thirteen

The woman in front of Josiah never ceased to amaze him. He'd not been able to contain his amusement as he'd watched her chase after that chicken. It was such a small space and no matter how hard she'd tried, Anna Mae couldn't bring herself to just grab the bird and hang on. He felt laughter bubbling up in his chest once more. When was the last time he'd been this happy?

Anna Mae nodded. "Go see for yourself." She tucked her left hand behind her.

What was she hiding? Josiah looked back at her sweet face. Her lips smiled, but something else was going on behind her eyes.

A loud clang in the kitchen had them both rushing out of the bedroom. Josiah knew Rose and Ruby were into something. When had his daughters slipped past him?

Sure enough. There they sat on the kitchen floor, playing in a new puddle of flour.

"Oh, you little scamps." Anna Mae hurried to get them out of the flour. "You know you aren't supposed to be in here," she scolded, even as she dusted the back side of their dresses.

He chuckled. "You seem to have this situation under control. I'll take the chickens out."

Her gasp stopped him in his tracks. He turned to see Anna Mae clutching her left hand against her chest and grimacing. What in the world?

Rose and Ruby had returned to the flour and were playing happily in the white powder, but Anna Mae seemed to have lost all interest in the little girls.

Josiah set the box of chickens down and hurried to see what she was hiding and what caused the intense look of pain. He took her hand gently in his and examined it. Her thumb had a big blood blister under the nail bed, a sure sign she'd hit it with a hammer. His fingers gently opened her hands to reveal broken blisters.

"Aw, Annie." He rested his forehead against hers. "Why didn't you tell me you were hurt?"

She shook her head. "It's nothing. Just a couple of blisters and a banged up thumb. I'm sure farmer's wives everywhere have to deal with a few blisters. I'll toughen up. I promise." Anna Mae pulled away from him.

Josiah wasn't having that. He gently drew her to the kitchen table and helped her into a chair. Not that she needed help, but he wanted her sitting while he cleaned her hands. "You aren't a farmer's wife. You are a sheriff's wife and most sheriffs live in town and their wives don't have to repair barns." He scooped up his girls and put them in their chairs. "You two stay put. Annie is hurt."

Big blue eyes turned to Anna Mae. "Owie?" Ruby asked, tearing up.

"Oh no," Rose added, her eyes wide.

"It's not so bad," Anna Mae assured them.

Josiah poured water into one of the wash basins. He stepped over the flour and placed the container in front of her. "Here, put your hands in this while I clean up the floor."

He turned stern eyes on his daughters. "Look at this mess you made. If you were older, I'd make you clean it up." Josiah set the flour bucket upright and grabbed Anna Mae's broom.

"Sawee," the girls chorused. Their little faces looked to him for forgiveness.

"Don't tell me, tell Annie. She's the one who has been cleaning up after you this week," Josiah scolded.

The twins each looked to Anna Mae. "Sawee, Awnie."

"Thank you, girls, that's very good that you are sorry." She offered them a sweet smile.

Josiah was glad that she didn't tell them it was all right. The twins needed to learn that they couldn't play in the flour and that they needed to respect their stepmother. He finished cleaning up the mess, put the flour back under the cabinet where Annie had set it and then turned back to check on her hands.

Once he had finished that, he looked at his girls. "You two stay there until I come back in."

"Josiah, you are making too much of this. I'm fine," Anna Mae protested.

He shook his head. "That goes for you, too. I'm going to release these birds into the barn and then I'll be back." Josiah didn't give her a chance to argue. He picked up the chickens and left.

What was he going to do with that woman? Anna Mae was a schoolteacher, and from what he gathered from her, she'd never lived in the country. Between the two of them they had no business living on a farm. She wasn't cut out for hard labor, and if the truth be told, he had no idea how to run a working farm.

The chickens squawked in gratitude as he released them into the stall. He watched as they immediately began scratching in the fresh hay that Anna Mae had spread for them. His gaze moved over the walls, inspecting her handiwork. She'd done a pretty good job.

Josiah grabbed the hammer and finished where she'd left off. It didn't take him more than a couple minutes to reinforce what she'd already done. He left the chickens happily scratching at the ground and clucking softly to one another.

As he started out the door, his gaze landed on the boards that Anna Mae had attempted to create a bookshelf out of. He sighed. If he didn't do it, she would. The woman was determined, he'd give her that.

Josiah stacked the wood into a pile, found the bag of nails and laid his hammer on top. Then he found the wheelbarrow and put it all inside. He pushed it to the house.

Anna Mae had moved to the couch and the girls sat at her feet, looking at some type of picture book. Satisfied his family was resting, Josiah headed back outside and collected the wood, nails and hammer. He set them inside the door and then ran the wheelbarrow back to the barn.

When he returned, Anna Mae had moved to the wood. She was about to pick up a piece when he stopped her. "What do you think you're doing?" Josiah demanded, pulling his coat off and hanging it up.

"I just wanted to help," she answered, standing up straighter and placing her bandaged hands on her hips. "I'm not going to sit around and do nothing because I have a couple of blisters." Her eyes dared him to argue.

The girls looked up at her raised voice, studying the grown-ups' every movement. Aware that his daughters were listening as well as watching, Josiah shook his head.

"Why don't you let me make the bookshelf? You can supervise." He offered her what he hoped was a compromising smile.

Anna Mae nodded. She handed him the board she'd been holding. "All right. I'm guessing this is my new bookshelf?"

"You guessed right."

"Why did you bring it inside?" she asked, gnawing on her bottom lip.

"Three reasons. One, if it's built in the house I won't have to lug it in from the barn when I'm done. Two, I wasn't sure how tall you wanted it, or how many shelves. And three, if I work on it in here we can both be warm and I can keep an eye on you." He knelt down and began sorting the wood, before glancing at his girls, who had regained interest in their book.

"Oh, why didn't I think of that?"

"What? That I want to keep an eye on you?" he teased.

Anna Mae looked troubled. "No, to bring it inside to work on it." She sat down on the arm of the couch. "I guess I'm not as clever as I thought I was."

Josiah laughed. His gaze moved about his home. It felt like a new place since she had arrived. Curtains hung on the windows; blankets and throws draped the furniture. The house smelled clean and fresh, not damp and musty. She'd managed to turn their house into a home in just a matter of days. He hadn't figured out how to do that during the whole time he'd been in Granite. "I wouldn't say you aren't smart. If you hadn't plowed forward and fixed that pen in the barn yourself, I wouldn't have decided to work on the shelves tonight."

She shook her head. "No, I could have saved us both time if I had brought the wood in."

Josiah stood up and walked over to her. He lifted her bandaged hands in his. "Now look here, Annie. This is all new to both of us. I am not a farmer, have never wanted to be a farmer, but here I am, corralling chickens and making bookshelves. You are a schoolteacher, and how often have *you* raised chickens or built furniture?" He didn't give her time to answer. "I'd say never to both. So don't go whipping yourself because you didn't think to bring the wood into the house."

Tears sprang into her eyes. "Do you regret marrying me?"

He shook his head. "Of course not. You are the best thing to happen to this place and my girls. Just look at what you've done to the house." Josiah released her hands. He motioned toward Rose and Ruby. "And look at the girls. I don't think they've ever been this happy and content."

Josiah knew he meant every word he said. What he didn't say was that he cared about her and was happy that she was his wife. He wouldn't say that out loud or even to himself. To do so would suggest that he'd developed feelings for Anna Mae Miller, and that scared him more than any bank robber ever could.

Chapter Fourteen

Anna Mae's hands healed over the next few days. Still amazed by Josiah's tenderness and kind ways, she washed and scrubbed the guest bedroom floor until it shone. The chickens had made a mess of the whole room, but the floor had been the worst part.

A glance at the clock told her she had a little while longer before the twins awoke from their morning nap. She pushed up from the floor and picked up the pail of dirty water. Her plans were to fix ham sandwiches and potato salad for lunch. She'd found a wonderful array of canned vegetables in the root cellar and couldn't wait to open a jar of pickles.

The sound of a wagon pulling into the front yard drew her to the door. The soft lowing of a cow came from the direction of the wagon. Emily Jane and Millie Westland, Levi's wife, waved from the seat.

Happy to see her friends, though a bit puzzled as to why they had a cow tied to the back of the wagon, Anna Mae tossed the dirty water to the right of the porch and hurriedly put the bucket away. She ran her hand over her hair and donned a fresh apron before going back to the door to greet her guests.

"Emily Jane, Millie, I'm so happy to see you both here." Anna Mae rushed down the stairs to stand behind Emily Jane as she disembarked from the wagon. It wouldn't do for her to fall in her condition.

Millie was already tying the horse and wagon to the porch rail. She looped a feed bag over the little mare's head and then walked around to the back of the wagon. "I hope you don't mind us just dropping in like this, but we wanted to get the milk cow out here before it got too late," she offered. "Levi has the baby, so we can't stay long." She started untying the cow from the tailgate.

Emily Jane turned to Anna Mae and grinned. "I brought chocolate cake, enough for now and more for your dessert tonight."

Anna Mae tilted to the right so she could see around Emily Jane to where Millie was undoing the cow's lead. "What is Millie doing with that animal?" she asked, feeling uneasy because she thought she knew the answer to her question.

"She's a wedding present from your neighbor Mr. Green," Millie answered, pulling the cow toward the porch. "The girls will have fresh milk every morning and her milk makes the best butter, according to him."

Should she refuse the cow? Her gaze darted between Emily Jane and Millie. They both looked so happy that she couldn't get her mouth to say what her mind was screaming: *Not another animal!* What was Josiah going to say?

"Where do you want her?" Millie asked, stroking the white streak down the center of the light brown cow's face. Big brown eyes looked up at Anna Mae. The cow let out a low cry.

Afraid she would wake the girls, Anna Mae made a quick decision. "Let's put her in the barn."

"I'll take the cake inside and check on my nieces," Emily Jane said, heading for the door.

Anna Mae shot her a stern look. "If you wake them up, you have to take them home with you." They both knew it was an empty threat.

"I'll be quiet. I just want to look at them and maybe steal a kiss."

Millie laughed. "Come on, Anna Mae. I'm getting cold."

As they walked toward the barn, Anna Mae asked, "Why did Mr. Green send us a cow? I mean, I know he did it for a wedding gift, but why a cow?"

The dismay in her voice prompted Millie to stop. "Mrs. Linker has been telling all your neighbors that you are going to make this a running farm, not just an orchard. Didn't you know?"

Anna Mae shook her head. "No, I can't think what I could have said to her to have given her that impression."

Millie shrugged. "Well, don't be surprised if more of your neighbors show up with other farm animals."

What Josiah would say about the cow didn't bear thinking about. "Did Mr. Green say if she has a name?"

"He called her Jersey. I guess that's her name." Millie pulled on the door to the barn. It opened and a whiff of warm air caressed their skin.

Anna Mae watched as Millie coaxed the animal inside. She'd seen bigger cows and was glad that theirs wasn't as big as those. She felt Millie studying her.

"You have to make friends with her, Anna Mae, or she'll think you don't like her and will probably quit giving milk."

"You're kidding." Anna Mae gazed at the cow. She'd planned on Josiah taking care of her. After all, she took care of the chickens every day. It sounded fair to her.

"Nope." Millie shook her head and pursed her lips.

"How do you become a friend to a cow?" Anna Mae asked, dreading the answer.

Her friend grinned. "Well, first off you need to pet her and talk in a nice voice to her."

"Pet her?" she squeaked.

Millie chuckled. "Yes, she's really gentle. You have nothing to fear from her."

Who ever heard of petting a cow to be friends with it? Anna Mae didn't believe her. For that matter, who ever heard of being friends with a cow in the first place? She eyed the big, brown-eyed animal with distaste. "Then what?"

"Well, Mr. Green said to tell you that she has to be milked at six every morning and evening." Millie looked about. "Where in here do you want her?"

Anna Mae pointed to the only available stall. "In there." Her finger shook. How was she going to befriend a cow? And she knew nothing about milking one. She only prayed Josiah knew how to do both. Anna Mae didn't think she could run a farm. What was she going to do if the neighbors continued to supply her with barn-yard animals?

Josiah heard the cow bawling long before he reached the yard. His gaze moved to the house and he thought he saw the curtain fall back into place. He dropped from Roy's back and waited for Anna Mae to join him in the yard.

It was well after eight o'clock and he was sure the twins were already in bed and sleeping. He continued to wait for Anna Mae, but after several long moments he realized that he must have been mistaken and she wasn't coming out.

The sound of an unhappy cow filled his ears. It came from the direction of his barn. "Oh, Lord, please don't let her have gotten another animal."

He pulled the door open. His gaze immediately landed on the cow. She was a Jersey with a white blaze down her nose. From her cries she was a cow who needed to be milked.

Josiah sighed. He put Roy in his stall and promised to return soon to complete their nightly ritual. Then he turned to the bovine.

"Hello, beautiful. What brings you into my barn?" He leaned on the door of her stall and waited until she brought her head closer before extending his hand to touch her velvety nose.

She snorted into his palm.

"Oh, my lovely new wife brought you in here, did she?" He worked his hand up her face, then gently scratched the stiff hair behind her right ear.

She twitched her tail and stomped a back hoof. He leaned to the side and looked at her swollen udder. "Just as I thought, you need to be milked."

Josiah found a rope and created a loop at one end. Then he approached the stall once more. He patted her nose and face and scratched behind her ear, and at the same time slowly lowered the rope around her neck.

After opening the stall door he gently led the cow out into the center aisle of the barn. He tied her to a sturdy post and grabbed a bucket of oats. Josiah set the bucket at her head and then placed the stool where he could milk her. "This won't take long," he told her, finding another clean bucket. He set it under her udders and slowly began to milk.

The barn door creaked open and a gust of cold air entered the barn. Josiah rested his forehead against the cow to soothe her. "Come inside, Anna Mae, but move very slowly," he instructed, continuing to milk.

She did as he said. Her skirts swished across the dirt floor as she inched closer to him and the cow. "I'm sorry. I didn't know how to do that. But Millie said it had to be done by six and, well, even though I'm late, I came out to try."

"You don't have to whisper. Just don't shout or move suddenly." He looked up at her.

Anna Mae wrung her hands in her apron. Her big eyes took in the animal with renewed anxiety. Why did she keep taking animals that she feared? Instead of asking her that, he asked instead, "Anna Mae, where did this cow come from?"

"Mr. Green gave it to us as a…"

"Wedding present," Josiah finished.

She nodded. "I'm afraid so."

"Why did you accept it?" He heard the frustration in his voice, but didn't know how to hide it from her. Josiah wasn't sure he should even try. She had to know he wouldn't be pleased.

Anna Mae mangled the apron. "Millie and Emily

Jane brought it out. I didn't know how to say no and I didn't want to hurt Mr. Green's feelings."

"What about how I would feel about it? I told you I'm no farmer, yet you keep accepting animals that have to be cared for. You are so scared of them you can't possibly help look after them. What are we going to do now with another animal that needs tending? Also, cows aren't cheap to feed, Anna Mae," he barked, not looking at her.

Josiah knew he was overtired from his day at the sheriff's office. Word had it that a gang of bank robbers had moved into the area. He'd spent all afternoon going over wanted posters, memorizing faces and names, just in case they came to Granite.

His town.

The town he'd vowed to protect.

Unless Anna Mae learned how to milk, the cow would have to go. The swish of the door opening and closing again met his ears. She'd left.

Josiah sighed. He finished milking the cow, took care of Roy and pitched fresh hay into all three stalls. By the time he entered the house, Josiah knew he owed Anna Mae an apology. He shouldn't have taken his stress out on her.

Pushing the door open, he found the sitting room and the kitchen empty. A covered plate of food sat at the back of the stove. Anna Mae had retired to her bedroom.

Maybe she would come out while he ate, he thought, pouring himself a cup of warm coffee. He took the plate and moved to the table. Josiah allowed the wood of the chair legs to scrape loudly against the floor.

Had he been too hard on her? He expected his wife

would come out any moment, telling him she knew exactly how much a cow cost to keep and that she'd learn to milk, just as she'd learned how to feed the chickens.

He finished his coffee and dinner, but Anna Mae never appeared. Josiah sighed. When he carried his dirty plate to the washbasin, he noticed a large slice of chocolate cake on the sideboard. The thought of eating it left a bitter taste in his mouth.

Josiah walked to the rocking chair by the fireplace and dropped into it. He reached over and picked up his Bible.

Thank God, when a man couldn't commune with his woman, the Lord always proved sufficient. His Bible fell open to Romans 8:25. *But if we hope for what we do not yet have, we wait for it patiently.* He sighed again. Patience was not a virtue he was known for.

He stood and blew out the lamp on the table. At least it would be warm in his room tonight, for Anna Mae had left his door open all day. Last night it had been so cold he could see his breath, and he'd burrowed under the covers like a mole.

She'd thought of him; that was a plus. The minus was that if she kept heating the whole house, he'd run out of firewood long before winter was over.

The bed groaned as it took his weight, and a still small voice from within whispered in his mind: *Tomorrow things will look much brighter.*

Chapter Fifteen

Anna Mae jerked awake. She'd overslept. Sunshine filtered through her window. She sat up quickly and found Rose and Ruby grinning at her from their bed.

She knew without being told that Josiah had gone already. He left every morning long before the sun rose, so why should today be any different? Anna Mae thought about the night before and his harsh words.

It had been childish to hide in her room, but she just couldn't face him. She'd known he wouldn't be happy about Jersey, but he'd never spoken harshly to her before. It had been unexpected but deserved. He could have said what he wanted in a kinder manner, but she couldn't fault him. Who knew what his day had been like before he'd come home to find even more responsibility?

"Good morning, ladies." She smiled at the girls and pushed the covers back. "I overslept. I bet you two are starving."

"Eat?" Rose asked hopefully.

Anna Mae laughed. "Yes, as soon as we're all

dressed and ready for our day." She quickly put her words to action and had the girls dressed and walking into the kitchen within ten minutes.

"How about we have pancakes for breakfast this morning?" she asked, looking down at them.

"Sounds really good to me."

Without glancing up, Anna Mae recognized her husband's voice. He hadn't gone to work. Was he sick? She looked up to find him studying her face. What did he hope to find? He didn't appear sick. Had he stayed home to finish what they'd started the night before?

"Then you shall have as many as you like." She offered him a wobbly smile. Why did she feel so close to tears again? Never in all her life had she felt the sting that his disappointment caused in her.

"Papa!" Rose and Ruby toddled as fast as their little legs would carry them, falling against his legs.

He swooped down and picked them both up at the same time. Josiah rubbed his face against theirs, causing more squeals.

The little girls' joy brought a genuine smile to Anna Mae's face. No matter what came their way, Josiah's daughters made it all worthwhile. She'd give up the cow, if that's what he wanted. Even though the previous afternoon she'd dreamed of all the things she could make. Soups, baked custards and cheese were at the top of her future menus.

Just thinking about them gave her renewed bravery. She'd try again to get him to let her keep the cow. He hadn't exactly said they were getting rid of it, just that she'd have to learn not to be afraid of it, and that it would cost more to have.

As she made pancake batter, Anna Mae began to think of ways she could earn a little money to help keep Jersey. Maybe she could make cream or cheese and sell it to Carolyn at the general store.

Lost in thought, she didn't realize Josiah was behind her until his arms snaked around her waist. She gave a little squeal, then tilted her head just as he fitted his face against hers.

"I'm sorry, Annie, for behaving like a raging boar yesterday. Can you forgive me?" Softly his breath fanned her face.

She sighed. How wonderful it felt to have a man apologize. She couldn't recall her father ever apologizing to her mother. And Josiah's arms felt so good around her, as if they were meant to enclose her.

Anna Mae tried hard not to read too much into it, but surely she could enjoy moments like this for what they were. He had hurt her feelings, and he recognized it and wasn't willing to let it pass.

But perhaps he was expecting more. She pushed the thought away. No, Josiah was asking for forgiveness. Even if he was looking for more, she wasn't. Her heart had been broken and still hadn't mended from that embarrassment. Still, that same heart sang with delight that he cared about their friendship and had asked her to forgive him.

She tried to act nonchalant, but her voice broke with huskiness when she spoke. "You are forgiven, with one condition."

He moved back but kept an arm about her waist. "I know, I know. I'll do my best not to ever take my tiredness and frustration out on you again."

Anna Mae shook her head, aware she hadn't put her hair up this morning because she'd thought he was out of the house. "That's not what I meant at all." She poured batter into the heated pan. "I need you to forgive me, too." She set the bowl down and wiped her hands on her apron. "Josiah, I'm so sorry I accepted the cow. A little voice in my head warned me you would be upset, but I was more afraid to offend the giver than I was you."

He gave her waist a little squeeze. "There's nothing to forgive. You did right in not wanting to hurt the old man's feelings. But that still leaves the question, what do you think we should do now?" Josiah released her and rubbed the back of his neck.

Anna Mae knew he was talking about the cow. Was he hoping she'd say to give it back or sell the beast? Had he asked her only out of politeness, and actually planned on selling it regardless of what her answer might be? Or was that just what he did while trying to figure out what to do next? She decided that instead of questioning his motive for asking her, she'd just tell him what she thought they should do now.

"I guess you better teach me how to milk the dreadful animal." Before he could protest, Anna Mae rushed on. "The girls need the fresh milk and I'm sure I can make cream and cheese with the excess and sell it to Carolyn at the store. That will help with the extra cost of hay and oats or whatever cows eat. What do you think?" She slid fluffy pancakes onto a plate and poured more batter into her hot pan.

Josiah nodded. "That might work." He paused, looked up and grinned wickedly. "But someone has to build a corral and a shed to keep it in. It can't stay in the barn forever."

"Why not? And who would you get to help you?" Anna Mae knew he meant for her to help him, but couldn't stop herself from teasing him back. Yet she really didn't understand why the cow couldn't stay in the barn.

"Cows are leaners. They like to lean against things. And they are heavy. Anything built for use around cattle must be very sturdy." He picked up a couple plates and put a pancake on each one, then carried them to the table.

Rose and Ruby hurried to meet him there. "Up, eat." They waved their arms in anticipation of being served breakfast.

"In a minute," he told them, brushing the tops of their heads with his big hands. Josiah returned and picked up two more plates, one for himself and one for Anna Mae. "As for who is going to help me, I think you have the muscles to do that."

Anna Mae jerked her arm away as he squeezed the upper part, testing her muscles. She giggled as if it had tickled. "So now we are building a lean shed for the cow and a chicken coop for the chickens." With a serious expression she added, "I suppose that's what I get for allowing the beasties on the farm." She carried the pancakes and butter to the table.

Josiah grabbed a jar of blackberry preserves from the icebox and followed her. "Yep." He set the jar down and proceeded to help the girls into their chairs.

Anna Mae wasn't sure what to say. Was he teasing again? His tone had sounded very serious.

He straightened, his gaze met hers and he wiggled his eyebrows playfully. "I guess you'll listen to that small voice next time someone gives us a wedding present. Especially if it's in the form of some sort of animal, like a pig or a goat."

She crinkled her nose at the thought of a dirty pig needing care. "I should say so." She laughed.

Josiah blessed the meal and he and the girls began to eat. He laughed and teased Rose and Ruby as he helped them with their pancakes. Blackberry preserves would have to be washed from their hands and faces and even possibly their hair. Anna Mae didn't mind. The girls never failed to put a smile on their father's handsome face, and that made her happy, as well.

Now that she thought about it, Josiah had been serious every time she'd seen him in town. It was only at home that he allowed his softer, fun side to show. A smile touched her lips, because now she was part of his home life, and she liked it and her new husband.

"If you are thinking about getting a pig, stop thinking. I hate taking care of those dirty animals." He shook his fork in her direction.

Anna Mae held her hands up in surrender. "No, I promise, no more barnyard animals." She looked to the girls. Purplish-blue goo covered their mouths and cheeks. "Except maybe a dog or a kitten." She laughed gleefully at the pained expression that covered his face. She could get used to married life if it stayed like this.

Josiah grinned at Anna Mae, enjoying the banter more than he ever expected to. "You know what this means now, don't you?" He wiped the grin from his face and studied her over his coffee.

Confusion laced her pretty features. Her hair hung about her oval-shaped face, giving her a soft, delicate look. "That we have to go dog hunting?"

He shook his head in mock frustration. "No, it means we have to go to town for supplies."

The thought of visiting town brightened her face. "Oh, that's a wonderful idea. I want to buy some fabric. The girls need new dresses. I'd love to make them Christmas dresses and..." Her gaze moved to the kitchen. "We need more sugar, coffee and bacon."

Josiah laughed. He found he laughed more around her than anyone. She brought joy out in him. Even Mary hadn't been able to make him laugh as much as Anna Mae had in the last couple weeks. The thought sobered him.

"You might want to make a list, but I think we also need corn and oats. Not to mention I'm going to have to go to Mr. Green and see if he has extra hay for the cow."

"Oh, that's a great idea." She jumped up and ran to her room.

Rose and Ruby looked at him in confusion. He shrugged. "I guess she went to get paper and pen. Who knows what that woman is doing?"

The little girls nodded as if they agreed. "Go," Ruby said, pushing at the table.

"Oh, no, you don't. You finish those pancakes and then we'll go."

Anna Mae returned with pencil and paper and an open book to make her writing neater. The pencil scraped rapidly across the page as she scribbled out her list. Her head was down and her hair created a curtain that hid her face. "I'd also like to get a few sheets of colored paper, if Carolyn has some." She spoke more to herself than him.

"Annie?"

She looked up. Her brown eyes sparkled with excitement. "Yes?"

Josiah pushed away from the table. "I need to go hitch up the wagon. Do you think you can take care of things in here until I get back?" He looked pointedly at his sticky girls.

"Oh. Sure. I'll give them a quick sponge bath and get them all prettied up." She stopped. "Oh, before we leave I'll need to feed the chickens." Her nose wrinkled in distaste. "And learn how to milk Jersey."

She looked so sweet with her nose all crinkled up and her lips curled. Josiah focused on pulling his boots on before answering. "I'll take care of the animals this morning. This afternoon or tomorrow will be soon enough for you to take over."

Her teeth flashed in a big smile. "Thanks, Josiah."

That smile brightened his outlook on things while he hitched up the horse and checked on the other animals. The mule brayed in her stall. She probably wanted to get out and kick up her heels. Josiah made a mental note to ask Anna Mae if the little mule belonged to her or if they should tie it to the wagon and take it back to the school.

The sounds in the barn had changed in the past month. Once Roy was the only animal in there, but now there was a mule, a cow and three chickens. It was a noisy and warmer place to be. Anna Mae had changed his life in more ways than one since her arrival.

How much more change would she bring to his life? He thought of them as good friends, but would that alter? Could he grow to love her? Josiah shook his head. No, he couldn't allow such thoughts to fill his mind. Mary had been the love of his life, and he could never allow anyone to take her place. Never.

Chapter Sixteen

At the general store, Anna Mae read the proclamation from President Grover Cleveland declaring a designated Thursday, the twenty-fourth of November, as a day of thanksgiving and prayer, to be observed by all the people of the land. She listened to Carolyn as she rushed about the store gathering up their supplies. Anna Mae's gaze moved to the back of the room where the men gathered, talking about the president's latest proclamation.

The Moores had placed several of the newspaper clippings about their store for their customers to read.

Carolyn's voice drew her attention once more. "We can't believe it. Can you imagine how many people will be buying more staples and food supplies here? I placed another order yesterday. I just hope it gets here before the twenty-fourth."

In her excitement, Carolyn didn't really want or need an answer, Anna Mae knew. Her gaze moved to Rose and Ruby, who sat on the floor, playing with a couple other children. The four of them rolled and played with wooden blocks. They would stack them up and knock them down with squeals of laughter.

Anna Mae walked over to the fabric and fingered the softness of the material. Her thoughts were more on Christmas than this new holiday called Thanksgiving. She already planned to make the girls Christmas dresses for the Sunday service and rag dolls with matching dresses. But for Josiah it had to be something special. The quilt on his bed was very worn. Perhaps she could make a new one. Something simple that wouldn't take a lot of time to do. She'd have to hand piece it. Her thoughts raced as she touched each fabric in turn.

A royal blue caught her attention, reminding her of the beauty in Josiah's eyes. She picked up the bolt and carried it to the counter. Then she returned to the fabric table once more. By the time Anna Mae finished her shopping, she had bolts of blue, yellow, white with blue swirls, pink and lavender resting on Carolyn's counter. She'd also picked up a package of needles, plus a few spools of white and black thread.

"You have been busy," Josiah said, coming up behind her.

How did he do that? The man walked more quietly than anyone she knew. She'd have to remember that around Christmastime. It might be hard to conceal his gifts from him.

He ran his hand over the blue fabric. "That's pretty. Are you going to make a dress out of it?"

She hadn't thought of making a dress for herself, but now she would. Anna Mae nodded. "I think so."

"It will look beautiful on you," Carolyn said, pulling the bolt to the side. "How many yards do you want?"

Anna Mae turned to Josiah. "I'm about done here. Would you mind putting those things in the wagon?" She pointed to the box of dry goods Carolyn had gathered for them.

A puzzled look crossed his face but he nodded. "I'll be happy to." He hefted the box and turned to the door.

She quickly turned to Carolyn and gave her the yardage she needed. "Be sure and put the fabric and sewing notions on my bill, Carolyn. It's a Christmas gift for Josiah and the girls."

Carolyn wrote up the bill and said, "Aw, that's why you sent him out of the store. Good thinking." After dropping the money in a drawer, she turned to cut the cloth.

Anna Mae walked over to where Rose and Ruby still played. "Tell your friends goodbye, girls. It's time to go." She waited to see if they would be obedient or throw a fit at having to leave.

Both little girls stood. "Bye-bye."

She took their hands and led them back to the counter. "Pick out a candy stick, girls. Thank you for obeying when I asked you to. Such good girls I have."

"They aren't puppies," Josiah said, coming to stand beside her once more. "You don't have to buy them a treat for behaving." Even though his voice sounded firm, when she looked up at him an unmistakable twinkle filled his eyes.

"No, I don't. But I want to." She picked up Ruby so she could look at the candy jars on the counter.

Josiah did the same with Rose.

As soon as the girls each had candy in their chubby hands, Josiah paid the bill. "We need to stop off at the feed store before heading home. Is there any place else you want to go first?"

"I wouldn't mind stopping in at the bakery and having a treat."

"Sounds good to me." Josiah set Rose up on the seat, took Ruby in turn and then helped Anna Mae up. He pulled himself onto the seat and grinned across at her. "Do you think Emily Jane might have some more of that chocolate cake for sale?"

Anna Mae chuckled. "I hope so. I really need to learn how she makes hers."

It felt as if they were a family as they rode down Main Street. The girls sucked on their candy, making slurping noises and giggling. Josiah sat in the driver's seat looking like a proud papa.

"Sheriff!"

Josiah pulled the wagon to a stop. Wade Cannon, his new young deputy, came running up to them.

Concern laced Josiah's face as he asked, "What is it, Wade?"

The deputy paused to catch his breath. Anna Mae realized he must have run all the way from the edge of town. "Mr. Caldron said to come get you. Someone butchered one of his cows. Took some of the meat and left the rest to rot." He squinted up at Josiah. "Who'd do a fool thing like that, Sheriff?"

"I don't know, Wade. Maybe a stranger was hungry and thought the cow had no owner. Was it outside the pasture?"

"Why, no, sir. He found it not too far from the barn. I looked about, but you know Mr. Caldron. He insisted you come look."

Anna Mae watched as Levi Westland walked up in time to hear the last of the conversation. He shook his head. "No one local would do something like this, so that can only mean one thing."

Josiah nodded. "Yep." He exhaled loudly. "We've got visitors."

"That could also explain the recent thefts," Levi added, looking studious.

Josiah studied his face. "What thefts? That's the first I've heard of it."

"Well, until right this minute I didn't think of them as anything to worry about, but Millie put two pies on the windowsill to cool and someone took them both. We thought it might be a couple of kids." He rubbed his newly grown mustache. "But then ole Asa, you know, that new fella in town, at the boardinghouse." At Josiah's blank expression, he continued, "Anyway, he hung his wash on the line and two pairs of his pants went missing. Ain't likely no one around here would want Asa's clothes. So again, we wrote it off as kids' pranks."

Anna Mae took the reins Josiah handed her before he swung down from the wagon. "Anything else?"

Levi shook his head. "As far as I know, that's it. Want some company? I assume you're heading over to the livery."

"Can't say as I'd mind a helping hand." He looked up at Anna Mae. "Annie, you take the wagon and go on over to Emily Jane's. Stay there till I come for you."

She looked at him, hoping he'd heed her gentle but firm warning. "You be careful, Josiah Miller." Anna Mae knew Josiah's job was dangerous but seeing him at work caused her heart to flutter with worry. *Lord, please keep him safe,* she silently prayed.

Josiah arrived at William and Emily Jane's house tired and frustrated. He was no closer to finding out who had butchered that cow than he'd been two hours ago when he and Levi had gone to the livery.

No one saw the deed done nor had heard anything. He'd noted two sets of footprints; which meant more than one culprit. The amount of meat they'd taken most likely would have fed four or five men. These thoughts rolled around in his mind, trying to find the right category to be placed in. Evidence or just circumstance?

At Josiah's knock, William opened the door. "Any news?" he asked, stepping back and letting him inside.

"Nope. But I do know it wasn't a random act. Whoever killed that cow knew what he was doing."

Emily Jane walked up behind her husband. "What do you mean?"

"They went for the choice cuts of meat and left the rest." He looked about, expecting his family but not seeing them. "Where are Annie and the girls?"

William coughed and moved back a few steps. "I tried to get her to wait, but she said that there was no telling when you'd return and that Jersey would need to be milked and the chickens put away for the night."

Josiah felt sucker punched. During the investigation, he'd felt a sense of power, as if he could do anything. He'd spotted the evidence clearly and decisively. He knew it was due to Annie's warning for him to be safe. It had lifted him up, made him do a better job, because he felt someone cared for his well-being. It had been a long time since he'd felt like that.

But now the woman had undone all those good feelings. Did she even realize the worry she put on him? Why couldn't that stubborn lady listen to him? She didn't even know how to milk the cow. Josiah took a deep, cleansing breath. "When did she leave?"

"About an hour ago," Emily Jane answered. She wiped flour off her apron, avoiding his eyes.

Josiah shook his head. "Well, that's a fine how do you do." She'd left him in town without a horse. How did she expect him to get home? Walk?

Chapter Seventeen

His temper continued to build as he bounced along in William's wagon. His sweet sister-in-law had insisted on taking him home.

Mary would never have acted so impulsively. She also wasn't quick to smile. Or quick to banter with him. The two women were as different as outlaws and lawmen.

Anna Mae came out of the barn when they rode up. She had one of the twins on her hip and the other by the hand.

As soon as the wagon came to a stop, Josiah jumped to the ground. He started walking toward the barn at a fast clip.

"Papa!" Ruby pulled her hand from Anna Mae's and ran for him as fast as her little legs would carry her. His girls were always happy to see him.

He swooped her up and continued toward his wife. When he got close enough for her to hear him without having to shout, Josiah said, "I thought I told you to stay at Emily Jane's until I returned."

Rose pushed against Anna Mae, trying to get to her Papa.

"You did. But I thought the animals should be taken care of before dark," she countered, as she handed Rose over to him.

Josiah stared into her pretty brown eyes. "How was I supposed to get home?"

She looked at him, confused. "I assumed you'd borrow a horse from William. I really don't understand why you are upset."

Emily Jane and William joined them. They each took a twin in their arms. "We'll take these two inside so you two can talk," Emily Jane said. She gave Anna Mae an apologetic look before turning to the house.

William hurried after her.

Josiah clasped Anna Mae by the arm and turned her toward the barn. He pulled the door open and ushered her inside. "Anna Mae, as my wife you have to do what I ask you to."

"No, I don't." She pulled free from his grasp and placed both her hands on her hips. "I did not stay in town, because I didn't know how long you would be. And whether you like it or not, we now have animals to take care of."

He inhaled deeply. "Those animals can be quickly sold."

"No, they can't." Her eyes took on a fiery glow that told him he would be in for a big fight if he threatened her with the animals.

Maybe he was going about this the wrong way. Josiah walked back to where the cow stood. She mooed in greeting. He heard the hay rustle behind him as Anna

Mae followed him. Without turning to face her, he asked, "Did you or did you not promise to 'love, honor and obey' me?"

Silence hung heavily in the air for a few minutes. Josiah didn't dare turn and look at her for fear she might be crying or close to tears at his words.

"I did. But since we took love out of our arrangement, honor and obey shouldn't be there, either." There was a softness to her voice that caused him to turn and look at her. She swallowed hard, then lifted her head and met his gaze head-on.

Josiah felt the fight run out of him. She was right. At no time had they discussed their marriage vows, but both had let the other know that this was no love arrangement. If anything it was more of a business deal. "You're right. You don't have to obey me."

He saw the barely hidden twitch of her lips. "I know."

He grabbed the milking stool and sat down on it, gesturing for her to sit on the bale of hay across from him. "I guess it's time we discussed our arrangement again."

"Do we have to?" The pretend defeat in her tone caused him to grin. She sank onto the hay bale and waited with a heavy sigh.

Josiah mimicked her sigh. "I'm afraid so. You see, when we got married I thought it would be real easy. You would watch the girls and I would work. But, woman, when you take my horse it makes it hard for me to work." He leaned his forearms on his knees and waited for her reaction.

Anna Mae nodded, as if in total agreement. "Yes, I can see where that might hinder your job. I'm sorry. I shouldn't have taken Roy."

"But that's not all."

Big brown eyes looked up at him. "It isn't?"

"No, ma'am, it isn't. You see, as the sheriff I have to keep law and order. Now, that's going to be hard for me to do if I have to worry about where you and the girls are at the same time. I don't mind telling you, it's a little distracting. Know what happens when a lawman chases outlaws and gets distracted?"

She shook her head. "No, but I'm sure it isn't good."

He sat up straighter. "No, it is not. I could get shot, hanged or worse." Josiah looked her straight in the eyes. He tried to convey that even though they'd been teasing earlier, now wasn't a time to joke or kid around. He needed to know that he could rely on her to keep herself and his girls safe.

Anna Mae knew he was serious, even though he kept his tone light. "I'm really sorry, Josiah. I don't want you getting shot, hanged or worse. I'll try to do as you ask in the future."

"That's all I'm asking," he said, standing. "Now, I think you need a lesson in milking a cow."

She curled her nose. "I suppose so. I fed the chickens and gave them fresh water. But, well, after I got here I realized I have no idea how to go about milking Jersey."

He nodded. "Well, first off we need to pull her out here so she's easier to manage."

Anna Mae watched him put a rope through one of the loops in the new halter she wore. He handed over the rope. "Now open the door and gently pull her out into the aisle."

Anna Mae nodded, a flicker of apprehension coursed

through her as the big animal took a step toward her. *Jersey is just a cow, Jersey is just a cow. She will not bite you. Or step on you.* The encouraging yet fearful thoughts kept her backing up.

"Whoa, Annie." Josiah stopped her by standing behind her. "The cow's not trying to get you. She's just coming out to be milked."

He placed his hands on her arms and gently rubbed them up and down in what she assumed was his way of trying to comfort her. Anna Mae knew it was silly to fear the cow, and she had no real basis for doing so other than she'd never been allowed around animals before. Well, horses didn't count, because they weren't farm animals—at least that's what her father always said. Anna Mae tried to halt her runaway thoughts and listen to Josiah.

"Tie the rope around that pole." He indicated a post that was part of the stall beside them.

When she'd done that, he continued, "Now, give her these oats." He put the bucket in her hands and watched.

Anna Mae closed her eyes. Could she get close enough to the cow's mouth to set the bucket down? What if it decided to bite her with those big teeth? She opened her eyes and looked to Josiah. "Maybe we should sell her. I don't know that I can do this."

He turned her to face him. "Think of the cow as one of the older, bigger boys in your classroom. Would you not teach him because he's bigger and older than the rest?"

"Of course I would teach him, but he isn't a cow!" Her voice and frustration rose with each word. Josiah simply didn't understand her fear. And how could he? She didn't even understand it.

"No, she's a dumb animal who is hurting because her bag is full of milk. By milking her, you are helping her. Just like you helped the bigger boys in your class-room get an education. Try thinking of her as an over-size dog that doesn't bite," Josiah suggested with a grin.

A big dog. Anna Mae turned back to the cow. She looked into her beautiful brown eyes and tried to imag-ine her as a dog. Then Anna Mae squared her shoulders, took two steps forward and set the bucket down within reach of the cow's head.

"See? That wasn't so bad." Josiah praised her from behind.

"For you," she murmured. Then she turned to face him with a nervous smile. "Now what?"

He shrugged. "Now we milk the cow." Josiah picked up the stool and a milk bucket and sat down. "It's really easy once you get the hang of it." He reached out, took a teat in his big hand and gave it a tug and a squeeze. Milk spurted into the bucket. "See? Nothing to it. And look, Jersey isn't paying us no never mind because she's happily eating."

Anna Mae nodded. She knew she had to try to milk the cow. Deep inside she told herself she wanted to, but her feet wouldn't move. "I seem to be stuck here, Josiah. Why don't you show me again how it's done?"

A grin split his handsome face. "All right." He dem-onstrated again. "Now it's your turn." He stood and moved aside so she could sit on the stool.

It took all Anna Mae's willpower to walk forward and sit down.

"Now reach out and do what I did."

She closed her eyes. *Lord, please help me.* That was as far as she got with her prayer. Big warm hands wrapped around hers. Heat from Josiah seeped into her back. He'd come up behind her and was guiding her hands toward Jersey.

Without another word, together they milked the cow. When the job was done, Josiah eased away from her. She turned around and faced him. Anna Mae whispered, "I did it."

He grinned. "Yes, you did. Now grab the milk and put it on the hay bale over there." He looked a little flustered and Anna Mae wondered if he felt all right.

She did as he said. The warm milk sloshed as she walked it over. She couldn't believe she'd milked a cow. The cow hadn't seemed to mind and she'd done it, with Josiah's help of course.

He set the stool off to the side and then instructed, "Untie Jersey and then take the feed bucket and hold it in front of her while pulling on the lead rope. Turn her around and lead her back into her stall."

Anna Mae looked at him. Was he nuts? A twinkle filled his eyes. He knew she couldn't do that. Was he making fun of her? Or was it a challenge? Tomorrow she'd try, but for today Anna Mae thought she'd come a long way. She smiled sweetly at him. "How about we make that a part of my lessons tomorrow and you do all that right now?"

Josiah walked over to her and leaned toward her. He kissed her on the cheek. "All right. I'm proud of you. You did good, but tomorrow you have to do it all."

The warmth of his lips lingered on her skin and it

was all she could do not to reach up and touch where he'd kissed. Anna Mae sighed, telling herself it was only because she was happy not to have to put the animal away. It had nothing to do with the sweet kiss he'd just delivered.

She watched as he and Jersey entered the stall. New fear pushed romantic thoughts away. Would she be able to milk the cow tomorrow morning? Or would Josiah have to help her again?

The thought of them milking together sent a shiver down her back. Maybe she really should try to do it on her own. Getting too close to him wasn't good for her mending heart.

By the end of the following week, Anna Mae had a handle on the milking thing; in fact, she felt accomplished about most everything she put her hand to these days. She could walk among the chickens to feed them, and though it took her much longer than Josiah to milk Jersey, she still got the job done. She'd even petted the brown-spotted cow a time or two.

Day by day the house took on more of her personality, and Josiah and the girls seemed pleased. While thoroughly cleaning one day she discovered that the bed in the third bedroom was broken. As fast as the girls were growing they'd soon be moving into the bedroom. Anna Mae decided she'd start working on it now.

She tried to repair the bed but couldn't, so she took it apart. She carried the frame piece by piece to the barn, then emptied the straw tick mattress and washed the covering. While working on this, she ran through different ideas of what to do with the room. The girls were too young to sleep in there still but maybe they could use it as a playroom.

There was an old table in the barn that had only three legs. She toyed with the idea of nailing a board in place of the missing leg. She could use it as a sewing table; a place to cut out material and quilt pieces. Then she thought about an office for Josiah. With the same plan, she could shorten the legs and make him a desk. Or maybe she should make something for the girls.

Anna Mae made her way back to the house to look the room over. It was a corner room with windows on both outside walls. The natural lighting was wonderful.

She stood looking at the room with fresh eyes, worrying her lower lip between her teeth. Excitement threatened to overwhelm her good sense from time to time, so she examined her new idea with extreme caution. It would work. After a long pause, she checked to make sure the girls still slept, and then she headed for the barn. In less than an hour the table was clean and a forth leg was nailed into place. She dragged the table onto the porch. All she needed was for the girls to wake so she could finish her plans.

Quietly she carried, from other parts of the house, things that were needed to make the room perfect. She made a little more noise each time she entered the room where the twins slept. Surely by now they were ready to get up. Finally Ruby wiggled around to peer through the slats in her crib, and Anna Mae ran back to the porch and in a few minutes had dragged the heavy table to its new home. By the time she finished, both girls stood in their cribs yelling "Out."

With happy expectation she set them on the floor and

led them to see what she'd been doing. Their squeals of delight caused her smile to broaden in relentless joy. They ran from the table to the dolls on the lower shelf of a small bookshelf, back to the table, then back to the higher shelf to get a book. They carried it to the table and sat to read, then were up again. Anna Mae watched with complete pleasure.

She'd chopped the three legs off the table and made it the exact height for the girls. The shelves also were within hand reach for them. It left a large part of the room unoccupied, but maybe she could make a rug for them to play upon. All in all, it had been a morning of hard work that had paid off for her little ones.

She left them playing and went to the kitchen to see what else she could tackle. Anna Mae felt an indefinable feeling of rightness. Who knew she could be so creative? Just the thought sent her confidence level soaring.

All this time, she'd thought teaching was all she had a talent for. Now Anna Mae saw that she could accomplish whatever she set her hand to. Philippians 4:13 immediately came to mind. *I can do all things through Christ which strengtheneth me.*

She looked at the churn Josiah had brought up from the cellar. His instructions were "You just mash this thing up and down till the milk turns hard. Then you have butter."

However, Anna Mae had helped her mother make butter a few times so she knew that wasn't all. Making butter had been one of the chores that her mother enjoyed as a child and so had continued to do, even though she hadn't needed to. A smile touched her lips at the memory.

Anna Mae washed the churn thoroughly and the paddle board, too. Then she packed snow into the churn to get it good and cold inside. She took the fat off the top of the milk Josiah had left covered and sitting on the porch this morning, and carried it back into the warm house. As she was churning the noise brought the girls to the kitchen, but they soon lost interest and went back to their room.

The whole process took about forty-five minutes, and then Anna Mae poured the butter onto a cold slab. She salted it, then rolled it into round balls. When finished, she had fifteen beautiful balls of butter, which she placed in a dish and put in the larder outside. She quickly cleaned up the kitchen, humming, with a dance in her steps.

Anna Mae played with the girls for a few minutes, then went to put on supper. She salted a slab of rabbit meat and put it on to fry. When it was almost done, she dropped a pat of butter in the pan and her mouth began to water. Biscuit dough rose in the side oven of the wood stove. It would taste wonderful tonight with fresh butter tucked between the flaky bread.

As she peeled potatoes, something kept niggling at her brain, something she'd forgotten to do. Or maybe it was something she'd promised to do. Anna Mae thought and thought, but nothing rang a bell. Maybe if she focused on something else, it would come to her. She washed the potatoes, intent on concentrating on dinner.

Finally she heard Josiah ride into the yard. Anna Mae felt giddy with excitement. She had accomplished so much today and knew he would be so pleased. Why, she might even get another hug. To be quite frank, she had enjoyed their hug from last week. Thoughts of it had occupied a lot of her time.

Ten minutes later, the back door swung open and hit the wall with a thud. "Anna Mae!" To say he roared would be putting it mildly.

She rushed from the kitchen. "Yes, Josiah. What is it?"

She watched him struggle for composure. "Did you use the turpentine today?"

A feeling of dread shook her from head to toe. "Yes, I mixed it with beeswax and polished a table for—"

He interrupted her. "And did you seal it up and put it back where you found it?"

She sank down into a chair, her legs too weak to hold her. "No, I—"

"No, you didn't. And the chickens turned it over and it's all over the barn floor. One strike of a match could burn our barn down right now, and Lord only knows how much the chickens have ingested."

Anna Mae's hands flew to her cheeks in dismay. "Oh, Josiah, are they dead?"

His lips puckered with annoyance, but his voice became calmer. "Not yet, but they are wobbling around like they're drunk. My main concern is getting the spill clean before an accident or fire breaks out. I carry the lantern out in the mornings to milk by. If it turned over, God forbid, the entire thing would go up in smoke."

"I'm so sorry. You stay with the girls and I'll go clean it up." She stood and reached for her coat.

"No, put the girls' coats on and we'll both clean it up." He paused, then turned back to her. "That won't work. The smell might overpower them. I'll do it. Hold supper, this will take a while."

He was gone before Anna Mae could even respond. Tears welled in her eyes and ran down her face. Josiah had seemed so disappointed in her. Smothering a sob, she checked the biscuits.

She'd had such a great day. Now this. Her joy in all she'd accomplished suddenly left her and she sat down at the table and wept. Why did it always seem she took two steps forward and three backward? Would Josiah ever see her as a suitable wife and mother?

Chapter Eighteen

Josiah pulled Roy to a stop. He searched for tracks in the mud. His prey were slicker than foxes when it came to hiding. They'd evaded him so many times over the past few weeks that he'd began to doubt his tracking ability.

With a heavy sigh, he turned the horse back toward town. It wasn't helping that his thoughts continued to dwell on Annie and the girls. His heart had leaped out of his chest at the turpentine on the barn floor and he'd snapped at Annie. To say things between them had been strained over the past few weeks would have been an understatement.

Now they'd been invited to William and Emily Jane's tonight to celebrate with a big meal, thanks to the new holiday that everyone was so excited about. He understood the need to be thankful to the Lord in all things, but wondered if this new holiday wasn't really just an excuse to get together and call off a day of work.

Josiah knew he was simply irritated that he'd lost the communication he'd begun to enjoy with Anna Mae, his Annie. It ate at him and he hated that he'd hurt her with the harshness of his words. Maybe he'd overreacted. No, she needed to understand the severity of what could have happened to the barn and the animals that lived inside it. Thankfully, the chickens had recovered.

He rubbed the back of his neck. Worry ate at him. Would she behave the same tonight as she had earlier in the day? They'd gone to church that morning and he'd endured her silence during the service. It was the first time they'd had to sit so closely since the turpentine incident weeks ago. The church had been packed due to it being Thanksgiving Day.

He'd been aware of the tension in her body. It felt as if she strained to get away from him. He might be sorry that he'd snapped at her, but Josiah wouldn't apologize.

When he arrived at the bakery, Roy snorted a greeting to the other horses in William's barn. Josiah patted his faithful companion on the neck. "We'll be heading home soon, ole boy."

William stepped out of a stall he'd been mucking. "Any news?"

Josiah grew so tired of that question. "No, just when I think I'm on the trail, I lose it."

"Are you even sure you're trailing the right men?" William asked, picking up a pitchfork and jabbing it into the hay.

"Yep, one of the horses has lost a shoe. Makes it easy to follow until they do something like cross the river, and then I lose them." Josiah helped William spread the hay in the stall. "What are you doing out here?"

"The women were all quiet and Emily Jane gave me 'the look' so I hightailed it out of there with the excuse

I needed to tend to these critters." He indicated the two mares and gelding that stood in stalls.

Josiah felt his ears turning red. Anna Mae was probably telling Emily Jane what a clod he'd been to her.

William leaned against the pitchfork and eyed him. "Yep, that's what I figured. What did you say or do? Maybe I can help you get back in her good graces."

He shook his head.

"Might as well tell me. You know Emily Jane will later, anyway." William grinned, knowing he was right.

"I didn't do anything but clean up her mess." He jerked the pitchfork from William's hands and stabbed it into the hay.

Catching his balance, William asked, "Before or after you scolded her?"

"What makes you think I scolded her?" Josiah wondered if he were truly that predictable.

William chuckled. "Let me guess. You came home, and she'd either left something out, burned dinner or done something even more ghastly. Your first instinct was to find her and tell her what she'd done wrong." Sensing he was on the right track, William continued with a dramatic flair. "Or if it was something dangerous that she did, you told her how foolish she was and then proceeded to condemn her for it, not out of spite but so that she'd learn her lesson and not do it again. And when she apologized, you didn't except it graciously but told her that now you had to fix whatever it was that she'd messed up."

Josiah sank onto a hay bale. "Now how do you know all that?" he asked, baffled. He was sure that Anna Mae would not confide in William, and she hadn't had time to convey to Emily Jane all the sordid details William had just supplied.

William joined him on the hay bale and slapped him on the back. "I'm married now, too, remember?"

"You've done that, too?" At William's questioning look, he clarified, "Accused her of all she did wrong? And all the other stuff you said?" Josiah dropped his head into his hands.

"Sure, a couple of months after we were married, I did just that. Emily Jane forgot about the bread and it burned to a crisp in the oven. I felt it was my place to tell her how dangerous, foolish and wasteful that was. I wasn't very smart back then, either."

"Well, burning bread isn't the same as leaving turpentine open in the barn and having the chickens tip it over and spill it on the floor." Josiah looked up, hoping for support.

William shook his head. "Doesn't matter. Did you hurt her feelings?"

He sighed. "I reckon so."

"So let me enlighten you, brother-in-law. She probably tried to do something nice for you, which was why she had the turpentine out in the first place. Did you ask why she used it?" When Josiah shook his head, William continued. "Trust me, when you find out, you'll feel like a dirt clod. When you yelled at her, you undermined her confidence, so now she's afraid to tell you. You can either eat crow now or eat it later, but it's for sure you're gonna eat crow." William shook his head as if in sad commiseration.

Josiah already felt the noose about his neck. "So what

should I do?" He was a doomed man. He picked up a piece of straw and began shredding it.

"Well, if it were me, I'd at least apologize for hurting her feelings. Especially if she's already said she was sorry." William stood and put the pitchfork away. He pulled one of his mares into the clean stall.

Low-down snakes couldn't get any lower than Josiah felt. Yes, she had apologized, even offered to clean up the mess, and he'd still left her feeling like the stupidest woman in the whole of Texas. And now he had to go in the house and face her. And by now Emily Jane knew what a sorry excuse he was. He heaved a sigh, tossed away the straw that he'd managed to destroy in a matter of seconds. "Might as well get this over with."

William clapped him on the back. "Wise move, my man. Face the music. Just remember to give her a hug and whisper in her ear that you're very sorry."

"I've been married before, too. I think I know how to make up." Josiah said the words, but did he really believe them? His and Anna Mae's relationship wasn't a true marriage. He just prayed he'd find the right words when the time came.

Inside the house, Anna Mae had just finished telling Emily Jane about the tension in her marriage. She couldn't believe how quickly her friend had figured out there was problem between herself and Josiah. She hadn't wanted to tell her, but seemingly Emily Jane already knew, and understood what was going on.

"Look, men sometimes react over the least things. It is our job as women to keep them grounded. It's obvious you didn't mean to do whatever it was that you did, so just let it go. In time, he'll come around and say he's sorry, too." Emily Jane pulled the roasted chicken out of the oven.

Even as she said it, Anna Mae felt foolish, but she wanted to be truthful with her friend. "I know, but he hurt my feelings."

Emily Jane placed the chicken on the side board. "And he will again."

Anna Mae poured hot green beans into a big bowl. "Just pretend it didn't happen? He practically called me stupid."

"If you want him to apologize, then yes." Emily Jane looked her straight in the eyes. "Do you want to continue the way it's been lately? Or go back to being happily married to your best friend?"

How little Emily Jane truly knew. Anna Mae and Josiah were far from happily married. They didn't even have a real marriage. As for them being best friends, well, that was a good description of their relationship from her viewpoint, but she doubted Josiah saw her that way. Still, if it would bring peace to their home once more… "I'll try."

Emily Jane hugged her. "That's all you can do." She released her. "Now, would you mind setting the table while I spread the rolls with this wonderful butter you brought? I can't wait to sample it."

Anna Mae nodded, then looked to the twins. They were content to peer at the picture book that she'd brought to entertain them. They pointed at pictures and communicated with each other in both English and baby talk. For the girls' sake, she'd try to forget that Josiah had hurt her feelings and made her cry. Lord willing, they'd be back to normal in no time.

The sound of the men stomping their boots on the porch alerted the women and children that they were coming in. "The table's ready," Anna Mae said, just as they entered the kitchen.

"Good, let's set this on the sideboard and eat buffet-style." Emily Jane handed Anna Mae two plates. "Why don't you go ahead and fix the girls' supper while I get them seated."

Anna Mae took the plates, very aware of Josiah walking toward her. She turned toward the food to avoid his gaze. *Lord, it's going to be hard acting as if my feelings aren't still hurt.*

"Here, let me help you with those." He placed a hand on her shoulder.

She nodded and handed him one of the plates. Together they chose green beans, mashed potatoes with gravy, a roll and a chicken leg for each of the girls.

William and Emily Jane talked to Rose and Ruby. The twins laughed as they squirmed in their chairs, trying to see around their aunt and uncle at the plates they knew were for them.

Anna Mae placed hers in front of Rose and Josiah did the same for Ruby. "Girls, wait for the rest of us," he instructed, joining William back at the sideboard.

Anna Mae filled the girls' milk glasses while Emily Jane poured coffee for William and Josiah. "Tell me more about the girls' room."

Josiah looked at her with a question in his eyes as he took his place at the table. Emily Jane set a steaming cup in front of him. Anna Mae looked away.

She didn't want to talk about the room she'd created for the girls. She hadn't shown it to him. As soon as Josiah had left to clean up her mess in the barn, she had taken the girls from their room and shut the door. Since they never used that third room, he hadn't had any reason to see it.

After the way he'd acted, Anna Mae was afraid to tell him what she'd used the turpentine for. She feared he'd think her foolish and the desk she'd created foolish, too.

Why had Emily Jane brought up the room when she knew it was a sore spot? Anna Mae wanted to kick her friend, but instead answered, "Oh, well. It's really nothing special, not even worth mentioning." She picked up a plate and turned her back to the table.

Emily Jane joined her. "I love the idea of them having a desk for reading and drawing. That was really smart of you to create such a space for the twins."

Anna Mae shot her a "hush up now" look. "Thank you," she answered, for the men's benefit.

Both she and Emily Jane returned to the table. After sitting down, William offered a grace of thanksgiving. While he prayed, Anna Mae felt Josiah's hand reach under the table and clasp hers.

Warmth spread up her arm and threatened to melt her reserve. When William said "amen," Josiah gave her hand a gentle squeeze before releasing it. She looked up to find him smiling at her. It seemed as if he looked straight into her soul.

Josiah leaned over and whispered for her ears only, "I'm sorry I hurt your feelings. I really didn't mean to." Then he sat back up and turned to help Rose with her chicken.

At that moment, Anna Mae knew he was forgiven. Would she regret forgiving him? She hoped not. She told herself it was time to let old hurts go. But a question plagued her. What did it mean that she could forgive him with one softly whispered sentence? What would letting it go cost her in the long run?

Chapter Nineteen

Life on the Miller farm fell into a routine over the next three weeks. Josiah went to work each morning after a hearty breakfast. While he was gone, Anna Mae cleaned, cooked and created Christmas gifts for her family.

While the girls napped she worked on Josiah's gifts. She had managed to crochet him a scarf and was in the process of piecing the blue-and-white nine-patch quilt together for his bed. While she worked, Anna Mae imagined his surprise at the gifts.

In the evenings, while Josiah read to them all from the Bible, she worked on the little girls' dresses. They were so small that she was sure they didn't realize what she was doing, but still kept the rag dolls and clothes a secret from them, working on them only after everyone went to bed. It felt good to have a family to create Christmas gifts for.

It saddened Anna Mae that her mother and father hadn't written back to her. She'd hoped to have their blessings on her marriage, but wasn't really surprised.

Father was busy with his business and Mother her social life. Time passed fast when you were busy, and her parents stayed busy.

A glance at the clock told her Josiah would be home soon. She went to the kitchen and stirred the stew she'd had simmering on the stove all day. Corn bread sat at the back, warming. She scooped out stew for each of the girls and set their bowls off to the side to cool. A sense of pride burst forth as she put fresh butter on the table.

She heard him stomping up the porch steps, and hurried to finish setting the table. "Rose! Ruby! Papa's home!"

The sound of the little girls scrambling from their room caused her to smile. They loved the room she'd created for them and spent most of the day playing in it.

Josiah had praised her on the job she'd done and suggested a way to finish the room. He'd asked Levi Westland to build the girls each a small bed that they would receive Christmas morning. Rose's would have tiny butterflies along the headboard and Ruby's little birds. Anna Mae couldn't wait to see them up and ready for the girls to sleep in.

"Papa! Papa!" they squealed, stumbling over themselves and each other as they attempted to race for their father.

Emily Jane had told her that the girls were small for their age. Anna Mae remembered laughing and responding, "Yes, but what they lack in size they more than make up for with their vocabulary." They'd developed so much since that fateful snowstorm.

Living out on the farm was lonely sometimes. She

missed seeing Emily Jane every day, but the little girls were plenty of company when they weren't napping.

Anna Mae set the last spoon on the table just as squeals of laughter burst from the front door. Without looking she knew Josiah had grabbed up his girls and was kissing their faces. She smiled at him as he entered the kitchen.

"Something sure smells good in here," Josiah said, coming over and giving her a hug.

Anna Mae pretended the hug didn't make her feel shaky inside. "It's rabbit stew. I hope you like it." She hurried to help Rose up into her chair.

"I'm sure I will. I'm as hungry as a starving coyote." He lifted Ruby into her chair and patted the girls on the head. "Were you two good today?"

The twins nodded and grinned at each other. From the mischievous expressions on their faces, Anna Mae wondered what their room looked like.

Within a few minutes, she had the stew, corn bread and their drinks on the table. As soon as she took her seat, Josiah said grace. The sounds of Rose and Ruby smacking their lips while they waited for him to finish made her smile.

"Amen." Josiah looked at the girls. "The way you two were smacking those lips, I'm not sure the good Lord even heard my prayer." He placed their bowls in front of them and inhaled. "From the smell of this, I really can't blame you."

The girls immediately began to eat. Anna Mae wondered if they were about to hit a growth spurt. Their appetites indicated they probably were. She made a mental note to add lace to the bottom of their Christmas dresses. More than likely they would need it to help cover their little knees.

She turned her attention to Josiah. "How was your day?"

He blew on his spoonful of stew. "Worrisome." He sighed. "Caldron found another dead cow today."

Anna Mae buttered a slab of corn bread and passed it over to him. "Oh, I'm sorry to hear that." She thought about Jersey out in the barn and worried that she might be in danger. Although it seemed the cows closer to town were more at risk than Jersey.

"Yeah, me, too. I had hoped since there hadn't been any incidents in over a week that the thieves had moved on, but now I know they haven't." He spooned the stew into his mouth and his eyes opened wide. Once he'd chewed and swallowed Josiah smiled. "That rabbit is so tender."

She couldn't hide her pleased expression. "Good, that's what I had hoped for."

He took a large bite of the corn bread and chewed with gusto. It did her heart good to see him enjoying her cooking. She nibbled at the edge of her corn bread, savoring the sweetness. Emily Jane had told her that adding a little sugar would make the best corn bread and she'd been right.

"You really are a good cook, Annie. I'm blessed to have you for a wife. Truly blessed."

Anna Mae looked up and found him looking down on his plate. Did he really mean that? Was he happy to have her as his wife? Her heart raced at the thought. She quickly tried to subdue it. *Don't read more into his words than what he said,* she mentally warned herself.

* * *

The next day, Josiah stomped his feet before entering the general store. The snow had all melted, but mud remained and seemed to coat everything in sight. Especially his boots. The sole had worn thin on the right one and he'd soon have to buy a new pair.

But not today. Today he was Christmas shopping for Annie and the girls. The smells of cinnamon, leather and pipe tobacco warred for his attention.

"Hello, Sheriff. Are you out of coffee over at the jail already?" Wilson Moore asked. He held a broom in his hand and wore a green apron.

Josiah shook his head. "Not today. I'm looking for gifts for Annie and the girls." He saw Carolyn come out of the side door and into the store. Josiah walked over to the counter where she stood pulling an apron over her head. "I'm glad you're here, Carolyn. Has Annie mentioned anything to you about what she'd like for Christmas?"

Carolyn's forehead crinkled and then cleared. "Oh, you're talking about Anna Mae. Took me a second to make the connection. Annie, that's cute."

He raised an eyebrow and waited for her to answer. Josiah leaned his hip on the counter and looked at the penny candy. The girls wouldn't mind having some of that, he felt sure.

"Well, she bought a lot of that blue fabric. She might like a blue ribbon to go in her hair that would match it." Carolyn moved around the counter and headed to where the ribbon was located.

Josiah followed. "I'll take some of that, but I thought something a little more…"

She picked up a spool of the ribbon and turned to face him. "Personal?"

He had the impression she fully enjoyed his discomfort. "Yes, but not anything frilly."

Carolyn laughed. "We just got some new necklaces in. Would you like to see those?"

Josiah leaped at the idea of a necklace. "Yes, please."

She continued to chuckle as they walked back to the counter. Carolyn moved behind it to where a glass case sat at the far end. "Here they are." She pointed down through the glass.

His gaze swept the necklaces. What he had in mind wasn't there. He wanted something that would suit her delicate beauty. Something good, wholesome and sweet. These were big flowers. Flowers were nice, but they just weren't what he wanted.

"Not what you had in mind, huh?"

Josiah straightened. "No, they are a little too big."

"Well, we also have these. No two are the same." She pulled out a small tray of rings.

They were simple gold bands, each with a different swirl or pattern on it. Josiah's gaze immediately fell on one that had an intricately woven vine engraved in the gold. He pointed to it. "How about that one?"

Carolyn pulled it from the tray and handed it to him. He slipped it on his little finger. "Do you think this will fit her?"

"Let me see it." She held out her hand.

He dropped it into her palm and watched her slip it onto her ring finger. "It's a little snug, but I think her hand is just a bit smaller than mine, so it will probably fit." Carolyn smiled up at him.

"I'll take it." *Surely it will fit one of her fingers,* he thought.

"Good. I'll find a pretty box to put it in while you decide what you want for the girls."

Josiah turned to the toy section. He'd already gotten the twins stuffed animals, so he eyed the other items. What else could he get Rose and Ruby? Anna Mae had shown him the rag dolls she worked on each night, so he wouldn't get them a doll. They had blocks and pull toys. Each of them had a favorite blanket. He sighed.

Maybe he'd choose something more practical, like a new pair of shoes for each of them. He walked to that section of the store and found little black shoes, but then realized he had no idea what size the girls wore. Mary had always taken care of their clothes and shoes, not him.

His thoughts turned to Mary. This would be his and the girls' first Christmas without her. She had enjoyed Christmas, but not in the same way Anna Mae seemed to.

Anna Mae went about the house humming Christmas hymns and talking about Christmas gifts. He was surprised she hadn't asked for a Christmas tree. Josiah realized he was grinning and frowned. How had his thoughts moved from Mary to Anna Mae?

He ran a hand around his collar. It was natural, he told himself. Anna Mae was his wife now. She was with him every day. They were friends. He nodded. Yep, that was it.

They were friends, only friends. A new and unexpected warmth surged through him as it slowly dawned on Josiah that Anna Mae had become his best friend.

The one he shared his day with over the supper table each evening. Who helped him get the girls ready for bed every night. He thought of things during the day he wanted to tell her; things he knew would bring a smile to her face or cause the little crease in her forehead when she puckered her face into a frown.

Wilson walked up beside him. "What's wrong with the shoes, Sheriff?"

"Huh?"

"You're staring at them as if perplexed. I just wondered what was wrong," Wilson answered.

Josiah shook his head. "There's nothing wrong with them. I just realized a few moments ago that I don't know what size to get the girls."

"Would you like for me to call Carolyn over here? She might know," he offered.

"No, I think I'll just wait and ask Annie if she thinks I should get them anything else for Christmas," Josiah answered, wishing he was out on the trail of an outlaw right now instead of in a store thinking about the women in his life.

"All right. Is there anything else I can help you find?" Wilson swept a clump of dirt out from under the shelf.

Josiah shook his head. "Naw, I think I'm about done for the day." He walked back to the counter, where Carolyn waited. He paid for the ring and the ribbon and slipped them into his pocket.

The cold air felt good against his warm cheeks as he stepped outside. He walked back to the jailhouse. The air tasted of snow and sent a shiver down his spine. Josiah decided to check in with Wade, and if everything was fine, he'd head home before the snow hit.

"Glad to see you back, Sheriff." The young deputy stood by the stove warming his hands.

"Why's that?"

He poured a cup of coffee and handed it to Josiah, then poured a second cup for himself. His boots clomped across the wood floor as he walked over to the desk. "These just arrived in the mail. Thought you might like to take them home and study them." He handed Josiah two wanted posters.

Josiah read them. "Looks like these're the fellas suspected of holdin' up the banks in these parts."

"That's what I got from reading them, too, but I don't think they're right," Wade said, leaning against the bars of the only cell.

Josiah moved to his desk and sat down. "No?"

The young man shook his head. "I think the cattle butchers and the bank robbers might be one and the same. And if that's the case, then we're looking for four or maybe even six men, instead of just two."

"What makes you think that?" Josiah leaned back in his chair and propped his feet up on the desk.

Wade sipped his coffee. "Well, it seems to me that a couple of days go by and during that time a bank gets robbed, thankfully not ours." He paused as if considering his words. Josiah had learned to just wait him out. "Then the next day we find a dead cow someplace."

Josiah had to agree that that was the way it seemed, but that still didn't mean they were the same men. He studied the wanted posters and waited. Wade would continue as soon as he got his thoughts together.

"If I was a robbin' them banks and I didn't want people to think it was me, I'd do something else to throw them off the scent. I think that's what the robbers are doing. They rob the bank and then butcher a cow to confuse the law." He took another sip of his coffee, then stood up straight. "'Course, I could be wrong. It might be different men, but my gut says I'm right, even if I ain't makin' a lick of sense." Wade finished his coffee and set the cup down.

Josiah pondered what the young man had said, then nodded. "Well, you could be right. I've learned to listen to my gut and if yours is saying they might be the same, well, they might just be." He folded the wanted papers and placed them on the desk. "We'll continue to keep our noses to the ground. They're sure to slip up somewhere along the way."

Josiah dropped his feet back down on the floor, took the ring box from his coat pocket and dropped it into the lap drawer of his desk. "When they do, we'll be there to get 'em." He tucked the blue ribbon deeper into his pocket to take out at home.

Wade nodded. "That sounds good to me, boss."

"Don't call me boss," Josiah scolded as he stood. He picked up the wanted papers and stuck them in his front coat pocket. "You ready to take over the town?" he asked, walking toward the door.

"Just for the night, Sheriff. She's all yours come morning." Wade pushed away from the bars and followed Josiah to the door.

"I'll see you then." Roy snorted as Josiah climbed up. "Sheriff?"

Josiah turned to see what his deputy wanted now. "Yes?"

The young man ran his hand along the back of his

neck. Josiah grinned. The lad was picking up his bad habits. Wade looked him straight in the eyes. "You be careful heading home. No tellin' where those mangy thieves are hiding out."

Josiah nodded. It pleased him that Wade cared enough to offer a warning. "Will do. You watch yourself, too." He turned the horse toward home. "Let's head home, boy. If I know Annie, she's got dinner on the stove and a fire in the fireplace."

Roy knew the way to his warm barn, oats and hay. The gelding wasted no time getting there.

For the next half hour, Josiah let Roy have his head while he thought about the robbers, the butchers and Wade's comparison of the two. Was it possible they were one and the same? If so, was his little family in danger out on the farm alone every day?

A bitter thought entered his mind. He hadn't been able to protect Mary in town. What made him think he could protect Annie and the girls out on the farm?

Chapter Twenty

Snowflakes, big and fluffy, cascaded gracefully to the ground at a fast pace. Anna Mae and the girls laughed and looked up into the gray sky. "I love this time of the year, don't you, girls?"

"Me wuv no," Rose answered, and stooped down to touch it.

"Uby wuv no, too." Ruby knelt beside her sister to examine the freshly fallen flakes. They giggled and shivered, all the while poking holes in the snow with their little gloved fingers.

Anna Mae set the bucket of warm milk beside the barn and then danced about in the snow. Thankfully, it hadn't gotten deep enough to keep her from her fun movements.

The girls jumped and leaped about also, laughing and trying to catch snowflakes on their tongues. Both fell and giggled, then pushed themselves up from the frozen ground, only to fall back down again.

"It's wet enough that we might be able to build a snowman tomorrow, if it keeps snowing," Anna Mae told them as they squealed and rolled about on the ground, looking like bundled-up snow babies.

She laughed at their antics. According to the locals, this winter was the harshest they'd had in many years. Anna Mae loved the snow and was glad to see it, even if the townspeople weren't thrilled. Still, the cold started seeping into her body, and sleet mixed into the snow, which began to fall faster. "Come along, girls. Time to go inside and warm up."

Anna Mae grinned as Rose and Ruby pushed themselves up from the frozen ground. They were a pair and a sweet pair at that. Once on their feet, they toddled after her.

She'd just gotten them out of their coats and into their high chairs when a knock sounded at the door. Anna Mae hurried to answer it, thinking that perhaps Josiah had his hands full and couldn't open it himself. She was surprised to see a large man with a big heavy coat standing in her doorway.

"I hate to disturb you, ma'am. My name is John Meeker and my horse has thrown a shoe. I'm afraid to ride him much farther. Would it be all right with you, if I put him up in the barn for the night?" He tilted back a flat brown hat, and green eyes the color of summer grass looked into hers.

Anna Mae swallowed hard. She should have called out to make sure that whoever was at the door was Josiah. Now here she stood, facing a mountain of a man and having to make a decision that only Josiah should be making. Cold air blew in and caused her to shiver.

If the man was telling the truth she couldn't leave him and his horse out in the cold. Anna Mae nodded.

"You and your horse are welcome to spend the night in the barn." She thought about adding that Josiah would be home soon, but decided it was better not to alert the stranger that she and the girls were alone.

He tipped his hat toward her. "Much obliged." John Meeker stomped as he went off the porch.

Was he angry that she'd said he and his horse could stay in the barn? Had the big man expected to be invited into the house for the night? Anna Mae didn't care what his expectations were, she would not endanger the twins by inviting a stranger into their home.

Her gaze went to the road. Darkness was falling almost as fast as the snow. Anna Mae closed the door and dropped the heavy bar over it. *Lord, please hurry Josiah home.*

Josiah followed the hoofprints and realized they were headed to his place. Like before, the prints were that of a horse with only three shoes. This horse usually seemed to trail the other outlaws, but this time the hoofprints were alone. Josiah's heartbeat picked up two paces. He kneed Roy. "Hurry, boy, he can't be that far ahead of us."

The night was quickly descending and so was the sleet and snow. Those prints had almost been filled in when he'd noticed them. Now Josiah was afraid he'd lose the man again in the snow and dark.

A few minutes from the house, he lost the tracks. Snow created a white blanket with no blemishes. Fear crawled up his spine and chilled him to the bone. He shivered both from the cold and the worry that the stranger would get to his place before he did.

Roy thundered into the front yard, kicking up snow as if driven by a need to spread the white stuff himself. Josiah was off and running up the porch steps before the horse came to a complete stop. Josiah pushed the door, only to find himself barred from the house. "Annie!"

He heard someone fumbling with the heavy piece of wood and then the door flew open. Anna Mae grabbed the front of his coat, pulling him through the opening, her eyes filled with a curious intensity. "I'm sorry it was locked, Josiah, but we have a visitor in the barn and I wasn't taking any chances."

He shut the door behind him and dropped the safety board into the slots. "Tell me about this visitor. Did he introduce himself? Or just head for the barn?"

His gaze darted to the girls, who quietly sat at the table in their high chairs. Their little bodies seemed poised for action, as if they knew something was up, but were uncertain if it would prove good for them or bad. He winked and they visibly relaxed, grinning at him around mouthfuls of bread.

Anna Mae answered, "He said his name is John Meeker and his horse is missing a shoe. I told him that he and his horse could stay in the barn tonight."

"What time did he arrive?" Josiah returned his attention to her. Her hair was down, giving her a soft, vulnerable look. He shouldn't have left her and the girls out on the farm alone. What had he been thinking?

She brushed her hair back. "About fifteen minutes ago."

Josiah placed his palm on her warm shoulder. "Did he threaten you or the girls in any way?"

"No, he was very polite. Just asked if the horse could

stay the night in our barn." She laid her hand on Josiah's and sighed. "I'm glad you're home."

He raised his fingers and touched her soft cheek. "Me, too."

"Papa!" Rose called from the table. She was bouncing in her chair, wanting attention from him, too.

Ruby swallowed her bread and echoed her sister's excited cry.

Josiah dropped his hand and turned to the twins. "Hello, girls. Papa has to go check on something in the barn. You be good for Annie. I'll be right back." He turned to Anna Mae. "Bar the door behind me. I'm going to go check on our visitor and put Roy away for the night." He could have mentioned that he speculated that they had a thief in their barn, but didn't want to alarm her more than she already was. Josiah reached for the bar.

Anna Mae put a light, restraining hand on his arm. "Josiah, please be careful. He's a big man."

For the second time in one day, someone had warned him to use caution. Josiah heeded both of them. "I will be. You just stay inside until I come back." He removed the bar.

At her nod, Josiah stepped out the door. He waited until he heard the bar fall into place before grabbing Roy's reins and heading out to the barn. What would he find there? He felt sure that this man was the same who had given him a merry chase all week.

Mentally, Josiah brought every wanted poster into his mind. He traced each face, checked that it was in his memory and then slowly pulled the barn door open. He intended to slip inside quietly.

"'Bout time you got home." The gravelly voice sounded familiar. Josiah ducked just as a beefy fist plowed into the door frame. And another punch knocked the gun from his hand.

Josiah turned and connected his fist with the big man's right rib cage. A grunt from his opponent gave him some satisfaction. He grinned.

"Faster than you used to be, too."

The sound of a rifle being cocked stopped both men in their tracks. "Take another step and I'll blow your big brains out." The threat was as cold as a rattlesnake's eyes and just as deadly.

Josiah recognized that voice, as well. Although he'd never heard it sound so lethal. He slowly turned to his bride. "Annie, put the gun down," he said, cautiously moving toward her.

She held the weapon steady as a rock, pointed dead center at the green eyes of the man she had in her sights. "I don't take kindly to anyone trying to kill my husband," Anna Mae threatened through clenched teeth, as if she hadn't heard him.

If the circumstances hadn't been so dire, Josiah would have grinned proudly, but right now he feared for Meeker's life. "Annie, we were just horse playing. I'd like you to meet Grady Meeker. Remember? I told you about him?"

Her gaze swept to Josiah, confusion in their beautiful brown depths. "Sheriff Grady?"

"One and the same," the big booming voice confirmed.

Anna Mae lowered the rifle. She handed it to Josiah, turned, and with stiff dignity stomped back to the house. At the porch she yelled back at them, "Since you forgot to mention that you know my husband, you'll definitely be staying in the barn." She sized up Josiah's grin. "You know what? You can both stay out here tonight." Her skirts swished as she slammed the front door.

Josiah watched her go. She'd followed him. Put herself in danger, put Grady in danger, and now she was mad at him. Josiah couldn't help but wonder if he wasn't the one in the most danger.

Booming laughter filled the barn and a hard hand slapped him on the back. "Well, I'll be. She's a little spitfire, isn't she?" Grady picked up the gun he'd knocked from Josiah's hand.

"It would seem so," Josiah answered, taking his gun and sliding it into his waistband.

"You didn't know she was a spitfire? How long you two been married? I saw a couple of young'uns in there that says you should have known her for at least three years. I declare, son, I thought you was smarter than that." Grady returned to the stall where his horse was stabled.

Josiah shook his head. "Annie is my second wife. We've only been married about six weeks."

"Looks like we've got a lot of catchin' up to do." Grady sat down on a bale of hay. "Why don't you start at the beginning and tell me what all you've been up to since last we met."

He nodded. That had been over three years ago. Maybe by the time he finished catching Grady up, Anna Mae would have cooled off some. Josiah knew he'd have to go into the house sooner or later, and decided later might be better. Anna Mae probably wasn't ready to hear that he'd had no idea Grady Meeker was in the area or going by the name John Meeker. Plus, he needed to find out what his old mentor was doing in Granite.

Two hours later, Josiah slipped into the house. He heard Anna Mae saying good-night prayers with the girls, and went into his room to consider what he should say to her.

Once she heard that Grady was on the trail of the bank robbers that were in the area, and that Josiah hadn't known about him being here, she'd understand. At least he prayed she would. He lit the lamp. The room had been cleared of his things. What had the woman done? Thrown them out the back door? Even his Bible was missing off the nightstand. This didn't bode well at all.

"I moved your things into our room." He jumped at the sound of her voice.

"Why?"

Anna Mae's brows drew together in an incredulous squint. "Because I assumed you wouldn't want your friend to freeze in the barn tonight." She walked out the door and into the kitchen.

Josiah followed like a dog with his tail tucked between his legs. She poured a cup of coffee and took a sip. Now why had he thought she was getting it for him? "Look, Annie. I didn't know Grady was in town or that he'd started using his given name when out on the hunt. He's a lawman, like me. After the same thieves as I am." Josiah paused. She still stared at him with steely brown eyes.

"Well, you both scared the living daylights out of me," she said, looking over her cup at him.

"How do you think I felt? There you stood, pointing a gun like you were willing to kill a man." He could no more stop the grin that crossed his face than he could stop breathing. "I sure hadn't expected you to come and protect me. But I'm glad you did. Thank you."

She sighed and let her shoulders drop. Anna Mae slipped into a chair at the table, as if her legs would no longer hold her up. "Why don't men just say hello like normal people?" She set the cup down and sighed again.

He shrugged. "No idea."

Picking up a clean cup and the coffeepot, he poured himself coffee, too. Josiah leaned his hip against the warm stove. "Now what's this about sharing a room?"

"I figured you didn't want him to guess that this is a marriage of convenience, so I moved you into mine and the girls' room. That way he won't know and no one else will find out, either." She traced a pine knot in the table.

He chuckled. "You told him he has to stay in the barn."

"I told you to stay there, too," she reminded him with a cheeky grin.

Josiah laughed, glad to see his good-humored wife back. "I don't think a woman's ever made Grady Meeker sleep in the barn."

She carried her cup to the sink. "Well, then, I don't want to be the first to make him, either. It's too cold out there for him, anyway. You go out and tell him to come inside. I'm going to bed."

"What about me? Am I to sleep on the couch tonight

because you're angry with me? After all, I did disobey and come inside." Josiah followed her to the sink.

She turned to face him. "I'm not angry with you. And no, you can sleep in our room. On the floor." Anna Mae left him standing in the kitchen.

The woman never ceased to amaze him. She'd thought of his reputation as a husband by moving him into her room, but also put him in his place by making him sleep on the floor. A proud grin slipped across his face. Anna Mae Miller was quite the woman. She was his Annie and tonight she'd proved she could hold her own against him or anyone who threatened him or the girls.

Anna Mae quietly cleaned the breakfast crumbs from the table, her mind on the conversation in the front room. She could see Josiah from where she worked, but Grady sat opposite him, hidden by the fireplace that partially divided the two rooms.

So, trouble had found its way to their little town. Not just mischievous pranks, but ugly, serious trouble that threatened their very livelihood. Someone might be robbed, or even worse, killed. It began to sink into her heart just how dangerous her husband's job could be.

It seemed Grady had turned into some kind of a bounty hunter. The older man had been trailing the outlaws for some time. He'd explained earlier that his horse had lost a shoe before he'd arrived in the Granite area and that he'd left it off to make the outlaws think he was just a drifter.

"So, you don't think the cow killing is a decoy to throw us off track?"

Josiah had explained Wade's theory earlier and Anna Mae felt pretty impressed with the young man's reasoning. At least Josiah had someone to help him figure things out. But as she listened to Grady, she realized her husband had been trained by one of the best.

Grady answered as though he'd really given the question some thought. "No, not to my way of thinking. Not a decoy, a weakness. They're never spotted in town till the day of the robbery and then they have their faces covered. They stake out the area thoroughly, get to know the comings and goings of the locals before they even strike."

Anna Mae heard the rocker creak as he set the chair in motion and then continued, "Killing cattle is a slipup, and the thing that's going to get them caught is their appetite."

Josiah nodded. "They like fresh meat." He ran a hand around the back of his neck.

"Yep." Grady answered matter-of-factly. "They're spoiled, too lazy to hunt, and have no shame at killing or stealing another man's possessions."

Josiah sat quietly for a moment. "I wonder when they will have enough money and quit robbing."

Grady barked a laugh. "Never. They will lose their lives over this."

Her husband sighed. "Why a man would sell his soul like that beats me."

Anna Mae stood looking out the kitchen window toward the barn. She'd been thinking the same thing. What would cause a man to continue a life of destruction?

"Well, I best be going. Going to get to the boardinghouse early so few people see me." Grady pushed himself up from the chair, straightened his shoulders and cleared his throat loudly. "Remember the protocol."

"Got it." Josiah followed him to the door.

"Thank you, Mrs. Miller, for the hearty breakfast." He patted his stomach. "Nothing like a good meal to start a man's day."

She stepped into the sitting room. "Please, call me Anna Mae."

He nodded, then opened the door. Anna Mae watched from the front window as the two men walked to the barn. When Josiah returned to the house she still hadn't moved.

"Brrr, it's cold out there." He held his hands out to the warmth of the fireplace. "Come away from the window, Annie. The air seeps through and you'll catch your death of cold."

She walked to the couch and settled into the fluffy pillows and quilt, her mind in turmoil as she worked through the morning's activities. "Josiah, do robbers ever straighten up? You know, get out of that lifestyle?"

"Sometimes. Depending on the circumstances that got them involved in the first place." He turned to allow the fire to warm his back.

"What do you mean?"

He shrugged out of his coat and hung it by the door. "Some men are just mean and too lazy to work. They see what another man has and they decide it should be theirs, so they take it." Josiah sat down on the rocker across from her. "Then you have the young men that fall on hard times and see no other way out. They steal to stay alive. They get sick of it, but once you sign your soul over to the first type of men, the evil ones, you never get it back. They won't let you stop."

Anna Mae felt bad for the young men. Surely some of them got away from that lifestyle. She looked up at Josiah. "But some do, right?"

He seemed to know what she wanted to hear. "Yes, on occasion one may take the higher road and straighten up his life."

She heard the skepticism in his voice. "You think it's few and far between?"

"Like I said, it does happen on occasion, but like Grady said, once they get an appetite for the lifestyle—drinking and gambling, women and traveling from town to town—it's hard to get them to turn away from it."

Josiah stood. He walked to the kitchen and put a pot on the stove. She watched as he poured cider into it. "It's sin, Anna Mae. Sin drags a man down, turns him into a person he never wanted to be. And sin doesn't stop until it has wrecked and ruined his life. There's only one thing that can rescue him and pull him up from the muck and the mire."

Anna Mae nodded. Her gaze moved to Josiah's large Bible. "The Lord."

He pulled two mugs down from the cabinet. "That's right. The saving grace of Jesus. It's a beautiful thing when that happens."

He poured them both a steaming mug of cider. Josiah returned to the sitting room and handed her one. Anna Mae wrapped her hands around the warm cup, impressed by her husband's thoughtfulness.

They sipped their drinks, each lost in thought. Anna

Mae knew that Josiah hoped to catch the outlaws before they could do more harm. She worried about their souls.

Josiah suddenly snapped his fingers. "I almost forgot. We've been invited to a taffy pull at the boarding-house Saturday evening. Sounds like there will be all kinds of activities and food."

Thankful for something else to think about, Anna Mae smiled. "Oh, good. I bet everyone's excited. When I lived in town and we planned something, the excitement was almost tangible. It lifted everyone's spirits and made life fulfilling."

"Do you miss living in town?" He set his cider on the floor and studied her intently.

"Some, but…" She knew that he watched her with curious intensity. "My life is completely fulfilled right here with my girls, my animals and my home."

"And what about your husband?" His intense blue eyes continued to study her face.

Anna Mae's heart pounded in an erratic rhythm. He seemed unsure of his place in her life. She hoped to ease his worry. "Oh, Josiah, when you explain things to me like you just did, I think I'm married to the smartest man in the world. You have such wisdom. And you keep getting me out of scrapes. You're kind and thoughtful, and I'm so thankful to be married to you. I just hope you aren't ashamed to be married to me." She set her cider on the side table and offered him a sweet smile.

Josiah reached over and took her hands in his. He rubbed the backs with his thumbs. "Don't ever let me hear you say those words again. I couldn't be more proud of you."

"But I keep messing up." When his eyebrows rose in

question, she continued. "With the turpentine, and then I chopped the table legs off and you had to saw them to make them even and smooth."

His jaw dropped and his thumbs stopped moving against her skin.

"What? You didn't think I'd notice the difference? How smooth and even the legs suddenly appeared? So I no longer had to worry about the girls getting splinters from my mess."

He burst out laughing and released her. "Now who's the wise one?"

Anna Mae missed the warmth of his hands holding hers, and picked her drink back up. "You gave me this beautiful life, Josiah, and I love it. I just wanted you to know that."

His eyes were gentle and contemplative. He'd just started to speak when a scream brought them both to their feet and racing to the girls' room.

Anna Mae didn't know whether to laugh or be serious. Ruby's head was stuck between the rungs of her crib.

Anna Mae held the bed as Josiah extricated the child, then listened as he softly scolded her, cautioning her to be more careful. Anna Mae took Rose from her crib and set her on the floor.

Ruby's lip pushed out and she glanced at her twin to see her reaction. Rose stood, hand on her hip, observing the situation. Then she walked over to her sister. She patted Ruby on the shoulder. "You o'tay, you alwite." That pronouncement did the trick, for both girls immediately began to play as if nothing had happened.

Anna Mae brought her hand up to stifle the giggles.

She looked up to find teasing laughter in Josiah's beautiful eyes.

He shook his head. "That one reminds me of someone else I know. You may not be her birth mother, but we'd never prove it to anyone else."

She smacked him playfully on the shoulder. Ruby was a bit of a daredevil. If the child could get into trouble, she did. Did Josiah really see Anna Mae that way, too? She grinned.

"At least Rose is like me. The voice of mighty wisdom." He placed his hand on his hip in mock Rose pose and repeated, "You o'tay, you alwite."

He and Anna Mae fell against each other, laughing; his arms went around her as hers closed around his waist. He looked down into her face, his eyes alight with pleasure, then fitted her head snugly under his chin. Anna Mae experienced happiness like never before.

"Annie?" His voice rumbled against her ear.

"Yes, Josiah?"

"There's one other thing we need to fix, if you're willing."

"What would that be?" Intrigued, she leaned back in his arms to see his face.

"The girls have a mother now. Don't you think it's time they called you that?"

Anna Mae pulled out of his grasp. For a brief moment she'd started to think of them as a family, but at the reminder of Mary, the idea seemed to evaporate like fog on a sunny morning. "No, they have a real mother. Her name is Mary. I know that I can't replace her in your heart, and I shouldn't try to replace her in theirs." Anna Mae returned to the cup of cider he'd poured for her, and sat down on the couch. So much for the fun, loving feelings they'd been sharing. Now she just felt deflated.

As if she'd ruined the moment for him, too, Josiah walked to the door and pulled his coat on. He turned to her and she saw in his eyes that he knew she spoke the truth. "Well, should you change your mind, you're welcome to allow them to call you Ma." The door slammed behind him.

So much for being wise. Anna Mae knew she'd handled that wrong, but she wasn't delusional enough to think he loved her and had replaced Mary in his heart with her. She should remember that next time she started feeling all mushy inside.

Telling herself to remember and being able to do so were two very different things. How much longer would she be able to protect herself from heartbreak? Josiah had said nothing about loving her and she'd do well to remember that.

Chapter Twenty-One

Saturday arrived with overcast skies, but the road was clear enough for them to drive to town and attend the taffy pull.

"I'm so glad you all could attend. You must stay with us tonight," Emily Jane said, smiling at Anna Mae with pleasure.

"Are you sure you don't mind us spending the night?" she asked, uncomfortable with the idea of staying at Emily Jane and William's overnight.

"Of course I'm sure," her friend answered. "It will be late when the fun is over and I'd hate to think of you all on the road home. Especially as cold as it is."

Beth Winters stood at the stove, making the taffy that would be pulled later. She'd already set several batches in bowls on the counter beside her. Hot water steamed under them to keep the taffy soft and manageable.

It was just the three of them standing in the kitchen. "Is it supposed to snow again?" Beth asked, measuring sugar, corn syrup, water and salt into a saucepan.

She blended it with a wooden spoon while the other two women watched.

"I hope not," Emily Jane answered, "I'm sick of snow and cold." She shivered.

Anna Mae smiled. She loved the snow, but not the cold so much. "I wouldn't mind having a white Christmas."

"That reminds me, William wanted me to ask if you and Josiah would mind coming into town Christmas Day instead of us going out there. He's concerned about the baby." Emily Jane rubbed her swollen belly.

Beth continued to stir the sugar concoction. "Men are always worried about the first baby."

"I'll have to ask Josiah, but I'm sure it won't be a problem." Anna Mae watched Beth's every movement. She loved taffy but had never gotten the knack of how to make it. If she learned today, maybe she could teach Rose and Ruby when they got older. Hers always came out crystalized. Crystalized candy wasn't bad, but it wasn't taffy.

"Ask me what?"

Anna Mae recognized her husband's voice and her heart greeted him. She turned with a smile. "If we'd come to town Christmas Day and save William and Emily Jane the hassle of coming out to our place."

"I don't see why not. Unless we get a white Christmas, and then it will depend on how much and how wet it is." He walked over and poured himself another cup of coffee. "Beth, is that first batch about ready to pull? We have some young'uns in there who are getting restless."

Beth touched the taffy she'd made. "I think it's cool enough for little hands to pull. Anna Mae, would you get the butter and start greasing palms? Emily Jane, will you make sure the kids stay on the floured sheet out there? I'd really rather not clean up a sticky floor when this party is over."

Both women nodded.

"Here, Josiah, you take the taffy and instruct the children to use only their fingertips to lift the edges of the warm, flowing candy, and then to pull it out about twelve inches from each other. As quick as possible they will need to fold the taffy and then pull it again."

Josiah took the big bowl and nodded. "How much should I give each pair of children?" he asked, looking puzzled and as if he regretted coming into the kitchen.

Anna Mae grabbed up the butter and grinned at him as she walked by. She'd expected the past few days with him to feel strained, but they hadn't. They'd both acted as if he'd never told her to ask the girls to call her Mother. It was easier to pretend it never happened and continue on with their friendship.

"Just give them a big hunk of it and let the pulling begin." Beth waved them all out the door.

"Line up, everyone. Time to grease your hands so you can pull taffy," Anna Mae said, as she hurried into the room. Several of her students were present and smiled at her in greeting.

Sometimes Anna Mae wished she were back in the classroom, but when they started pushing and arguing the way they were now, she didn't miss it a bit. "If you children don't settle down I'm not going to give you any butter, and that means no taffy pulling."

Immediately the kids formed a nice straight line. She

smiled at each of them as she scooped out a little bit of butter and told them, "Rub that all over your hands."

As soon as they were ready, Emily Jane called them over to the sheet that had been covered in white flour.

Anna Mae watched with pleasure as Josiah divided the children into teams of two and began giving them taffy to pull. Laughter immediately rang out as the kids began to tug at the sticky candy. The longer they pulled the harder it became to do so.

"Adults, time to get your hands dirty," Beth called as she came from the kitchen carrying another big bowl. "Husbands find your wives. Singles find a partner."

Levi and Millie stood with Josiah and William. Levi raised his voice for all to hear. "Better do as she says, or no candy for you to take home."

Several of the men grunted and the women giggled. It was amusing to watch those same grunting men hurry across the room to their wives. Anna Mae smiled as Josiah came to stand before her. She coated his big hands with butter, very aware of the callused skin that set her fingertips to tingling as she smeared it on.

She took a glob of butter for herself and then passed the bowl to the woman closest to her. Anna Mae tried to ignore Josiah's waiting eyes as she applied the butter to her hands as she would lotion.

Beth came by and gave them a large glob of candy. Together they followed her earlier directions, working the candy between them and laughing as they tried to keep it from oozing to the floor.

"This is really fun. I'm glad I told Levi we'd come," Josiah said, glancing at the twins, who sat on the sidelines in high chairs with other children around their age. They all had taffy and were eating it faster than it could harden. "The girls are having a grand ole time."

"Yes, and the added sugar will keep them up most of the night, too." Anna Mae felt the taffy becoming harder. She grunted as they pulled again. When they came together once more she said, "Emily Jane has invited us to spend the night." She pulled away again.

They came back together. "No can do. We have a cow to milk and she's not going to be happy to be getting milked late as it is."

Anna Mae stopped and looked at him. She'd forgotten all about Jersey. She should be grateful for an excuse not to have to sleep in the same room with Josiah, but she found herself feeling a little disappointed. The one night they had to share a room she hadn't slept a wink. Josiah had tossed and turned on the floor so much that she was sure Mr. Meeker had heard him through the wall.

"Let's see if this is ready to cut," Josiah said, pulling her and the taffy as he made his way to the table.

They found an empty platter and laid their candy down. Beth walked past and thrust a pair of scissors into Anna Mae's hand. "Get to cutting. I'll have one of the older boys come get it to wrap."

Anna Mae laughed. Beth Winters could be very bossy. She watched as the older woman walked about the room, praising the children on their wrapping and rushing the adults to hurry and get the candy cut.

Josiah's warm breath tickled her ear. "You might want to get started. I believe if you don't have that cut by the time her boy comes by for it, Mrs. Miller, we'll be in big trouble and get no candy."

A giggle eased from her throat. "While I'm cutting what will you be doing?" she asked, looking up into his bright blue eyes.

"Supervising, of course." His face was only a few inches from her.

If she wanted to, Anna Mae could easily lean forward and kiss him. She ducked her head. Now where had that thought come from?

She snipped the candy into small pieces, aware that Josiah watched her every move. Why? Why was he studying her as if he'd never seen her before? Had he thought about kissing her, too?

Josiah knew he had to get away from his sweet wife. She smelled of candy and he'd felt the urge to kiss her just now. Kiss her right in front of everyone, something he was sure she wouldn't appreciate. "I'm going to go let Emily Jane and William know that we won't be able to spend the night."

As he approached his brother-in-law and wife, he heard their teasing remarks. "I can't remember the last time I had this much fun making candy." William winked at his wife, who was busy cutting their candy into bite-size pieces.

Emily Jane giggled and her cheeks flushed a pretty shade of pink. "Probably when you were a little boy."

"Probably so." He hugged her growing waist. "But I bet it wasn't nearly as much fun as this."

Josiah shook his head. Even though they'd been married several months now, they still behaved as newlyweds. For a few short moments he'd shared similar happiness with Anna Mae. Not like "in love" newly-weds, but fun just the same.

He cleared his throat. When they both looked at him expectantly, Josiah said, "Can you help me with something outside?" He motioned for William to follow him.

Emily Jane frowned. "Josiah, are you sure? It's pretty cold out there." Her brow furrowed with worry.

"This won't take long, Emily Jane."

William didn't seem to want to leave his wife any more than she wanted him to leave. "I'll be right there, Josiah."

"All right. I'm heading out for some fresh air." Josiah crossed the room and then reached for the front door handle.

"Pssst."

As natural as breathing, Josiah's hand lowered slowly to his holster. He turned to face the stairs behind him.

Grady leaned over the rails and whispered, "Come here, Josiah."

His shoulders sagged in relief and he removed his hand from his gun. Josiah took the stairs two at a time.

"Where you headed?" Grady asked in a low voice, as soon as he was close enough to talk.

"I invited William to meet me outside. I planned to tell him me and Annie can't spend the night at his place." He didn't add that the desire to kiss his wife had him hankering for much needed fresh air.

Grady frowned. "Why not?"

Not used to having to answer to another man, Josiah all but snapped, "We have animals to take care of."

It wasn't lost on Josiah that his friend had slipped into the shadows to avoid being seen below.

"Why are you living in the country, Josiah? You're not a farmer, you're a lawman. Shouldn't you be near the town you swore to protect?"

Irritation rose in him again. Josiah had no intention of discussing his situation with anyone at the moment, so he shrugged casually. "It works right now."

Grady shook his head and probably would have argued if Josiah hadn't changed the subject. "You find out anything?"

That did the trick. Grady growled. "Yes, no thanks to that bumbling deputy of yours."

Weariness settled between Josiah's shoulder blades. "What happened?"

"Had a situation back of the stable the other night about an hour after you went home. Saw two fellows ride up the back alley, so I hid in the loft. It's not good, Josiah."

Unease joined the weariness. "Did you know them?"

"One of them. It's Jose Garza."

Josiah's misgivings increased by the minute. "Jose Garza of the James gang?"

"The one and only."

"But why would a notorious gang want to mess with a little town like this? We're not even on the map. Our bank won't have enough money in it to make it worth their while." His head was beginning to pound at the seriousness of their situation.

"Not sure. They could be looking for a town to make their home. They may check out Granite and decide there's not enough law here to keep them from taking over." Grady grimaced. "Or they could be looking for towns with newspapers so the tales of their actions can be recorded."

Josiah resented the first remark, but knew it was true. "But our newspaper is just local stuff. Probably not more than fifty copies per week."

"Doesn't matter. Newspapermen, like your Mr. Lupan, tend to write about all these shenanigans. Other newspapermen will take what your Mr. Lupan wrote back to their syndicated presses and make heroes of criminals. The story could go all over the United States."

"You met Mr. Lupan, our newspaper editor?"

Grady nodded. "You might want to deputize him. He's a much better tracker than the one you've got. I've been dodging him for days. He knows I'm staying here at the boardinghouse. He plans to find out who I am and why."

Josiah couldn't help but smile at Grady's description of Mr. Lupan, who wasn't above spreading a little bit of gossip, since he'd learned it sold more papers than the news. "Speaking of plans, did you overhear the James gang plans?"

"Enough to know they're waiting on someone else to arrive on the stage. I'd have learned more but your deputy came down the alley and heard voices. He cocked his pistol, Josiah." Grady's voice reflected his scorn at the error. "Gave his position away before they ever saw him. They would have ambushed him had they not been waiting on this other feller to arrive. He'd be a dead man right now."

"I'll have a talk with him." Josiah felt momentary

panic when he thought of young Wade trying to protect the town by himself.

Steely green eyes stared into his. "He needs to be trained, Josiah, not talked to. And who's going to train him when he's out on patrol at night and you're thirty minutes away on the farm?"

He didn't need a lecture from his mentor. What he needed was to move to town. But how to approach Anna Mae about the sensitive subject? She liked living on their farm and taking care of the animals. "I'll see to it, Grady."

An hour and a half later, Josiah handed the twins down to Anna Mae. Neither awoke and he knew she would have them tucked in for the night before he ever finished with the chores.

He turned Roy and the wagon toward the barn. Once the horse was unhitched, Josiah started the dreaded process. He looked at the chickens. He didn't much care if he ever saw one again. Unless it appeared on his Sunday plate. He led Jersey out of the stall and reached for the stool.

What was the James gang doing in his town? He should have been the one to learn of them, not Grady. And then there was the training of Wade. If the James gang shot the boy, there'd be no reason to train him. Josiah leaned his head against the cow's side. He couldn't afford to let his deputy make mistakes like cocking his gun before he even knew what he'd be shooting at.

"What's on your mind, Josiah?"

Warning spasms jolted him around. Lost in thought, he hadn't heard her approach. Had she opened the barn door? He must not have closed it, which was even worse.

He was losing his touch. And any good lawman knew that was a dangerous thing.

Pretending her sudden appearance hadn't shaken him up, Josiah asked, "What do you mean, Annie? And what are you doing out here? You'll catch your death of cold."

"I came to help with the chores so you wouldn't have to be out here so long." She pulled her cloak tighter around her. "You didn't say a word all the way home."

Josiah raised his head but continued to milk the cow. "Neither did you."

"But I was reliving the excitement of the day, and I would have shared with you except that you seemed so withdrawn." She placed a palm on his arm.

He stared at her fingers while some illusive thought tugged at his memory. She jerked her hand away and clasped it against her chest. "I'm sorry. I didn't mean to be forward. And I don't deliberately try to intrude. I just wanted to help if something is troubling you."

He recovered her hand. "Oh, Annie. You could never be any of those things." Suddenly the chores didn't look so dreadful, and fresh eggs, butter and milk sure did make a man's stomach feel good. He saw the uncertainty in her eyes and felt strongly compelled to convince her of her worth. "Annie, you make things look so much better, easier. When I feel things are impossible, you challenge me to rethink. I feel like I can accomplish anything if I work hard enough."

She made a slight gesture with her right hand. "That's exactly how I feel, Josiah. I make a mess of things, but you don't treat me like I'm hopeless. You help me without making me think I'm an idiot."

He lifted an eyebrow inquiringly.

"Like with the legs on the girls' table. Or your patience teaching me to tend these animals," she reminded him.

He couldn't contain the grin that overtook his face. "Well, I need your help out here."

"Exactly, and you trust me to help." She shifted from foot to foot. "What I'm trying to say is that I love my life with you. We're connected somehow."

He finished milking the cow and moved the bucket off to the side. He stood and pulled her close for a hug. "I agree."

Carried away by emotions they both seemed to feel, he watched as she straightened the lapels of his coat. He felt the shy yet eager affection coming from her. Anna Mae looked down as if focused on the material under her fingertips.

Josiah couldn't have stopped his reaction to her if the barn had been on fire. He placed a hand on either side of her face and tilted her head. He touched her lips with his like a whisper. She closed her eyes, waiting, and he kissed her again, tender and light as a summer breeze.

She opened her eyes, then bumped awkwardly against him. He barely managed to keep them from falling. His kisses had never had that effect on Mary. Josiah searched Anna Mae's startled face.

"Jersey pushed me!" Anna Mae accused, pointing at the cow. "Can you believe that? She knocked me against you." Her eyes widened in understanding. "She's jealous."

Josiah laughed out loud. "Most likely she wants to be back in her warm stall. She figures you need to quit lollygagging and get to work."

He dodged Anna Mae's friendly slap against his arm and set about putting the cow back in her stall. Farmer Miller to the rescue. How long would he be able to keep this up?

Grady was right. Josiah did belong in town, but how would he tell Anna Mae? Could he tell her? So many unanswered questions plagued his mind as he added fresh hay to the stall. And any good sheriff knew that the sooner you solved a case the quicker your mind could rest. But if he continued to kiss his wife, his mind would continue to remain mush and the case would never get solved. He sighed, knowing he'd enjoyed the kiss more than he should have. Now what? Had their relationship just changed again? And if so, what did the future hold for them?

Chapter Twenty-Two

A few days later, Anna Mae gathered all her scraps of fabric and carried them in a basket to the sitting room. "Rose, Ruby, come help me please."

The twins entered the room with big grins. They spotted the basket and hurried over. Each grabbed the colorful strips and started pulling them out.

"Pitty," Ruby said, grinning as if she'd just had another piece of taffy.

Rose nodded. "Pitty."

Anna Mae touched their soft curls. "Would you like to help me make pretty decorations for Christmas?"

They looked at each other and then nodded.

"Good." Anna Mae pulled her scissors out and began cutting the strips into smaller pieces. "We're going to make Christmas garlands so that we can decorate our house. Won't that be fun?"

They nodded and giggled. For the next hour Anna Mae worked with the girls tying the fabric strips into loops and then tying the loops together.

The little girls played with the cloth and took turns

helping her string their homemade garland about the house. The brightly colored fabric brightened the room.

"Pitty," Rose said, pointing at the garland Anna Mae had hung about the bedroom door.

Ruby clapped her hands together and grabbed the next string. She hurried to the playroom, tripping on her little legs and hurriedly picking herself up. Rose, hot on her trail, picked up the tail of the string and followed her sister, laughing and chattering a mile a minute. Some of the words were intelligible, most were not. They both were doing much better in that department.

Anna Mae adored the little girls. They were such sweet babies and they loved to laugh. She grinned and followed them inside. They stood in the middle of the room, looking about.

"How about we hang that one above the window?" she asked, walking toward it and pulling a chair over as she went.

Again the girls nodded in agreement, so Anna Mae climbed on the chair, then reached down for the string of bright fabric.

As she hung it, she recognized the blue from her dress and the quilt she'd made for Josiah's bed, the pink and yellow from the little girls' dresses, and green, purple and red that she'd used to make doll clothes. The scraps represented their first Christmas together and the many hours she'd worked to create gifts for her family.

Once garlands hung from every available space about the house, Anna Mae turned to the twins. Their eyes darted back and forth as they admired the decorations they'd put up. "Would you like a warm glass of milk?" she asked them, heading to the kitchen.

The sound of little feet following caused her smile to broaden in approval. It seemed these days she smiled a lot.

It took only a few minutes to get the girls in their chairs and the milk on the stove warming.

Josiah came through the door, stomping his feet. "Boy, it's cold out there." He took his coat off and hung it up, then walked to where the girls sat. It was sweet the way he kissed the tops of their heads.

He looked at Anna Mae, eyebrows raised inquiringly. "So what have you ladies been up to?"

"Pitty!" Rose squealed, pointing at the garland.

Anna Mae laughed, amazed he hadn't noticed the many colorful swags that decorated his home. "Getting ready for Christmas."

Josiah looked about at the various strings of looped fabric. "It is very pretty."

"Yep, pitty," Ruby agreed, with a nod at her father.

"We're having warm milk and cookies. Would you like some?" Anna Mae asked, stirring the milk to make sure it didn't scorch.

He pulled out a chair and sat down. "I was hoping for something a little heavier. I've not had lunch yet."

She poured the warm milk and grabbed four cookies from the cookie jar. "How about a couple of ham biscuits and a pickle?" She handed the twins their cookies, then set their glasses of milk just a little out of their reach.

"Sounds wonderful. Do you have any cold milk left?" He snatched up one of Ruby's cookies from her chubby hand and pretended to take a bite from it.

When the little girl sent her a wide-eyed look, Anna

Mae hid her smile. "I do." She turned around so that Ruby wouldn't see her pleasure at Josiah's teasing.

While she made Josiah's lunch, Anna Mae listened to him talk to his daughters, his voice filled with love and warmth. What would it be like if he spoke to her like that? Anna Mae pushed the thought away and finished fixing his food. She hadn't expected him to come home for lunch. She'd hoped to be able to go to town and finish her Christmas shopping.

She set Josiah's plate in front of him. "You're home early."

He looked up at her. "I decided to come home this afternoon and after dinner return to town. Would you like to go Christmas tree hunting after I finish this sandwich?"

Anna Mae couldn't contain her excitement. "You mean it?"

"Why not? It will be a fun outing for the girls." He bowed his head and quietly thanked the Lord for his meal.

When he finished Anna Mae pulled four more cookies from the cookie jar and poured herself a glass of milk. She placed two of the cookies on his plate before sitting down. "They will need to go down for a nap before it gets too late."

"No nap!" the girls said in unison.

Josiah laughed. "See? They don't want to nap." He tipped his glass up and drank about half his milk in one big gulp.

Anna Mae shook her head. "You are not helping me keep their schedule, but today, it's all right. I'm looking forward to getting a tree." Joy bubbled within her.

Her husband had been paying attention. He'd noticed how much the tree would mean to her. Did she dare hope that he was finding something to love about her?

Josiah pulled a sled behind him as he and Anna Mae made their way into the woods. Rose and Ruby sat on the toboggan, giggling. The breeze was cold as it blew against his cheeks.

"Do you think they will be all right? It's a little chilly out here," Anna Mae said, looking over her shoulder at the twins.

"They will be fine. It won't take long to chop down a tree and get them back to the house. We might even have time to get them down for—" he lowered his voice "—that nap you mentioned earlier."

Her pink cheeks and the soft tendrils about her face gave her a youthful look. Anna Mae's eyes sparkled as she turned to face him. "That would be good."

He pushed on through the light snow. She didn't know it but he'd already found the perfect tree. He just hoped Anna Mae thought it was perfect, too.

"Did you have a Christmas tree when you were a kid?" she asked, looking at all the evergreens around them.

Josiah sighed. "No, Grady didn't think Christmas trees were safe. He didn't allow one."

"That's too bad. What about before you went to work for him?" she pressed, again checking on the girls.

"My dad enjoyed his bottle more than he did Christmas trees." How could Josiah change the subject? He searched his mind and then it dawned on him to just ask her the same question. "Did you?"

Her gaze swept back to him. Big brown eyes studied his face knowingly. "Yes, my parents threw a big party every year, so we had a large tree in the entry."

Josiah arrived at the tree he'd picked out. "What do you think of this one?"

Anna Mae walked around it and studied its branches. "It's not very tall." She touched the vibrant green pine needles.

"I don't know that we want it too tall." Josiah ran his hand around the back of his neck.

She turned with a smile. "You're right. I think it will work fine." She glanced at the girls again. "Uh-oh."

Josiah spun around to see what she was looking at. His sweet daughters were curled up like little foxes on the sled. "Well, you got your wish. They are napping now." He leaned down and tucked the blanket tighter around them.

Anna Mae sighed. "Yes, but I kind of hoped they'd wait until we got home."

He gently turned the sled back toward home. "I'll take you home and then come back for the tree."

Her shoulders slumped as she walked along beside him. His girls often interfered in things Anna Mae wanted to do. Feeling bad, Josiah draped his arm around her. "I know you wanted to be there when I cut it. I'm sorry."

"It's all right. I'll get them down for their nap, then start looking for things to decorate the tree with."

The brave smile she gave him melted a small part of his heart. Josiah leaned over and kissed her temple. "You are some woman, Annie Miller." He'd been looking for a reason to get this close to her since he'd seen her stirring milk at his cookstove. He only wished she'd offered her lips for his kiss and not just her temple. He could get used to kissing Anna Mae and deep down he knew his feelings for her were growing stronger every day.

Chapter Twenty-Three

The next morning, Anna Mae walked up Main Street. Many of the houses sported Christmas decorations and store windows displayed the best of their goods. In some shop entryways Anna Mae spotted mistletoe.

She grinned and blushed at the same time, remembering the kiss Josiah had given her in the barn. How many times would she relive that sweet kiss? Yesterday, she'd enjoyed his lips on her temple. Heat fill her face as she remembered, wishing it were another true kiss on the lips. She pushed the thoughts away and focused on the reason she was in town.

She'd dropped the twins off at Emily Jane's, with plans for a little time to herself. It felt odd not to have the girls with her. Over the past two months she'd grown used to having them around at all times.

What would Josiah think of her sneaking off with the girls so that she could buy a pair of boots for him? His looked worn and needed to be replaced. She knew he didn't like not knowing where she was, but for Christmas Anna Mae wanted to buy him new boots, and the twins ribbons and penny candy.

Anna Mae knew Josiah wasn't in Granite. Wade had come by the house earlier in the morning to tell her that Grady wanted Josiah to meet him on the edge of town. Later the deputy had returned, saying Josiah would be gone for the rest of the day.

Anna Mae had seen it as the perfect time to come into town, do her last-minute Christmas shopping and then get back home. He would never even know she'd left the farm.

She made her way to the bank. It wouldn't do to buy Josiah's Christmas boots with his money. Anna Mae had saved her teaching salary, and along with the money she'd earned selling eggs and butter to Carolyn at the general store, she would have just enough to take care of Christmas.

Pulling the bank door open, she stepped inside. Its interior seemed dim after the brilliant sunshine she'd just left. Anna Mae waited until her eyes adjusted and then made her way toward the tellers.

An older woman, a younger one and two children stood in line ahead of her. The children were too young to attend school, so she didn't know them. Even so, Anna Mae smiled at them.

As she waited she glanced about the bank's interior. There were two offices, but both were empty. Heavy dark furniture filled the rooms. A chair was positioned beside the main entry to the bank. She wondered if a guard sat there.

Turning her attention back to the line, she noted that the teller was a middle-aged man who had a bald spot on top of his head. He seemed focused on the papers that the older woman had handed him.

Anna Mae glanced over as the bank clock chimed the hour. It was probably the largest clock she'd ever seen, shaped like the sun, with big numbers on its face. She realized that she'd already been gone from the girls for over thirty minutes. She'd promised Emily Jane that she would be back in an hour.

Wishing she hadn't dawdled, Anna Mae turned back to see what was taking so long. The woman was arguing with the teller in a low voice and pointing at the papers in question.

The younger woman held on to her children's hands and tapped her toe. Anna Mae thought about telling her that as long as they were waiting in line, at least nothing was expected of them. But she, too, felt her impatience growing as the big clock ticked loudly.

Sunlight briefly filtered into the room as two sets of heavy boots clomped into the bank. Anna Mae turned to look at their owners, and her blood froze. The lower halves of the men's faces were covered by bandannas and they both held guns pointed at the bank occupants. One of them stopped and locked the door, while the other continued walking toward them as if he owned the place.

The other two women and the bank teller paid the men no mind. Anna Mae wasn't sure what to do. If she alerted them to the danger they were in, would they overreact and get shot?

Two seconds later the decision was taken out of her hands. "Put your hands in the air, keep your mouths shut and we won't have any trouble," the bank robber closest to them growled.

The two women immediately did exactly what he'd just told them not to do. The younger one started to cry out, and the older one argued, "Why, you good-for-nothing scoundrels, how dare you threaten us?"

Anna Mae watched in horror as the man shoved the old woman to the floor, effectively silencing her. He grabbed one of the kids and raised his eyebrows menacingly at the mother. "Your choice, woman. Either close your mouth or lose your kid." The child, a little boy of about five, reached for his mom, his lips trembling and his face crumpling.

The woman shook her head quickly. Not another sound issued from her and she caught her son tightly against her as he was shoved into her arms.

Fear knotted inside Anna Mae's chest. Why had Josiah chosen today of all days to go out of town? Wade had pulled the second night patrol, so he most likely had returned to the jailhouse to sleep for a few hours.

As Anna Mae studied the scene in front of her, reality sank in. She might never see Josiah or the girls again. Now she wished she'd told them that she loved them. Would she ever get the chance?

Would Josiah ever know that his wife cared for him as a wife should?

Josiah's stomach tightened once again, a sure sign something wasn't quite right. One of the first things Grady had taught him was to follow his instincts, and his instincts today shouted that he was headed in the wrong direction. From the moment they'd left Granite for Hancock, that little warning voice had whispered in his head.

Hancock was a small town with a bank about the size of Granite's. Grady had said he'd overheard a couple men saying that the Hancock bank was in for a surprise. Feeling sure it was going to be the location of the next bank robbery, Grady had asked Josiah to help him capture the James gang.

Josiah looked across at his mentor. "How many men do you suppose are in the gang?"

The older man pulled his horse to a walk. "Rumor has it that they are up to six strong, but I'm not real sure on the numbers. I've only seen the two scouts hanging out in Granite. Why do you ask?"

"The night before Mary was killed, I had been stalking a couple of men who I suspected were bank robbers. While they sat around their campfire, I hid in the bushes. They plotted their next robbery, and because I had to catch them in the act, I listened. Sure 'nuff, the next morning I hightailed it to the bank I thought they'd be at, only they never showed up. Instead, they robbed the town I was sworn to protect, and killed my wife." He paused.

"Son, that wasn't your fault," Grady said, before setting his horse into an easy gallop.

Josiah caught up to him. "In a way it was. I learned later that they had planted a false trail for me to follow." The knot in his stomach tightened. "They knew, Grady. They knew that I was listening." He pulled on Roy's reins. "They caught on to the fact that I was trailing them and they set me up."

Grady slowed in turn. "What are you trying to say, son? That you want to turn back?"

"I'm trying to tell you that this situation feels the same, Grady. What if they split up and are hitting two banks on the same day?" Josiah rubbed the hairs that stood up on the back of his neck. "They could have caught on that you were on their trail and deliberately set you up, just like they did me."

Grady's hand rested on his gun. "It's possible, I suppose."

The two lawmen studied each other, both knowing that if they split up they could possibly be facing several bank robbers alone.

Josiah had friends and family in Granite. He couldn't leave them vulnerable to a gang of thieves. Wade wasn't experienced enough to know what to do should the men come out with guns blazing. Plus if Josiah knew his deputy, Wade was probably asleep on one of the jail bunks. "You taught me to trust my gut. My gut says to go back."

The old man nodded. "Go on," Grady said. "Take care of your town. I'd do the same thing, if I was you."

Josiah sighed. "What if I'm wrong? You'll be facing the gang by yourself."

"Naw, I won't. I'll scout out the situation. If there are too many of them for me to handle, I'll wait and capture them another day." Grady edged his horse up close to Josiah's and clasped him on the shoulder. "And if I have to track them down again, you can be sure you're going with me."

That was all he needed to hear. Josiah nodded once and then spun Roy around. The wind tore at his hat as they raced back to town. The closer he got the more apprehensive he felt. *Thank you, God, that Annie and the girls are home safe.*

His horse's sides heaved and white foam sprayed against his sleek coat as they finally arrived in town. When Josiah reached the bank, Levi was pulling at the door, but it didn't open. Josiah looked at the sun. By now, the bank should be open for business. As casually as he could manage, he slid off Roy's back and called Levi's name. He looped Roy's reins over the hitching post and patted his nose.

His friend strolled toward him. "What's up with the bank being closed, Josiah? It's not a holiday." Levi didn't try to hide his irritation.

When he got close enough to hear him, Josiah answered in a soft voice, priding himself on sounding calm. "Levi, I figure the bank is being robbed. Go home and keep your wife and family safe. Let me handle this."

To his credit, Levi never reacted, just turned and walked down the street. Josiah crept around to the back of the bank, cocked his gun and eased open the door. Mr. Anderson should know better than to keep this door unlocked. However, up until today, the town had never had reason for caution.

Silent as a church mouse, Josiah passed the safe and stepped into the main part of the bank. Bitter, cold despair twisted inside him. Just as he'd figured, the place was being robbed.

He took in the situation swiftly. There were only two outlaws visible, one standing by the door with his gun aimed at the customers, and one holding his weapon on the teller, who trembled so badly he had trouble putting the money into a bag.

Then Josiah's gaze moved to the customers. His heart stopped. Anna Mae stood between the robber and the small group of distraught women and children.

Just as Josiah stepped out to confront the robbers, the sound of keys jingling in the lock of the front door drew everyone's attention. Mr. Anderson and Levi burst through the door. The bank president shot the man closest to him.

The young woman screamed. Anna Mae and the other woman dropped to the floor. His Annie grabbed the child closest to her and pulled her down, too. When the young woman saw them on the floor, she dropped, too.

The other robber turned to run out the back door, and saw Josiah. Shock held the man immobile for a few seconds, then the assailant aimed and fired. Pain ripped through Josiah's shoulder as the outlaw's bullet found its mark.

Josiah fired off a shot as he went down. Two things registered at once: the outlaw falling forward into the hardwood floor, and the look of horror that crossed Anna Mae's face when she saw the blood spreading across Josiah's chest.

Searing pain took his breath away as his legs gave out under him. With extreme effort, he fought off the beckoning darkness. Everything seemed to move in slow motion, especially Anna Mae rising to her feet and struggling to get to him.

Why was she here? Why did she have to see him get shot? She should have been home taking care of the kids. She could have been killed, like Mary. Anger that his job had once more put someone he loved in danger, filled him.

Chapter Twenty-Four

Anna Mae watched the events unfold before her like a bad dream. A raw groan of despair erupted from her throat as she saw Josiah stagger backward, then slump to the floor. She pushed herself up, untangled her skirt and ran to him. Anna Mae collapsed beside him, reaching to touch his chest.

For a brief moment she clung to him, but within seconds Josiah shoved her behind him. "Stay down," he growled. His gun arm raised and he kept it on the robber who lay a few feet away from them.

Why? Both robbers had been shot. Anna Mae didn't care about them or herself. All she wanted was to make sure that Josiah wasn't going to die from his wound. "You're hurt," she protested.

"I am very aware of that, Anna Mae."

Anna Mae. He'd called her by her given name, not Annie. Anger poured from him like hot butter. She felt it scorch her heart, and the withering look stopped her from attempting to touch him again.

Levi pushed the robber over and shook his head. "This one is dead," he said.

"This one's not," the bank president called from across the room. "But he's not going anywhere." He pointed his gun at the man's head and growled, "Get up."

Moisture began to flow down Anna Mae's face. She swiped at it with her hands. One man was dead, two were injured and Josiah was angry with her. Disconcerted, she crossed her arms and looked away.

Josiah lowered his head and looked down at his shoulder, where blood seeped into his shirt. "Levi, would you escort these people out of here and help Mr. Anderson get that man over to the jail?" He waved his hand toward the injured robber.

"What about you?" Levi asked, coming to stand beside him. "You've been shot."

A harsh laugh echoed in Anna Mae's ears and then Josiah stopped laughing and looked up at Levi. "I'm very aware I've been shot, Levi. My wife has already pointed that out to me."

"Come along, folks." Anna Mae watched as the women and children practically ran from the bank at Mr. Anderson's command.

"Anderson, do you need help getting that man to jail?" Levi asked, holding Josiah's gaze.

"Nope, Mr. Sheridan can help me." He motioned for the bank teller to join him. Together they lifted the injured man and then pushed him out the door.

When he was outside, Anna Mae heard the bank president say, "There's nothing to see here, folks. The sheriff has stopped an attempted bank robbery. Go on home. Mr. Lupan, if you will come with me, I'll give you the whole story for your paper."

Her husband's voice pulled her attention back inside. "Anna Mae, where are the girls?" Josiah still didn't look at her.

"With Emily Jane."

Speaking between gritted teeth, he commanded, "Get them and go home."

"You need to go to the doctor," she protested, wanting to pull him into her arms and give him comfort from the pain.

"Do as I say!" he growled.

Levi knelt down to look into her tearstained face. "I'll make sure he goes, Anna Mae. Please, do as he says."

She jerked awkwardly to her feet, then spoke in a suffocated whisper. "But how will I know you are all right?"

His voice softened. "Annie, it's only a shoulder wound. I'm fine. Please, get out of town. I don't know where the rest of the James gang is and I want you and the girls home safe." Pain-filled blue eyes slowly rose and met hers. "Please."

Anna Mae nodded. She stumbled and a desperate sob escaped before she managed to walk away with stiff dignity. She paused just inside the door and looked back. Josiah stared after her, an unusual play of emotions on his face.

Thankfully, everyone had followed Mr. Anderson's orders and left. She turned in the direction of the general store and ducked around the building. Holding her breath, Anna Mae waited for her husband and Levi to come out of the bank. She wanted to make sure Josiah could walk on his own.

Both men exited the bank, and though Josiah bent forward slightly, he walked without assistance. His face appeared pale in the bright sunlight. He pulled his hat down low and turned in the opposite direction from Anna Mae, straight toward the doctor's office. When they were out of sight, she returned to the boardwalk and headed to the general store.

She'd come to get the girls hair ribbons and penny candy for Christmas, and that's what she planned to do. The boots would have to wait for another time. Anna Mae still refused to buy Josiah's Christmas gift with his own money.

The pleasure of the morning had been poisoned by ugly events. She ached with an inner pain.

As soon as she walked inside, Carolyn exclaimed, "Please tell me you weren't in the bank."

Anna Mae couldn't speak for the lump in her throat, so she nodded.

"Is everyone all right?"

A small crowd of men stood at the back of the store. They inched forward, waiting for her answer. "One of the bank robbers was killed and the other was injured. Mr. Lupan is with Mr. Anderson, who's giving him a full report. You'll all get to read it in this week's paper, I'm sure."

She didn't want to talk about the attempted robbery. Anna Mae hurried to the ribbons, chose two spools that matched Rose's and Ruby's dresses, and carried it to the counter.

"Praise the Lord," Carolyn said, taking the ribbon.

"I'd like half a yard of both of those." Anna Mae tried to smile, but knew her lips wobbled too much for a genuine one.

Carolyn nodded. "Are you all right?" she asked as she cut the ribbon.

"Yes, just a little shaken up. Can I also get three peppermint sticks, a small bag of lemon drops, three apples, three oranges and three of those sweet potatoes?" She'd make a sweet potato pie for Christmas. The potatoes were huge and knobbed, and might even be enough for two pies. Anna Mae kept her mind on mundane things in an effort not to break down.

She paid for her purchases, left the store and ran to the side of the building. Her stomach roiled and she lost her breakfast. With one arm clasping the bag and the other hand propped securely against the wall she stumbled along till she found the steps at the back of the store and sank down wearily.

Anna Mae rocked back and forth, weeping hot cleansing tears until she captured her composure. She saw with abrupt clarity that she had fallen in love with Josiah Miller. She thought she should feel sorry about that, but instead it felt right.

A sense of strength came to her and serene peace wove its way into her heart. Her husband lived. God had protected him. She was grateful.

She gathered her purchases and walked calmly to Emily Jane's house. Her friend pulled her quickly through the door, exclaiming with fear, "You're hurt."

Anna Mae looked at the front of her dress and saw spots of Josiah's blood where she'd held him close for those few seconds before he'd shoved her behind him.

She wrung her hands. "I'm not hurt. That's Josiah's blood." Why hadn't Carolyn mentioned the blood? Maybe she hadn't noticed.

Emily Jane's hands went to her cheeks. "Oh, no."

Anna Mae held up her trembling palm. "He's alive. He was shot in the shoulder by a bank robber. He will be fine." *Lord, please let him be fine.*

She managed to give Emily Jane the shortened version of the robbery. Remembering her promise to leave town, Anna Mae announced, "We have to go." She started gathering the girls' coats, blankets and toys. "Thank you, Emily Jane, for watching them this morning. I was able to get their Christmas gifts bought and a few groceries for special holiday dishes."

They said their goodbyes and she headed out of town.

"Mrs. Miller!"

Anna Mae pulled the wagon to a stop and looked over her shoulder. Amos, the delivery boy for Carolyn, came running up to the wagon.

Breathlessly, he panted, "Mrs. Moore asked me to give this to you." He handed her a letter.

"Oh, thank you, Amos."

"You're welcome." He turned and ran back the way he'd come.

Anna Mae turned the envelope over and immediately recognized her mother's penmanship. She tucked the letter into her bag and continued on home.

When she pulled into the yard a cry of relief broke from her lips. She'd never before been so glad to see the place. Rose and Ruby clapped their little hands and laughed. They, too, seemed to be glad to be home.

Once the girls were down for their afternoon nap,

Anna Mae pulled the letter out of her bag and opened it. For weeks she'd wondered what her mother thought about her marriage, and now she'd find out. With trembling fingers, she pulled the letter out and began to read.

My dear, sweet Anna Mae,
I know you say you recently got married, and I respect that. Your father and I have to wonder why you married so quickly. We know how devastated you were when Mark left and then when that dreadful Mr. Westland chose another over you. We hope you didn't get married for the mere sake of being married. But I fear the worse.

I spoke with my dear friend Grace Hardy, and she tells me that a teaching position has come up at the school and she'd love to have you back. You were one of her best teachers, after all. I told her I'd let you know as soon as possible. She would like for you to be here to start after the Christmas break.

Honey, I know you are married, but are you happy? If not, this is the perfect opportunity for you to come home and start anew. No one has to know you were married.

Please write me back as soon as possible so that I can give Grace your answer.
We love you,
Mother and Father

So that was it. After months of humiliation, now the school board wanted her to return to her old job as if nothing had happened. As if they hadn't rejected her when she'd asked for her job back after Mark had left her standing at the altar. She laid the letter down and began making a fresh pot of coffee.

Anna Mae knew she'd never be able to leave Josiah and the girls. She no longer thought about Mark and even wondered if she'd ever really loved him. Her feelings for Josiah were so much stronger than they'd ever been for her old fiancé. Anna Mae closed her eyes and tried to pull up Mark's handsome image. For a moment she felt confused. She remembered him, but his face no longer appealed to her.

Josiah's laughing blue eyes and handsome features eased forward in her mind's eye. She loved him. She'd never loved like this before. And if he didn't ever return those feelings, at least she knew what it meant to be head over heels. She exhaled a long sigh of contentment.

In comparison, Josiah was the better man. He treated her like an equal, not a thing that belonged to him. Her opinions mattered to Josiah; Mark had never consulted her on anything. Josiah never talked of money and Mark lived for the almighty dollar. The more she compared the two men, the more Anna Mae realized that she'd never loved Mark, and it really hadn't been her heart that had been broken, but her pride.

Josiah had given her back her self-esteem without either of them realizing it. He might never love her as he had Mary, but Anna Mae knew that she loved him. Her husband was a good man and he'd made her feel worthy and confident.

Although, at the bank he'd been angry. Angrier than she'd ever seen a man. Was that anger at her? The robbers? Maybe after the robbery he'd want her to leave.

A knock sounded on the door, pulling Anna Mae from her thoughts. Her heart soaring with her new-found knowledge, she swung the door wide, then fought to keep the disappointment from showing on her face.

For the second time in less than a month, Grady filled the entryway. "Woman, have you lost your mind? What if I'd been one of the James gang?" He growled down at her like a concerned father.

Anna Mae gasped. He was right. She should have realized that the gang might come after Josiah's family. But then again, Josiah wouldn't have sent her and the girls to the farm if he hadn't thought it was safe.

"Are you going to let me in or continue staring at me as if I've grown horns on my head?" The lawman placed both large arms on the door frame.

A feminine voice sounded and two small hands pushed him from behind. "John Grady Meeker, get out of the way. Can't you tell she's in shock?"

"Susanna?"

"Yep, it's me." She poked her head under Grady's arm and smiled. "Do me a favor and invite this mountain of a man in so I can give you a hug."

Anna Mae opened the door wider. "Of course, come in. Both of you."

Grady cleared the doorway and Susanna shot around him. She grabbed Anna Mae in a tight hug. The sweet scent of roses filled her nostrils.

"When I heard from Carolyn what had happened and that you had blood on your dress, I just had to come. You poor dear. Are you hurt anywhere?" Susanna pulled back and searched Anna Mae for injuries.

"No, I'm fine. The blood Carolyn saw is Josiah's, but he's all right, too."

"Oh, good." Susanna pulled her toward the couch. "Sit down and tell me all about it."

"Sure, you do that. I'll shut the door," Grady said in a disgruntled tone.

Anna Mae turned to him. "I'm sorry, Mr. Meeker. Did Josiah send you out? Is he all right?"

"Nobody sends me anyplace, young lady," he grumped, and then sat in Josiah's rocker. "But yes."

Susanna continued to rub Anna Mae's back as one would a small child. "You really should change dresses so we can try to get the blood out of that one."

Anna Mae inched away from her friend. "I will, Susanna, but let me find out about Josiah first." She turned her attention back to Grady. "Have you seen him? What did the doctor say?"

The big man leaned forward and rested his arms on his knees. "Yes, I saw him. Josiah's shoulder is going to hurt for a while, but the doctor says he'll heal."

She heaved a sigh of relief. It had pained Anna Mae to leave him in town, but she'd seen for herself that he could walk to the doctor. "I'm glad." If he was fine, then why had he asked Grady to come out to the farm?

Susanna sat forward. "So if Josiah didn't send you out here, what are you doing here?" she asked in her no-nonsense way.

The lawman leaned back in his chair. "Young lady, there are still four bank robbers running loose. I came to check on Anna Mae and the girls. Josiah wasn't thinking straight when he sent them out here alone."

Grady propped his fingers in a steeple and stared

at her with steely green eyes. "I'd thought to persuade Anna Mae into returning to town, where she belongs."

Anna Mae shook her head. "I'm sorry, Mr. Meeker, but I have animals out here that need tending to. I appreciate your concern, but I'll be fine."

Grady stood. "He said you'd say something like that. Mrs. Marsh, are you going to stay out here for a while?"

For the first time ever, Anna Mae saw a serious, determined side of Susanna. "I brought a bag with me. I didn't like the idea of them being alone out here, either."

The two exchanged a look of understanding and respect. Anna Mae stared at her friend.

Susanna Marsh had been one of four mail-order brides who had arrived to marry Levi Westland months ago. She was the oldest and the only one who had been married before. When they'd arrived, Susanna had seemed the most determined to marry Levi, but was also the first to give up on him. She had seemed bossy, arrogant and a little flighty.

But the woman sitting beside her now seemed more mature, in control and caring. Anna Mae realized at that moment that she had developed close friendships here in Granite, another reason not to return to her parents.

"Well, then, I'll be going. We still have four men to catch." Grady walked to the door.

Anna Mae hurried to catch up with him. "Mr. Meeker, is Josiah heading home?" She didn't like the idea of him being injured and out chasing outlaws.

"No, ma'am. He's planning on catching those other men. When I left town, he was in the process of questioning the prisoner to find the location of their hideout. If I know Josiah, he won't rest until he has all five of them behind bars." Grady looked down at her with kind eyes.

She nodded. Tears felt close to the surface once more.

He walked back to her and turned her to face him. "Josiah is a good lawman. He knows how to take care of himself."

Through a tight throat she managed to say, "And yet today he got shot."

"Yes, ma'am, he did." Grady lifted her face to look up at him. "But I believe he was distracted by a pretty lady. That won't happen again." Grady winked at her and then turned to leave.

As soon as the door closed, Susanna said, "You know, I'd like for a man to find me distracting." She sighed dramatically and patted her lips with her pointer finger. "I think I'm going to do some advertising of my own."

Anna Mae turned to face her. "What?"

A comical expression crossed Susanna's face. "Wouldn't it be fun to place an ad in Mr. Lupan's paper? Something like 'Husband wanted: See Mrs. Marsh for details.'"

Anna Mae giggled. Now there was the friend she recognized. She felt grateful for the company, but she knew she wouldn't relax until her husband was home safe.

Josiah slid from his horse but hung on to the saddle horn while he gained his balance. His body felt too weary to stand, let alone walk the distance from the barn to the house. His shoulder felt as if it were on fire. It had been two days since he'd been home and the relief he felt walking up to the porch knew no bounds. How he had missed Anna Mae and the girls, but thanks to the help of Grady and Wade, all the remaining James gang members were in the paddy wagon headed to Austin.

Grady would travel with the prisoners there and then return to Denver. Saying goodbye had been hard, but he knew his old friend and mentor needed to get home to his own community. Before he'd left, Grady had pressed him once more to move his family to town.

Josiah twisted the door handle and pushed lightly. To his utter surprise the door swung open. He quietly closed it behind him. The fact that Anna Mae hadn't dropped the bar into place across it proved Grady was correct. Josiah shook his head in disbelief. It was way past the midnight hour and she'd left the door open. What was wrong with her? Anyone could have come in.

The click of a hammer being cocked froze him in his tracks. He raised his hands out to the side and slowly turned to face his attacker. The glint of metal eased from the shadows. The scent of roses wafted toward him, and had he not been about to crumble to the floor he would have laughed.

"Either shoot me or lower the gun, Mrs. Marsh."

"Sheriff?" Her voice sounded sleepy.

"Yes, it's me." He moved into the light from the fireplace so that she could see him better.

Susanna eased the hammer off, lowered the gun and joined him in the firelight. "I'm glad you're home." She yawned.

"Where is Annie?" He looked about the room for his wife.

"Sleeping." Susanna sat on the couch and yawned again. "Midnight to six is my night-watch time. Hers is bedtime to midnight. It works better that way, since she has to get up with the girls in the mornings."

"Whose idea was this?" he asked, as he sank into his rocker. What a blessed relief to be off his feet.

"Anna Mae's. She didn't want to lock you out and she didn't want to invite outlaws in." Susanna pushed herself up from the couch. "Since you're home, I'm going to bed." Just before she walked away, she whispered, "Did you catch them all?"

He grinned. "Yes, they are on their way to Austin."

"Good, a body can rest now. Night, Josiah." Susanna walked to the girls' playroom.

Josiah leaned back and closed his eyes. So his Annie hadn't been foolish. She'd thought of a way to keep them safe and also make sure that he felt welcomed home. Which surprised him, considering the treatment she'd received at his hand the day of the robbery. He'd been downright mean to her. He figured he had a lot of explaining to do.

One thing he was certain of—he'd died a slow death when he saw Annie with her arms spread wide, trying to protect the other bank customers. He'd felt gutted. Weak. He began to shake as his mind spiraled to what could have happened. Could have happened, but didn't. His mouth suddenly felt dry.

Josiah walked to the kitchen for a sip of water. He was bone tired. Drinking from the dipper, he sat down at the table, happy to be home.

His gaze fell upon a piece of paper. It was open for anyone to read, so he did. His heart clinched in his chest as he read Anna Mae's mother's words. Just to be certain of what he'd read, Josiah went through it again.

They wanted her to come home. To a teaching job. Would she go? After the way he'd treated her he wouldn't be surprised if she did leave. Just the thought of it caused his heart to contract in a way that almost took his breath away. Josiah silently prayed that God would supply a way for him to explain to Anna Mae that he loved her. And a chance to ask her not to leave.

Chapter Twenty-Five

Anna Mae paced from window to window, waiting for Josiah to arrive home. This was the third day, and still no word came from town, saying whether he was safe or not.

Over the past few days she'd worried about Josiah, and yet she also wondered if he wanted her to leave. He'd been so angry, and now that she'd had more time to reflect on it, Anna Mae knew he was upset with her. Was he angry enough to ask her to leave once he'd captured the outlaws and secured his girls' safety?

Thoughts of the twins had her looking over her shoulder at them. She'd brought them into the kitchen so they wouldn't awaken Susanna, but it proved harder each moment to keep them occupied. They wanted to go to their playroom. She'd let them help mash the sweet potatoes she'd cooked earlier, then they'd helped pat out cookies. Now they ran their hands through the dried beans she'd poured on the table in a desperate attempt to silence their whining.

"Papa."

Anna Mae whirled around to shush or comfort the girls, whichever was needed, and her senses leaped to life. Josiah stood in the doorway to his bedroom, hair tousled. He had a big white bandage covering one shoulder and wrapped around his chest and back.

"Josiah." She could barely get his name past the lump in her throat. She moved toward him, compelled by an unseen force. He stepped forward and clasped her body tightly to his. She buried her face against the corded muscles of his neck, her heart bursting with love and anguish at the same time. She could no more stop the tears than she could stop breathing.

She felt him swallow and then he kissed her forehead.

"Shh, Annie girl. I'm fine."

She refused to budge from his arms, her face against his unhurt shoulder. He murmured words of encouragement and sweetness. "Seeing you in danger..." He paused and swallowed again. "You are so brave." His hand softly brushed the hair flowing down her back. "I'm sorry."

"I'm so thankful you're alive." Her voice was a weak, tremulous whisper. She leaned back to look up into his face.

He started to answer her then gave her a gentle squeeze, a grin the size of Texas tilting the corners of his mouth. Josiah looked down.

She had no problem identifying the source of his amusement as the twin now climbing his leg was almost to her waist, fingers digging into the fabric of her dress. She stepped back to give the child more room.

Once Anna Mae was out of his arms, Josiah lifted

Ruby on up to his shoulder as Anna Mae clasped Rose in front of her.

"I guess all her climbing has made her strong." She laughed.

He nuzzled his two-day bearded chin into Ruby's neck, making her shriek and giggle, then leaned forward to snuggle Rose, as well. Rose patted his face, then buried her head against Anna Mae as if she might cry.

"What's wrong, Rose?" Anna Mae had a notion she knew what troubled the child. "Does Papa's hurt scare you?"

Ruby gingerly touched her father's bandage, then looked him in the eyes. "You falled?"

"Something like that." Anna Mae saw the uncertainty that crept into his expression even as tears welled up in his beautiful blue eyes. That was all it took for Rose's soft heart and she launched herself from Anna Mae's arms to Josiah's, effectively pushing her twin to the side. Anna Mae's frantic grab was all that saved Ruby from landing on the floor.

It lightened the situation and Anna Mae laughed happily. Rose's little arms tightened around her papa's neck until he walked to the table and sat down. Only then did she lean back and look into his face. There was no sign of tears. Instead, Rose's beaming smile melted Anna Mae's heart, and from the look of love in Josiah's eyes, it did the same to him.

Anna Mae also saw pain in the depths of his gaze. It was time to get his arms free and to fix her husband some much needed breakfast. He was starting to look a little thin to her.

"What's going on in here? A person can't sleep with

all this caterwauling." Susanna took Ruby from Anna Mae and swung her round and round. Anna Mae wondered how long Susanna had been watching. The rims of her eyes appeared a little red and puffy, as if she'd been crying. Had her friend been listening in on her small family and been touched by the sweetness of it all?

Anna Mae took Rose from Josiah and put her in her high chair. "I'll start breakfast and we can eat in a jiffy."

"If you don't mind, Anna Mae, I'd rather get on back to town." Susanna set Ruby in her high chair as well and cleared her throat. "I've been gone three days and I figure work has piled up."

"I'll saddle your horse. Just give me a few minutes to get dressed." Josiah turned to go into his bedroom. Only then did Anna Mae notice the bare parts of his chest, back and shoulder.

"I've been saddling my horse for as long as I remember, Josiah Miller, and I'll not have you insulting me. I'll be gone before you get your boots on." She pointedly looked down at his bare feet, pulled on her scarf, then her coat, and picked up her valise.

Josiah shook his head and went to his room. His door closed softly and Anna Mae rushed to hug Susanna, who hugged her back, then released her. "You have a wonderful family now, Anna Mae. I'm happy for you." She turned and blew kisses to the twins.

Anna Mae wasn't quite ready to let her go just yet. She caught Susanna's sleeve. "Thank you for staying with us. I don't know if I would be sane now if it hadn't been for you and your assurances that Josiah was fine."

Susanna smiled. "It was my pleasure. I'll see you Sunday." The door closed behind her.

Anna Mae turned to find three sets of eyes on her. Josiah's were gentle and contemplative and held a gleam of interest she returned wholeheartedly. The other two identical sets said, "You mentioned breakfast, so what's the holdup?"

She clapped her hands together. "So, what shall we do?"

"Eat."

Ruby echoed Rose and then grinned as if she'd just been offered a prize at the fair.

Josiah and Anna Mae exchanged open looks of amusement.

She nodded and walked to the stove. "Then breakfast it is." Anna Mae noticed the letter from her mother still lying on the table where she'd left it the night before. She'd read it every night since its arrival, and she still felt her place was here with Josiah and the twins. Anna Mae stopped and picked it up, folded it and stuffed it into her apron pocket.

That letter, along with worrying about Josiah, had kept her awake most of the nights he'd been gone. At times she knew she'd be writing her mother back saying she was happily married and not coming home. Other times she thought about her unrequited love for Josiah, who could never love her like a true wife should be loved. It was all just too confusing.

"Annie, if it wouldn't be too much trouble, would you mind rustling up a batch of biscuits and gravy?" Josiah asked. He sounded sad, as if he thought she wouldn't be making them for him again soon.

She looked over at him. Had he read her letter? And if so, what was he thinking? That she was going home? Or that she should go on home? "I'll be happy to."

"Egg," Rose called. Josiah handed her a cloth ball to play with.

"All right, one egg for Rose." Anna Mae looked to Ruby. "Ruby, would you like an egg, too?"

The child shook her head and took the picture book Josiah was handing to her. "Bikit."

Josiah eased into a chair at the kitchen table. "I hope you don't mind, but I read your letter."

Anna Mae turned to the counter and began mixing dough for the biscuits. "I don't mind." She poured milk into the dry ingredients.

"Have you given any thought to what your mother told you?" He paused, waited, then continued. "About the teaching job?" His voice sounded pained.

She stirred the batter. "I've done nothing but think about it." She folded the batter over with her hands, adding a little more flour each time till the mixture was stiffer. Then she pinched off a little section, rolled it in her palms and patted it flat in the pan.

He waited until she'd finished making the biscuits and had put them in the oven before asking, "And?"

Anna Mae wiped her hands and came to sit at the table. "I guess that depends on you." She held up a palm to stop him from interrupting her. "I've prayed about that letter for three days. I don't believe God wants me to leave you and the girls. But if you truly feel you don't need me or that you want me to go—" she swallowed hard "—I'll go."

There. She heaved a sigh. *I said it*. Silent prayers

began flying heavenward. Anna Mae didn't want to leave Josiah. It would break her heart. She loved him and the girls with everything that was in her, but she also knew it wouldn't be fair to keep him in a marriage where he felt no husbandly love for his wife. *Lord, it's in Your hands now.*

Josiah felt as if a big piece of the puzzle finally fell into place. Love shone from her eyes. He'd been afraid Anna Mae would reject him after he'd treated her so poorly at the bank, but now he knew she cared for him as much as he did her. He patted his front pocket to make sure that Anna Mae's ring was still there.

He reached across the table and took her hands in his. "I never want you to leave me, Anna Mae Miller." He searched her face, her eyes, noted the trembling in her fingers, all evidence that her emotions were involved. That was a positive. But would they return to the advance-and-retreat actions of the past? Could he allow her to see what was in his heart?

Now was the time. He'd spent the past three days studying his heart and he knew Anna Mae held it as surely as he knew anything. He could hold back no longer. She had to know that he loved her.

Josiah pulled the ring box from his pocket and set it on the table. "Things have changed, Annie. Three days ago I walked into a bank and my wife stood between a gunslinger and banking customers. My heart leaped into my throat. I died a slow death. I knew right then and there that if we lived through that bank robbery, I would never let you go. It just took my heart three days to convince my head it was true." He prayed she'd see all that he felt for her in his smile and eyes.

A lone tear escaped the corner of her eye and slowly trickled down her face. Josiah used his thumb to wipe it away. He continued, "I've been an idiot, Annie. I realize that now. I thought I could only ever love one woman. I thought that to love you, I'd have to forget Mary and the relationship we had together. But that was wrong, too."

"I never want you and the girls to forget Mary," she protested.

He scooted his chair around the table so that he could wrap his good arm around her shoulder. "Thank you. I'm glad you feel that way." She rested her head on his chest and it felt good. It felt right. "I need to explain something, so hear me out."

She leaned back to look up at him. The trust he saw in the depths of her eyes gave him the assurance that Anna Mae was listening to him.

"I grew up without a mother. When I married Mary, she'd run a hand over my hair or touch my arm and I'd feel special, and it fed something that had been missing in my life. The softness of a woman's touch and the desire to matter to someone. But over time, she was as happy to see me leave on the trail as I was to get away. Neither of us minded being apart for weeks, sometimes even months."

Josiah kissed Anna Mae's cheek and smiled secretly to himself when her face reddened. "With you, my precious Annie, I hate leaving you to go to work in the mornings. I'm dying to run home for a bite of lunch, and I really resent the thirty minutes it takes to come home. That's half an hour I could be spending loving my family."

"Oh, Josiah, I feel exactly the same." She snuggled against his side. "When I was engaged to Mark, it felt scary and like I had to do what was required. But when I am with you, I feel safe and happy. It comes naturally to try and make you happy. I search for things that will please you."

Josiah laughed joyfully. "Don't look now, Annie, but I think we are in love." He reached for the ring box and opened it. "Merry Christmas, my sweet Annie."

She giggled and raised her face. "I love you, too, Josiah. I have for a long time, just was too afraid to admit it to myself and to you."

All he had to do was lower his head and he could kiss her. Josiah did just that. His lips touched hers and he knew he'd finally found where he belonged. Kissing Anna Mae was as necessary as breathing.

He would have been perfectly content to sit and kiss her all day, but a tugging on his shirt interrupted him. "Tisses!" Rose demanded. "Div me tisses, Papa."

"Me tisses, too." Ruby joined in, pushing at her sister to get closer to their papa.

Reluctantly he released his wife. "In the very near future we have to teach them to wait their turn."

Anna Mae laughed and slipped out of his arms. "I better check on the biscuits while you give these babies their kisses."

Josiah grabbed her hand and slipped his gift upon it. The ring fit perfectly on her finger. He held her hand for several more seconds. Leaned over and kissed the back of it.

"Peases, tisses," Ruby begged.

Josiah laughed. He looked up at Anna Mae. Her eyes, as she moved away, promised she wouldn't be gone long. If she didn't return soon enough to suit him, he'd just go after her. Simple.

Josiah turned to his girls and gave their little faces kisses. One of the Psalms suddenly came to mind and his heart blessed the Lord. *Delight thyself also in the Lord, and He shall give thee the desires of thine heart.*

Josiah hadn't even known what those desires were, but his Father had, and had given him his heart's desire. His soul sang as he realized that he was loved not just by his little girls, but his Annie loved him, too.

Chapter Twenty-Six

The next day was Christmas. The night before, Josiah had enjoyed watching Annie and the girls open their gifts. They'd read the Christmas story from the Bible and sang hymns.

He sighed, almost hating to share them with Emily Jane and William. He finished hitching Roy to the wagon and smiled. But it was Christmas Day and everything was perfect. He wanted to climb up on the highest peak of the barn and crow like an old rooster.

Annie and the girls stood on the front porch waiting when he led Roy toward them. Annie's eyes sparkled and her hair fell in beautiful waves about her shoulders. She wore her blue Christmas dress, with matching cloak.

Anna Mae lit up the morning. His stomach clenched tight. He wondered if she truly knew how desperately he needed her in his life. The gold ring caught the light and he smiled.

Rose and Ruby clutched their Christmas babies to their chests and wore big smiles on their little faces.

Rose wore a new green dress with a matching ribbon in her hair, while Ruby sported a new red dress and ribbon. They both looked cute and happy.

Anna Mae held a large package in her arms. "What's that?"

"Emily Jane and William's Christmas gift," she answered, handing it to him.

"Oh." He took the present. "I thought it might be for me," he teased. "After all, I do have a surprise for you."

"You do?" She stepped back up on the porch to retrieve something else.

"Yes, and I'll show you when the time is right."

Josiah put the gift in the wagon and then swung each of the girls up. When he turned back around, Anna handed him a box filled with dishes. "What's all this?" he asked, placing it carefully in the back.

"Part of our Christmas dinner." She propped both hands on her hips. "What did you think I was doing in the kitchen all morning?"

"Reading a book." He laughed at the expression on her face. "It wouldn't be the first time I've caught you in there reading when you were supposed to be cooking," he teased.

She playfully slapped him on the arm. "That may be true, but not today. Today I cooked up a feast." Anna Mae pulled herself up onto the wagon. "Scoot over, girls," she said.

"Alwite, Mama." Rose answered with a grin.

"Mama?" Her eyes grew round.

Ruby pulled at Rose's coat. "Me sits wif Mama."

The girls scrabbled back and forth till Josiah raised his voice. "If that don't beat all. No one wants to sit with me?" He faked a pout and Rose patted him on top of his head.

"Me will, me will." She immediately climbed into her place beside Ruby, both girls unaware that they had made their new mother the happiest woman in the world.

Josiah watched his Annie surreptitiously wipe at her eyes. Then she gathered both girls as close as she could and kissed them soundly.

Truth be told, he was just as surprised as Anna Mae appeared. He'd never heard them call her Mama, or anything, for that matter. Carolyn at the general store referred to Annie as their mama so maybe that's where they got it from.

"Thank you, my sweet girls. I think that's the best Christmas gift I have ever received." She couldn't seem to let them go until they squirmed, wanting out of her arms.

Josiah pulled himself up into the wagon. He looked at Anna Mae. She'd once told him that she didn't want them to call her Mother. Looking into her eyes now, he knew she was ready. More than ready.

"They called me Mama." She reached across and squeezed his arm. Her eyes flashed with happiness like silver lightning. "Did you hear that?"

"I sure did. It's about time, too." He tickled Rose until she scooted over.

He slapped the reins on Roy's back and clicked his tongue. Then Josiah's eyes drifted right back to his wife. He couldn't seem to quit looking at her. The satisfied expression on her face spoke volumes about what was in her heart. He should know; it was a reflection of his own.

He ignored the little twinge in his gut. If he'd learned anything the past few days, it was that his gut instincts about Annie were not always right. But he had also learned something important from his marriage that would work equally well on his job. Communication was the key to success.

That's why he knew he'd better start talking. They had thirty minutes tops for him to present an idea to his wife and pray she'd like it. He drew a deep breath.

"Josiah, I've been thinking hard about something these last couple of days."

He closed his mouth with a snap and all but groaned. He'd missed his chance. His gaze moved to hers and he forgot that he'd wanted to talk first. "What is it, Annie?"

She played with the folds on her cloak. "Well, the things you mentioned the other day about coming home for lunch and not caring for the long drive home." She paused, waited until he nodded and then continued. "I've been thinking how much I would love seeing you at different times during the day."

He gave her a sidelong glance of utter disbelief. Had she read his mind?

"Would you be very upset if we sold the farm and moved to town?"

Joy filled him. Josiah pulled Roy to a stop and twisted sideways on the wagon bench. "Annie, that's my surprise." At her look of confusion, he clarified, "Remember the house that wasn't destroyed by the storm? That sat about four down from yours and Emily Jane's?"

"You mean Mr. Parker's place?"

"Yes, that's the one. Mr. Parker passed away and Mrs. Parker plans to move back East to live with her children, just as soon as she sells her home. I wanted to show it to you today to see if you'd consider moving back to town and living there."

She bounced on the seat in her excitement. "Oh, Josiah, I love that place. It has a wraparound porch and three fireplaces."

He nodded. A smile the size of the Rio Grande split his face. "Right, and a huge fenced in backyard. The girls can play without us worrying about them wandering off."

"You wouldn't miss the farm?"

He studied her intently. Then decided honesty was the best policy. He squinted, but kept eye contact. "No?"

She giggled. "That's a question, Josiah, not an answer." She picked Ruby up and slid into her place on the seat, then plopped her on the other side of her. Depositing Rose right next to her sister, Anna Mae effectively closed the space between herself and Josiah. She was near enough to kiss with the barest of movement from him. From the look in her eyes, that's exactly what she planned.

"Will you miss the farm, Annie?"

"Like the plague."

He threw back his head and let out a great peal of laughter. His Annie was a minx. She brought her hand up to stifle her giggles, but he caught it and kissed her. As though his kiss drove her, she wrapped her arms around his waist. When he released her, Anna Mae laid her head against his shoulder.

The sound of whispered "tisses, tisses" echoed from

the girls' side of the wagon. But it seemed they understood that these were special kisses, and didn't demand they be included this time.

Josiah had never felt happier in all his born days. He silently began to thank the Lord above for all his blessings.

For the birth of Christ that they celebrated on this special day; for coming to earth to die for the sins of mankind, and last but most certainly not least, for sending Anna Mae into his life on a cold winter night. Josiah had never dreamed he could feel this happy and loved.

Her soft voice drifted up to him. "Merry Christmas, Josiah. I love you."

Those were words he'd never get tired of hearing. His wife loved him.

"Wuv you, Papa." Rose and Ruby chimed in.

"I wuv *you*, too." He placed his lips against Anna Mae's brow. His Annie. He hoped she felt the depth of his love. Thanks to her they were a family. A family full of love.

* * * * *

Sherri Shackelford is an award-winning author of inspirational books featuring ordinary people discovering extraordinary love. A reformed pessimist, Sherri has a passion for storytelling. Her books are fast-paced and heartfelt with a generous dose of humor. She loves to hear from readers at sherri@sherrishackelford.com. Visit her website at sherrishackelford.com.

THE RANCHER'S
CHRISTMAS PROPOSAL

Sherri Shackelford

Being confident of this very thing,
that he which hath begun a good work in you
will perform it until the day of Jesus Christ.
—*Philippians* 1:6

To my editor, Tina James,
because she can work miracles with even the most
disjointed manuscripts. Even though I'm convinced
that each book I turn in will end my career, she
always manages to dig out a little magic. And
sometimes she has to dig really, really deep.

Chapter One

Train Depot, Wichita, Kansas, 1886

For one brief, idyllic interlude, Tessa Spencer had believed her days of living on the run were behind her.

That time was over.

Perched on her steamer trunk, she considered the list of cities chalked across the destination board, searching for inspiration. Her hasty exit had left her with few options and even less money.

Earlier that morning, a member of the notorious Fulton Gang had been asking some very pointed questions about her at the Harvey House café where she worked serving tables. She'd packed her belongings and set off for the train station before the outlaw's coffee had cooled. Since her regular shift began with the dinner service, she had until this evening before Dead Eye Dan Fulton discovered she'd flown the coop.

Her stomach pitched. Time was slipping away at an alarming rate.

"Ball," a small voice said.

She searched for the source of the interruption.

"Ball."

She glanced down.

A bright-eyed toddler with shiny blond hair smiled up at her. The boy was smartly dressed in a sky blue sailor shirt tied with a red scarf, his feet encased in gleaming black patent leather shoes.

Tessa frowned. "Where are your parents, little fellow?"

"Ball."

The wooden sphere he proudly displayed was obviously well loved, the painted stripes faded.

"Yes," Tessa replied. "That's quite lovely. Except you've gone and gotten yourself lost, haven't you?"

Most likely the boy's frantic parents had already begun their search. Keeping an eye out for stray members of the Fulton Gang, she studied the passengers milling beneath the awning of the train station, seeking any sign of a disturbance.

The boy tugged on her apricot-colored skirts. "Ga."

"You'd best be careful," she admonished gently. "Being lost is a lonely business."

The toddler extended his chubby hand, offering up his most prized possession.

Tessa waved off his gift. "Oh no, I couldn't possibly take your toy. Although I thank you kindly for the offer."

The boy grinned. He clambered onto the trunk, and she instinctively aided his ascent. He perched beside her and scooted close, pressing the warmth of his small body against her side.

"Best to stay put when you're lost," she said. "Or

you only become more lost. That's what my dad always told me."

The boy tilted his head and stared at her. "Da-da."

"Yes, Emmett is my da-da." Tessa rolled her eyes. "He's a bit of a rogue. Not that he thinks of himself that way. Oh no. Emmett fancies himself a righter of wrongs, earning his living playing cards with folks who can afford to lose. Except lawmen don't appreciate that fine moral distinction, do they? And now he's run afoul of Dead Eye Dan and the Fulton Gang, which is even worse—I'll tell you that."

Heedless of her startling confession, the boy merrily kicked his heels against the trunk. She braced her hands on her knees and locked her elbows straight. Yep. She'd gone loopy, all right. At least talking to this little fellow was better than talking to herself, and she'd done plenty of that since Emmett's disastrous attempt at robbing a bank. He'd been tasked with concealing himself inside and letting the others in after closing. Except the bank vault had already been emptied when the Fultons arrived, leaving Emmett the only suspect.

"As you can imagine," she continued, "Dead Eye Dan is fit to be tied if he's come looking for me. I don't know where Emmett is hiding any more than he does, but I'm not sticking around to argue the point."

Obviously Dead Eye didn't know about her falling out with Emmett. Her throat tightened. She hadn't realized until recently how gloriously unsuited she was to a solitary life. The longing to see Emmett once more had become an almost physical ache. His love had been negligent, but as she'd learned over these past months, a slipshod sort of affection was better than nothing at all.

A nearby commotion snagged her attention. A towering gentleman in a cowboy hat and boots held a crying toddler—a girl, about the same age as the boy who'd taken up residence beside her. Though handsome, everything about the man was slightly askew. His hat sat at an angle, his collar was bent on one side, and the hem of his trouser legs was partially snagged on the stitching of his boot. He frowned and studied the area immediately surrounding his feet.

Tessa reluctantly stood. Though the boy's conversation was limited, he'd been a welcome diversion from her own difficulties. "Come along little fellow. I believe your da-da has discovered your absence. You will be my good deed for the day."

The boy eagerly took her hand. "Ga."

The distinctive word was obviously all encompassing. "*Ga* to you as well."

The gentleman's back was turned, although the woman beside him noticed the boy soon enough. From her sharp chin to the pointed tips of her black boots, she was about as welcoming as a barbed wire fence.

Her lips pinched, the woman extended her arm toward them, palm up. "The child is safe. There's no need to fuss."

Tessa narrowed her gaze and scrutinized the details. Emmett always said a good lookout needed to know who belonged where and why. Folks tended to pair up by status and temperament, and these two were opposites in both, meaning they were clearly not husband and wife.

The man whipped around. At the sight of the boy, his face flooded with relief.

He crouched and balanced on the balls of his feet. "Owen. You gave me a fright."

His obvious affection touched something kindred in Tessa, and she blinked rapidly. With her hopes of ever seeing Emmett again growing dimmer by the day, the sight was all the more poignant.

Everyone should have at least one person in their life who minded when they were lost.

The woman slanted a glance down the blunt edge of her nose. "Don't reward the boy. He'll only run off again."

Her tone pricked Tessa like a nettle. Memories from the year following her mother's death came rushing back. Only eight at the time, she'd been sent to live with distant relatives who begrudged having another child underfoot. Unaware of their simmering resentment, Emmett had arrived for a visit some months later. He'd discovered her huddled on the front porch, her arms covered in bruises.

Lawless or not, life with Emmett had at least been far more peaceful and far less painful.

"See, Alyce," the gentleman assured the toddler in his arms. "I told you we'd find Owen."

The two siblings greeted one another in a flurry of incomprehensible gibberish. They were a striking pair with their large, cobalt blue eyes and matching blond hair. Twins by the looks of them. The resemblance was even more pronounced by their clothing. Alyce wore a starched blue empire-waist gown cut from the same sky blue fabric as her brother's sailor shirt.

The children must have inherited their mother's looks, because the gentleman's hair was a deep, rich brown, and his eyes were the translucent green of a tender new leaf.

"Ball," Owen offered by way of explanation.

The gentleman flashed a boyish half grin, sending a little flutter through Tessa's stomach.

"The name is McCoy," the man said. "Shane McCoy. Thank you for returning Owen. He's quite the escape artist."

"Tessa Spencer," she replied, extending her hand.

The quick clasp of his fingers sent a stirring of gooseflesh up her arm.

He angled his body toward his companion. "This is the children's aunt, Mrs. Lund."

"Pleasure," Tessa replied, her tone clipped. The woman had her on edge.

As though addressing someone beneath her notice, Mrs. Lund gave only a slight incline of her head. "God rest Abby's soul. She always did have a knack for leaving her troubles on someone else's doorstep."

Tessa absently rubbed her arms. The poor man was a widower. No wonder he was overwhelmed. Especially considering his sister-in-law hadn't offered any additional help. Without a word of explanation, Mrs. Lund had set off in the direction of the ticket office.

"You must excuse her," Mr. McCoy said. "She's still in mourning."

Tessa smothered a snort. *Not hardly.* She'd seen people express more grief over the loss of a wooden nickel.

Unlike his acerbic sister-in-law, the bleak look on the widower's face mirrored her own despair. As much as it shamed her to admit it, she'd gladly assist Emmett with one of his swindles if only to see him once more.

She'd taken for granted how much her world had orbited around caring for him. Oh, he was a capable grown man, certainly, but of the two—she'd always been more of the parent. Maybe that was why the haunted look in Mr. McCoy's eyes resonated with her.

At a loss, she gestured toward the heap of bags and coats at his feet. "Is there anything I can do to help?"

"Thank you for the offer," he replied, his light tone not quite ringing true. "But as you can see, I'm beyond help." He nuzzled the top of Alyce's head. "Isn't that right, my dear?"

Alyce bussed his cheek with a delighted squeal, and something inside Tessa melted a little. "I don't believe that for a moment."

Mr. McCoy flashed his boyish grin once more. "Perhaps not."

Certainly it was the early fall sun warming her cheeks. If only her own troubles weren't quite so overwhelming. The little family was obviously in need of a good deed, and good deeds were her new stock-in-trade.

The previous year, she and Emmett had attended a tent revival on a lark. The edifying experience had set her on a path of atonement. While she hadn't been completely sold on the itinerant religion, the preacher's words had given voice to the nagging unease in her heart.

That little voice had turned out to be her conscience. Each day with Emmett, that pesky voice had grown louder until she'd realized there was only one way to silence the clamoring. Since Emmett's moral compass had never been set to true north anyway, he'd taken her desertion badly.

Tessa squared her shoulders. "It was a pleasure to meet you, Mr. McCoy. I wish you all the best on your journey."

She wasn't certain if he was coming or going, and she didn't suppose it mattered.

"Likewise," he said. "What about you? Are you on the first leg of some grand adventure?"

"Actually." She let a small, self-indulgent sigh escape. "I'm not certain where I'm going."

"You're all alone, then?"

His innocent question had her eyes burning once more. If only her last words with Emmett hadn't been harsh. Her change of heart concerning his dubious activities had driven a wedge between them, and she should have tried harder to make him understand. If they'd been on better terms when the Fultons had approached him, she'd have talked him out of consorting with the dangerous gang.

The Fultons.

Her heartbeat picked up rhythm and her gaze darted around the platform. "Being alone isn't such a bad thing."

She'd been standing here like a dolt instead of keeping an eye out for trouble. A dangerous mistake.

Satisfied her lapse hadn't been fatal, she assumed her most serene smile. "I believe I'll go wherever the wind takes me."

She sure hoped the wind picked up soon.

"I miss those days," Mr. McCoy replied a touch wistfully. "Enjoy the freedom."

Alyce snatched his ear and tugged, replacing his melancholy expression with an indulgent chuckle.

Tessa's gaze lingered on his face. My, but he had striking eyes. She gave herself a mental shake. What sort of woman mooned after a widower? Quite a few, judging by the admiring gazes he received from several female passengers strolling past.

Bending to Owen's eye level, she smiled. "Stay out of trouble."

"Ga."

Unable to resist, she ruffled his hair, prolonging the moment. Her gaze locked with Mr. McCoy and they remained frozen, cocooned among the porter's calls and the shouted greetings tossed toward departing passengers. Never in her life had she felt such an immediate connection to someone. Or was her continued solitude simply taking its toll?

"I'm in your debt," Mr. McCoy said, breaking the taut thread of awareness stretching between them.

"Anyone would do the same." She tightened the ribbons on her bonnet and turned away. She mustn't leave her trunk unattended for long. As she knew firsthand, there were thieves lurking everywhere. "Perhaps we'll cross paths again one day."

Tessa tossed the last comment over her shoulder, wondering if he'd felt the same instant kinship. Probably not. Her shoulders sagged a notch before she straightened them. That sort of nonsense wouldn't do at all. She wasn't the sort of person who indulged in fits of melancholy. His obvious affection for his children had stirred up her guilt over Emmett, nothing more.

Mr. McCoy appeared lost and overwhelmed, emotions she understood all too well. Though the encounter felt unresolved, she resumed her seat on her trunk, retrieved her ledger and carefully searched out an offense.

Distracted shop owner while Emmett stole a hat.

In the opposite column she wrote "Returned lost toddler to his father."

Tapping her pencil against her bottom lip, she considered her admiration of the children's father and then discarded the lapse as an offense. He was a fetching gentleman and she'd always been drawn to kindness. No harm in that. Maybe someday, after this was all over... She shook her head. *No.* That was a foolish thought.

Love always came with expectations, and if one fought against those expectations, life was a misery. Her mother had expected a child would domesticate Emmett, but he'd left all the same. Emmett had expected her unwavering loyalty for his rescue, though he conveniently forgot he'd left her with those awful people in the first place.

While there were things about her years with Emmett that she'd genuinely enjoyed, her ledger of offenses was thick and her bank balance thin. She sensed Mr. McCoy was someone who lived by a rigid code of honor. A man who'd expect the same in others.

She closed her book with a snap, blocking out her pages of dishonorable deeds.

After tucking away her ledger, she studied the chalked destinations once more. Her spotty schooling had left her without much knowledge of geography, and she was at a loss. She'd settled in Wichita only because she'd liked the sound of the name.

"If You're up there..." she began, lifting her face to

the warming sun. "If You're up there and You have any ideas, I sure could use one now."

A distinctive wooden toy struck the base of her trunk.

"Ball," a familiar small voice declared.

Planting her hands on her hips, Tessa leaned forward. "You are a troublemaker, aren't you?"

Looking inordinately pleased with himself, Owen grinned. "Ga."

Tessa squinted at the sky. "You and I need to work on our communication."

The train whistle blew, startling Alyce, and Shane murmured soothing nonsense. He forced his thoughts away from the lovely Miss Spencer and concentrated on the task at hand. *I am doing the right thing.* Maybe if he kept repeating those words, they'd feel right, they'd feel true.

Unaware of the changes about to upturn her young life, Alyce fiddled with his collar and kicked her feet. *I am doing the right thing.*

Having left Owen with the pinch-faced Mrs. Lund, he arranged for the twins' baggage as well as his own return ticket. Crowds of people surged around them, agitating Alyce and further darkening his mood. This was Abby's dying wish—she wanted her children raised by her family. Only Abby wasn't here anymore, and she didn't see how the children's smiles had faded beneath her sister's dour countenance.

When he returned to where Mrs. Lund was standing, Owen was nowhere to be seen.

"Where is he?" Shane demanded.

Mrs. Lund lifted one shoulder in an unconcerned shrug. "Perhaps if he isn't showered with attention upon his return, the boy will cease running off."

Taller than average, Shane quickly spotted Owen pestering Miss Spencer once more. His rush of relief quickly morphed into anger. There was no way Mrs. Lund had seen Owen from this distance. For all she knew, he'd wandered onto the tracks.

Singularly unrepentant, she crossed her arms over her chest. "Proper discipline is what the boy needs, not coddling. I hope these sorts of antics won't be common-place with the children."

Her voice grated on Shane's nerves. The woman had all the warmth of a root cellar in winter, but she was also the twin's closest kin.

"They've been cooped up," he replied shortly. "They're bound to wander."

He and Abby had been childhood sweethearts. They'd paired up mostly because their ages matched and they were always seated together in the one-room schoolhouse. At seventeen, Abby had pressured him for an engagement. He'd thought them too young and he was already overwhelmed with his own responsibilities. His father had abandoned the family three years before, and Shane had taken over as the man of the house. Despite his best efforts to soften the blow, urging Abby to wait instead, his refusal had incensed her.

They'd gradually lost touch after her parents had died and she'd moved away. Years later, she'd arrived at his ranch, pregnant and alone. Compelled by honor and loyalty, he'd thought he was doing the right thing by marrying her, hoping their past friendship might grow into something deeper. Except she'd never stopped loving the man who'd betrayed her.

Mrs. Lund harrumphed, and her gaze shifted. "Have you made the arrangements with the bank?"

His jaw worked. "I'll finish up this morning."

That figured. Abby's older sister may have lost sight of Owen, but she hadn't lost sight of the money he'd offered for the twins' care.

How had such a simple arrangement become this complicated? Ten years older than Abby, her sister had been married and gone by the time he and Abby had started school together. After Abby's death, their correspondence had been brief, but Mrs. Lund had been well aware of her sister's wishes and hadn't balked. He'd put off the inevitable for as long as he could, but the time had finally arrived.

As though sensing his tension, Alyce squeezed her small hands around his neck. He absently rubbed her back in soothing circles.

"Everything will be fine," he said, though his blood simmered. He turned toward Mrs. Lund and, with an effort born of sheer will, kept his tone calm. "It's been hard on them, losing Abby. They need patience."

"Fine talk coming from you," she snapped. "A man foisting off his children as though they were so much chattel."

"You know what Abby wanted," he said quietly. "The ranch is isolated. If anything happened over the winter…"

"Or perhaps my sister regretted her choice of a husband."

Her words slashed at his conscience. "We can finish this discussion later."

As though his day couldn't get any worse, he locked gazes with a pair of sparkling blue eyes. A flush crept up his neck. He didn't know how much Miss Spencer had heard, but it was probably too much.

"We meet again, Mr. McCoy." Despite her casual words, Miss Spencer clenched her hands before her stomach, her knuckles white. "I believe this little fellow belongs to you."

Assuming his most stern expression, Shane switched Alyce to his opposite shoulder and reached down. "Owen, that's twice today."

The boy grinned, not at all sorry. Shane raised his eyebrows. Leave it to Owen to find the prettiest girl at the depot. The child was a positive flirt.

Miss Spencer's gaze darted around the platform. "I believe Owen was chasing his ball and became a little lost."

The tight coil he kept around his emotions eased a notch. Owen's champion was smartly dressed in a traveling suit the color of a ripe peach. The cheerful hue brought out the luster in her flaxen hair and the flecks of gold in her sharp blue eyes. Though clearly nervous about something or someone, she exuded an air of confidence and grace.

Her presence felt out of place on the crowded platform. As though she belonged in a private parlor—sipping tea and waiting for her Pullman car. She was the sort of woman Abby had always admired. The rope around his emotions tightened once more. The sort of woman who'd find him boring and suffocating, no doubt, just as Abby had.

"Thank you," he said. "For returning Owen. *Again.*"

"My pleasure."

Her voice had a husky quality that stirred long-dormant yearnings. Though she kept a calm visage, there was something troubled about the way Miss Spencer kept glancing over her shoulder. The more time he spent with her, the more he realized there was an air of mystery surrounding his lovely Good Samaritan. That ambiguity made her all the more alluring, and he fought against his curiosity. Mysteries had a way of ending badly.

While Shane struggled for a suitable reply, Owen tossed the ball toward Mrs. Lund.

She squeaked and dodged sideways, then snatched the boy's shirt and cocked back her arm. "You did that on purpose, you little—"

"No!" Shane shouted helplessly. With Alyce in his arms, he struggled to reach Owen.

Miss Spencer threw herself before the boy and grasped Mrs. Lund's wrist.

Gratitude rushed through him.

Mrs. Lund's face suffused with color. "Get your hands off of me!"

"I will not stand by and watch you hit a child," Miss Spencer declared.

Sensing the trouble he'd caused, Owen whimpered behind her skirts.

"I wasn't going to harm the boy." Mrs. Lund sniffed. "Not that it's any business of yours. A woman, traveling alone. You're no better than you should be."

Shane moved between the two combatants. "I won't have you insulting Miss Spencer."

"And I won't have this…this *person* questioning my intentions."

"What were your intentions?" he challenged.

His sister-in-law gasped. "How dare you question me!"

Now what? It sure looked as if Mrs. Lund was getting ready to haul off and wallop the boy. And if that was the case, then her actions changed everything. No matter how desperate, he wasn't leaving the children with an abusive guardian. They might not be his children by blood, but he loved them all the same, and he was honor bound to ensure they were well cared for, no matter what Abby's wishes.

Mrs. Lund's mouth worked, and after several tense seconds, she gathered herself. "We had an agreement. There's no need to fuss."

Shane rubbed his forehead. *Impossible situations.* He had a singular talent for landing in impossible situations. With winter coming, he'd lose the help he hired from town. The weather isolated the ranch, sometimes for weeks. He'd kept Abby's secret about the babies— everyone assumed he was their father—and he was bound to abide by her request concerning the children's care. Yet he questioned her sister's intentions.

People were always hiding their true motivations. Abby had claimed she still loved him, even though she was pregnant with another man's children. Mrs. Lund had claimed she wanted to raise the twins, when clearly she was more interested in the money. Even he was keeping secrets—Abby's secrets. Of the three of them, only Miss Spencer had no reason for duplicity.

As though only just deciphering the situation, Miss Spencer looked between the two of them. "You're leaving the children with *her*?"

Mrs. Lund tossed her head. "After seeing how he manages them, I can understand Abby's insistence that I raise the children. They are in need of a firm hand."

Shane turned his back on his sister-in-law and faced Miss Spencer. The disappointment in her eyes sent his words spilling forth in a hasty confession. "I live on an isolated ranch. We're cut off from everything during the winter. It's just my men and me."

Miss Spencer swayed forward. "Your ranch is isolated?"

"It's just south of Cimarron Springs. Completely off the map."

"That sounds quite remote." Her voice grew breathless. "And inaccessible."

"Uh." He wasn't certain if there was a question buried in her statement. "Yes."

Shane reached for Owen, who clutched Miss Spencer's skirts all the tighter. His chest constricted. He wasn't leaving them with Mrs. Lund, even if that meant defying Abby's wishes. Though she was the children's closest relative, he'd known her for less than twenty minutes. In that short time he'd seen how truly unsuitable she was for the task.

Twenty minutes.

About the same amount of time he'd known Miss Spencer. His gaze lit on Owen's lovely rescuer. She obviously feared something or someone, though she was doing her best to cover her anxiety. She wasn't as excited about her travels as she'd have them believe. He sensed her independent nature and her stubborn resolve, but he had his own streak of obstinacy as well.

For a moment he imagined the world from her viewpoint, and his thoughts left him unsettled. An unmarried woman without the protection of relatives had few resources. Traveling alone was dangerous, more so farther west. Did she know the trouble she courted? Was she aware of the admiring stares she evoked? A very male sense of protectiveness tightened his jaw.

Mrs. Lund reached for Owen, who cowered away. "Come along," she ordered. "We've wasted enough time."

The boy burst out crying.

"No." Shane spoke more forcibly than he'd intended. His gaze fastened on Miss Spencer. "I'll find another way."

Chapter Two

Searching for a way to gently extract herself from the tense situation, Tessa took a discreet step back. She'd already caused enough trouble for Mr. McCoy, and the more she delayed, the more trouble she caused for herself as well.

Mrs. Lund smoothed the hair from her temple. "I blame Abby for this. She never had a lick of sense. Always running with the wrong sorts of people. Look at what it got her. I suppose I should have known she'd marry someone cut from the same cloth. Blood will out, as they say."

Tessa gazed at the two beautiful children. "Yes, blood will out." If the twins were any indication, Abby had not been cut from the same cloth as her sister. "By way of apology, perhaps I could distract the children while the two of you speak alone."

Shocked by her impulsive suggestion, she froze. Really, this was none of her business, and she was being terribly forward, but the poor widower looked as though he had a few choice words for his sister-in-law that were best exchanged in private.

A muscle ticked in his cheek. "I believe you're right, Miss Spencer. Mrs. Lund and I have a great deal to discuss."

"Call me Tessa."

"Then you must call me Shane."

His sister-in-law made an exaggerated show of straightening her hair and pressing her clothing with flattened palms. Tessa glanced warily between the two. There were fireworks coming, that much was certain. Mrs. Lund had best not underestimate her brother-in-law. Tessa sensed a spine of steel behind that even-tempered exterior.

Clearing her throat, Tessa drew their attention. "There's an ice cream parlor across the street. Why don't I arrange a treat for the children and let you and Mrs. Lund have a moment in private?"

Shane hesitated. "Are you certain?"

"Positive." Despite his assurances, she *did* feel somewhat responsible. When she'd thought Mrs. Lund might strike the boy, she'd seen red, and her instincts had taken over. Though she didn't regret her actions, she *had* set this chain of events into motion. "We'll take a seat by the window. That way, you can see us as well."

He gestured toward a young porter standing vigil near the ticket office. "Can you store the lady's trunk?"

"Right away, sir."

Tessa noted the cut of the freckle-faced porter's clothing and took stock of his shiny new shoes. He was obviously well paid, which meant there was no reason for him to rifle through her belongings for valuables.

"Thank you, Shane," she said. "For your thoughtfulness."

"Enough." Mrs. Lund snorted. "I don't have all day while the two of you chatter about nonsense."

"I believe that's my cue." Tessa knelt and gathered the twins close. Emmett had always discouraged the wasting of one's charm on the charmless. "Your dad says it's all right if I take you for ice cream. Is that all right with you?"

The two exchanged a glance.

Owen nodded. "Ga."

"High praise indeed."

She led them across the street and took a table near the window. Their vantage was doubly useful since Shane could keep sight of his children, and she could keep watch for Dead Eye. She didn't suppose outlaws frequented ice cream parlors. So long as she didn't attract more attention to herself, she was safe. For the moment.

Oblivious to the drama unfolding on their behalf, the twins were instead fascinated with the intricacies of the metal scrollwork chairs. Alyce knelt backward on the seat and traced her finger around the twisted heart pattern. Attempting to climb up as well, Owen pushed her aside. Alyce shoved him back.

"There's no need to fight." Tessa scraped another chair closer. "Wouldn't you like your very own seat, Owen?"

He squinted, then crossed his arms over his chest and stubbornly glared at his sister.

Shrugging, Tessa sat and pivoted her legs beneath the

table. "How very nice it is to have a chair all to oneself. Makes one feel very grown up."

From the corner of her eye, she watched as Owen carefully rested his ball on the table and claimed his own seat. Though pleased with her success, she kept her emotions hidden lest Owen catch on.

Only a few tables in the parlor were occupied, showcasing the black-and-white tile floor and the blue-and-white-checkered curtains hanging from the windows. During the height of the summer season, the shop must burst at the seams. With a slight chill in the fall air, business had obviously slowed.

She studied the list of choices. "I believe the special today is chocolate. Chocolate is a fine choice, on any occasion."

After taking their order, the grandmotherly shop owner clasped her hands. "My, but your children are well behaved. And so lovely, too. If you don't mind me saying so, they're the spitting image of you, ma'am."

Without waiting for an answer, the woman circled back around the counter.

Tessa tugged her lower lip between her teeth. Explaining her actual relationship with the children seemed unnecessarily complicated. She'd always adored children, though life with Emmett hadn't afforded much opportunity to be around them. Considering her current predicament, she didn't suppose there'd be much opportunity in the future either. A pall fell over her once more. Always before she'd had hope, but the passing of time had relentlessly drained her optimism.

She rolled the ball across the table and Owen stopped it before it tumbled off. Alyce found the game more entertaining than tracing the metal scrollwork and joined in the fun. The task took a great deal of concentration and giggling.

An elderly couple seated nearby watched their antics with indulgent smiles.

The woman leaned toward Tessa. "You have a lovely family. Makes me think of my own children at that age. Enjoy this time. It passes quickly."

Feeling a fraud, Tessa murmured a few polite words in response. They were strangers. She'd never see them again. And yet she was no better than Emmett was— playing a game of smoke and mirrors based on assumptions. Worse yet, the game was all too familiar, almost comfortable, like donning one's winter coat after a long summer.

The shop owner returned and handed Tessa two folded flour sacks.

"Their outfits are so pretty," the woman said. "I'd hate to see them mussed."

Grateful for the shopkeeper's thoughtfulness, and still feeling a touch guilty, Tessa knotted the sacks around the squirming children. A tug of longing surprised her once again. There was no reason to be maudlin. Emmett had loved her dearly, she'd never doubted that, but he'd always been slightly befuddled with having a little girl around.

Over the years, ladies from the boardinghouses and saloons where they'd stayed had occasionally taken her under their wing, showing her how to fix her hair and dress properly. Sometimes she felt as though she'd had scores of mothers, and other times she felt as though she'd had none at all. Everyone had different expectations, and she'd spent much of her life puzzling out her role with new people.

One way or another, she'd been searching for something elusive all her life. Just once she wanted affection without expectations. Someone who knew who she really was and loved her all the same. Her fingers tightened around Owen's ball. An impossible hope considering her past.

As the shop owner placed two bowls of ice cream before the children, a grim-faced Mr. McCoy stepped inside. He doffed his hat and took the remaining seat.

Alyce snatched her bowl and lapped at the ice cream. Laughing, Tessa pulled the bowl away. Now sporting a chocolate beard, the toddler groped for her spoon. Tugging the utensil out of reach, Tessa wiped the sticky mess from Alyce's face.

Shane lifted his spoon and turned toward Owen. The boy worked his mouth like a baby bird.

"They haven't mastered the fork and spoon yet," he said. "Sometimes it's best if we assist."

"Of course." Tessa stole a glance at him from beneath her eyelashes. "Is everything all right?"

"We've decided Mrs. Lund is far too busy to watch the children over the winter."

"Perhaps that's for the best. You're a good father, keeping them with you. You've done the right thing."

He flushed beneath her praise and looked away. "Miss Spencer, thank you for your help. I hadn't met Mrs. Lund before today. I had no idea she was quite so…harsh."

Tessa tilted her head. How odd the widower had

never met his sister-in-law before today. Then again, she didn't know much about how regular families worked.

His expression turned severe. "She had other reasons for wanting the children. I can't abide falsehoods."

Instantly chilled, Tessa ducked her head. "Have you considered placing an advertisement? An older woman, perhaps a widow, would not attract gossip."

There was a hopeful gleam in his eyes that had her wary. For a moment the idea of living in the wilds had struck her as the perfect solution. Before she'd realized the impossibility of such a plan. Despite having been raised by an unconventional parent, she understood propriety all too well. While she wasn't particularly vain, she was too young and too unattached for the role of housekeeper. Which made losing her job at the Harvey House all the more catastrophic. There were few opportunities for single ladies. She'd seen the life of a saloon girl firsthand living with Emmett, and while she understood desperation, she'd do anything to avoid *that* fate.

Shane collapsed back in his chair and raked his hands through his hair. "Abby had certain…wishes." A shadow passed over his face. "I've backed myself into a corner. With winter coming, I'm running out of time. An advertisement could take weeks. I'd have to wait on the post. Then the applicants must be carefully scrutinized. We live in tight quarters on the ranch."

Tessa stared at the spoon clutched between her fingers. "I should never have interfered in something that was none of my concern. I've had a lot on my mind recently."

"You're afraid of someone, aren't you?"

Her head snapped up. "Why would you say that?"

Her acting skills had obviously rusted.

"A few things. Like the way you sat so you could keep an eye on the door. And before, at the train station, you were as jumpy as an outlaw in a room full of deputies. Are you a runaway heiress or something?"

Tessa fiddled with the lace at her collar. "Nothing so romantic, I'm afraid."

Clearing her throat, she glanced away. The outlaw-and-deputies analogy had struck a little too close to home.

"If someone is bothering you," he said, "perhaps I can help."

"We're quite a pair, aren't we?" Though she hadn't expected an instant shower of riches, she'd thought living a moral life might result in a bit more reward and a bit less trouble. Carefully choosing her next words, she said, "I've attracted the attention of a somewhat shady character."

That wasn't too far from the truth. Nor was it a lie. Dead Eye Dan was definitely a shady character.

Shane's eyes widened. "Who is this person?"

"He, uh…he came into the Harvey House where I work. *Worked.* He's been asking about me." Which was also the truth. Maybe not the entire truth, but a good portion of it. "I have reason to believe he's an outlaw."

A really, *really* good reason.

She imagined Dead Eye Dan trolling through town with the daguerreotype picture of her that he'd flashed at the Harvey House. The picture he'd obviously stolen from her father. She'd seen such events play out before with startling predictability. As long as the outlaw concocted a believable tale, each person she'd met this morning would proudly declare her whereabouts. People enjoyed feeling helpful. Meaning the more time she spent with Mr. McCoy, the more she put him and his family in danger as well.

Shane offered Owen another bite and caught her gaze. "Outlaws dine at the Harvey House?"

"Everyone dines at the Harvey House. We have the best prices and our service is impeccable."

"I don't doubt it." He paused. "You don't happen to know this fellow's name?"

Skirting the truth had the unfortunate side effect of leaving too many openings for pointed questions. Tessa considered making a run for the door, then discarded the idea. She'd only attract more attention. And, really, what harm was in a name?

"He's called Dead Eye Dan Fulton."

Shane scoffed, "That is the worst outlaw name I've ever heard."

"Not very clever, I know." Tessa laughed in spite of herself. "He has a meandering eye. It's terribly difficult to carry on a conversation with him because you never can tell which eye is looking at you... I'm rambling again."

"I'm curious." Shane removed the flour sacking from around Owen's neck and wiped his chocolate-covered fingers. "Why don't you simply turn him over to the sheriff?"

"Staying out of his way seemed the best solution. I wouldn't want to anger him."

Or his brothers. She couldn't very well tell Shane about the rest of the Fultons either. Just like she couldn't tell him that if she turned in Dead Eye, the outlaw would guess her involvement in a heartbeat.

The Fultons might not be the smartest men, but they weren't the dumbest either. "As you can probably imagine, one does not rebuke the advances of an outlaw without consequence."

"I see your point." Shane tipped the glass bowl and scooped out another bite. "Then you've decided to abscond like a thief in the night."

Tessa sighed. There it was again, that unfortunate reference to thievery. "Despite what the poets say, absence does not make the heart grow fonder. He'll forget about me soon enough once I'm out of his sight."

She hoped.

The door opened and she leaped halfway out of her chair then sat back down with a thud. The elderly couple who'd admired the children earlier were leaving. No need for panic.

"Sorry," she said. "Thought I saw someone I knew."

To her immense relief, Shane appeared unfazed by her weak excuse. "You've had a rough go of it, haven't you?"

A sharp pain throbbed in her temple. She wasn't lying, though, not exactly. She was withholding certain facts for his protection. Men like Mr. McCoy didn't understand men like Dead Eye.

Despite the bolstering thought, or maybe because of it, she averted her gaze before biting the inside of her cheek.

Emmett had been certain she'd fail on her own, certain she'd come crawling back, begging for his help. He could have at least had the courtesy to be available for the begging-and-crawling portion when the time arrived. "I'm starting on a new adventure. It's very exciting."

Exciting in the sort of way a catastrophic train wreck was exciting, but rousing all the same.

A shadow passed before the window, and she shrank back, dipping her head and covering her face. Everyone simply assumed they were a loving family enjoying the afternoon, and she'd relaxed into the illusion. She'd taken for granted the respectability of traveling with Emmett. Alone, she attracted all sorts of unwanted stares and attention.

Bolstering her courage, she stood. She'd made her choice, and she had no one to blame but herself if the going was difficult. Her heart heavy, she reached out and brushed the backs of her knuckles along the cushion of Alyce's cheek, then ruffled Owen's hair.

The twins had devoured what ice cream hadn't melted and claimed their spoons. They were having great fun sweeping their fingers around the glass bowl, seeking every last drop. The task took a great deal of concentration, which meant Tessa had lost her last excuse for lingering.

The ticking clock above the counter propelled her forward. "It was a pleasure meeting you, Mr. McCoy. You have a beautiful family. Despite your difficulties this morning, I feel certain you will prevail."

She squared her shoulders and focused on the door. The important part was not looking back. Emmett always said that life was not meant to be traveled backward.

Shane caught her hand. "Wait."

She mustn't turn around. All of her instincts screamed that he expected something from her. She knew full well she'd never live up to those expectations.

Certainly she'd never been one to linger over little heartbreaks and trivial disappointments. This morning when she'd realized her time at the Harvey House was at an end, she'd set out with dogged resolve. Though she mourned the loss of her delicate new friendships, she hadn't faltered.

Yet her feet remained rooted in place. She didn't believe in fate, but something had brought them together on that platform. Of all the people passing through the station, Owen had found her. Surely that meant something in the grand scheme of things.

The preacher at the tent revival had said that in helping others one helped oneself. But what did a retired thief have to offer?

Shane released her hand. "Hear me out. Please."

The appeal in his voice scattered the last vestiges of her good sense. "I'm listening."

Chapter Three

Miss Spencer's direct gaze had Shane tied up in knots again, and he immediately forgot what he was about to say. There was a chance they might help each other—if he took care of the problem plaguing her first. Just once he wanted to do the right thing and have something good come of it.

Before Shane could speak, Owen reached for his spoon and slipped. His body fell forward and he splayed his hands, nicking the edge of his bowl. The glassware slid across the table. Tessa lunged. The bowl dodged between her fingers and careened off the edge. Melted chocolate splattered her skirts before the glass shattered.

Owen sobbed and rubbed the spot on his chin where he'd bumped the table. The boy reached for Tessa and she immediately resumed her seat, pulling him onto her lap while carefully avoiding the shattered glass. Owen grasped at her white lace collar with sticky fingers and buried his chocolate-covered face in her neck. Oblivious of the damage marring her pristine outfit, Tessa rubbed his back and murmured soothing words.

Shane swallowed hard once. Then twice. The twins had sought that affection from Abby, craved her attention. Instead, she'd drifted through their lives like a marionette, going through the motions without any more warmth than a carved wooden block. Everything he'd done to help had only made matters worse.

As Owen's cries turned into hiccups and eventually subsided, Tessa glanced up, her expression troubled. "I have to go. My shift normally starts at dinner. When I don't arrive, Dead Eye will start looking for me."

She was paler by the moment, her movements jerky and frightened. Shane blew out a breath. He'd always had a weakness for the marginalized. All the men he'd hired on the ranch had conquered adversity in one way or another. Finch had lost his right arm and the vision in his left eye during the war. Wheeler was a freed slave Shane had met on a tortuous stagecoach ride through the sweltering Texas heat.

The others…well, the others had seen more than their fair share of hardship. Probably that was why Abby had returned once she'd realized she was in trouble. She knew he'd never turn her away. Yet he suspected a difference in Tessa. As though she'd take any offer of protection as an affront, though clearly she was in need of assistance.

Shane scowled. The outlaw deserved a throttling for terrifying her. Barring that, he'd do the next best thing.

"Let me help," he said quickly. "Please."

Owen fidgeted in her lap and she produced a coin he hadn't noticed before. With a deft flick of her wrist, the coin disappeared. Owen snatched at her fingers and frowned in confusion. She fisted her hands a few times, turning her arm this way and that. With an exaggerated frown of confusion, she brushed Owen's temple.

"Hmm," she said solemnly. "What have we here?"

With a flourish she produced the coin from behind Owen's ear. The boy squealed in delight.

Alyce stood in her chair and leaned over, eagerly joining the game. Without answering him, Tessa absently repeated the trick. Much to the delight of the children, the coin dropped from noses and sprang from beneath dimpled chins with an elegant and imperceptible sleight of hand. Shane was as mesmerized as the children with the rapid disappearance and reappearances of the coin. Only when she dropped the money into her reticule was the spell broken.

She glanced up and he shook his thoughts back to the problem at hand, grasping for a convincing argument.

"The next train doesn't leave for hours." He charged ahead. "I have an idea that may help us both."

Her face softened and his persuasions died on his lips. Abby had an odd habit of staring at a spot over his shoulder, never looking directly at him. The practice had left him feeling invisible. Tessa met his gaze dead-on, her expression open and forthright.

"I'm not sure how you can help." She quirked an eyebrow. "Unless you have a freshly pressed dress handy or a private stage for a hasty exit out of town?"

"No." Her directness was refreshing and disconcerting at the same time. "I'm afraid not, but I can offer you a room at the hotel." At the startled look in her eyes, he quickly added, "To freshen up."

She gave a sad shake of her head. "I wouldn't mind

staying out of sight and cleaning up, but I can't displace you."

"As you can see, our plans have changed."

A riot of color suffused her cheeks. "Because of me."

"Never say that. My plans have altered because Mrs. Lund wasn't a good choice for a guardian. I might not have realized her unsuitability," he added, "if Owen hadn't pestered you into returning him."

Owen grinned at the sound of his name, revealing his two front teeth. "Ball."

"Don't paint me as the hero," Tessa replied, raising her delicately arched eyebrows. "I was a little reluctant to return him. He's a very good listener."

Shane dug through his pockets, producing the metal key. "This is the only key. I have some business in town. If you need to change, I can fetch your trunk as well."

"Not the trunk! I mean to say, that won't be necessary. I'm sure a dab of water will take care of this."

Shane didn't know much about laundry, but he figured it was going to take a lot more than a spot cleaning to erase that damage.

His doubts were forestalled by a flutter of activity. Summoned by the commotion, a woman in an apron bustled over. Together they plucked shards of glass from the floor and wiped up the mess.

Tessa brushed at the stains on her gown. "I can't very well travel like this."

"Definitely not."

Reaching out, she rested her hand over the key. "You said there's only one key."

"Only the one." He'd bought himself some time. With a little effort, his plan would erase the fear in her eyes and make up for the trouble they'd caused her. Then maybe he could convince her they each had something the other needed. "I'll walk you the distance and be on my way."

Owen showed no signs of surrendering his perch, and Tessa absently tucked him closer. The boy rested his head in the crook of her neck and stared at the shiny locket nestled at the base of her throat.

With a last glance over her shoulder, she nodded. "I accept your offer."

Shane blew out a relieved breath. "You'll be on your way in no time."

Keeping vigil for outlaws with wandering eyes, Shane escorted his motley bunch to the hotel and made arrangements with the clerk. Miss Spencer was obviously not well-known in town, as none of the staff showed even a flicker of recognition.

Not that anyone could get a good look at her anyway. She spent much of the time helpfully chasing after Owen and Alyce as they reached for the vase of flowers on the round table in the lobby and crawled between the spindly legs of a settee.

The room he'd procured was at the end of the corridor and he walked her that way, then gathered the twins. Owen yawned.

Tessa hesitated. "How long will your business take?"

"An hour. Maybe two."

"The children appear tired."

"They usually nap around this time."

She reached for Alyce, who eagerly took her hand. "I could...I could watch them. You know, while you accomplished your task."

He hesitated, not wanting to take advantage of her. "If you're certain."

Her offer was ideal. Better than he could have hoped. While he was fully prepared to take the twins on his errand, he moved faster without them.

"Aren't you afraid I'll abscond with your children?" she asked, turning the key in the lock.

Her bright smile stole his breath. Her eyes sparkled and a delightful dimple appeared in her left cheek. He'd been immersed in his own troubles for so long, he'd forgotten the simple pleasure of a moment of joy.

"I'm more afraid they'll send you screaming into the streets," he said at last.

"I'm much stronger than I look."

Her dimple disappeared and he mourned the loss. "I don't doubt it."

Tessa turned the key a few times, but no click of the lock sounded.

She removed the key and studied it closely. "The numbers match but one of the teeth is bent. That must be the problem."

"I'll see if they have another."

"No need."

She reached behind her head and pulled a hairpin from the coil at the nape of her neck, then inserted the slender metal into the space beneath the key. Her brow knit in concentration, she jiggled the hairpin a few times and the door sprang open.

Shane gaped, nonplussed by her odd talent for disappearing coins and difficult locks.

"I—uh," Tessa stuttered. "I once had a temperamental lock on a boardinghouse door. I learned a few tricks."

He supposed there was nothing too odd in that. "You're quite the locksmith."

"It comes in handy at the oddest times."

The twins hugged him around the legs before he left, but seemed content to remain with Miss Spencer. Relieved at Owen and Alyce's easy acceptance of the situation, he made his way toward the train depot with only a twinge of guilt for taking advantage of Tessa's good nature. The twins had been roused earlier than usual this morning and should sleep easily. Tessa appeared as though she could use the rest as well.

Her intervention with Owen, though unplanned and unexpected, had pushed him out of his stupor. While he'd like to believe he'd have seen Mrs. Lund's duplicity eventually, viewing her through Tessa's eyes had forced him into acknowledging her unsuitability.

The telegraph office was devoid of customers, and he accomplished his task in short order. Having a cousin who served as a telegraph operator was convenient. Having a telegraph operator for a cousin who was also married to a lawman was even more helpful.

A flurry of messages were received and dispatched over the following hour, and he took a seat on the bench tucked into a corner of the small office, impatiently tapping his heel. A fine bead of sweat formed on his brow. Miss Spencer must be pacing the floors by now. He checked his watch for the thousandth time. Another forty-five minutes passed before the sheriff appeared. Shane met him at the door in three long strides.

The man was tall and slender and as weathered and thin as a strip of beef jerky.

He presented Shane with a wanted poster. "There's a reward for Dead Eye. Where would you like it sent?"

A reward. His stomach twisted. Glancing at the picture, his eyes widened at the sum listed on the bottom of the page. Tessa could hire her own private Pullman car with that amount. She certainly wouldn't need a housekeeping job. He stuffed his free hand into his pocket and shook his head. At least one good thing had come out of this mess.

"You've got him, then?" Shane prodded. "He's locked up?"

"Picked him up straightaway. Didn't put up too much of a fight. I suppose he didn't figure anyone around these parts would recognize him."

For once, doing the right thing had resulted in something good. Maybe not for him, but that wasn't the point anyway. "Excellent."

The sheriff pushed his hat back on his head with the tip of his index finger. "And how did you come to recognize him, Mr. McCoy?"

Shane scratched his temple and stared at the floor. "Long story."

The question had nagged him as well. How had Tessa known the identity of the outlaw? He shrugged. She probably saw all sorts with people coming and going from the café.

"Understood." The slender man touched the gun strapped against his thigh. "You'd best not stick around, just in case."

"Trust me, there's not a chance he'll connect me with his capture, but I'll be on my way all the same."

"Not so fast. You haven't told me where you'd like the reward sent."

Shane considered and discarded several possibilities. Best not to leave a trail that might lead back to Miss Spencer. "Send the money to Marshal Cain in Cimarron Springs. He'll know what to do."

Once Miss Spencer was settled, he'd make arrangements to have the money transferred. She'd spotted Dead Eye first, after all, and the money was hers. The sheriff jotted down a few notes and went about his business.

His steps dragging, Shane returned to the hotel. Separating from Tessa was for the best. Being around her stirred up a sting of loneliness. Always before he'd thrown himself into work when the yearnings for companionship had grown too distracting, exhausting himself in body and spirit. The children had forced him to keep a part of his heart open, and he'd be wise to be on his guard in the future. Tessa reminded him of Abby when they were young, full of hope and hungry for adventure. He didn't want to see that optimism fade.

He rapped on the door and Miss Spencer appeared, holding a finger over her lips. A scowl darkened her brow.

"Shh," she ordered. "They've fallen asleep."

Somehow or another she'd draped the stained portion of her skirt like a fall around her waist, cleverly disguising the spots. There were damp portions around her collar where she'd scrubbed at the rest of the marks, and he forced his gaze from the charming sight. His was an honorable mission, and he did her a disservice by thinking of her in any way other than an unexpected acquaintance.

She slipped into the corridor and quietly shut the door behind her. "Where have you been? What took so long?"

"I'm sorry. I can explain." He handed over the wanted poster. "They've picked up Dead Eye Dan. You're safe now."

Her face grew ashen. "What have you done?"

He gripped her shoulders, shocked by her violent trembling. "He's behind bars. He can't bother you anymore."

She vigorously shook her head and backed away. "You don't understand. This is worse. This is much worse."

"There's a reward." His declaration only sent her stumbling farther back, and his hands dropped away. "I had it sent to Marshal Cain in Cimarron Springs. The outlaw will never guess your identity. Contact the marshal and he'll make the arrangements."

Her pale lips pinched together. "I wouldn't touch a dime of that money if my life depended upon it."

"Why not? You spotted him. You've earned that reward."

"Because it's dangerous, that's why. Claiming the reward money will lead the rest of his gang directly to me."

Her fear instantly made sense, but there was an easy enough solution. "Come with us to Cimarron Springs, help me with the children. I'll pay you for your trouble. I'll even claim the money myself and hand it over to you. That way, you're not involved."

She jerked her head in a negative gesture. "You'll put yourself in danger. I won't allow that."

"I'm a grown man."

"You're a father. You should consider your children. Lawmen aren't always honest."

The skeptical edge in her voice stiffened his spine. "I trust the marshal in town. He's married to my cousin. He won't put either of us in danger."

Her shoulders slumped. She opened the door once more and stared into the room. He caught a glimpse of Alyce and Owen asleep on the bed, curled around each other like puppies, a bolster of pillows surrounding them.

"I know you're strong," he said. "I know you don't need my help, but I need yours."

Blood rushed in his ears. He couldn't recall the last time he'd asked someone for help. He'd been independent since the moment his father had walked out on them, and he liked it that way. As long as he didn't count on people, they didn't let him down. Since arriving in Wichita, he'd felt as though he was unraveling bit by bit. If he let this go on any longer, there'd be nothing left of him.

"Never mind," he said, reaching for the key. "It's been a long day. I appreciate everything you've done. I had no right to ask for more."

She yanked her hand out of his reach. "I'll help you."

It was too late to take back his offer, and gratitude and shame warred in his chest. She'd agreed to help him. She'd agreed because she'd seen him weak.

Tessa hesitated. "I'll leave Cimarron Springs as soon as the reward arrives. You know that, right?"

"I know." Earlier, a selfish part of him had hoped she might consider staying on, just until he found a suitable replacement, but she'd obviously anticipated his appeal. "I understand."

Tessa had called him a good father before. She'd said he was doing the right thing by keeping the children with him. The truth was far less charitable. He wasn't a fit parent for the children any more than Mrs. Lund. By refusing to face the impossibility of the situation, he'd been lying to himself rather than doing what was best for the children.

"Four o'clock," he said, replacing his hat. He was done being weak. Once they were all back home, he'd finally make things right, even if it shattered him. He'd put himself back together before; he knew how the pieces fit. "We leave at four."

Now that he'd committed to his decision, a cynical relief surged through his veins. The reward money made everyone's life simpler. Without Tessa, there'd be one less person in town who'd been disappointed by him.

As long as nothing unforeseen happened, they'd never see each other again after the journey's end. She was as good as gone. At least there was nothing left to go wrong.

"The reward money has hit a snag." Marshal Garrett Cain spoke from his seat behind his desk.

"What kind of a snag?" Tessa demanded, covering the panic in her voice. "I was hoping to avoid a delay."

She needed the money quickly. She'd already been in town for three days. That was long enough. Too long, really. She feared she'd run into Shane once more, and the cold shoulder he'd given her upon their arrival had made it abundantly clear that her presence was unwelcome.

"Let's give Shane a few more minutes." The marshal shook his head. "He needs to hear this, too."

Tessa stifled a groan. Perched on the edge of her seat in Marshal Cain's office, she tucked the edges of her skirts around her frozen ankles. Wind whistled beneath the door and frost coated the windowpanes.

She shivered and tugged her coat tighter. "There's no need to bother Mr. McCoy, is there? This really doesn't concern him."

Though Shane's rejection had hurt her more than she cared to admit, his absence was for the best. She was putting them all in danger the longer she stuck around.

"He's on his way already," the marshal said.

Perfect. She offered a tight-lipped smile of acknowledgment. Just what this day needed.

All the little nagging worries she'd harbored piled up around her in a suffocating heap. She'd had no more success in contacting Emmett, which meant her meager savings must stretch indefinitely. Though she'd scoffed at the reward before, a few days of introspection had given her clarity on the matter. Considering her situation, money was a good thing. Someone was going to collect that reward, and it might as well be her. Since she was no longer an outlaw, the code didn't apply anyway.

She glanced across the desk separating them. The marshal held her gaze with a benevolent expression she imagined he normally reserved for relaying the news of untimely deaths.

"I don't suppose your news is good news?" she asked.

"Nope."

On that less-than-cheerful note, he stood, plucked several pieces of wood from the stack near the potbellied stove and stoked the fire. Though clearly not the best conversationalist, he was a fine-looking man with dark hair showing a feathering of gray at the temples. The lawman had a forthright manner and a direct approach that compelled honesty. The kind of man Emmett avoided at all costs.

Her mouth went dry. "You have me worried, Marshal Cain."

And that was saying something.

The door burst open in a flurry of cold air and a young girl scooted inside. Realizing she had a brief reprieve before Mr. McCoy arrived, Tessa forced the tension from her shoulders. The newcomer flipped back her coat hood and stomped the snow from her boots on the rag rug.

The young beauty was in her midteens, showing the first blush of womanhood with her bright blue eyes and curly corn silk hair. "Shane is on his way," the girl said. "He's talking with Mama now."

The marshal assisted her with her coat. "This is my daughter, Cora. Cora, this is Miss Spencer."

The girl held out her hand. "Hello. I've heard so much about you."

Tessa tucked an escaped tendril of hair behind one ear. "Surely not. I only met your father this morning."

"I didn't hear about you from Papa."

Heat crept up Tessa's neck. Shane must have spoken of her—but why? She doubted she'd made much of an impression. Touching her cheeks, she hoped they weren't flaming as hotly as they felt.

The marshal ushered his daughter through a second door at the rear of the office. Tessa caught sight of a jail cell and a flight of stairs through the opening.

"Enough, Cora," the marshal ordered. "You're making our guest uncomfortable. I'm guessing your mother will be along soon. Why don't you run along upstairs and put on some coffee? You know where to find everything."

Yep. Tessa's cheeks were definitely flaming.

A gust of winter bluster indicated another arrival. Her heartbeat thundered and the freshly stoked fire suddenly turned the room blistering hot. Shane stepped inside and turned toward the coat hooks, presenting her with his profile. The corners of his mouth drooped at the edges and his eyes were tired and bloodshot, as though he hadn't slept in a month of Sundays.

He hung his hat on the peg near the door and ducked his head. "Miss Spencer."

"Mr. McCoy," she replied, matching his formal tone.

He didn't appear at all happy to see her. Not that she'd expected cartwheels and a jig, but a friendly smile might have been nice. He'd asked for her help before and she was only here at his request, yet he was treating her as though she'd somehow offended him. Crossing her arms, she looked away.

He didn't even have the courtesy to bring the children. Certainly he knew how much she missed them.

The marshal resumed his seat behind the desk. "Thanks for coming out, Shane. I figured the two of you should hear this at the same time. I just got word from Wichita. Dead Eye Dan Fulton has busted out of jail."

Chapter Four

Tessa gasped and bolted upright. "When?"

"Last night."

Panic rose like bile in her throat. "Who broke him out?"

As though she had to ask.

"His brothers," the marshal replied grimly.

She didn't believe in luck, but she was starting to believe in bad luck. Here she'd been lulled into a false sense of safety, thinking she might actually claim the reward money and sleep a full night through for once.

Tessa turned her fear on Mr. McCoy. "I knew this would happen."

"I was trying to help," he wearily replied.

She splayed her fingers over her eyes. Terror definitely had a way of making her forget herself. While she had perfectly valid reasons for being angry with Shane, the outlaw's escape wasn't one of them. If she'd told him the truth about her connection to Dead Eye in the first place, then they wouldn't be in this mess. She had no one to blame but herself for this particular disaster.

"I'm sorry," she said. "Of course you meant well. I was surprised, that's all."

"What about the reward?" Shane demanded.

"Rescinded." The marshal held up his hands in supplication. "Didn't say I agreed with the decision."

"We caught him." Shane's voice vibrated with suppressed anger. "It's not our fault they couldn't hold him."

Tessa unconsciously touched his hand, instantly realized her mistake and snatched it back. "The money is the least of our worries. What if he follows us here?"

Ten minutes ago all she'd cared about was the reward money. This news had her caring more about saving her own hide. She'd given the Fultons two reasons for tracking her down: she'd serve as bait for Emmett, and they'd have their revenge as well.

Her hands trembled and she balled her fingers into tight fists. She had no desire to experience Fulton revenge.

The marshal kicked back in his seat. "Without the reward, there's no way the Fultons can trace the money back here. You're sheltered in that regard."

"I suppose that's something," Tessa muttered. The men gaped at her. "That's good for us. For both of us," she amended.

Talk about a tangled web. If only her father had been a cook or blacksmith or a farmer. Something simple and ordinary. At least Mr. McCoy and the children were safe. Dead Eye was much more likely to connect the dots between her disappearance and his capture than a handsome widower and his children passing through Wichita.

"I have some contacts," the marshal said. "People I trust. I'll put out the word, see if we can track them."

"I'd appreciate that," Shane replied.

Her slim hope of ever living openly as Tessa Spencer evaporated like the mist. Here she'd been twiddling her thumbs while searching for Emmett, thinking he'd fix his problem and solve hers as well. No more. She had to disappear. Really disappear. Not this skulking about, hoping for the best. She'd go so deep into hiding, not even Emmett could find her. She'd become an entirely new person, with a new name and a new identity, someone no one would suspect.

She'd worry about honesty and good deeds later. Staying alive was a key factor in accomplishing those tasks anyway.

She tipped back her head. "Why are You doing this to me? I'm trying. I'm really, really trying."

You'd think there'd be a little more grace and a little less punishment for those folks who put in the effort. Why did it always seem the dreadful people of the world like Dead Eye always landed on their feet like spry cats, whereas she'd only tried to right a wrong and tumbled right off the ledge and into the abyss? Even Emmett had a talent for squeezing out of difficult situations, and he wasn't exactly a saintly figure.

The marshal frowned. "Who are you talking to?"

"God," Tessa replied with an apologetic wave toward the ceiling.

Railing against God probably wasn't the best solution. Clearly she had more work to do on her spiritual training.

Shane followed her gaze upward. "Does He answer?"

"Yes." Tessa grimaced. "Only His answers are very perplexing."

The lawman didn't appear shocked by her outburst, which was something at least. In his profession, he'd probably seen far more unusual things than a woman talking to the ceiling.

"Do you mind sticking around for a moment?" The marshal straightened. "Shane and I have another matter to clear up as long as he's here."

"Don't give me a second thought," she replied gingerly, ignoring his piercing stare.

He was making excuses to hold her here, no doubt, waiting her out in case she collapsed into hysteria. Which she had no plans on doing. She was made of sterner stuff. Emmett hadn't raised a wilting flower. She might have drooped a touch, but she definitely wasn't wilting.

Hugging her arms over her chest, she stood, crossed the short distance and stared out the window. Towns had personalities, the same as people. This one screamed *respectability*! The boardwalks had been swept clean of snow, lethal icicles had been chipped from the eaves and black smoke pumped merrily from the chimneys. Emmett had never lingered in towns like this. Respectability made him nervous. Perhaps that was why Shane had been so cold once they'd reached town. Maybe he sensed she didn't belong.

Which begged the question—where *did* she belong?

Since arriving on the train, she'd known there was no way of watching the children without attracting unwanted attention. Her previous hunch had been correct; she was too young and too, well, too unattached. She'd spent twenty minutes escaping an interrogation from Mrs. Stuart in the mercantile yesterday. Even arriving on the same train with Shane had piqued the woman's curiosity.

The marshal focused his attention on Shane. "How's that mare? The one that ran into the barbed wire?"

Letting the conversation ebb and flow behind her, Tessa formulated a new plan. First, she'd take on an assumed name. While the subterfuge went against everything she'd fought for, in order to live an honest life, she had to remain alive. Even God had to understand that. Next, she needed an income. She'd checked the board outside the church the day of her arrival, but the only listings were for cattle hands and train workers. Neither of which was suitable. She wasn't returning to Wichita with Dead Eye on the loose, and the next larger city was even farther away. She was counting her pennies already.

"Shane, you're wound up tighter than an eight-day watch," the marshal said. He indicated the fresh blanket of snow outside his window. "You'll end up frozen in a snowdrift if you insist on traveling in this weather."

"It's not so bad," Shane said.

"Jo is worried."

"About the children?" Shane scooted forward. "What's wrong?"

Tessa's attention perked.

"They're fine," the marshal said. "It's you she's worried about."

Rubbing his forehead with the heel of his hand, Shane slumped back. "Jo's got no cause for worry."

"Don't do this to yourself," the marshal continued.

"The kids miss you. Of course they do. They'll get used to the change. You might as well let them adjust now. When the weather turns ugly, you won't be able to make the trip anyway. We all know that. Things will all work out. You'll see."

The space between them thrummed with emotion. Tessa held her tongue for a full minute before blurting, "What do you mean the kids miss you?"

The two men blinked.

Shane spoke first. "The marshal and his wife, my cousin, are watching the twins over the winter."

"You didn't keep them with you?"

"You said I was a good father." He stared at his clasped hands. "I'm trying to be. They're better off this way, with people who can give them attention. This is my solution. It's for the best. Better than Mrs. Lund, that's for certain." His startling admission ignited a flurry of self-recriminations. All this time she'd thought she'd done something wrong, that he was annoyed with her or, worse yet, embarrassed by her. Even with his face averted, she sensed his guilt.

A tumble of comforting words balanced on the tip of her tongue and she held them there, hugging herself tighter. He didn't want or need her pity. Having faced tough times herself, she knew the frustration of trite phrases and meaningless assurances.

Why hadn't she listened closer before? What had the marshal said? Something about the weather. And Shane *did* look exhausted.

Tessa's thoughts raced. Instead of running again, what if she stayed put? The town was far and gone from all the Fultons' usual haunts. Dead Eye would stand out like a sore thumb around here.

"Mrs. Lund was not a good choice," Tessa agreed. Perhaps Agnes would consider letting her stay on at the boardinghouse full-time. There'd be no changing her name, the cat was already out of the bag, but she'd worry about that minor detail later. "Anyone can see you only want to do the right thing."

"It's a big change." He heaved a sigh. "We're all doing our best."

Her stomach rumbled, and she pressed one hand over the noise. The boardinghouse provided a nice breakfast and lunch, but she'd been hoarding the bread and cheese for the next leg of her journey. Though she'd counted on the reward money, she'd also been prepared for a hasty exit. Another one of Emmett's rules: hope for the best, and plan for the worst. If she ever saw him again, she'd thank him for all the excellent advice.

Right after she read him the riot act.

She recalled the reason she was in the marshal's office in the first place and her optimism faded. She couldn't put these kind people in danger.

The door Cora had disappeared into earlier opened once more and Owen and Alyce raced through. They caught sight of Tessa and charged. A wave of pure longing sprang forth. With a shriek she knelt and gathered them into her arms.

Cora followed close behind. "I tried to stop them, but when they found out Tessa was here, they were determined."

"It's all right," Shane said. "I planned on fetching them after the marshal said his piece."

"I've missed you," Tessa squealed in delight. "Have you been keeping busy?"

Owen held out his hand. "My ball."

"Yes, your ball." Tessa beamed at Shane. "That's two words together."

His grin was tinged with pride. "He started that just yesterday."

Alyce patted the ribbon at Tessa's neck. "Pretty."

Tessa's eyes burned. She'd been away from them for only a few days, and already they'd changed. They'd changed but they remembered her. She couldn't recall a time when someone had greeted her with such unabashed joy.

She scooped them close and laughed, then glanced at Shane and her smile faded. She'd never seen a man more crushed, more defeated. Being separated from his children was obviously tearing him apart, and her heart went out to him.

Though they were little more than strangers, she'd give anything to take away that pain, even for a moment. He reminded her of Emmett, making all the wrong choices for all the right reasons. Trying his best in a bewildering situation. While she assumed the marshal and his wife were good people, clearly the twins belonged with their father.

Cora planted her hands on her hips. "Shane, what you need is a wife. Why don't you send away for one of them mail-order brides like the blacksmith did a few years ago? I've never seen that man smile so much since he got hitched."

Marriage.

Tessa smothered a gasp. How had she overlooked

such an obvious solution? She'd been so wrapped up in the details that she hadn't seen the broader picture. The most obvious solution had been sitting right in front of her all along. Like it or not, the only guarantee of respectability was marriage.

The edge of her ledger protruded from her satchel. The project was a lifetime of work. Instead of piecemeal efforts, what if one grand good deed erased all the other entries?

The idea took hold and gained shape. She'd have everything she ever wanted: security, safety and, best of all, anonymity. Well, everything but authenticity. Her past must be left in the past.

Owen touched the locket at her throat, fascinated by the shiny metal. The twins seemed genuinely fond of her. They adored her in the way only children could, without artifice of expectations. She envisioned their future in light of their current arrangement, shuttled from family to family, always searching for a place where they belonged. Memories of her own childhood returned with an unsettling jolt. They deserved better.

Although this was hardly a perfect solution for all of them, it was the best one she could think of. What other choices did any of them have? She glanced at Shane and a curious sensation passed through her, a gentle warmth, like the heat of the sun shining through a glass windowpane.

She'd learned his wife had passed away almost six months before. How much did he miss her? What would he think of such a suggestion? She sensed an unyielding resolution about him. Most folks took the easy way of things, drifting along like flotsam. Not Shane. He hadn't given up his children because that was the easy way out; he'd given them up because he felt it was the right thing to do.

What of her own situation? This was a clean slate. A new start. They were strangers with no preconceived notions about each other. He was a kind man, and she was a good person at heart. She'd simply never had the opportunity for demonstrating her better qualities.

There was only one little snag in her plan. Unlike the children, Shane definitely didn't adore her. She wasn't certain if he even liked her. Then again, he was a widower, and no one expected him to fall at her feet. They only needed to get along. She'd seen too much of the darker side of human nature to harbor any hope of a fairy-tale ending anyway.

"Find yourself a wife, Shane," Cora declared. "I'm brilliant. A mail-order bride solves all your problems."

Cora was brilliant, all right. The idea was as inspired as it was obvious.

All Tessa had to do was convince a virtual stranger to spend the rest of his life with her.

Brilliant indeed.

Alyce tugged on Shane's pant leg, and he hoisted her into his arms.

The marshal shook his head. "Leave Shane alone, Cora. He doesn't want to marry a stranger."

"You did."

Garrett's ears flamed. "I knew your mother. She wasn't a stranger. She was from town."

Shane had never seen the marshal shaken, but Garrett sure looked shaken now. Wondering if Tessa was enjoying the exchange as well, Shane grinned at her, but her expression was distant and shuttered, as though she was puzzling out some great difficulty.

"Yes, Mama was from town." Cora rolled her eyes. "But you weren't. You'd only been here a few months. You barely knew her."

"I knew her well enough," Garrett muttered, his scarlet ears turning even redder. "You've been listening to rumors again, haven't you?"

"Mrs. Stuart does ramble on," Cora continued. "But that doesn't mean getting married isn't the perfect solution. Shane is quite a catch. Any lady would be privileged to have him. Let's put his picture on the church bulletin boards in Wichita."

"No." Instantly panicked, Shane broke into the conversation. He figured his ears matched the marshal's right about now. "No one is putting my picture anywhere. Ever."

Agitated by his raised voice, Alyce hugged his neck. Shane tickled her stomach until she grinned. Taking good-natured enjoyment from the marshal's discomfort was one thing; hearing Cora talk about him as "a catch" was a whole different matter.

Garrett scrubbed his hand down his face. "Your mother and I didn't know each other very well, I'll admit that. But not everyone can be as fortunate."

Shane's amusement faded, and their friendly quarrel disappeared into the background. Alyce was staring at him with her wise, solemn eyes, and his whole chest ached. Freezing in a snowdrift didn't seem so bad if it meant seeing the children. Even if he saw them only once a week. Even if he didn't get a full night's rest until they were full-grown. He was used to hardship.

Cora's voice grew exasperated. "Maybe if Shane left the ranch once in a while, he might have more options. Except for that trip to Wichita, he doesn't go anywhere. How's he supposed to meet anyone around here? Miss Spencer is the only new single female we've had in town in months."

A strangled noise sounded from Tessa's direction, and Shane kept his attention averted. Cora was three for three—she'd mortified all the adults in the room.

The marshal ushered his daughter toward the back of his office once more. "This conversation is over. We'd best check on that coffee and find your mother. Can't leave the stove unattended." He motioned for Shane. "Bring the kids by the house when you're ready." He touched his forehead. "Miss Spencer, it was a pleasure meeting you. Let me know if I can be of any further assistance during your stay."

The door closed resolutely behind them.

While grateful the awkward conversation was at an end, Shane didn't relish being alone with Tessa after that mortifying exchange.

She craned her neck, following their hasty retreat. "What is behind that door, anyway?"

"A jail cell and stairs to an apartment on the second level. The marshal keeps the space closed off unless there's a prisoner. The deputy lives upstairs when there's an inmate overnight."

Cora's words rang in his ears. Tessa was definitely the only single female they'd had in town in a while. He almost laughed out loud before catching himself. Even if she didn't have one foot out the door, she'd never settle for someone like him. She was too smart and too pretty for a lonely widower who lived on an isolated ranch with nothing but a bunch of uncouth men for company.

All the same reasons she couldn't watch the children. Mrs. Stuart at the mercantile had practically tackled him when he'd stepped off the train with Tessa by his side. No doubt the old busybody had been watching them like a hawk, searching for any sign of impropriety.

At least Tessa didn't appear shocked by the Cains' ribbing. Their candor could be disconcerting. He shook his head. The idea was crazy. Out of the question. He'd already got married once for the sake of the children. What kind of fool made the same mistake twice? Clearly he wasn't marriage material. As for sending away for a bride, who in their right mind would come all this way to marry a man sight unseen? The idea was ludicrous.

Tessa perched on a chair and lifted Owen into her lap. "I was starting to think that door had mysterious properties."

Shane chuckled. "JoBeth, the marshal's wife, comes in through the back as well. It's a shortcut from the telegraph office where she works. She must be around here someplace. The kids didn't make that walk alone. She's probably upstairs."

Voices and footsteps rumbled overhead, and a welter of emotions swirled around him. He envied the Cains' easy camaraderie and close-knit family. After his father left, he'd quit school and supported his mother by working as a cattle hand. A man's job that hadn't left him much time for anything but eating and sleeping.

Following his mother's death, he'd worked even

harder, saving up money for his own place. That was all he'd ever known—work and responsibilities. The kids were the best thing that had ever happened to him. They deserved a childhood. Although he supposed most folks didn't think about such frivolous things, having surrendered his own youth, he wanted more for them.

A burst of laughter from overhead filtered through the vents. The Cains liked each other and enjoyed spending time together. Sometimes they tried to pull him into their antics, like this afternoon, but he always kept a distance. Even when his family had been together, they'd never shared that sort of lighthearted connection, and he wasn't certain how to fit in.

He caught sight of Owen and grimaced.

The boy had turned away, making an exaggerated point of ignoring Shane. Of the two children, Owen had taken the change the hardest. He'd been sullen and withdrawn since the move. While understandable, his rejection still hurt.

Owen glared. "Want Scout."

The demand had Shane shuffling his feet. "He's at home. I'll bring him for a visit next time."

Tessa glanced between the two. "Who is Scout?"

"A horse." Visiting Scout each morning had been part of their daily routine since before Owen could walk. He'd even had his own currycomb and took great pride in brushing the feathered hair above the animal's hooves. Over seventeen hands high, the enormous draft horse had taken a shine to Owen as well and always remained docile beneath his ministration. "Owen wasn't happy about leaving him behind."

That was an understatement. Shane briefly closed his eyes against the memory of the boy's pitiful sobs.

Tessa pressed a hand against her stomach, and Shane recalled the rumblings he'd heard earlier.

He'd been almost rude with her before. The decision to leave Alyce and Owen with the Cains had weighed heavily on him, and he hadn't been very good company on the train ride back or even today, for that matter.

In an effort to atone for his previous behavior, he asked, "Have you eaten yet?"

She glanced up. "Not yet."

He studied Tessa's upturned face and his gut knotted. Lines of tension framed her mouth and dark circles showed beneath her eyes. He recalled the trunk he'd seen in the haberdashery window and realized why the familiar-looking luggage had caught his eye. She must be pawning her belongings. Most telling of all, she'd been frantic about the reward this morning when she'd been hesitant about the money before. Those hints might have clued him in earlier if he hadn't been wrapped up in his own concerns.

Tessa was obviously short on funds.

She'd been adamant about leaving town as soon as the reward arrived. What was she going to do now? What were her plans for the future? Forcing his questions aside, he reached for his coat.

Curiosity was holding up what needed to be done. "Join me for lunch at the hotel. I could use a bite." Actually, he'd eaten an hour ago. "I insist. You can fill me in on the gossip from town."

Owen had practically attached himself to Tessa. Most likely she'd be gone soon, another disappointment for the boy, yet he couldn't deny them their visit. At least the twins were smiling for once. All three of them had been more somber than usual lately. The finality of their situation had left Shane troubled and distracted. Assisting someone else was the perfect way to take his mind off his worries.

"Um," Tessa began. "There is one small matter I'd like to discuss over lunch."

Chapter Five

Alyce and Owen were bundled into their coats and Shane assisted Tessa with hers. After a quick scurry down the boardwalk, their heads bent against the wind, the hotel dining room was warm and inviting with the mouthwatering aroma of fried chicken filling the air. Chairs were quickly arranged and orders placed.

Tessa rested her hands on either side of her plate and straightened her silverware. "The marshal and his wife, are they happy?"

Rolling his eyes, Shane said, "Sickeningly so."

He laughed and Tessa's mood lightened. She'd tread carefully. This was an extremely delicate situation and she must present her solution with the utmost care. If she structured the conversation correctly, he might even make the suggestion himself. Another one of Emmett's handy tricks.

Shane removed his hat and threaded his fingers through his hair. "JoBeth's courtship was the talk of the town some years back. Garrett and JoBeth married after the marshal accepted guardianship of his niece,

Cora. She calls them Mom and Dad now, which seems fitting enough. It's a tough job, being the only parent. Around these parts, marriages are arranged for practical reasons as often as not."

Excellent. His story fit her plan perfectly. Already he must be thinking about the two of them together. Cora had set the wheels in motion by mentioning mail-order brides and the fact that Tessa was the only single woman available. Soon he'd put the pieces together and catch the drift of her thoughts.

"People get married for all sorts of reasons, you say." She nodded slowly, her eyes locked with his. "Like caring for children?"

He rubbed his chest as though something pained him. "Yep."

Well, that wasn't a good sign. He didn't appear to comprehend her meaning at all. He looked as if he had indigestion. "You must miss the children terribly. Not being able to see them every day. If only there was another way."

Surely that was obvious enough. She was dropping all the hints she could think of. Giving him every opportunity to realize she was open to his offer.

"Owen and Alyce love the Cains," he said quietly. "And certainly Jo and Garrett are excellent guardians, but nothing replaces seeing them every day."

Tessa drummed her fingers. Perhaps if she approached this from another direction. "And you can't possibly hire anyone because folks will gossip."

"Exactly."

"I thought before…" She inhaled deeply. "On the trip back from Wichita, the children and I did well together."

Maybe if she backed up the conversation and reminded him of the time they'd spent together already, he'd catch the drift of her thoughts. Once he recalled the past, maybe he'd look to the future.

He fumbled for the coffee mug the server had set before him. "You did real fine with them."

Though she'd never been around small children before, they'd got along well. There'd been the usual tantrums and spills. She'd even scolded Owen and he hadn't appeared to hold it against her. Children didn't seem to hold grudges.

Owen teetered and Tessa instinctively steadied him. Yep. She was definitely developing her instincts with the children.

She folded her hands before her. "And we got along well, too, didn't we?"

"You know I'd hire you in an instant," he blurted. "After meeting Mrs. Stuart, you can understand the difficulties. I won't let you endure that sort of gossip. That doesn't mean you can't see them as often as you want."

"Don't misunderstand me," she added quickly. "I realize now how impossible it would be for you to hire me as a housekeeper."

"Exactly," he declared. "I couldn't put you in that situation. There'd be talk. There's always talk. You're a fine-looking woman."

A jolt of pure feminine pleasure surprised her.

She'd never much thought about her looks one way or the other before. Discreetly rubbing her damp palms against her skirts, she caught sight of Owen and Alyce peacefully rearranging their table settings. Those two never got along for this long.

Shane jolted upright. "You need money, don't you? I should have realized that sooner. What with losing out on the reward and all. You just have to ask. I'm happy to help."

Tessa nearly pounded her fists on the table. He'd picked up on the clues, all right. The wrong clues. "I don't want to borrow money from you. I want to help out with the children. But not as your housekeeper."

He frowned. "I can talk to JoBeth. I'm sure she'd appreciate the help."

Nope. He was not catching the drift of her meaning at all. Not even close. Worse yet, they were drifting further off point with every word.

"All three of you get along real well." He rushed ahead before she could say anything else. "Both Owen and Alyce adore you. If you settle here, the Cains will let you visit as often as you like."

"I'd like that." Her knuckles whitened around her own coffee mug. "Sometimes we have to change our plans. Sometimes things don't work out as easily as we think they should."

"No. They don't."

Shane cleared his throat. "I think I know what you're hinting at."

"Excellent." She resisted adding a *hallelujah*. "I was beginning to think we'd be here all day."

"You think I should consider Cora's suggestion."

"Yes!" *Finally.* At last they were on the right track.

"I can't send for a mail-order bride," he declared forcefully. "Even for the children. I know you're all trying to help. I appreciate it. Truly, I do. But it's out of the question." Owen tipped a cup and he lunged before the liquid spilled. "I'm not really the mail-order bride kind of fellow."

Tessa covered her face with her hands. What did a woman have to do to get a marriage proposal around here? She lowered her hands and sucked in a restorative breath. If he wasn't catching the hints, she'd have to do this herself.

"Why don't we get married?" she declared just as forcefully. They'd be here all afternoon if she waited on Shane to decipher her hints. "We already know each other. Sort of. And you said it yourself before. We each have something the other needs." Before he could speak, she rushed ahead. "No one could take the place of your first wife, I'm sure."

Something flashed across his face, an emotion she couldn't read. "I wouldn't expect anyone to."

"It's what you said before," Tessa went on, relieved they were at least finally speaking on the same topic. "Things are different out West. Marriages are arranged for practical reasons. We're simply being practical."

"I just want to get this straight," he said, not appearing at all eager. "You're saying we ought to get married? You and me?"

Her enthusiasm deflated, and she pressed two fingers against her temple. This had seemed much more logical back in the marshal's office. Sitting here before Shane, trying to think of a good way to convince him that she was the perfect choice for a bride, nothing seemed clear. What qualifications did she have? She could pick a pocket and spot a cardsharp from across the room. Not necessarily what most men were looking for in a bride.

Now that the words were out, her courage fled. Covering her unease, she snapped, "Of course you and me!"

"You caught me off guard." Shane forced the pent-up air from his lungs, remembering to breathe. "Just making sure. You see, um, you said you had a small matter you'd like to discuss."

"Yes. Marriage."

"I think I see the problem," he replied, still feeling a bit dazed. "Maybe next time you should say that you have something important to discuss rather than something small. That way I'm prepared."

For a moment she appeared annoyed, but her expression quickly shifted to one of uncertainty. The sudden change left him even more confused.

Tessa sighed and studied the tines on her fork as though they were the most fascinating things on earth. "When Cora spoke of mail-order brides before, I couldn't help but think about the children."

"The children?" He was still catching up with the conversation. And who could blame him? Usually when someone wanted to discuss a small matter, they meant a broken heel on a shoe or an overdue bill at the boardinghouse.

Something small.

A marriage proposal was not a small matter.

"Clearly they're better off with their father," Tessa said. "They're better off with the person who loves them most." Her eyes took on a misty appeal. "This all must be very confusing for them. Losing their mother, moving from the only home they've ever known."

Her reasoning put him at ease. She liked the children. Maybe it was because they were twins that they had that effect on people. But was affection for Alyce and Owen enough for a lifetime together? He'd been down this road before with disastrous results.

Her too-pale lips pinched together. "I realize we haven't known each other very long, and this is an enormous decision, but I really think we could make this work."

While he was busy reeling from the unexpected announcement, she'd obviously thought through the details already. Any man would jump at the offer, himself included. Except he didn't want her making a lifelong decision because she was backed into a corner. He didn't want her to do something she'd regret later.

His collar had grown alarmingly tight, and he tugged on his string tie. Adding the minutes together, they'd known each other only a matter of hours, and yet he'd known Abby for most of his childhood and still managed to marry a stranger.

"We could make a list—" her voice quivered "—of all the reasons for and against the marriage."

She had the look of a wide-eyed doe, softly innocent, ready to flee at the least disturbance. She'd been strong and brave since the moment he'd met her, and he'd never considered how much energy that courage cost her. For a woman on her own, harassment from men like Dead Eye must be all too familiar. He felt her desperation as though her plea had taken on a physical presence. If he refused, if he turned her away, where would she go next? Because of his interference with the outlaw, she appeared more frightened than ever.

"Like I said before, you caught me off guard." A

fierce need to shelter her from harm welled up inside him, and he stalled for time. "It's not a bad idea. Unexpected, sure. But not crazy."

These past few days without the children had been miserable. Being together again was right and good, the way things were supposed to be. He desperately wanted that feeling back. He wanted the same peace he'd felt the first time he'd held Alyce and Owen in his arms nearly two years ago. There was only one problem. He didn't want that peace at the price of someone else's misery.

Snared in his memories, the quiet stretched out.

Tessa held out her locket for Owen's fascinated inspection, and Shane marveled at the silky lashes sweeping against her cheeks, the delicate translucency of her eyelids and the brilliance of her hair catching a shaft of afternoon sun.

She broke the silence, jarring him from his musing.

"What?" he asked. "I didn't catch that."

"I should go," she said. "I've kept you too long."

"We don't need a list." Her hesitant uncertainty spurred him into action. "After thinking things through, getting married is the best solution."

He wasn't exactly a silver-tongued charmer. Tessa deserved a proper courting, but that wasn't in the cards. He didn't have the time or the skills. Best not to give her false hope anyway. He'd begin this relationship as he meant to go on. He was a practical man and this was a practical decision.

"Are you certain?" Tessa asked softly, a heartbreaking note of doubt in her voice.

"I'd ask you the same. It's a hard life. Be sure you

know the bargain you're making. They'll catch those outlaws sooner or later. You'll see."

No regrets. If they agreed to this marriage, he wanted no regrets for either of them.

He didn't doubt her abilities or her resolve. She wasn't weak, not by a long shot. He'd eaten in Harvey House restaurants plenty of times during his travels. He'd seen waitresses lift trays that would bend a grown man. Though she was little more than a slip of a thing, she'd taken care of herself well enough up until now. It wasn't her fault she'd attracted the notice of Dead Eye.

Owen wrapped his arms around Tessa's neck and snuggled close.

She had an effortless, nurturing quality about her that left him curious about her past. "Do you have brothers and sisters? Family?"

Why wasn't someone looking out for her? He'd settled in Cimarron Springs because of his family. His aunt was the closest thing he had to a mother with his own gone. His uncle, guilty about his brother abandoning the family, had taken it upon himself to fill in the empty space. Though their attention was occasionally stifling, he appreciated their concern.

"No brothers or sisters, I'm afraid." Tessa's smile was strained. "I'm an only child. My mother died when I was eight. My father raised me after that. He's not around anymore." Her gaze skittered away. "That's all there is to know about me."

Shane very much doubted that. Her face had got that shuttered look once more, and he didn't press her any further. There'd be time enough for them to get to know one another later. A lifetime.

The thread between them was fragile, and he feared one wrong word might snap the delicate connection. "You can change your mind, you know."

"I know." She rested her cheek on Owen's head and sighed. "This is about something different."

In the first months of his marriage, he'd wondered about the man who'd abandoned Abby. The man who'd made her so miserable, she'd wasted away from the heartbreak. He didn't think about it anymore, because thinking didn't change anything and only made the hurting worse. He didn't care beyond a lingering sadness for what might have been.

Something weighty and ragged settled in his chest. "I don't want you making a mistake you can't take back."

"You're not a mistake, Mr. McCoy."

"Shane," he said, his throat working. "Call me Shane."

The last time he'd plunged into a marriage, he'd been confident that friendship would turn into love. Never again. He'd go about things differently this time. With this marriage, he'd keep his distance, treat the relationship as a partnership in the business. He'd give her space instead of stifling her.

He wouldn't give either of them a reason for regrets.

Her eyes grew unfocused and looked beyond him. "My father raised me after my mother died. Just him alone. I know the challenge. I'm well aware of the sacrifice."

The distant look in her eyes returned. Already she was shutting him out. He bent his head. At least this time there were no surprises.

"Cimarron Springs is a nice town, but it's small," he

said. His initial impression of her came rushing back. In another life, she might have been the tea-sipping heiress. Fate had left her in a far different situation. She hadn't given up yet, and he admired her pluck. "There's not much excitement around these parts."

"I've had all the excitement I can stand in one lifetime." Her gaze turned intense. "I've lived everywhere, Shane. Just once I'd like to live *somewhere*. I want to feel safe."

Owen slapped his hands on the table, rattling the dishes. "Ga."

Tessa smiled. "Even Owen agrees."

She was more than he deserved. How could he explain that his hesitation had sprung from his own unsuitability, not hers? At least they'd have the twins between them. Her affection for the children had obviously instigated her precipitous suggestion. Though he lauded her compassion, someday Owen and Alyce would be grown and gone, and there'd be only the two of them. What then? Would they have enough in common after the years to survive the loss of what had brought them together in the first place?

"You're certain?" he asked.

Her chin came up a notch. "There's one thing you should know about me. Once I make up my mind, I don't change it. I'll feel the same in a day, a week, a month and a year. There's no reason to wait."

The twins, normally full of energy and chatter, were oddly, blissfully quiet. Their silence gave him the opportunity for reflection. Too much opportunity. Just once he wished for a little noise. A tantrum or another spill.

For this union to work, he required Tessa's unfailing loyalty, which meant giving his in return. "This isn't just about finding a caretaker for the children. I want this to be a partnership. My ranch is doing well, growing. I need someone I can build a life with."

Growing bashful, she smoothed Owen's hair. "I don't know much about running a household."

"We'll take things slow. Real slow." He might have been married before, but he'd wager he knew even less about being a husband than Tessa knew about being a wife. This time, though, neither of them would have any false expectations. "We'll figure out the relationship together. There's no need for love or any of that nonsense gumming up the works."

There. He'd said it. There'd be no awkward scenes like the one with Abby. Her last words to him rang in his ears. *I tried to love you—really, I did.* He wondered if his father had thought the same thing. Had he tried to love his only child, but simply couldn't?

"No need at all," Tessa scoffed. "Love. Really? I shudder at the thought."

He ignored his unexpected shock of disappointment. "Absolutely. We'll have something that's better—mutual respect."

This was going well. He'd set the expectations. There were no secrets, no false hopes. Only an agreement between two people brought together by fate. He'd finally be in control of his own destiny, not pushed along by forces outside his control. He should have felt powerful. Instead, he felt hollow. Empty.

"Yes," she agreed with a faint, polite inclination of her head. "Respect. That's far, far better."

"We should shake on it."

"Shake?"

He stuck out his hand. "Yeah. We'll shake on it. Like a true business deal."

She clasped his fingers and his resolve immediately disintegrated. Everything about her was soft, gentle and unintentionally inviting. From the touch of her hand to the curve of her cheek, she embodied all that was feminine. A good mother for the children, she was everything they needed, everything they'd been lacking in their short lives. She was loyal, he sensed that, and he owed her loyalty in return. He'd made her a promise and he'd keep that promise. They could be business partners, all right, as long as they never touched.

Two people, living in close quarters in the middle of nowhere, never touching. That shouldn't be too difficult, right?

He lifted his gaze to the window and groaned. He'd been so focused on Tessa, he'd missed the fat snowflakes sheeting before the window. The ominous haze that had been hanging in the air had finally broken loose in a squall. If this weather continued, they'd be snowed in before long. He'd run out of time already. It wasn't unusual for a foot or more of snow to fall in a day. He'd find out soon enough if Tessa had spoken truthfully about her resolve.

She followed his gaze and gasped. "Oh my. When did that start?"

"I'm sorry—truly, I am," he said. "That weather changes everything. I can't afford to be stranded in town. I have to stay ahead of that weather. I'll come back with the next thaw. If you're…if you're still here. If you haven't changed your mind."

They'd been granted an unexpected reprieve. Why, then, was this irrational panic welling in his chest?

"Today." She spoke with gritty determination. "There's no reason for waiting. I'll leave with you today."

Shane's heartbeat thundered in his ears. Now which one of them had lost their nerve? "There'll be no going back."

She leaned forward, her earnest gaze pinning him in place. "I'm ready to start over. Now. Today. There's no reason to wait any longer. I'll be a good wife to you, I promise. I've taken care of my father for years. I'll be a good mother to the children. You wanted a partnership, and that's what I'm offering you. We both know what we expect from each other."

Doubts clung to his resolve like cobwebs. He didn't want her regrets turning into resentment. "And what is it you expect of me?"

Her eyes glittered and he unconsciously took her hand once more. She squeezed his fingers. "I don't want to be afraid anymore. We barely know one another, but you make me feel safe. I haven't felt that way in a very, very long time."

As though the confession had cost her, all the fight drained out of her.

His determination crystallized. He tucked two fingers beneath her chin and gently forced her to meet his steady gaze. "I'll keep you safe, I promise."

Her lovely, expressive eyes wreaked havoc with his senses. She should have been nestled safely away in a warm house, with someone looking out for her. He could do that much for her at least.

The weather outside gave him an idea. From now until Christmas he'd give her plenty of space. That way, if she eventually decided they didn't suit and she wanted to leave him, she wouldn't feel beholden.

He doubted she expected anything different. She'd wanted only safety.

Safety...the one thing he could offer her. He only hoped that would be enough for a lifetime, because that was all he had to give.

Chapter Six

"You look like a tea person. Am I right?" JoBeth McCoy, the marshal's wife, squinted at Tessa.

Tessa waved away the tin. "Tea is far too extravagant."

Everything was moving at a wonderfully brisk pace—the preparations, the wedding, even Jo's rapid-fire speech. Tessa hadn't gathered a breath since she'd agreed on marrying Shane within the hour. Things were definitely different out West, as she was quickly learning. Without batting an eye, Shane's family had sprung into action. They hadn't seemed shocked by the announcement at all.

Cora had even winked. *Winked.* She'd deliberately dropped those hints about marriage. Although someone should tell the poor girl that Shane was oblivious to hints. Tessa sighed inwardly. The whole town had clearly been trying to marry off the widower, and Tessa was, as Cora had so bluntly stated, the only new single woman in town in ages. They'd obviously exhausted all the other possibilities.

Ignoring her refusal of the tea, Jo stuffed the tin into the crate before the counter. "Never underestimate the edifying powers of small luxuries."

A twinge of guilt nagged Tessa. She should have waited out the weather, given Shane more time. Except whenever he was near, the heavy weight on her chest eased. For the first time since she'd parted ways from Emmett, she felt as though she could take a full breath. The sensation was heady, intoxicating.

She'd give their relationship until Christmas to take hold. If Shane was still indifferent to her by then, she'd reassess the situation. Although she didn't plan on giving him any reason to be indifferent.

She'd be a good wife, a good mother. She was a quick learner, and she'd figure things out along the way. "Never mind the tea. Tea is a waste of money."

"You'll thank me later." The dark-haired woman gestured out the window. "We don't have much time. The boys are meeting us at the church in twenty minutes. I'm guessing you won't be back in town for another few weeks. Maybe a month. Better be quick about your purchases."

"I don't even know where to begin." The boxes and cans blurred together in one overwhelming mass.

While she'd taken care of all the purchases with Emmett, she'd never taken care of little ones before. "I'm not certain what I'll need. What the children will need."

"That's why I'm here," Jo said brusquely. "Why don't you pick out a nice shawl? Something special for the wedding since there isn't time to change."

She steered Tessa toward an out-of-the-way display of fabrics and continued shopping. Tessa grimaced.

Clearly Jo didn't want or need her help. Probably for the best—she was only slowing down the process. Though she hadn't lied about her resolve before, she was still adjusting to the abrupt change. The inclement weather had sent everyone into a flurry of activity that left her little time to think.

The preacher had been fetched, Shane had ordered the horses hitched and the marshal had returned home for the twins' belongings. The bustle hadn't given her any chance for second thoughts or regrets. She only hoped Shane felt the same. The intense look on his face had worried her.

A book caught her attention and she touched the faded cover. *Bartleby's Encyclopedia of Household Management.* On impulse, she snatched the heavy volume and added it to her purchases. If Bartleby had written that tome, he must know a whole lot more about household management than she did. Caring for her and Emmett was one thing, but she had two children counting on her as well.

A gust of snowflakes and a blast of frigid air signaled the arrival of another customer. Marshal Cain appeared, his hat dusted with snow.

He shook off the flakes and grinned. "The wagon is hitched, the kids are packed and Shane is waiting at the church. How are you two doing?"

"Almost ready," Jo said brusquely. "Walk Tessa over and I'll join you in a tick."

Her nerves drew taut and Tessa hesitated. "I should stay and help."

Jo marched over, carrying a heap of crocheted items crafted in a cheerful emerald green. "You'll need these as well. Mrs. Edwards makes the warmest hats and mittens. That piece of felt you're wearing won't offer much protection in this weather."

Touching the brim of her sad little bonnet, Tessa acknowledged the thin material. "It was the warmest hat I own."

Her winter wardrobe had been designed for a brisk walk from a train station to a hotel or a quick scamper across a crowded street. She'd never had to choose clothing for anything more rigorous than a short dash.

"Don't worry." Jo filled her arms with the woolens. "You'll be fine. I'll take care of everything."

"Are you certain?" Tessa asked, hoping they hadn't caught the wobble in her voice.

The marshal drew his wife into his arms and kissed her forehead, then turned toward Tessa. "Leave the supplies to Jo. She knows what you'll need better than anyone."

At their affectionate display, Tessa stifled a sigh. How she missed the warmth of companionship. She'd always considered herself independent. These past few months had taught her the difference between independence and solitude.

With a resolute nod, Tessa wrapped the emerald green scarf around her throat and replaced her felt bonnet with her new cap.

A young boy hovering over the penny candy caught her attention. Tessa snapped her fingers and the boy cast a guilty look over his shoulder. The temptation of the penny candy was no match for the sight of the marshal's tall figure by her side. The boy stuffed his hands in his pockets and scurried away.

The marshal frowned down at her. "What was that all about?"

"Saving him from himself, that's all. Everyone needs a reminder about right and wrong now and again." Although some people clearly never got the message. "It's best to turn them young, before they can get into any real trouble."

Before they became caught up in the thrill of danger and lost sight of good and bad altogether.

"Ah, sticky fingers." The marshal nodded sagely. "I'll keep my eye on him."

She'd recognized the boy's look well enough. She'd seen the slightly glazed longing on Emmett's face plenty of times. Over the years she'd gradually realized he loved the game more than the prize. Why he couldn't receive that same thrill from an honest day's work, she'd never know. Life would have been so much simpler for everyone.

As she reached for the door, Jo called out. Tessa whirled around.

"Take this." Jo thrust a cinnamon-colored silk scarf into her outstretched hands. "Something new. We'll figure out the old, borrowed and blue later."

Tessa touched the collar of her dress. "This will serve as something old. And if the temperature drops any lower, my lips will serve as the blue."

"You look lovely." Jo squeezed Tessa's shoulders. "Stop worrying."

"I'm not worried." That was mostly the truth. She wasn't worried, more like uncertain. While she didn't regret her decision, she feared the unknown. "Thank you. For everything."

Her chin trembled and she clenched her jaw. The only opinions Emmett had ever trusted were those of babies and animals. He always said that children and beasts saw the true heart of people and not what was falsely presented on the outside. She'd seen Shane with his children; she'd seen how they adored him. He was an honorable man. Except she wasn't drawn to him only because he was a good man. Her decision was based on far more than his fatherly abilities.

There was a spark between them. She ticked off her self-imposed time frame in her head. She had until Christmas to fan that spark into something beyond companionship. Surely by then the Fulton brothers would have given up on her as well.

The more time they spent together, the more her past would recede. She'd watch it fade into the distance like a departing train. Would Shane do the same? His affection for his first wife obviously ran deep. Could he ever feel that same affection for her?

Jo flipped the dark hair from her forehead. "A few jitters are normal. If this is something more, only say the word. We'll put a stop to this whole event at once."

Though she'd known Jo only a short time, Tessa didn't doubt her words. "No, no. It's not that."

"You'll do well together." Jo placed a reassuring hand on her shoulder. "Take good care of him."

"What if I can't?" she asked in a ragged whisper.

Tessa was grateful when the marshal moved away and studied a display of tinned milk, giving them a moment of privacy.

"You can." Bending her head, Jo spoke quietly. "Be patient with Shane. He's had a rough time these past few years. It's not my place to say, but I don't think life with Abby was easy."

Tessa grasped for an appropriate response, but the marshal interrupted her reply. She had so many questions and yet she feared the answers.

"We'd better go," the marshal said. "This weather isn't letting up, and Shane will be waiting."

With a last glance at the heap of purchases piling up on the counter, Tessa followed him into the frigid afternoon. She sure hoped Shane wasn't angry about all the money she'd spent. She hated starting off their marriage on a bad note. Up until this point, saving money had consisted of what she'd managed to squirrel away beneath her mattress. The only budgeting she'd done had been hiding the surplus from Emmett—his taste ran to the expensive. Life with her father had been a series of ups and downs. He spent money freely when they were flush, and Tessa economized when they weren't.

After stepping outside, the marshal held out his hand. "It's slippery. Be careful."

Clutching his arm, she ducked her head against the howling wind. Snowflakes blurred her vision and she blindly followed his lead. The cold whipped at her legs and a sharp, stinging gust brought tears to her eyes. By the time the marshal escorted her into the warmth of the church, her toes had gone numb. They shuffled into a small vestibule brightened with twin glass lanterns.

The marshal gestured toward his right. "There's a room over there where you can hang up your coat."

The cramped office space was overflowing with books. They were stacked and stuffed on every available space. Considering the variety of subjects, she wondered if the collection served as a sort of library for the town. Cautiously navigating the clutter, she removed her coat and cap and smoothed her hair. Standing on her tiptoes, she checked her reflection in an oval mirror perched on a shelf. At least the wind had whipped some color into her cheeks. She brushed at her skirts before abandoning the effort. The scarf Jo had chosen added a bit of elegance to her outfit.

A soft knock sounded at the door, and Tessa greeted a kindly gray-haired man with pale blue eyes.

"I'm Reverend Miller," he introduced himself with an outstretched hand.

She clasped his fingers in greeting. "Tessa Spencer."

"Are you settling in all right? Is there anything I can get you?"

"I'm fine. Thank you for asking. I appreciate your help on such, um, on such short notice."

He offered a gentle smile. "You have to be ready for anything in this neck of the woods."

"I'm learning that."

He studied her face and she resisted the desire to squirm beneath his piercing scrutiny. After a moment he nodded, as though coming to a decision.

He reached for the door and hesitated. "Shane is a good man."

How many people had said the same? She hoped she was worthy of him. "I know."

He expelled his breath in an audible rush. "I'll see you inside, then. Welcome to Cimarron Springs, Miss Spencer."

Feeling as though she'd passed some sort of test, Tessa followed him out the door. The marshal was patiently waiting for her. He'd removed his hat and heavy coat and his hair had obviously been finger combed into place. While she appreciated his solicitous behavior, she hadn't had a moment alone since they'd set the wedding into motion. She felt as though she was under scrutiny, and any moment they'd discover a flaw.

"Shane is inside with Cora and the children," Marshal Garrett said. "Jo will be here any minute. We'll start the ceremony then."

"All right." She tucked a lock of hair behind one ear. "Thank you for helping to arrange everything."

He nodded. "Life can be tough out here. If you need anything, Jo and I are close."

Feeling a fraud, she stared at the plank wood floor. "You're all being so kind."

They were all loyal to Shane, and she didn't know if she deserved their kindness. When she'd imagined the marriage, she'd pictured the isolated ranch. She hadn't given much thought to Shane's friends and family. What did they think of her? Were they worried?

The marshal circled the brim of his hat with his fingers. "Shane is a grown man. He knows what he's doing."

While his words didn't exactly put her at ease, she appreciated his honesty.

"Since your father isn't here," the marshal continued, "I was wondering if I could have the honor of walking you down the aisle."

Tessa touched her locket and swallowed around the lump in her throat. "Thank you. I'd like that."

The familiar ache took hold once more. Emmett would have enjoyed playing the father of the bride. He had a way of attracting a party even when there was nothing to celebrate. He'd have enjoyed her wedding if only for a new audience to regale with his stories.

Though wary of the lawman, she appreciated his thoughtfulness. She'd listened as the other girls at the Harvey House had waxed poetic about their future wedding days, but she'd never joined in the game. She'd never been one for daydreaming.

The marshal checked his watch and rocked back on his heels. "I did a lot of traveling before I settled in Cimarron Springs. Met a lot of people in that time."

"I imagine your job was very exciting," Tessa offered.

While she preferred the silence, she supposed he thought small talk might pass the time. She glanced over her shoulder. What was taking Jo so long?

The marshal shrugged. "Sometimes it was exciting. Sometimes not. The thing about traveling is that you meet all kinds of folks. I met a fellow named Spencer once. I think his first name was Earl or Edgar or something."

He knew. Tessa jerked her head up and sucked in a sharp, frightened breath. Why else would he mention the name? She searched his face for any sign of condemnation and found none. Pressing her hand against her racing heart, she masked her expression. Perhaps it was a coincidence. There was no reason to assume he knew about her father. Or her.

"Spencer is a common name." She kept her reply deliberately vague and her voice dispassionate.

"I'll never forget him." The marshal rubbed his chin and gazed at the door. "Craziest thing I ever saw. There was a poker game in the saloon and old Frank was in deep to this stranger named Spencer. Frank was a known drinker and a known gambler, but he also had three children and a wife at home, so the regulars had a gentleman's agreement. They steered clear of Frank when he got wound up that way. Only Spencer wasn't exactly obliged to honor that agreement."

"I suppose not."

Her legs grew wobbly and she locked her knees. The story sounded all too familiar. He was almost certainly speaking of Emmett.

Voices sounded from deep in the church and she started. Had the marshal orchestrated a delay to expose her? Why was he toying with her? If he planned on revealing her past before Shane, she wished he'd speed up the story. Or was he simply baiting her? While she hadn't pegged the marshal as a blackmailer, she didn't know him well enough to decipher his motivation.

The marshal gave a slow shake of his head. "By the time I got to the saloon, poor Frank had gambled away all his money. Frank was desperate. The very next deal of the cards, he bet the deed to his farm. Now, I might have been the law in that town, but a game is a game and I had no right to interfere. Near broke my heart when Frank lost his home to Spencer. I've never seen a man look like that before, like he'd lost his spirit."

Tessa took a cautious step toward the door. She wasn't certain where this story was leading, and she had a bad feeling about the ending. Either way, she was hedging her own bets this time. "Gambling is a wicked addiction."

"Most of the regulars lit out real quick. No one likes

to see a man like that, trounced. I stayed behind, worried about Frank's state of mind. Spencer stayed behind as well." The marshal scratched his temple. "Spencer waited until it was just us three, then handed Frank back the note for the deed and all but twenty dollars of his winnings. Old Frank was blubbering and crying like a baby. Spencer said, *Some lessons you gotta learn the hard way.* Those words, they stuck with me."

She glanced behind her, searching for any sign of a deputy waiting with wrist shackles. "This Mr. Spencer sounds like a wise man."

There was a three o'clock train. If she scraped together all her pennies, she just might make the fare. Her shoulders sagged. There probably wasn't a place west of the Mississippi that wasn't plagued by Emmett's past capers. She was well and truly trapped.

"Don't get me wrong." Marshal Cain chuckled. "I'm certain Spencer was cheating, though I never could prove it. But Frank never gambled again. He'd learned his lesson, all right, and cheaper than he might have with a less compassionate cardsharp. That's the trouble with being a lawman sometimes. Figuring out what to do with people like that Spencer fellow. I couldn't decide if I should put him in jail or give him a medal."

"What did you do?" Tessa pressed her quaking hands together. "You said you couldn't prove he was cheating."

Emmett might not have been out-and-out cheating, but he was most certainly double-dealing. He had a whole bag of tricks. Often his strategy was as simple as counting the cards or ensuring the other man drank too much. He was adept at noticing the little ticks people assumed when they were dealt a winning or a losing hand. Nothing with Emmett was ever as entirely straightforward or as simple as cheating.

"You know what I did?" The marshal studied her intently. "I tipped my hat to him. Then I suggested he move on to another town. I'll tell you this—I wouldn't mind meeting up with that fellow again someday."

She narrowed her gaze, wary of the trap in his words. "You're a very tolerant lawman."

"Experienced, more like. After a while in this job, you stop seeing everything as black-and-white and you notice a whole lot of gray."

As Tessa cautiously eyed the marshal, JoBeth arrived in a breathless rush.

She skidded into the vestibule and pecked her husband on the cheek. "Sorry I'm late."

After giving Tessa a brief hug, she rushed inside. Tessa stole a peek through the narrow opening in the double doors, hoping for a glimpse of Shane.

Marshal Cain stuck out his elbow. "Ready?"

She looped her hand through the bend in his arm and nodded.

He gave her hand a quick squeeze. "As long as you're honest with each other, the rest will take care of itself."

An uncomfortable sensation settled in the pit of her stomach. *Honesty.* His random tale hadn't been so random after all. Did he know for certain, or did he simply suspect she and Emmett were related? Either way, according to the marshal, the one thing she needed for a successful marriage was the one thing she couldn't give.

The doors from the vestibule opened and Shane stood, tugging on his coat sleeves, then lifted his gaze

and flinched. Her face pale, Tessa clung to Garrett like
a prisoner being led to the gallows. Shane sighed quietly. Just once he'd like a bride who didn't appear as
though she was ready to bolt for the nearest exit at any
moment. Tessa greeted him at the altar with a tremulous smile and he offered what he hoped was a reassuring smile in return.

The rest of the ceremony passed in a blur. Reverend
Miller was well aware of the time press and moved
the ceremony along at a clipped pace. This wasn't the
first hasty marriage the reverend had overseen, and it
wouldn't be his last. Tessa didn't hesitate over the promise to "love," but he doubted she even knew what she
was saying. Her gasping responses sounded slightly
dazed. Owen lost his ball during Shane's portion of
the vows, briefly halting the ceremony, which meant
no one noticed his garbled replies.

Since there'd been no time for procuring rings, Reverend Miller simply skipped over that part of the ceremony. Shane cast a sidelong glance at Tessa, wondering
if she'd noticed the oversight, but she appeared unper-
turbed.

When the preacher pronounced them man and wife,
Shane cupped her cheeks and leaned down, directing
his kiss toward her forehead. She tipped back her head
and their lips collided. Her hands fluttered gently to his
shoulders, then drifted upward, entwining in the hair
brushing the nape of his neck. Time slowed and everything drifted away, leaving only the two of them. A tender flood of emotion shuddered through him.

A movement caught his attention and he wrestled hold

of his senses, pulling back. Her eyes glassy, Tessa swayed forward. Shane steadied her before scooting away.

Garrett reached between them and clasped his hand, covering the awkward moment. Following a few hasty goodbyes and promises of future meetings, the children were bundled onto a makeshift bed in the back of the covered wagon. Snow sheeted around him, catching on his collar and trickling wetly down his back. He pulled his woolen muffler tighter.

Tessa lifted her foot onto a spoke of the wagon wheel and reached for the buckboard. He caught a glimpse of her trim ankles encased in wholly impractical half boots. He adjusted his leather gloves, hoping JoBeth had followed his instructions and outfitted his new wife with some sensible winter clothing. Judging by the stack of boxes in the back of the wagon, his cousin had taken him at his word.

Tessa kicked off and raised herself only halfway up before collapsing back onto the snow-packed street. Tipping back her head, she glared at the high seat. Without giving her time for protest, Shane gathered her around the waist and easily lifted her onto the bench. She squeaked and quickly scooted toward the opposite side. As he pulled himself up, the wagon tipped, and Tessa slid across the seat, bumping against his shoulder. She lurched away with a muffled apology.

"You warm enough?" he asked.

Her head jerked in a nod. "I'm fine."

The sudden change in her demeanor had him on edge. She'd seemed fine before the ceremony. During, even. Had the reality of her situation finally set in? Was she afraid of him? The thought was like a punch in the gut. What had he done to frighten her?

He cast her a cautious glance. "The trip takes an hour on a good day. Probably two hours in this weather."

"All right."

His new wife wore matching bright green woolen mittens, a hat and a muffler in a familiar pattern he recognized as the work of Mrs. Edwards. She'd wrapped the muffler completely around her face, leaving only her eyes visible. Crystal snowflakes clung to her eyelashes like cottony powder. He reached beneath the seat and produced a red plaid blanket, offering her the warmth without quite meeting her eyes. She dutifully tucked the material around her legs.

Flipping back the domed canvas cover, he made certain the twins were warmly bundled as well. Tessa followed his gaze and frowned.

"They'll be fine." He answered her unspoken question. "The canvas covering and the blankets trap the warmth. They'll be a lot more comfortable than you and me. Don't worry. You tell me if you need another blanket."

She tugged down her emerald woolen scarf, revealing her pert nose and full, pink lips. "I will." Then she quickly replaced the covering.

Gazing at the sky, he considered putting off the trip and quickly realized the futility of such a plan. If he hadn't been able to talk her out of a wedding, he doubted she'd be content with staying in town another night.

He didn't feel the cold like other folks. The kids were fine, so he didn't worry about them. Even if the wagon became stuck in the snow, they had plenty of supplies and his ranch hands would fetch them soon enough. He was worried about Tessa and her impractical boots of the thinnest kid leather. The horses jerked their heads, jangling their harnesses, and he reached for the brake. He'd worry about her shoes later. It wasn't as though she was walking the distance.

He'd know by Christmas whether or not she regretted her decision. All he could do until then was wait and keep his distance. He'd come this far—there was no use turning back now.

Chapter Seven

As Shane made to flick the reins, Garrett shouted from the stairs of the church. The marshal loped the distance and lifted a bundle toward Shane.

"JoBeth thought you might need this," Garrett said.

He touched the brim of his hat in Tessa's direction and dashed for cover once more.

The wrapped bundle warmed Shane's hands and he flipped back the covering, revealing a heated brick. He leaned toward Tessa and she recoiled.

"It's a warm brick," he said tersely. "For your feet."

She hadn't jolted away from him in the church. She'd actually leaned toward him. If they hadn't been standing before other people, he'd have been sorely tempted to take the moment further. She hadn't been protesting then. What had changed?

As the wagon lurched into motion, she braced her mittened fingers against the buckboard, her hand appearing impossibly small and almost childlike. He must have at least a foot of height on her as well as a hundred pounds. Some people were intimidated by his size. Next time he was in town, he'd ask JoBeth for advice. He'd see if she had any insight on how to put Tessa at ease. His cousin sure wasn't scared of him. Then again, JoBeth wasn't scared of anything. Maybe she wasn't the best person to ask.

For now, he'd keep his distance. It was what he'd planned on doing anyway. With that settled, Shane slapped the reins against the horses' backs and the horses picked up speed. Glancing over her shoulder, Tessa sketched a wave at the Cains.

They smiled and waved in return. Before long, the swirling white curtain of snow obscured everything but the faintest outlines of the buildings in town. The children fussed for the first half an hour or so, and Tessa spent most of that time with her back turned, quieting Owen and Alyce and keeping them warm and occupied. By the second half hour, the movement of the wagon had lulled them, and they curled around one another and dozed.

A sound caught his attention and his head swiveled. Tessa sat tall and straight, her hands clasped in her lap. Without turning his head, he kept an eye on her.

When he thought he caught her shivering, he whipped around. "I can rearrange the boxes, make some room with the children. It's warmer."

"I don't think there's any room even if you rearranged things." Worry clouded her face. "Jo near bought out the whole store."

"You're probably right. I hope cattle prices are good this spring to pay off the tab," he said, hoping to lighten the moment.

"You don't mind, do you?" She asked with tentative

uncertainty. "About all the things Jo bought? I'm not even certain what she purchased. I'm sure we can return some things if it's too much. Or not."

Her continued hesitancy troubled him. They were too new to each other. They didn't know each other's moods yet. They hadn't developed the shorthand of shared experiences and private jokes. "I don't mind. Jo knows what she's doing." He glanced at the supplies heaped in the back of the wagon. "I told you before. This is a partnership. Don't feel like you're beholden to me."

She didn't appear convinced, and he caught a glimpse of her knotted hands once more.

"Looks like the weather might let up," he offered hopefully.

"Don't worry about me. I'm fine. And I promise you, I'll keep a good budget. I'm good at saving money."

"You won't beggar me anytime soon," he said easily. "You can help me tend the books. That way, you'll know how much you can spend."

He understood pinching pennies. The first year after his father left had been miserable. There'd been no money. His mother hadn't known the first thing about their financial situation. He'd ensure Tessa had a better grasp of their capital.

"I'm not good with numbers." Weariness showed in her eyes. "I know my letters. I can read," she continued with a hint of challenge in her voice. "I can keep a budget—truly, I can. Just as long as the numbers aren't complicated."

"Keeping the books isn't difficult. I'll teach you."

"You will?"

"Sure."

He caught the gratitude in her wide blue eyes and faced forward once more, remorse settling in his gut. After her bold proposal, he hadn't expected the emergence of this shy, uncertain creature. He much preferred the cheeky Tessa he'd first met in Wichita. He racked his brain for ideas, but couldn't think of a single thing that might put her at ease.

"Are you certain you're warm enough?" he asked lamely.

"Quite comfortable," she replied primly.

He lifted his shoulder in a slight shrug. She must be all right. Why lie about something as simple as whether or not she was cold? That didn't make any sense.

She tipped her head to look at him. "I know it must not seem like I'm very capable, but I can manage quite well, even in the leanest of times. Emmett always spent just a bit more than whatever we had. I grew quite adept at economizing when necessary."

"Some folks are like that." The snippets she dropped about her past made him curious for more information. "How did your father make a living?"

"A little of everything. Emmett was easily distracted. We moved around quite a bit."

"Hmm," he replied noncommittally.

At least they had that much in common. His own father had been a drifter. The similarity explained why Tessa was eager for the permanence of ranch life, and he prayed she didn't regret her decision. Sometimes wanting something and getting that something were two different things.

Snowflakes melted against his cheeks and dampened his collar. Tessa tugged her knit hat lower over her ears.

He thought he caught her shivering again from the corner of his eye, but when he turned, she was stock-still.

The wagon wheels cut a path in the snow and he followed the hazy tree line, stark, leafless branches the only things visible against the white. Dense sheets of snow churned in a mesmerizing dance on the wind. With visibility down to a few yards at best, the sight was hypnotic, isolating them in the winter storm.

Tessa brushed the flakes from her lap, her head swiveling to and fro. "How can you tell where you're going? Everything looks the same to me."

"I've done this enough, I can see the landmarks." Without thinking, he gave her hand a quick squeeze. "I know the way. I won't get lost."

"I trust you."

His chest swelled with both pride and trepidation. She trusted him. She must—she'd married him, after all. In the coming months she'd realize any lingering doubts she might have about his intentions were unfounded. She'd find out soon enough she had nothing to fear from him.

He studied her face, searching for a clue to her thoughts. What had she said before? *You're not a mistake, Shane.*

He sure hoped she felt that way once she'd settled into ranch life.

"Don't worry," he said, his anticipation building the nearer he got to home. The past week had been full of change. Once they were at the ranch, they'd develop their own routine. Things would go back to normal. A different sort of normal, maybe, but they'd work out the details later. "We're almost home."

The worst of the trip was behind them.

* * *

Home.

This trip was interminable. Tessa clamped her teeth against their chattering and nodded rather than answering outright. Something had happened back there in the church. She couldn't explain it. One minute she was mumbling her vows; the next minute the touch of his lips had sent her nerves sizzling. When the pitch of the wagon had thrown her against him, the result was electrifying. He'd pulled back just as quickly, and she'd been keeping a space between them ever since.

Clenching her jaw, she repressed a shiver. She was freezing. Doing her best to hide her misery, she wrapped her arms around her body and concentrated on taking deep, even breaths. By her calculations, they had less than a half hour before they arrived at his ranch. She'd prove herself worthy of the task she'd undertaken even though her lungs had practically crystallized with the cold. At that moment, she feared the blizzard just might do her in before she'd passed a single day as Mrs. McCoy.

This was her first test, and she'd endure. Shane had warned her against the harsh conditions, and she'd assured him of her fortitude. She wasn't showing weakness now. Pride held her tongue. She wasn't giving voice to her misery. Not after he'd offered her every chance of staying in a nice, warm hotel, and she'd insisted on traveling instead. Her own discomforts were of little significance anyway. As long as the children were cozy and safe, nothing else mattered.

Aching from holding herself still, she groaned into her muffler. There might be a few things other than the children's comfort that mattered. The sensation in her toes probably mattered. She'd lost all feeling in her feet sometime during the past mile or so. Probably that wasn't a good thing. The tantalizing heat of Shane's body beckoned, but she kept her distance. Being close to him did something odd to her stomach.

A shudder racked her body and his head spun toward her. "I can stop, you know. Clear out a space in the back and you can sit with the children."

"I'm fine," she replied, her lips stiff with the cold. Pride was a powerful motivation. She'd practically railroaded him into marrying her; she wasn't giving him a reason to doubt her now. "Don't worry on my account."

"Suit yourself," he said, his voice clipped.

Another uncontrollable shudder caught her unaware. She rubbed her upper arms and peered at her new husband. He didn't seem the least bit chilled or uncomfortable. As all the little discomforts piled together, the realization left her unaccountably annoyed. Emmett had never taken to the cold weather. He tended to drift south during the winter and north during the summer. At the thought of him, a curious mixture of grief and anger gripped her.

She was exhausted and spent from worrying about him. He should have at least sent a telegraph. Didn't he care about her? Even a little? Perhaps something dire had happened that prevented him from reaching out. She'd know if he was dead, wouldn't she? Surely she'd feel his loss in her soul. What if he was injured? *No.* That didn't make any sense either. Emmett had never been much of a brave patient when ill. If he needed assistance, he'd have no qualms about contacting her.

He wasn't a prideful man when it came to his own discomfort.

More than anything she sensed his absence was typical of Emmett's abiding negligence. Since he clearly wasn't worried about her, it probably never occurred to him that she might be worried about *his* safety. He'd reach out when he was good and ready, no matter how much his silence frightened her. Not because he was a cruel man, only thoughtless.

Blurry figures appeared in the distance, a line of horse and riders remaining ominously still, and she clutched Shane's arm. "Who are they? What do you think they want?"

There was no good reason for anyone to be out in this miserable weather, which left the alternative.

He switched the enormous tangle of reins to one hand and brushed a spot of snow from the tip of her nose. Her stomach did that odd flip once more.

"Those are my men." A tinge of pride crept into his voice. "They must have been keeping watch. I'm later than usual. With the weather, they'd have been keeping a lookout."

She scooted farther away lest he feel her chilled trembling. "Will they mind? About m-me, I mean?"

Shane frowned. "Why should they mind about you?"

"Well, um, won't our marriage be a s-surprise?"

He shrugged. "I suppose. They'll get over it."

Not for the first time she found his economy of words frustrating. Emmett had always managed to fit three sentences into a place where one would do. While the quirk had sometimes been annoying, at least she'd never had to guess what he was thinking. Other worries crowded out thoughts of Emmett. Despite her best efforts, the shaking began anew. It seemed her body had a will of its own.

She considered asking Shane how long until they arrived, then abandoned the idea. If she appeared impatient, he might catch on to her misery. Instead she concentrated on the approaching riders, squinting through the snow as they took shape.

One man separated from the other three and took the lead. Something covered part of his face, and as he approached, she realized he wore a patch over his left eye.

The man's good eye widened at the sight of her while the other three riders openly gaped.

The man with the patch turned toward Shane, his right arm tucked at an awkward angle against his side. "You're late, boss."

By his tone, the words were a statement rather than an accusation.

Shane shrugged. "I'm surprised you spotted me."

"Parker saw the movement. He's got eyes like an eagle." Though clearly curious about Tessa, the man was obviously waiting for an explanation from Shane. "We were saddled and ready. Thought you might have trouble in the whiteout."

"No trouble. The kids are in the back. This is my wife."

The man's good eye nearly bugged out of his head. "Pleasure to meet you, Mrs. McCoy."

Tessa started. No one had spoken her new name before now, and the sound of it brought home the permanence of her situation. This was her new life, her new home. She'd best get used to the change. Though aching from the bitter cold, she assumed her most polite expression.

She leaned around Shane, seeking a better view of the men he employed. "Call me Tessa. I didn't catch your name."

Shane had gone oddly silent. He hadn't even attempted an introduction. She wondered if he was embarrassed or uncertain.

The first ranch hand touched the brim of his hat with one hand, his other still bent against his side. "Call me Finch. This here is Red, Milt and Wheeler."

Tessa's violent trembling hadn't yet abated and she gritted her teeth against the chattering once more. "It's a pleasure to meet y-you all."

Even bundled in their winter gear, the men were distinctive. There was Finch with his patched eye, Milt with his ragged gray beard and Red with a shock of ginger hair peeking out from beneath his hat. Wheeler was the most striking of all, a tall black man with an amused expression in his dark eyes. He kept looking between her and Shane, a smile twitching at the corner of his mouth.

When he caught her staring at him, his grin widened as though someone had told a joke and he was the only one who understood the humor. "Nice to make your acquaintance, Mrs. McCoy."

The men's mounts seemed oversized for horses. Even sitting in the wagon, they towered above her. Their breath puffed white and they pawed at the ground.

"We can finish the introductions later," Shane said. "Finch, drive the wagon the rest of the way. I'll ride your horse back with Tessa. Red can stay behind and make sure you don't get stuck. Wheeler, why don't you head on up to the house and get the fire started, maybe put on a pot of coffee."

Wheeler glanced between Tessa and Shane once more, his dark eyes glistening with suppressed laughter, then nodded. "Sure thing, boss."

She touched her head and caught sight of her mittened hand, recalling her matching woolen muffler with a grimace. He was probably wondering what was beneath all that knitting. No doubt she appeared two stones heavier as well. They were probably curious as to what had possessed their boss to marry such an odd creature.

Shane and Finch quickly swapped places and Shane urged his behemoth mount around to Tessa's side of the wagon. The animal was as dark as midnight with flecks of snow catching in its hide and melting just as quickly. She kept her gaze focused ahead, blinking her watering eyes against the flakes pelting her face.

Shane motioned with one hand. "You'll ride with me."

She gazed up at him, light-headed at his superior height atop the enormous horse. There were limits to one's endurance, and she'd just discovered hers. "I'll stay with the children."

Finch stiffened beside her and she considered offering him an apology. Continuing back to the house with a woman swathed in green knitting was probably not to his liking, but she'd reached her boundary for new adventures as well. She absolutely wasn't giving up the safety of the wagon for that enormous beast, no matter how chilled.

"Finch can handle things," Shane said. "They'll only be twenty minutes behind us."

"*We'll* only be twenty minutes behind," she corrected him. Even if she was frozen solid by the time they arrived, she wasn't budging. "Right, Finch?"

Finch blanched and looked away.

Shane leaned down and pitched his voice low. "Riding is quicker. And it's a whole lot warmer back at the house."

"I doubt I'll ever be warm again," she grumbled, having exhausted her good nature as well as the limits of her resilience. The frigid cold had seeped into her very marrow and she figured it'd stay that way until the spring thaw. "I'll be fine."

His jaw tightened and he extended his arm. "You're making Finch nervous. Now give me your hand."

"I'm not making Finch nervous. He's perfectly fine."

Finch shrugged.

Shane's fingers waggled encouragement and his face reflected command. There was compassion and understanding there, too, but the command remained. If he'd ordered her, she could have resisted easily. Instead he'd gentled his voice into a soft appeal.

"Please."

She huffed. "All right."

With obvious hesitation, she gathered her skirts and rose unsteadily. Before she reconsidered, he grasped her around the waist and tossed her onto the horse before him.

She yelped and clutched the arm he'd wrapped around her waist, then glanced down at the nauseating expanse between her new perch and the ground. "Why are all your horses so tall?"

"I raise draft horses. They're bigger than average. I train the runts for saddle. No sense in wasting good horseflesh."

Tessa gaped. "This horse is considered a runt?"

His chuckle rumbled against her back. "Yes. This horse is small by dray standards."

Her fingers dug into his arm and he eased her closer. "Hook your right knee around the saddle horn and brace your left foot on my boot. You'll have more balance and feel more secure that way."

She didn't exactly feel insecure. Though she was alarmed by the height, the arm holding her steady was strong and sure. Settling into position with her frozen and stiff limbs was awkward at best, painful at worst. After elbowing Shane in the stomach and butting the back of her head against his chin, she stilled.

He grunted and she muttered an apology before saying, "I'm ready."

Finch had taken on an amused expression remarkably similar to the one Wheeler had assumed earlier. Tessa sighed. If nothing else, at least she'd been a source of entertainment for the men.

As Shane expertly spun the horse around she stifled a squeak.

"Meet you back at the house," Shane called.

Tessa peered around. "Will you be all right, Finch?" She gazed up at Shane, her thoughts veering into panic. "What if the children wake up? Won't they be scared?"

"They'll be fine. They know Finch. Since Abby

died, the men have taken turns helping with Alyce and Owen."

His eyes were inches away, and she noticed the flecks of amber surrounding his irises and the way the green darkened around the edges. Her breath hitched. Already the heat of his body had seeped through his jacket, promising the first hint of a thaw. The tantalizing warmth relaxed her and eased the ache in her bones.

He kicked his horse into step and Tessa yelped once more. "A little warning, if you please."

He tightened the arm holding her. "I won't let you fall."

"I know."

"Relax, Tessa." He pried her grasping fingers from the folds of his shirt. "You're cutting off my circulation."

She tried to loosen her grasp—really, she did. But her fingers wouldn't mind. Self-preservation had taken over her muscles, and they refused to loosen. In order to keep her seat, she remained staunchly upright. Never the best of riders, she hadn't been on a horse in years. Usually Emmett borrowed some horribly expensive animal from a friend of a friend if he needed a mount. Those horses were always delicately boned and much, much closer to the ground.

The jerky gait sent her bumping against Shane. Taut and sore from the cold, she collapsed deeper into abject misery with every step. Feeling wretchedly sorry for herself, she cataloged her discomforts. Beginning with her frozen ears and ending with her frozen toes, she mentally counted her list of aches and pains.

"Relax," Shane soothed. "Don't fight the horse's gait. Sink into the movement."

She'd much rather be sinking into a hot bath with lavender-scented oil. "I've never ridden double before," she offered by way of excuse.

Of all the things she'd worried about, neither freezing to death nor breaking her neck in a tumble from an oversized horse had been on the list. She hadn't considered whether riding would be part of her new life. Considering Shane lived on a ranch, she probably should have thought that one through. What other surprises did her future hold?

She'd face whatever came next with courage and grit. Well, with grit at least. The courage might come later.

"Don't worry," Shane said. "If you like, I'll buy you a nice, docile mare. Something small and meek. Perhaps a Shetland?"

"Absolutely not! A poor little pony amongst all these dray horses? They'll trample the wee thing underfoot."

"You might be right. Something a little larger, then."

"Yes, but not too large."

The conversation had temporarily distracted her from her dangerous perch, and she gradually relaxed back into the gait. After a few strides, she caught the rhythm of the animal and swayed in unison. Nothing could distract her from the miserable weather. Snowflakes pelted her face, stinging her cheeks. She turned her face into Shane's jacket, clutching his lapel. Raising his arm, he adjusted the fluttering edge of her muffler, tucking the loose end between their bodies. The gesture was absurdly comforting and protective, banishing some of her earlier fears.

Fatigue crept up on her once more, and her eyes grew drowsy. She was exhausted, but the cold wouldn't let her rest. Though she fought against them, violent tremors racked her body, and there was no hiding her suffering from Shane. Though he said nothing, she felt him urge the horse into a faster pace.

"Just a little bit longer," he said near her ear, his warm breath puffing against her temple, "and we'll be out of this weather."

"I'll be f-fine once we're inside."

The past few weeks caught up with her in a rush, sapping her strength. She'd set out from Emmett with all sorts of lofty aspirations and high hopes, and she'd failed on all accounts. Truth be told, she'd left with more than her fair share of arrogance as well. Like an errant child, she'd harbored a bit of an "I'll show you" attitude toward Emmett. She'd come to believe that she'd done most of the work in keeping them afloat, and maybe she had. But Emmett had always solved their most pressing problems. Perhaps not in the most conventional way, or even the most legal way, but he'd always kept them one step ahead of disaster.

What a fool she'd been. She'd apologize to him for her foolish overconfidence if they ever met up again. He'd treated her as a child and she'd behaved like one. Emmett had preferred her as a little girl, staring up at him with wide-eyed devotion. He preferred being adored to being chastised. Didn't everyone?

Slackening his hold, Shane tucked her arms between them and adjusted the lapels of his coat, cocooning her against his body. "You'll be warmer this way."

His masculine scent teased her nostrils and a tremor

that had nothing to do with the cold shook her. The familiarity was foreign and disturbing, but exhaustion prevented her from resisting his comfort. Sagging into the solid wall of his chest, she slipped her arms inside his coat and anchored them around his waist. The heat of his body sparked life back into her icy fingers.

She'd never been this close to a man before. That same foolish longing for unconditional love pierced her heart like a spear, overwhelming any vestige of good sense or restraint. Husbands and wives were allowed a greater degree of affection, and she'd only just realized how much she craved the touch of another human being. She felt as though she'd been given her first sip of water and discovered a desperate, unquenchable thirst.

The rough wool of Shane's coat scratched against the chilled patch of skin exposed between her forehead and her muffler, the discomfort barely registering against the rest of her complaints. "R-really, I'm f-fine. Just a little ch-chilly."

"Sure."

"I don't want you to think that I'm ill-suited for the w-weather."

His chuckle rumbled beneath her ear. "Out here, everyone is ill-suited for the weather."

"You don't s-seem to mind the cold."

"I mind. Not as much as other folks, but I mind."

She angled her head and caught sight of a modest ranch house, the chimney already billowing dark smoke into the sky. Relief flooded through her. The building was a neat structure, one story with a porch that stretched across the entire front. The house was dwarfed by enormous buildings set farther back and a third, smaller structure off to the left.

Shane leaned away and slipped two fingers against her chin, lifting her head a notch.

"Look, we're nearly there."

Wind whistled between their bodies, robbing what little warmth she'd captured.

Home.

She was damp, cold, miserable and homesick for something she couldn't even name. She craved a sense of familiarity, of recognition. Her life had changed in the blink of an eye this morning. No one could blame her if it was all too much to absorb. This wasn't her home. Not yet. None of this felt any more memorable than the copious number of hotels and boardinghouses she'd stayed in over the years.

She glanced at the silent man she'd married. Could she make this her home? How did someone who'd never had a home make a home for someone else?

Chapter Eight

Tessa's violent trembling reminded Shane that she was huddled against him only for his shared warmth. He should have left her in town, though a part of him knew she'd have refused. His new wife definitely had a stubborn streak.

He watched her reaction to his homestead, unable to read her response. He'd never much considered how his place looked to other folks. The ranch had been arranged with the house facing the road, two enormous barns sitting back and to the east, the bunkhouse between them. He'd built every structure on this land alongside his men. He'd planted all the trees a decade before. Fast-growing elms and poplars, along with slower-growing evergreens that were already making a fine windbreak. Though sturdily built and neatly arranged, the ranch house was woefully inadequate. He hadn't been thinking of a family when he'd laid out his plans.

After Abby had arrived, the small space had quickly filled with supplies for the babies. His aunt Edith, the local midwife, had taken one look at Abby and warned them of the possibility of twins. Abby had been miserable in those last months, and his presence had only aggravated her. Eventually, he'd moved to the bunkhouse. Even after the children were born, he'd stayed away. The ladies from town had clustered around, taking turns and helping out. His presence had seemed unnecessary.

Tessa blinked, her eyes welling with tears in the sharp wind. "This all belongs to you?" she asked, her voice filled with wonder.

"To us," he replied. "You're my partner now, remember? This all belongs to us."

Something had been missing from his life for a long time. Too long. He sensed a kinship with Tessa and a renewed sense of purpose. The past couple of years had been difficult, harder than he'd even admitted to himself. He hadn't realized how glum he'd been until the first ember of hope had illuminated his discontent.

Between the twins' birth and Abby's illness, there'd been no time to plan for the future. All the change and tragedies had narrowed his focus. Like moving through this blizzard, he'd only been able to take the steps immediately before him. For the first time in a long time he caught a glimpse of a fresh start, and he felt the faint stirrings of enthusiasm once more.

He'd planned on adding a second story to the house after the twins were born, but the addition had no longer seemed necessary after Abby's death. He'd dig out the plans this winter and get Tessa's opinion.

She shook her head, her encompassing gaze full of wonder. "How many acres do you own?"

"A thousand." At her gasp he added, "Only about

one-third of that is fenced for pasture. The rest is prairie. I'll fence more as needed."

"Was this your parents' farm?"

"Nope," he replied, his pride evident. "I saved and bought a couple hundred acres, then bought a couple hundred more. Everything added up over time."

She pressed back into his chest, her head ducked against the wind. Though he'd insisted they ride as a matter of expediency, he hadn't counted on the way she'd melt against him. Her trust in him was part of the reason he'd agreed to the hasty marriage, after all. She put on a fine air of sophistication, but it hadn't taken long to realize she was little more than a babe in the woods. She was far too innocent for her own good. How had she got this far without someone taking advantage of her?

"You didn't tell me you were a land baron," she said, her voice muffled against his jacket. "I guess there's a lot of things we don't know about each other."

"I know. I rushed things."

She stiffened and he immediately regretted his words.

"Don't worry," he said. "We've got plenty of time to find out about each other."

"A-ages," she replied, her words nearly incomprehensible over her chattering teeth.

Everything had seemed more urgent in town. Here, the wind biting like a thousand teeth, her suffering apparent, he questioned his choice. He should have given her more time, no matter the weather. His men were plenty able to look out for the ranch while he was gone. He wasn't so all-fired important they couldn't last a few days without him. Part of keeping her safe was keeping her warm and dry.

Except he didn't like being away. When he was gone, even for a short time, he felt the pull of home.

The arms wrapped around his middle tightened and Tessa nestled her head beneath his chin. "I know you think we should have waited, but I'm glad Owen found me that day at the train station. I'm glad we met."

"Me, too," he said, truly meaning his words. "Me, too."

She murmured something unintelligible, her words garbled by her shivering, and his worry over her comfort increased. Illness was always a risk. Abby had suffered from a vague malaise even before the children were born, but the fever that had taken her life had been swift and unexpected. A sense of urgency tightened his knees against the horse's flanks, urging the animal into a faster step. The sooner Tessa was inside, the better.

She was still trembling when they reached the house. He looped the reins around one of the posts anchoring the porch, knowing Wheeler was near and would care for the animal. The snow had lightened but the cold hadn't let up yet. The wind alone was brutal.

He swung down first and reached for Tessa. He grasped her waist and she braced her hands on his shoulders. She stared at him with her wide blue eyes revealed between the silly green muffler and knit cap.

"I look ridiculous, don't I?" she asked.

"You look charming. Mrs. Edwards does enjoy bright colors. I recognize her work. Or her color choice at least."

He set Tessa on her feet and her legs collapsed beneath her.

Catching her against his chest, he scooped her into his arms. She was solidly built, but not heavy.

"Oh my," she gasped and circled her arms around his neck. "I guess I'm not used to riding. I'm far too heavy for you to carry."

"Do you doubt my strength?"

"Not your strength—your endurance."

Wheeler had unlatched the door and Shane nudged it open with his foot. A burst of warm air ruffled his hair.

She tugged down her muffler and grinned. "You've carried me over the threshold like a proper bride."

His chest constricted. The gesture was more personal than he'd imagined, more intimate. The stove had been lit and a pot of coffee percolated on the burner. Books and papers lay scattered over the kitchen table. A pile of clothing was visible through the open door of his bedroom. He grimaced at the mess. After leaving the children with JoBeth and Garrett, he hadn't felt like doing much of anything, and his lack of enthusiasm showed. Dishes were piled in the dry sink and he caught sight of the muddy prints his boots had tracked.

He set Tessa on her feet and she teetered a bit before catching her balance. "I'm getting my sea legs again."

Hovering near as she took a seat beside the pot-bellied stove, he stepped away only once she'd been safely seated. She scraped her chair nearer the fire and whipped off her gloves, warming her fingers.

"Be careful," he said. "Don't warm them too quickly."

Her face screwed up and she groaned, folding her

hands against her stomach. "It feels like pins and needles."

He knelt before her and forced open her fingers, chafing them between his own. "They're like ice. Why didn't you say something earlier?"

"It's not bad."

Her violent trembling intensified and he realized this wasn't the time for lectures. He slipped her damp coat off her shoulders and draped a blanket around her. Kneeling before her again, he reached for the laces of her boots.

She brushed his fingers aside but her own were too stiff and clumsy for the sodden laces. He pulled them off and realized her socks were damp as well. "You're fortunate you didn't get frostbite."

Her small toe peeked out from a hole in her sock, and she curled her feet, covering the hole with her opposite foot. The gesture was guileless and endearing.

She offered a weak smile. "At least I can feel them. My feet."

He carefully wrapped her chilled toes in a woolen blanket and pulled over a footstool, resting her heels on the surface with her feet toward the fire. "No closer," he admonished.

He crossed to his room and dug out a pair of clean wool socks from his drawer, then draped them over the warmer atop the stove.

A knock sounded on the door and he discovered Parker on the threshold holding a steaming covered dish. "Thought you might like some leftover stew." Parker lifted the pot. "Wheeler said, uh… He said you had a guest."

Parker was the second man Shane had hired after Wheeler. The old cook was stout and solid, his beard as gray as his squinted eyes. He peered around Shane with unabashed curiosity. Word of their unexpected visitor traveled fast.

"This is my wife, Tessa. Tessa, this is Parker. He does most of the cooking around the ranch."

The grizzled cook advanced farther into the house. "Pleasure to meet you, miss."

"Mine as well," she said. "You'll excuse me if I don't get up. I'm afraid the ride from town has left me a little worse for wear."

Parker grunted and cast a reproving glare at Shane. "It's not fit for man nor beast out there. Not sure why anyone would want to travel in this weather."

"I—" Shane began.

"I'm afraid that's my fault," Tessa interrupted smoothly. "I forced the matter. I was anxious to see my new home."

Parker flushed beneath her warm smile. "You let me know if you need anything settling in. I'm just across the way."

"Did Wheeler take care of Scout?" Shane asked. He couldn't have anything happening to Owen's favorite horse.

"The animals are tucked away in the barn already."

"Excellent."

Clearly they'd exhausted their pleasantries, yet Parker lingered in the cozy heat of the house. "I can see the wagon just over the rise. They'll be here soon. Wheeler says you brought the children. The place isn't the same without them younglings running underfoot."

"My thoughts exactly."

Parker remained just inside the door, appearing as though his feet had sprouted roots and anchored him to the floor. "Do you need anything else?"

"We'll be fine." Shane steered him toward the door. "I'll explain everything to the boys later." He spoke low enough that only Parker could hear.

The man grinned. "I can't decide whether we should send you into town more or less often."

"Some discretion is in order."

"All right, all right. Don't get your back up. You better take care of your missus, there. She looks a mite chilled."

"As soon as you finally leave, I'll see to Tessa. Except you don't seem to be able to leave, do you? Did someone nail your feet to the floor when neither of us was looking?" Shane muttered, growing more exasperated by the minute.

"Right, boss."

After firmly shutting the door behind Parker, Shane crossed back over to Tessa. She'd wrapped her arms around her body and was rocking back and forth in an effort to chafe some heat into her arms. He took the socks from the warmer on the stove and knelt before her.

As he pulled back the wool blanket, she gasped in protest. He slipped the warmed wool socks over her feet and her expression instantly transformed. She went from ragged annoyance into pure bliss in the space of a heartbeat.

"Oh my," she breathed out in a sigh. "That is absolutely the most wonderful thing I've ever felt. I had no idea I could be that miserable and cold."

Shane ducked his head. Not even three hours married and he'd nearly frozen his wife. Things were not starting off well at all.

Things were not starting off well at all. Tessa woke before the children the following morning and soon realized Shane was gone.

Not just gone. Most of his belongings were gone as well and all the drawers in the bureau were empty. The previous evening, she'd fallen asleep in the enormous bed while reading Alyce and Owen a bedtime story. This morning they were safely tucked in their cribs in the adjoining room, the covers neatly tucked over their shoulders.

An ignominious start to any marriage. Shane had promised her space while they got to know each other, and while she hadn't been entirely certain of the living and sleeping arrangements, she hadn't expected completely separate dwellings. Near as she could figure, he must be staying in the bunkhouse with the men. Where else would he be?

She padded into the kitchen and took stock of her dwellings. This was a new chance for a first impression, and she was making the most of the opportunity.

The house wasn't terribly large, featuring a long main room with a kitchen on one end and a living area at the other with a table and chairs for eating in the middle. Having a kitchen open to the rest of the house left her feeling oddly exposed, but she wasn't exactly in a position to complain. Off the main living area, two bedrooms flanked the west side of the space with a washroom in the middle.

The pantry was well stocked, and the crates filled with JoBeth's purchases were stacked along the wall. Her trunk was there as well, and a blush crept up her neck. Shane must have seen it in the window of the haberdashery. Though embarrassed, she appreciated the gesture.

Like a child on Christmas morning, she carefully unwrapped each item and marveled at the selection. Jo had even thrown in two calico dresses, a sturdy pair of boots and several pairs of wool socks. Tessa savored the memory of her warmed socks from the previous evening. Stove-warmed socks were her new favorite thing.

After everything was unpacked and neatly arranged, she opened *Bartleby's Book of Household Management* and discovered a recipe for biscuits. She'd seen the cooks at the Harvey House rolling out the dough plenty of times, and with only a few wrong turns, she soon had a fine batch of biscuits prepared.

Her cooking skills were adequate and she relished the time for improving them. She'd always found baking an enjoyable activity. Since the cooks at Harvey's were always complaining that stoves could be temperamental, she carefully monitored the progress of her first batch until they'd achieved a perfect golden brown. By the time Owen and Alyce called from their room, she had six dozen biscuits cooling on every available surface.

Frowning at the surplus, she penciled a note into the margin of the book. *Recipe makes 72 biscuits. Considering cutting recipe by ½ or ¼.*

In the following hours, she had Alyce and Owen fed and dressed, the coffee percolated and the kitchen back in order. In all that time, Shane had yet to make an appearance. While she accepted full responsibility for falling asleep before they'd spoken of their plans for the day, she'd expected he'd at least check in on her and the children.

Planting her hands on her hips, Tessa pivoted. "How about we go exploring?"

Owen clapped his hands. "Ga. Scout."

"Would you like to see Scout?"

"Ga."

"Excellent."

Soon she had the two children bundled into coats, gloves, hats and scarves. Sweating, Tessa sat back on her heels and swiped the moisture from her forehead. She'd never considered the difficulties of pressing tiny feet into tiny boots and tying wool hats beneath dimpled chins.

The moment she had them both prepared, Owen tore off his hat. "Hot."

"No, no," Tessa admonished. "I'll be ready in an instant."

By the time she'd donned her own hat, gloves and coat, the twins had shed theirs. With tears of frustration burning behind her eyes, she quickly accomplished the task once more. Owen wailed and tugged at the knot she'd tied in his hat strings, and she quickly opened the door.

"There." She pointed. "Why don't you wait on the porch?"

Owen's tears instantly dried and he toddled outside, Alyce close on his heels. Sweat trickled down Tessa's back from her exertions, and her skin itched. She scrounged a burlap sack and had it filled with biscuits in record time, the door open and the cabin filling with cold air. Her attention darted back and forth between the children as she clumsily finished her task.

Once she'd stepped outside and closed the door behind her, the sheen of moisture covering her instantly chilled.

"Really," she said in Owen's direction. "There simply must be a better or more efficient way of doing things."

Owen only pointed toward the red barn. "Ga. Scout."

Hoisting her bag into the air, she gestured in the opposite direction. "First we're delivering these to the bunkhouse, and then we'll visit Scout."

Stubbornly shaking his head, Owen pointed. "Scout."

"Bunkhouse."

Owen shook his head.

Tessa shrugged. "Then I guess we can't visit Scout after all. Back inside, everyone."

This time Alyce burst into tears. Tessa scrubbed one hand down her face, smothering a sound of frustration. Children were proving much more difficult than she'd expected.

She felt a tug on her sleeve and glanced down. Owen stared up at her. He pointed toward the bunkhouse. "There. Ga there."

The battle of wills had been struck. Alyce hiccuped and ceased her tears. Tessa warily eyed Owen. She might have won this skirmish, but she anticipated resistance at every turn. It appeared Owen enjoyed testing his limits with her. She'd keep a close eye on that one.

"That's better," she said brightly. "Off we go."

Feeling both excited and apprehensive, she set off down the shallow stairs. The ranch featured the main house, a bunkhouse that was quite a bit larger, an enormous red barn and another barn that had been painted an indistinguishable shade of mud brown. Trees dotted the area and a lengthy line of enormous evergreens had been planted as a windbreak. In the distance, fenced pastureland stretched as far as the eye could see. She spotted horses, cattle and even what looked to be a sheep.

The men had already cleared paths leading to all the buildings. Fascinated by the fresh blanket of snow, the twins dutifully trailed behind her, occasionally sticking their mittened fingers into a drift and licking off the snow.

"Remember, only clean snow," she admonished, brushing a patch of grayed flakes from Owen's mitten.

Once she reached the bunkhouse door, she rapped sharply. A moment later Finch appeared.

"Mrs. McCoy," he said, blinking his good eye rapidly. "Shane isn't here. He's in the barn."

A noisy burst of activity sounded from inside and several figures darted past. A distinct mixture of scents wafted through the door. She recognized tobacco, bacon and coffee, all blended together into something that undeniably declared the bunkhouse a male-only domain.

She lifted her burlap sack. "I'm actually here to see you."

Finch silently opened and closed his mouth a few times, then said, "Well, uh, come in. Don't stand out there in the cold."

Tessa and the twins shuffled inside. One of the men stood at attention as though waiting for an inspection. Wheeler straightened his collar while Red hopped on one stockinged foot, clumsily tugging his boot onto the opposite limb.

Finch cleared his throat. "You met the boys last evening. You remember Red, Wheeler and Parker."

Only Parker appeared at ease. He sat before an enormous tin washtub filled with a pile of peeled potatoes, his shirtsleeves rolled up while he scraped the peel from yet another. As she nodded a greeting, she caught Finch shoving playing cards beneath his pillow out of the corner of her eye.

Alyce plucked something from the floor and lifted it to her mouth.

Wheeler lunged and pried the object from her fingers. "You don't want to eat anything off this floor, little missy." He stuffed the offending object into his pocket. "You be careful, Mrs. McCoy. They'll give you a run for your money at that age."

"Everything to the mouth." Red planted his hands on his hips. "That's what my mother always used to say about my little brothers. Everything to the mouth."

"I'm learning that," Tessa said with a roll of her eyes. "I can't thank you enough for taking care of the children and unloading the wagon."

Owen reached for Parker's sidearm and the man scooted away. "No, no, little partner. Remember, we talked about that."

Alyce approached Wheeler and reached out her chubby arms. He held up his hands and took a step back, casting a wary glance in Tessa's direction. The move had her wondering about his past. Had his family been touched by slavery? Considering his age, older than Shane, but younger than Parker, the idea wasn't that unlikely. Clearly the man was uncertain of her welcome, and Tessa's heart ached for the past. Over twenty years since the war, and he was still guarded around newcomers. Not that she blamed him.

She lifted Alyce into her arms and crowded the man. "You'd best accept the inevitable, Wheeler, and hold her. She's quite persistent."

Clearly wary, he accepted the child. Alyce grasped his cheeks with both hands and gurgled. Wheeler's broad grin revealed his white teeth against his dark skin.

Tessa turned toward Finch. "I made far too many biscuits this morning. I was hoping you gentlemen could assist."

She held out the bag and he reached for it with his left hand. Only then did she notice his right sleeve was pinned back. He'd lost his arm beneath the elbow. She'd thought he'd held the limb at an odd angle the previous evening, but she'd been too immersed in her own misery for closer inspection. Anchoring the bag against his side with what remained of his upper arm, he retrieved one of the biscuits.

She fidgeted beneath his close scrutiny. This was her first real effort, after all, and there was no need for such a meticulous critique, was there?

After turning the biscuit this way and that, he took a bite and nodded. "This is good."

Tessa expelled a breath she hadn't even known she was holding. "Thank you."

"Where did you learn to cook like this?"

"I cooked for my father some. I bought a book from the mercantile in town. I simply followed the recipe.

The first batch didn't turn out as well. The stove was too hot, I think."

"That stove runs hot. Let me know if you need any help."

"I will."

He glanced at the biscuit and back at her. "You just followed the recipe?"

She wasn't quite certain what he found odd about her explanation. "Yes. The instructions were quite clear. There are more recipes in the book I'd like to try. I'm short of ingredients, though."

"There's a meat shed around back and root cellar near the house." He jerked one thumb over his shoulder, indicating the general direction. "I'm sure Shane will show you around today. Do you need anything else?"

She had to give them credit. If the men were surprised Shane had brought a wife home from town as well as the supplies, they kept their curiosity well hidden.

"That was all. It was nice meeting you." She reached for Alyce. "You said Shane was in the barn?"

"Yep."

After that brief reply, the silence stretched out uncomfortably. Okay, maybe their curiosity wasn't that well hidden. The four men stared at her as though some exotic creature had wandered into their midst. As she stepped outside once more, the cold hit her like a blast and she held Alyce closer. At least the wind wasn't blowing and the snow wasn't falling. With the bright morning sun sparkling off the snow, she might have lingered over the enchanting sight.

The barn was only a few degrees warmer than the

outdoors, but even the slight change was welcome. A man she recognized from the previous evening, Milt, sat on a low stool surrounded by heaps of corn he patiently shucked, tossing the cobs into the center.

Shane stepped from one of the stalls and halted. "What are you doing here?"

Tessa hesitated. It was more than a little disconcerting how surprised he was to see her. The easy companionship they'd shared the previous evening had vanished, leaving a wary edge to Shane.

What had she done to make him watchful of her? They barely knew one another. What about her, then, made him brace for a showdown each time she appeared?

Chapter Nine

Taken aback by his demand, she halted. "Well, uh, looking for you."

Owen dashed toward the open stall door. "Scout!"

She caught him beneath one arm midstride and hoisted him onto her opposite hip. "Let's hear what Papa has to say first."

Her arms strained against the increased weight of carrying both children. Though Alyce remained still, Owen squirmed against her hold. The men were clearly working, and she didn't want to disturb them more than necessary.

Milt stood and brushed the corn dust from his hands. "I can take the little fellow around for a visit."

Alyce cantilevered her body toward the man and Tessa set her down.

The little girl tugged on his pant leg. "Scout."

Milt grinned. "Yes. You can come, too."

Tessa set Owen down as well, rolling her shoulder in relief. "Are you certain?"

She turned her head toward Shane, and he gave a slight nod.

Tessa followed their progress. "He'll keep a close eye on them, won't he?"

"You can trust Milt."

She nibbled on the inside of her cheek. Left alone with her husband, Tessa's unease increased. There were no road maps for this new relationship, no past experiences on which to build. She wasn't certain how wives were supposed to act, but judging from the odd look on Shane's face, she wasn't hitting the mark.

She stared at her clasped hands. "I thought I'd see you at breakfast."

"I ate with the boys."

"I figured as much. I made biscuits."

Well, that was certainly a good start. *I made biscuits.* She'd have him swooning at her feet in no time with those honeyed words.

"I'll probably eat with the boys most meals," he said, his gaze not quite meeting hers. "You don't have to cook for me."

By her self-imposed timeline, she had until Christmas to convince him they suited. How was she supposed to do that if they never saw each other?

"How about dinner?" She scuffed at the ground. "Will you at least have dinner with us? For the children," she added quickly. "You can spend time with the children that way. We can develop a proper routine. From what I read in Bartleby's book, routine is very important for a successful family life."

Then again, Bartleby had also stressed the importance of accurate references when acquiring new servants and the proper etiquette for receiving morning callers, neither of which applied here. As she'd discovered after reading the first few pages, Bartleby must have been English, and the English obviously had far more rigid procedures and customs.

The chapter on entertaining sprang to mind. If she ever threw a formal ball, she knew the lady of the house should perform the first quadrille. Whatever that was. Yet the basic advice throughout the book had seemed sound, and stressing the importance of having a routine felt a whole lot more acceptable than begging for a scrap of companionship like an eager chicken pecking for feed.

"Good idea." Shane rubbed his chin. "The ladies from town were big on routine as well."

"They sound like very wise ladies."

"Dinner is a good idea, then, too. What time?"

Wow. She'd had two whole good ideas in a row. She was on a roll. "Six o'clock."

The concession rang of victory, though she felt anything but victorious. Too bad Bartleby hadn't included a chapter on wooing widowers. She craved something more than this stilted awkwardness. She'd find a way for them to work comfortably together as friends, with or without his cooperation.

She sucked in a breath and started over. "Finch said you'd show me the root cellar and the meat shed."

He tilted his head. "When did you see Finch?"

"Just now." She motioned in the vague direction of the outbuilding. "I stopped at the bunkhouse before I found you."

"You went to the bunkhouse?"

Tessa narrowed her gaze. His tone did not sound encouraging. "Yes."

His grim expression had her taking another cautious step back. "Was that wrong?"

His eyes softened and he speared his hands through his dark hair. "Not wrong, exactly, but steer clear of there in the future."

His impervious tone raised her hackles. She wasn't one of the children and he'd best remember that.

"How come?" She sounded like a recalcitrant child, but since that summed up how she felt, she didn't care. "Why can't I visit the bunkhouse?"

"Because they're doing stuff."

"What kind of stuff?"

"I don't know. Man stuff." He threw up his hands. "They need their privacy. They shouldn't have to worry if you're going to barge in."

He might have a valid point, she conceded. They had seemed rather shocked by her presence. There'd been all that hasty tucking away of shirttails and secreting away of playing cards.

Despite the allowance, she wasn't ready to let him off the hook. "I didn't barge in. I knocked." She huffed. "What if I need you for something? Can I knock then?"

It wasn't as though they were sharing the same quarters. Concessions must be made. He made it seem as though she was a great inconvenience, and she didn't relish being thought of as an imposition.

"Yes," he replied, clearly exasperated by the run of questions. "You can knock if you need anything. Just try not to need anything too often."

Tessa crossed her arms over her chest. "I'll try and

keep my knocking at a minimum. I wouldn't want to interrupt all your *man* stuff."

Their conversation smacked of the ridiculous, and the whole arrangement struck her as a bit irregular. Didn't Shane realize that he might be the person she needed? She might not know much about being a wife, but she didn't suppose this was the usual way men and women went about things. Shane had been married before. Surely he knew… She blew out an inward sigh. She mustn't forget about his previous relationship. She'd practice her patience. As long as he didn't take too long to come around.

Battling a surge of remorse for her curt attitude, she searched for a change of subject.

Alyce and Owen had emerged from the stall and discovered the corn. Owen plucked a cob from the dirt floor and stuffed it in his mouth.

"No!" Tessa called.

Owen grimaced and spit out the dried kernels. "Blech. Bad."

"Yes, bad." She took the cob and wiped the drool from his chin. "You needn't taste everything, you know."

Milt gave a slight shrug of one shoulder. "A little dirt never hurt none. My ma always said dirt had healing powers. Why don't you leave the young'uns with me and take a look around the spread. That sun won't stay up forever."

Rather than debate the healing powers of dirt, Tessa hooked Alyce beneath her arms and set her on one of the low stools. "Would you mind helping Mr. Milt while Papa and I take a walk?"

Alyce opened and closed her fists with a nod. "Me help. Me help."

Crouching, Owen lifted another ear from the floor and tossed the whole thing into the center, husk and all. Milt retrieved the corn.

Tessa lifted her eyes heavenward. "Don't help the man too much." She turned toward Milt. "You're sure you'll be all right for fifteen minutes or so?"

"Right as rain."

Shane heaved open the barn door enough for them to pass, then called over his shoulder, "Holler if you need anything."

Once outside, he glanced at her feet and paused. "Those are better boots than the ones you had on yesterday."

"JoBeth picked them out for me."

He halted in his tracks. "Then why didn't you wear them yesterday? They'd have kept your feet a whole lot warmer. You nearly froze."

"Because they're ugly work boots," she grumbled. "I wanted to look nice on my wedding day."

And there hadn't been time to change since he'd been all fired up about the weather. She glanced around the serene setting and the light dusting of fresh snow. Clearly his fears had been unfounded, but she wasn't pointing out *his* mistakes.

He pinched the bridge of his nose. "Never mind. I'm sorry. Let's get on with the tour. We only have a short time before the twins tire of their current activity." He paused before a building not much bigger than an outhouse. "This is the meat shed."

He swung open the door and Tessa gasped. An

enormous carcass hung from a hook in the center. She gagged and spun around, holding one hand to her mouth.

Shane heaved a sigh.

Oh no, she wasn't giving him any more fodder. She didn't know why he'd woken up on the surly side of the bed this morning, but she wasn't letting him ruin her day. If Mr. Shane High-and-Mighty McCoy thought she was too much of a tenderfoot for the ranch, she'd prove him wrong.

Him and his big, gusty disappointed sighs.

"How long…?" She swallowed hard. "How long does it hang there?"

"Weather like this, when it stays below freezing, it'll keep for a bit. The meat is cooked or dried or salted. I keep two thousand head of cattle and three hundred horses. The cattle business keeps me afloat when the horses aren't selling. Horses are an unpredictable business, but the cattle is steady. Everybody has to eat."

The carcass wasn't quite as shocking anymore. She'd been surprised, that was all. She'd noted a drawing of prime cuts in *Mr. Bartleby's Book of Household Management*. Although the penciled drawing of that animal had been much less detailed and colorful than the real thing. No matter. With each experience she gained a thicker skin. Later, she'd ask Finch how to carve up the parts. If she caught him outside the bunkhouse, that was. Who knew if butchering was considered important enough for *knocking* and interrupting *man stuff*?

Tessa snorted, her warmed breath puffing vapor into the air. She'd have to skulk around and pounce the instant he walked past. Man stuff indeed.

Shane turned. "Did you say something?"

"I was wondering about the root cellar," she answered blandly.

He led her across the grounds following a well-worn path scraped clear of snow toward a lean-to cut into the side of the hill. He crouched and flipped open the door set at an angle. "Be careful when you go down the steps. When there's a melt, sometimes the water leaks inside and freezes."

She peered over his shoulder.

He motioned with one hand. "Ladies first."

Stooping, she squinted into the darkness. "Are there spiders?"

"In the summer, yes. Now they're mostly dormant."

"What about snakes?"

He heaved another one of his annoying sighs. "The snakes are hibernating as well," he said with exaggerated patience. "As long as you wear your ankle boots, they can't bite you anyway."

Ankle boots were quickly becoming the bane of her existence.

She recalled her morning routine with frustrating clarity. She'd practically torn Owen's boots asunder trying to jam them on his feet. She'd had such enthusiasm this morning.

Six dozen biscuits, three sinks full of dishes and two pairs of boots later, her cheery mood had waned. Suddenly it was all too much. The cold, the spiders, the snakes, the side of beef swinging from a jagged hook and how abominably difficult it was for a grown and capable woman to place tiny shoes on tiny, squirming feet.

Shane wasn't the only one who was a touch cranky

this morning. She stared at the jagged edge of the fingernail she'd torn while dressing Owen. A burn on her thumb from the stove throbbed as well. Her new husband's unexpected dour mood didn't do anything to lighten her own thoughts either. The sooner this was finished, the sooner she could sit down with a cup of tea and nurse all her bumps and bruises, the mental ones as well as the physical ones.

She pressed a stiff arm against Shane's chest. "Never mind. Ladies first, remember?"

He staggered back a step. Her torn nail caught on his wool coat and she winced, then glared at the spot of blood.

"I'll rip out their tongues tomorrow," she grumbled.

Shane blanched. "Whose tongues?"

"The shoes. The boots. Those tiny little boots with a bend where a foot doesn't bend."

"Oh yes. It's quite a chore, isn't it?"

His weary resignation softened her anger. They were in this together, the two of them, by design, by agreement and by the vows they'd declared before a man of God. This was no time for turning on each other.

"Yes," she returned shortly. "It's quite a chore."

Already this morning she'd changed their diapers twice. Bartleby needed a chapter on child rearing. That thought brought her up short. How did one transition a toddler out of diapers, anyway? She made a mental note to ask Jo the next time they saw one another.

Yes, Bartleby definitely needed a chapter on child rearing. Instructions on dealing with tantrums seemed far more useful than knowing where to sit a baroness at the dinner table.

With Shane staring expectantly at her, she took a cautious step into the abyss, then another. She'd never been overly fond of the dark. Emmett had conducted most of his more nefarious business after nightfall. He'd slip out after he assumed she was asleep, padding across the floor and slipping out the door. She'd listen for the thud, thud of his shoes as he replaced them in the corridor followed by the raspy turn of the key in the lock.

The moment his shadow disappeared from beneath the door, she'd roll over and light the wick on the oil lamp. After that, she'd wait. The waiting was the loneliest part. She'd imagine all manner of catastrophes the longer the evening wore on. One question had always worried her most. What would she do if he never came home?

At least now she knew. She'd succumb to a keening sense of loneliness within months and marry a handsome stranger with two adorable children. Ah well. She gave a mental sigh. There were worse fates out there.

She wasn't dancing with a smelly cowboy in a saloon for a nickel a song with bells jangling around her ankles. That was something. She wasn't in a shallow, unmarked grave with one of Dead Eye's bullets in her chest. That was another something. All in all, things might have turned out worse.

The stairs had been cut into the dirt and topped with embedded wood slats. Three steps down her false courage ran out and she whirled. "Perhaps we should get a lamp."

"There's plenty of light," Shane assured her. "We're not here to read the newspaper."

"Right. Of course."

She faced the darkness once more and traversed the last three steps. The space was no bigger than the washroom in the ranch house, the ceiling low enough that Shane had to stoop. The air smelled dank and loamy and a fine sheen of dirt covered every surface. Wooden shelves holding jars of neatly arranged preserves lined the walls. There were pickles, peaches, even tomatoes.

"Who did all this work?" she asked, covering her unease.

Shane stood before the door, blocking both the exit and what little light penetrated the inky blackness.

"Finch and Parker, mostly," Shane said. "Finch grows a garden out behind the barn in the summer."

"Even with his…" Her voice trailed off and she made a vague motion with her arm.

"The loss of his hand has never slowed him down, near as I can tell." He cleared his throat. "Abby liked to keep the household supplies separate from the rest. This set of shelves is for the main house. Everything else is for the men."

"How come?"

"How come what?"

"Why did Abby want the supplies separated?"

"I don't know," Shane replied, a touch of sorrow in his voice. "She liked things a certain way."

Tessa frowned at his halting explanation. Something brushed her arm and she yelped. Leaping aside, she collided with Shane.

He stumbled back and crashed into a shelf, rattling the jars.

She scooted away and brushed at her arms. "Something touched me."

"Probably cobwebs."

Shivering, she backed toward the stairs. "You said there were no spiders."

"The cobwebs are left over from summer. It's winter. Like I said, they're mostly dormant. Spring is when you have to watch out."

The more she thought about spiders, the more she felt the cobwebs everywhere. In her hair, grazing her legs, touching her cheek. She discreetly brushed at her arms, concealing her unease from Shane. If he knew she was terrified of this tiny, cramped space filled with who-knew-what kind of creepy crawlies scurrying about, he'd sigh and take up what little oxygen remained in the heavy air.

"As long as we're down here," he said, then snatched a jar from a shelf and extended his arm. "Apple jelly. It's excellent on flapjacks."

"Bartleby has a recipe for French pancakes."

"Are those like flapjacks?"

"I think so."

At least he was matching her for witty conversation. What a pair they made. If this was an example of the scintillating conversation they'd have over the next twenty years, they were both in trouble. Once they'd exhausted the fruits and vegetables in the pantry, they'd be well out of topics unless they planted something more exotic next spring.

"That reminds me." Shane tilted his head. "Who is Bartleby?"

"Something I found at the mercantile. *Bartleby's Book of Household Management*. It's quite useful. Well, mostly useful. For example, in England, lobsters are best purchased during July and August. I don't suppose I'll ever use that little tidbit."

Shane chuckled. "Cimarron Springs is a long way from the coast."

A rare burst of insight had her clutching the jar against her chest. They were no good with each other alone; they needed the children between them. Each encounter they'd had up until this point had been with the children. As time wore on, would they become better or worse at dealing with each other when the children weren't present? She didn't want to contemplate the answer.

The walls closed in around her and her future pressed against her with suffocating and endless finality. She had to escape. Scurrying past him, she bolted up the stairs. The brush of cobwebs swept against her face and she batted them aside.

Her annoyance sprang from her insecurity. What if he never developed an affection for her?

In the sunlight once more, she brushed her face and arms. A shudder swept through her from head to toe.

Shane followed close behind her and the silence stretched out between them.

Tessa set her jaw. She'd always thought she was a strong woman, but this relationship was testing her courage more than the spiders had. She'd rather face the dark cellar than his disappointment. When she'd given herself the arbitrary deadline of Christmas, she'd been certain she'd prevail. No more.

Even as she worried for the future, the idea of never seeing him sent an ache through her soul. They'd figure things out eventually. They had to.

"Since this is all new to me," Tessa began, "I thought it best we keep things out in the open. What exactly do you expect of me?"

Shane blanched. "Expect? How do you mean?"

She didn't know whether to laugh or cry at his panicked expression, but at least they were having a conversation about something more than preserves.

"You know, we need to talk."

She mustn't panic. This was only their first day together. There were bound to be a few bumps in the road. Things would get better. They had to. Except Shane didn't seem to want her around the men, and the children weren't the same as having the company of another adult.

Surely he'd want to spend more time with her eventually. Because if they didn't find some common ground between them, she feared she'd drown in her own loneliness.

Chapter Ten

Since this was only their first full day together as man and wife, Shane wasn't prepared for the questions. All his previous experience had taught him that women mostly wanted to be left alone. That didn't seem to be the case with Tessa, and he wasn't ready for such personal questions.

She turned her head aside and glanced at him askance. "What do you mean what do I mean? You know, what do you expect of me in regard to the chores and such."

"Oh yeah. Chores. Sure." He scratched his chin. "Whatever needs to be done. The men take care of themselves. Wheeler does the washing and the mending. Parker does the cooking. Everyone chips in."

"I'll need to speak with Wheeler."

"About what?"

"About the washing and the mending, of course." The slightest hint of a glare appeared on her face. "As long as my questions don't interrupt his *man stuff*."

She seemed awfully stuck on that one particular

phrase. "I mentioned before, we live in close quarters around here. It's best everyone respect each other's space."

"Can I speak with Wheeler or not?" she demanded, her voice sharp.

"Yes."

"Excellent."

This was all new territory. Abby had rarely left the house, let alone approached the men. He'd never addressed the problem before because he'd never had a problem before. Tessa was not Abby, a fact he was reminded of more and more often.

"Any other questions?"

"Not that I can think of right now."

As they crossed the distance, Milt emerged from the barn, Owen and Alyce trailing behind him.

The older man nudged Owen forward with a gentle hand on the boy's shoulder. "I think this little fellow needs some attention."

Tessa held her hand before her nose. "If our conversation is finished…"

"Yes." He hesitated, then moved closer. "Are your feet and toes all right? No lingering damage from the cold after last night?"

"Not at all." She lifted her chin a notch. "Dinner at six? You promised."

The censure in her voice raised his hackles. At least give him a chance to do something wrong first. He'd already agreed. Why was she hounding the point? Why did he feel as though he'd already been tested and failed? "I'll come by in the evenings."

"Excellent."

She pivoted on her heel and marched back to the house, Owen and Alyce in tow. Shane blew out a breath.

Beside him, Milt grinned. "Sure is a nice day today."

More than nice, the day was positively gorgeous. The sun was shining, the wind was calm—not a cloud marred the sky. A perfect day for being outside. "Yep."

"Good day for a ride from town."

"Something you want to get off your chest, Milt?" He'd taken the children and Tessa into a dangerous storm, when clearly there'd been no need. For all its bluster, the storm had left only a few inches of snow, making the trip appear all the more absurd. "It might have gotten worse."

"But it didn't."

"Is there a point to all this?"

"You seem a little cranky this morning. Everything all right?"

"Remind me why I hired you."

Milt chuckled. "Because I don't let you get away with anything."

"Fair enough."

It wasn't Milt's fault that Shane had made a poor decision, but he sure didn't need the point driven home. "The weather might have turned. This time of year, you never can tell."

"You never can." Milt slapped him on the back. "How long will you be living in the bunkhouse? The boys are a mite confused. Especially if the new wife will be stopping in to see you during all hours of the day."

"We're figuring things out." Shane pressed a thumb and forefinger against his eyes until he saw stars. "I told her the bunkhouse was off-limits except for an emergency."

"Ah, she's all right. The boys were surprised, that's all. They'll get used to her being around by and by. We all grew accustomed to things being a certain way. Abby rarely came outside."

"Things are going to be different, that's for certain." Shane watched as Tessa bundled the children into the house. There was something about her, something vibrant and alive. She breathed excitement into every space she occupied. When she entered a room, it was as though she expected something to happen—as though she planned on making something happen if it didn't.

He wasn't really all that comfortable with excitement. "Things are going to be very different."

"Be good to shake things up. We're all too set in our ways."

"I don't know if everyone else will agree." Shane had known these men a long time. Long before he and Abby had married. He couldn't have built the ranch without their help. Even though they were hired hands, he owed them. None of them had to stay; they were free to leave anytime the mood struck. "You don't mind if things change?"

"Owen and Alyce seem comfortable with Tessa. She's good with them."

"She is."

"What about you? Are you happy?"

Shane stopped in his tracks. "What kind of question is that?"

"It's a fair question. A man should have at least one thing in his life that makes him happy."

"I didn't realize we were sharing our feelings this afternoon. What makes you happy, Milt?"

The older man tugged on his ragged gray beard. "I like being a part of something. I like waking each morning knowing that I'll put in a good day's work. I like going to bed bone weary, knowing I did my share."

Shane hooked his thumbs into his belt loops. Leave it to Milt to actually answer the question and turn the tables on him. "What does happiness matter? Happiness doesn't pay the taxes or put food on the table."

Why, then, did he feel such a steadfast pull toward Tessa? He was terrified of examining his reasons too closely. There was a part of him that was missing, something Tessa would never understand. He'd lost that youthful optimism the day his father had left them. Life was precarious, lived on a razor's edge. He'd learned to make his way cautiously, never investing too much hope or too much sorrow in any one event. He didn't want to know what made him happy, because he didn't want to lose out once again. Thinking about happiness only drove it away.

With no place for his anger, he glared into the distance. "I don't know what makes me happy. I never stopped long enough to think about it. I like having the kids around. I don't like when they're gone. I hated the idea of them living in Wichita. I didn't even like the idea of them living down the road. The house feels like home when they're here and empty when they're gone."

Milt hoisted his bushy gray eyebrows. "For a man who's never thought about something, you sure have a lot to say on the subject."

"You asked me a question," he nearly shouted. "I'm answering."

"All I'm saying is that maybe you should think about these things before you go traipsing into town and bringing home a wife."

Milt was an old friend, but even Shane had his limits. "I don't traipse."

"You did bring home a wife. Maybe you should think about what makes you happy and unhappy the next time you make a lifelong decision."

"Why does it matter?"

"It matters because you're shouting at me and all I did was ask a simple question. I could ask Wheeler, Red, Parker or Finch, and I bet they wouldn't be hollering at me. All the years I've known you, and I ain't never heard you raise your voice. Why does thinking about what makes you happy send your blood boiling? Seems like that means something."

What made Tessa happy? Shane was afraid to ask. Afraid to find out. What if he couldn't provide her with what she needed? The questions rattled around in his brain and gave him a throbbing headache. "Everything seemed so simple in town. I'm trying, Milt. I'm really trying. What if I can't make her like me?"

"Is that what you want? You want her to like you?"

"It seems like a good place to start, yes. She seemed really annoyed with me this morning. Do I sigh a lot? What's wrong with men doing man stuff? She seemed really annoyed by that as well."

"Yep." Milt cackled. "There's a great place to start. Maybe next time you should hold off getting married until you decide whether she likes you or not."

"That's the thing." Shane whipped off his hat and slapped his leg with the brim. "I don't pick them. They pick me. She asked me to marry her. What's a guy supposed to say when a beautiful woman wants to marry him? What would you say?"

Sure, there were other men who'd probably make better husbands, but he couldn't imagine Tessa with someone else.

His frustrated admission only sent Milt laughing harder. "I can't help you there. I never once heard of a fellow with that sort of problem. I don't know what you're doing, but I think I'll follow you into town next time. See if I can get me a wife, too. Especially one with pretty blue eyes like Mrs. McCoy."

"They are pretty," Shane conceded. There was no harm in admitting the truth. He may not have married her for her looks, but there was no point in denying her beauty. Even when she was annoyed at him, he caught a glimpse of sardonic merriment, as though she was laughing at a joke only she understood. "She's beautiful," he added, almost to himself.

The next few weeks were bound to be difficult for both of them. Despite their shared concern for the children, they were strangers. How did a pair of strangers go about feeling married? At least he and Abby had had common memories, common friends. He and Tessa had nothing but an awkward meeting on a train platform and a love for a precocious pair of toddlers.

"You and Tessa will do fine by and by," Milt said. "She reminds me of my own missus."

Shane gaped. "You were married? You?"

"Don't act so all-fired surprised," Milt grumbled.

"I was a handsome man in my youth. Had my pick of the girls."

Shane chucked him on the shoulder. "I don't doubt it."

Milt's expression grew sorrowful. "I was eighteen when I married Sarah. She was as pretty as a new penny. We only had six months together. It was the typhus. Things were different back then. It was the war, and I was gone. There were no doctors. She never had a chance."

Almost a decade Shane had known the man, and he'd never once realized Milt had been married. "I never suspected."

"I never told you. You did right by Abby, and I'm proud of you for that."

"I never truly loved her. Not like she wanted me to," Shane said, the admission ripping through him. "I sure never made her happy."

They'd reached the corral and Milt braced his arms on the top railing. "People can make their mind up about being happy or unhappy. Abby was like that. She made up her mind to be unhappy. That wasn't your fault."

"Abby and I were kids together, climbing trees and fishing in the stream. We were friends. How could I have been so wrong about everything? We were married a year and I never really knew her." What a fool he'd been then. What a fool he was now. "I was the wrong man for her."

He'd lied before. He wanted things to be different with Tessa. He craved something more. He wanted to be the right man this time. That was his curse. No matter what happened, he'd never let on. He'd never let her know. She'd agreed on the basis of a partnership, and he was sticking by his bargain.

If she seemed content by Christmas, maybe he'd try to move their relationship forward a bit. Until then, he was hanging back and giving her space.

He took a step away and Milt blocked his path. "Six months was all I had with Sarah, and we fought almost every minute. People die and it's easy to forget all the little things that annoyed you about 'em. Sarah was a real pain sometimes. Opinionated. Stubborn. Dying didn't change that, didn't make her a saint."

"But you loved her."

"We loved each other, sure." Milt braced his arms on the corral fence once more. "Abby is gone now and nothing can change that, but you and I both know she didn't come here for love. She came here because she knew you wouldn't turn her away. I don't know who she got mixed up with after she left town, but I know when a person is ate up by regret. Felt that way myself a time or two. Some people get hooked on suffering the same as people get hooked on drinking and gambling." He fisted his hand. "That's your weakness—you think everything can be fixed. Except you were never going to fix Abby because she didn't want to be fixed. She came here because she wanted a good home to raise those children, and you gave her that."

Shane's chest squeezed with pent-up frustration. "Then why did she insist on sending the children to her sister? Why didn't she want me to keep them?"

"The same reason you went traipsing off to town and got yourself a wife. She didn't expect to die. A man can't raise children alone around these parts. You tried. Everyone knows you did. No one blames you."

"For the last time, I do not traipse. You make it sound like I was skipping down Main Street with a basket of daisies." Turning the topic helped Shane catch his breath. He'd never had a conversation longer than a sentence or two with Milt, and here they were, dissecting his life like a gaggle of women at a quilting bee. "You've been reading Wheeler's penny dreadfuls again, haven't you? Those books will rot your brain."

"Those are good books. Exciting. And don't change the subject. I might not know what you were thinking bringing home another wife, but I do know this—Tessa is different. You can't go expecting she'll be like Abby, because she's not. Things are going to change around here. I can smell it as surely as I can smell a change in the weather."

"That's what I'm afraid of."

Milt guffawed. "You know what your problem is? You think change is a bad thing."

"I thought my problem was trying to fix everything," Shane began, then stopped himself. There was no use arguing. "Never mind. We'll move the smaller herd to the south pasture today. If this thaw keeps up, we'll be knee-deep in mud soon enough. Let's keep the cattle closer to the ranch. I want to keep an eye on things."

He'd leave her alone. Give her space for the next few weeks. Let her settle in and learn the routine. Things would change, certainly, but not that much.

"Sure thing, boss."

Milt took the abrupt change of conversation in stride, though his words haunted Shane in the following weeks.

* * *

Tessa was going crazy.

She was going absolutely, stark raving mad. There was absolutely no reason this should be happening. Everything was going wonderfully. Swimmingly. Perfectly. She and Shane had developed a perfectly wonderful, easy routine. He'd done exactly what she'd asked of him.

And yet she wanted to strangle him.

Everything he did annoyed her. She couldn't explain it. She had nothing to complain about—nothing.

She punched down the bread dough, then stuck out her lower lip, blowing a breath and ruffling the hair plastered against her forehead. She wasn't feeling generous toward Shane *or* Bartleby at that moment. She flipped the bread dough and sent up a cloud of flour. Coughing, she waved her hand before her face. Neither man understood what it was like being a woman. Bartleby clearly thought menial labor was for servants. Which was all well and good if one actually had servants.

Shane breezed in each evening and played with the children. Never mind if there were dishes in the sink or laundry hanging from the eaves. Why should he be concerned? He'd clearly had a hard day of work. He clearly needed a relaxing evening.

She punched the dough again. What about her? Did it ever occur to Shane that she might have had a difficult day? That *she* might need some time alone? Oh no. Never. Shane rolled around on the floor like her third child, whooping it up with the twins.

Flipping the dough aside, she nicked the edge of

the flour tin and sent the whole thing tumbling off the counter. A plume of flour rose from the floor like a white explosion.

"Drat."

Owen toddled over. "Drat."

"Don't say that word, dear. That's a grown-up word."

"Drat," he repeated.

Tessa wiped the damp hair from her forehead with the back of her hand and reached for the broom. Already she was a day behind in her chores. Alyce had torn down the clothesline the previous day and she'd had to begin the washing all over again.

As she swept up the mess, Owen toddled over. With her hands full, she lifted her foot and carefully nudged him back with a toe against his shoulder. "No, no. Let Tessa clean up the mess."

He appeared mutinous before turning away. With a huff she reached for the dustpan, sweeping up the flour as best she could. It seeped into the floorboards and mixed with the water she'd spilled from the dishes earlier, turning into a thick paste.

"Of all the stupid messes," she muttered. "Never mind. I will finish this later."

She rounded the tall kitchen worktable and gaped. Owen and Alyce had snatched her rising bread from the counter and were tugging it apart.

"No!"

Her teeth gritted, Tessa engaged in a brief tug-of-war, managing to wrest more than half of the dough away. She set the mounds onto the worktable once more and inspected the damage. Bits of dirt and dust adhered to the sticky surface.

"Ruined!" she exclaimed. "It's all ruined."

"Drat," Owen declared.

Her heart pounded against her chest and she had an inexplicable urge to scream. She was going batty and she had no one with whom she could share her frustrations. She'd assured Shane she was fit for ranch life.

He'd explained everything clearly. He'd told her all about the isolation and the hard work. He'd been perfectly honest about the trials she'd be facing. She'd been confident that she was prepared.

She'd been wrong. Horribly, horribly wrong.

She was lonely. She was bored. No, that wasn't right. She had plenty to do. She wasn't so much bored as stagnant. She was heartily sick of doing the laundry on Thursday and baking the bread on Friday. Or was it the other way around? She didn't even know which day it was anymore. She was used to being surrounded by scores of people. She was used to being around Emmett. Emmett was a person who liked to talk. Emmett actually carried on a conversation.

She wasn't used to being in the same house day after day after day conversing with two tiny little people who had only a twenty-five word vocabulary between them. Not that she didn't love the children. She absolutely loved them. Feeling lonely around them felt like a betrayal, which only made her feel worse.

Closing her eyes, she sucked in a few breaths, letting her chest rise and fall. She thought about the brilliant sunset they'd had the previous evening and the time her mother had taken her to see Lake Michigan and she'd thought it was the ocean.

Yes. That was better.

She opened her eyes and formed a plan. "Let's build a fort!"

While the children watched, she arranged the chairs in a square and gathered several blankets from the bedroom, then draped them over the backs.

"There," she declared. "Isn't that lovely? Now you can play in the fort."

A crash sounded.

She whipped around. Alyce had tipped over the pan of beans she'd been soaking for supper. They'd landed on the floor in a splatter, the water mixing with the flour and the bread dough the children had smeared around earlier.

The pressure in her head throbbed. She couldn't do this. She was a failure. Twice in her life she'd set out to do something difficult, and twice in her life she'd fallen flat on her face.

With a sob, she turned and crawled beneath the blanketed fort.

Chapter Eleven

Shane sensed something was not quite right as soon as he neared the house. No enticing aroma of dinner wafted from the kitchen; no little people toddled outside to greet him. He cautiously pushed open the door and discovered Owen without his trousers sitting in a mess of water and beans, while Alyce wore Owen's pants and perched on a mound of flour.

Anxiety danced along his spine.

"Tessa," he called softly.

Upon seeing him, Alyce and Owen greeted him with their usual unabashed delight, then quickly returned to their mess. The children reveled in the unsupervised disorder, drawing pictures in the dust and arranging the beans into piles. The kitchen chairs were arranged in a square and draped with a blanket.

"Tessa," he called again. "Are you here?"

He heard it then. A quiet noise. A soft sniffle sounded from beneath the makeshift fort.

Anticipating trouble, he brought Alyce and Owen

a cup of milk as added insurance against a few more minutes of peace.

Shane crouched and peered beneath the blanket. Tessa was sitting with her legs crossed, her fist against her mouth while tears glistened on her eyelashes.

He cleared his throat. "How was your day?"

"Fine." She sniffled. "How was yours?"

He scooted into the fort she'd arranged and let the blanket fall back into place, plunging them into darkness.

"You sure you're fine?" he asked.

"No." Tessa's voice broke in a sob. "Owen won't wear pants, and Alyce will only wear Owen's pants. They knocked over the beans and the flour, and then they started playing in the mess. Oh, and they ruined the bread dough. It's all covered in dirt. Don't worry. They're not eating the beans. They both tasted one, though, and spit them out. They didn't take a nap this afternoon, which meant I didn't get the washing done, and Bartleby says the washing should be done on Tuesday. I shouldn't have even been doing the wash except Alyce tore down the clothesline yesterday."

"Can you switch the days around?"

"No. Wednesday is the day I make bread. There's the kneading and the rising and then the baking. It's exhausting. Have you ever made bread?"

"Can't say that I have. Biscuits sometimes."

"Bread is much more difficult than biscuits." He felt rather than saw her scowl. "You don't understand."

"We could have biscuits next week instead of bread," he prompted.

"Why would we do that?"

"Because biscuits are easier and you said all the bread dough got ruined."

Her hiccup turned into another sob. "You're not helping. You don't understand."

"Then help me understand."

His eyes had adjusted to the dark, and he made out her disheveled appearance.

She swiped at her nose with the back of her sleeve. Reaching into his back pocket, he retrieved his handkerchief and handed it over.

With a hiccup, she fisted her hand over the square. "I lied to you. I can't do this. It's too much."

Why hadn't he seen the signs sooner? Everyone had their breaking point. Tessa had gone through a lot. She'd come to a strange place and married someone she hardly knew, assuming the care of two rambunctious children. She'd tried to make everything perfect. Too perfect. She'd set an impossible standard for herself.

He should have noticed that she was growing overwhelmed sooner. "Sure you can. This is one bad day. Everyone has bad days. You've had lots of good ones, too, haven't you?"

"Yes." She took a few uneven breaths. "I hate Bartleby."

"Then I'll burn his book. I'll have the boys start a bonfire right now."

"No." She hiccuped. "I like his recipe for potted chicken."

Clearly she didn't want her problems solved, which was too bad, because he excelled at fixing things. Instead, he tried another tack. "How about this? First, I'll clean up the kitchen. Then I'll take Owen and Alyce to visit Scout. You can have some time alone to catch up on things. If you're feeling better later, we can all go sledding together."

"That is the worst idea I've ever heard." She huffed. "That's the whole problem. Don't you see?"

He frowned. "I don't."

"Except for the cleanup part. That part wasn't a bad idea. You can clean up all you want. Whenever you want. The sledding is a terrible idea."

"Why?" He pinched the bridge of his nose. "I can't help you unless you talk to me."

"If you must know, I don't want to go sledding." She crossed her arms rebelliously over her chest. "I'll have to bundle the children and that will take hours because Owen will undress while I'm putting on Alyce's coat and Alyce will undress while I'm putting on my coat and nothing will ever get done."

"We'll bundle them as a team. That way, no one can undress."

"All right." A loud sniffle. "Only if you help clean up and bundle the children."

He would have offered more help earlier, except she'd never asked and everything had seemed fine. If she'd let him know sooner she was growing overwhelmed, things might not have spiraled out of control.

She brushed the tangled hair from her forehead. This didn't seem to be the time to point that out.

The agreement was struck and he emerged from beneath the blanket. He spent the next hour and a half cleaning the house, though he left Tessa and the fort undisturbed. He bundled the children, which took just as long as Tessa had complained about, and led them outside. They visited Scout, feeding the horse a winter dried carrot, then dug the sled out of the loft.

After an hour alone Tessa joined them outside, as cheerful as ever. Her eyes were dried and she looked as bright as the morning sun. He didn't even mention the blob of bread dough in her hair, figuring she'd discover it soon enough.

Following that memorable evening, he'd made a point of ensuring Tessa had time alone each day. Sometimes she'd finish her tasks and join them in sledding or building a snowman or a snow fort; sometimes she simply stayed in the cabin and brewed a cup of tea. While his daily intervention didn't solve all the problems that cropped up, it seemed to provide Tessa with the endurance to handle whatever the children threw her way.

They were friends of a sort. He'd asked for companionship, and he'd got companionship. Except he feared with Tessa, he wanted something more. Only he'd made a promise, and he was honor bound to keep that promise. Since those first hesitant days together, she'd given no hint that she wanted anything more from him. Nothing. Not even the slightest indication.

Whatever tender feelings she may have harbored in the beginning, those feelings obviously hadn't survived time and proximity. Tessa had kept her end of the bargain. She was a good mother to the children. She'd kept her promise to him, too. She was a good wife in all the tasks he'd set before her. He didn't have the heart, or the courage, to ask for more.

Only one problem nagged him. She was holding something back, and until she trusted him with her secret, a wall remained between them. If he pushed her to trust him, he'd only push her away. He'd been through this with Abby and lost, and he feared he was losing again.

For the second time in his life, he was the wrong man.

Shane was holding something back, and yet Tessa couldn't quite put her finger on the problem. Following her slight hiccup with the beans and the flour and the all-around mess, they'd fallen into a much easier routine. Some of the ice had thawed between them. They didn't exactly share the easy camaraderie of old friends, but at least they'd developed a level of comfort around one another.

Despite this newfound partnership, there was still something missing. She told herself he was mourning his first wife, that he was exhausted, that he just needed more time. No matter what she told herself, she'd begun to suspect the problem wasn't with Shane. She'd started to wonder if she simply wasn't the sort of person who inspired affection in others.

Despite her misgiving, one evening after the children had gone to bed, she blocked his exit. There was no time like the present.

"Shane," she began haltingly. "I was wondering if you'd help me with something."

"Sure. What?"

She reached for *Bartleby's Book of Household Management*. Also following her slight mishap with the beans and the flour and the all-around mess, she and Bartleby had come to an agreement as well. She stuck to the recipes and mostly ignored his other advice. She'd do the washing when she was good and ready, and not adhere to an arbitrary schedule created by some crazy Englishman for the torture of frontier wives.

She set the book on the table with a thump. "Do you know fractions?"

"Sure." He scratched his temple. "Some. Nothing real complicated."

"Hopefully this won't be too complicated." She indicated a list of ingredients. "Some of the recipes make too much, and some of them make too little, but I don't know how to calculate the adjustments."

He grinned and her eyes were drawn to his mouth. Memories of the way his lips felt against hers flooded her senses. Too bad she didn't inspire affection in others, because she sure experienced it herself.

"That's easy," he said. "I can show you how to do that."

She felt a little breathless. "Right now?"

"Absolutely." He glanced right and left. "I thought we had a slate board around here. That's probably the easiest way to start."

After retrieving the twins' slate board and chalk, she indicated the recipe again. "This made seventy-two biscuits, which is too many. I'd like to cut the recipe in half."

"Let's see here. Knowing how to do something and explaining how to do something are two entirely different things."

Shane prowled around the kitchen. He gathered the measuring cups along with the tin of flour and set them on the table.

She gazed at his eyes, recalling how she'd thought

they were the green of a tender new leaf. They reminded her of spring, when everything was fresh and new again. She liked the way he moved. There was an unconscious grace about him, an economy of motion.

As he arranged the flour and measuring cups, her apprehension grew. "I don't need to actually make the biscuits. I just need to know how to change the recipe."

"We're not making anything. I'm showing you how this works in practice."

She lowered herself onto a chair and planted her chin in her cupped hands. "I can't wait to see what you have up your sleeve."

And she definitely liked looking at his arms. His rippling muscles were undeniably masculine and unconsciously enticing.

"I suppose we should start out with something easy. Like a cup."

She studied his shaggy hair, the way it curled over his ears. He really needed a haircut. She'd clipped Emmett's hair before. Maybe he'd let her give him a trim. "That one is easy, silly. Half of a cup is a half a cup."

"Fair enough. Then let's take this next measurement."

Scooping the flour, he filled two measuring cups, then reached for a third. She liked his hands. The dusting of dark hair across the knuckles, the scars from the nicks and cuts he'd suffered over the years, the callouses on his fingers. Most of the men she'd encountered growing up had worked in saloons or storefronts. They'd had soft hands with neatly clipped nails. Shane's were jagged. His thumbnail even had a dip in the center, as though he'd crushed it once and it had never healed.

She'd never considered someone's hands in detail before, but she found Shane's fascinating.

"Are you listening?" His voice interrupted her inspection.

"I missed that last part."

The next hour passed in a blink. After seeing him with the children, she shouldn't have been surprised at how incredibly patient he was with teaching her. Nothing quite made sense at first. He wrote the problems on the slate board and solved them, then showed her the solution using the measuring cups.

She scooted closer and followed his directions on the slate board. Their shoulders touched and he didn't move away. Fearful of spooking him, she didn't press nearer. He erased the problem and wrote another. After a few false starts, she completed the task with a frown. "That doesn't look right."

"There's one way to check it."

She scooped equal amounts of flour into a smaller cup and measured them both into a larger cup, eyeing the results. "That's right! That worked."

"Of course it worked. It's math."

Tessa grinned. Reaching above her, she brushed a dusting of flour from his forehead. "You'll need a wash after this."

He caught her hand against his temple. With infinite care, he turned his head and her knuckles scraped along the shadow of his beard. Dragging out the moment, she placed her other hand against his chest, noticing the strength there, the gentle beat of his heart against her fingertips. A soul-deep yearning filled her.

As though it was the most natural thing in the world,

he tipped his head and kissed her, his mouth wooing hers. She threaded her hands through his hair, marveling at the sleek texture.

As she sank into the sensation, a call sounded from the children's bedroom and they broke apart.

Her gaze skittered away.

Shane stuffed his hands in his pockets. "Sounds like Owen."

The call sounded again.

"He wants water," Tessa said. "He always wants one last drink of water."

"He doesn't like being left alone."

"This will just take a moment."

While Tessa saw to Owen, the sounds of Shane cleaning up the kitchen drifted through the door. The noise of dishes clinking together was comforting. Such a small thing she'd taken for granted before. Right now the simple task filled her with longing. The familiar sounds of another person bustling in the kitchen were music to her soul.

By the time she'd settled both Alyce and Owen, he was gone. Tears of frustration sprang in her eyes. She longed to turn back the clock and play out the moment once more. She sat in the kitchen for a long time after that, trying to figure out what she'd done wrong.

He wasn't indifferent to her, and yet whenever she approached him, he turned away. Which had her wondering once again if he found some problem with her, if he found something lacking in her. She pressed two fingers against her lips and recalled their earlier kiss.

Her chest ached. Owen wasn't the only one in this house who didn't like to be left alone.

Chapter Twelve

The temperate weather melted all but a few patches of snow, making Shane's life easier while he worked outside. The change also meant Tessa and the children were enjoying the subtle shift in temperature. They weren't underfoot exactly, she took great pains avoiding him during the working portion of the day, but she left an indelible mark wherever she went.

The ranch hands adored her. Each evening in the bunkhouse he lay with his hands threaded behind his head as they spoke of her in glowing terms. She and Parker exchanged recipes. Wheeler, whose mother had been a seamstress, was teaching her how to sew. The other men treated her with kid gloves, watching her from a fascinated distance.

A gradual shift took place in the general mood of the ranch, a change in the rhythm of everyone's routine. Though a perpetual winter haze hung low over the horizon, a quiet sense of anticipation took hold. Usually about this time the men grew surly with the shortened days and he was hard-pressed to keep them in line. Petty fights erupted. Tiny irritations exploded into fisticuffs. Not this year.

Everyone was happy with the changes. Which didn't explain why everything annoyed Shane. He knew his frustrations were unfounded, and that annoyed him all the more. His reactions were irrational and out of proportion. There was no reason or explanation for his surly mood. He'd got exactly what he'd envisioned. If anything, the marriage was turning out even better than he'd hoped for at the start.

The four of them had sunk into a comfortable routine. The exact sort of comfortable routine he'd always desired. Each evening they ate dinner together. Then he played with the children for an hour or two while Tessa worked on one of her numerous projects. She never sat still for long. Either she was knitting a lumpy scarf, mending some stray piece of clothing or experimenting with a new recipe. Like a metronome, she kept up a steady beat of activity.

He had no cause for complaint and yet something bugged him, something he couldn't quite put a finger on. She respected his time with the children, even encouraged their interaction. The house was neat and tidy. Everyone was happy.

Everyone but him. Lord help him if Milt ever found out. The man would never let him live it down.

She'd kissed him, and yet he still felt her hesitancy, as though she withheld a part of herself. She didn't show that same hesitancy around the other men, and that troubled him. Why was she holding back with him and not the others? Why did she prefer their company to his?

The next morning, enmeshed in his troubled

thoughts, he rounded the corner and collided with the source of his agitation. Tessa stumbled back with a warm smile.

"I didn't think you'd be around today," she said. "Last night you mentioned checking the cattle pastures."

Glancing over his shoulder, he gauged her trajectory. "Is that why you're on the way to the bunkhouse? Because you knew I wouldn't be there? Where are Alyce and Owen?"

Her cheeks flamed. "The children are napping and I need Wheeler's help."

"Can it wait? He has other work." They were behind on chores already. He'd let the men know already that today was all about catching up. He didn't want the weather trapping them unaware, and he had a bad feeling there was another storm on the horizon. "Why don't you check back with him tomorrow?"

A flicker of apprehension crossed her face. "Are you angry with me? Have I done something wrong?"

"It's not that." He was torn between wanting to draw her closer and needing to keep her at arm's distance. "The next few days will be busy. The men have other work to do."

She drew back her shoulders. "I always ask if they have time."

Shane heaved a breath. "They're not going to refuse you. You're the boss's wife. Or had you forgotten that?"

"Stop it." She jabbed a finger into his chest. "Stop sucking in your breath whenever you speak with me. I'm sick of it."

"Easy there." Her sudden fury startled him. "What's gotten into you?"

"What's gotten into me? Your stupid heaving sighs. That's what's gotten into me. Have I done one thing over the past weeks to disappoint you?"

He held up his hands in a placating gesture. "No."

Not once since he'd known her had he seen this side of Tessa. She was quaking with anger, her lips trembling, her face mottled red.

"Then why are you always glaring at me? Why are you always sighing and muttering as though I'm some problem that can't be fixed? I don't know what you want from me. I'm trying. Truly, I am. I don't know what else you expect of me."

Trapped by his regrets, he shook his head. "I'm sorry. I didn't mean to upset you." That wasn't entirely truthful. He'd been itching to lash out at someone for days. He'd felt his control slipping away and he desperately wanted it back. "We both knew this wasn't going to be easy."

"It doesn't have to be this difficult either. You're not helping."

"Me?" Her tirade set him back on his heels. "I've done everything *you've* asked of me as well. I come for dinner each evening and I promptly leave as soon as you usher me out the door."

"I don't ask you to leave." Her stance faltered. "Once the children are asleep, there's nothing left to say, is there?"

Shane rubbed the back of his neck. He was reliving his first marriage all over again. Abby had accused him of being too withdrawn on more than one occasion.

Instead of telling Tessa that it didn't matter how hard he tried, he'd still be a rancher, he paced back and forth before her. He knew cattle and horses and hard work. He'd always be a disappointment because he had nothing else to offer. There was no use trying.

He was making her unhappy. Christmas was around the corner, and though they'd fallen into a comfortable routine, Tessa remained elusively distant. He'd given her space, and she'd drifted further away.

"We did our best," he began, his voice thick with an apology. "Maybe this was a mistake."

He didn't know women. He didn't know Tessa. They had nothing in common but the children. He was making her miserable. That alone was reason enough for ending things.

Her face paled. "This isn't a mistake. We can make this work but you must meet me halfway."

He'd thought she'd leap at the chance of an escape. Instead she was staring at him as though he'd betrayed her, treating him as though he'd gone and done her some great wrong. "I won't keep you from the children, if that's what you're worried about."

"I love them. You know I do. I need you as well."

She didn't need him and they both knew it. That was the whole problem.

"Don't you see? This is all I am." He swept his arms in an encompassing gesture. "This is all I have to give you."

Her eyes wide and pleading, she looked up into his face. "I don't believe that."

All at once he felt vulnerable and exposed. Raw emotion knifed through his chest, sending his heart hammering. He didn't have the words. She wasn't the enemy, this wasn't an attack, and yet he was threatened in a way he couldn't explain.

His mood was precarious, balancing between panic and fear. He needed space between them because his thoughts became muddled when she was near. Away from her, his path was clear and unfettered. Knowing she was near and didn't return his affection would drown him. He needed a firm grip on his emotions. Somehow he was going to find a way to handle this crazy mess he'd drawn them both into.

He watched her shoulders slump, and a cloud of tenderness enveloped him. If he didn't even know what made him happy, how did he make someone else happy? Her fears were not unfounded. He'd offered her safety and he wouldn't renege on his bargain.

"It's all right," he soothed, stalling for time. "We don't have to make a decision this minute." He drew in a breath, then recalled her earlier complaint about his sighing. He expelled the air from his lungs slowly, quietly. What was she thinking? How did he fix the turmoil he'd set in motion? "We can talk more about this tonight."

Her eyes glistened. "Do you promise? Can we actually have a conversation for once?"

"Sure."

"I mean actually talk. Not about the weather or the cattle or the children, but really talk."

"We talk about other stuff every day."

She stamped her foot and made a noise that sounded suspiciously like a growl. "Sometimes I think you deliberately misunderstand me."

If that were actually true, this particular conversation might be easier. "I promise you, the only thing I'm trying to do is understand. You have to meet me half-way as well."

"All right. Tonight. I have to go," she declared abruptly. "The children are napping. I have to be back before they wake up."

Maybe he should try a different approach. "Tessa, wait."

She spun around. "What?"

He'd hurt her just now, and his heart wrenched at the thought. He burned to see beyond her mystified expression into the very heart of her. Maybe then he'd know what to say, what to do. Maybe then he'd know what she needed. He was a man who'd never had tenderness in his life, and he had no tenderness to give.

"It'll all work out one way or another," he hedged carefully. "You'll see."

He'd caused her pain because he was thinking only of himself. How did he become more than what he was? Was that even possible?

"Sure," she said, her reply decidedly lacking in conviction. "See you tonight. Don't be late. We're having potted chicken."

He definitely enjoyed her cooking and eagerly anticipated dinner each night. Sometimes the ingredients were a touch imaginative for his taste, but he couldn't fault her effort. "You cook really well. I like that thing you made the other night. You know, with the potatoes that were sliced and there was a kind of a sauce."

She tossed him a look tinged with suspicion. "Those are called potatoes in the German style, according to Bartleby."

"I liked those."

"Then I'll make them tonight."

He looked forward to the potatoes even though he was developing a definite annoyance with constant mention of Bartleby's name. He wished he'd burned the book when he'd had the chance. The man was everywhere. In the laundry, in the household cleaning, in the cooking. If he didn't know better, he'd think he was jealous of the man. The only thing Bartleby needed was a chapter on the care and nurturing of wives.

"That book seems really useful," he said, wondering if he sounded as inane as he felt. "Maybe I could borrow it sometime?"

"If you ever make potatoes in the German style, I penciled some notes about the recipe in the margin." She flashed him a cheeky grin. "Bartleby uses too much salt."

"I didn't know Bartleby made mistakes. I thought he was infallible."

"Everyone makes mistakes."

You're not a mistake, Shane.

Was she haunted by her own words? "Tonight, then."

"Tonight."

Despite her attempt at lightening the mood, she was still annoyed with him. He felt her lingering ire in the stiff set of her shoulders as she marched in the direction of the house. He ached to bang his head against something hard and unyielding. He'd failed miserably in his first marriage, and the same uncertainty returned. Each time he felt the faint stirrings of something more, a door slammed in his face. Instead of repeating the old mistakes, he was simply creating all sorts of new mistakes.

As if that weren't bad enough, he took three steps and ran into Wheeler, who didn't appear happy to see him.

Normally ready with a joke or a sly remark, Wheeler's dark face was set in a grim mask of annoyance. "When you hired me, you hired me as a free man, right?"

"Yes," Shane cautiously replied. He didn't know much about Wheeler's past, and he'd never asked. Sometimes details slipped out in conversation. Wheeler's parents were dead, and he had a brother who'd fought and died for the Union Army. Other than that, the man was a mystery. "You can come and go as you please. You know that."

"Do you have any complaints with my work?"

"None."

"Then as a free man, my free time is mine to do with as I please." Wheeler crossed his arms over his chest. "Or have things changed? I'm helping Tessa learn to stitch. Nothing more."

"Nothing has changed. I don't want you to feel obligated toward Tessa because she's my wife."

"When have I ever felt obligated to do something?"

"Never." Shane scraped a hand down his face. "I've been short-tempered, I know. I'm sorry. I'm figuring things out."

"You better figure things out faster, or you're going to lose that little lady." Wheeler's white teeth flashed against his dark skin, and he relaxed his defensive stance. "We've been through a lot together. I've never seen you tied up in knots like this."

He was making Tessa miserable, driving her away.

And he didn't know how to stop. Shane absently rubbed a hand across his chest. "What if I make a mistake, Wheeler, and I can't fix it?"

Wheeler threw back his head and roared with laughter. "You made a mistake, all right."

"What's funny about that?" Shane demanded.

"You'll figure it out."

With that oblique response, Wheeler turned his back and set off for the barn. Nettled, Shane adjusted his hat low on his head. He was a man who acted with methodical precision. He'd never been one for introspection. He mostly trusted his gut. He'd built this ranch on a solid foundation of hard work and perseverance. From the beginning, he'd surrounded himself with people he trusted. No matter how hard he worked or how much he gained, something had always been missing.

The children had changed him. He'd seen a glimpse of something more. They were innocent, and seeing the world through their eyes, he'd seen a chance at a different future. For them, for himself. He'd desperately wanted to share that vision with Abby, and she'd shunned it. Owen and Alyce were not his by blood, and yet they were a part of him. They'd shattered his defenses and left him exposed.

He wanted to share his vision with Tessa, but something held him back. The moment was never right. It was always too soon or too late. The lingering doubt that he was the wrong man held him in check. He'd rushed things before. Made assumptions. Not this time.

Except the gulf between him and Tessa was widening. He should apologize. He *would* apologize. He'd give her time first, let her cool down. Her apprehension had brought a renewed sense of clarity. He'd promised her safety, and he'd left her feeling as though he might turn her out at any moment. Sometimes he felt as though she was testing him, seeing how far he'd let her go. Yet that made no sense either. She was terrified of being out on her own again. Why push him in that direction?

She was bored by him, and he had to change. If he kept doing what he'd always done, he'd get what he'd always got.

A nagging thought held him back. What if he changed, and he still wasn't good enough?

Tessa stomped across the clearing. A freeze and thaw had left the ground slippery, slowing her progress. She'd thought the men genuinely liked her. How naive she'd been. A loyal worker mustn't refuse the boss's wife. Then again, if her husband ever strung more than two words together in a sentence, she wouldn't need their help all the time.

Why hadn't she seen the obvious sooner? As she recalled the number of times she'd asked the men for help over the past days, her humiliation came rushing back. They must have been simmering with annoyance.

Her steps slowed. She *had* been a pest. Shane had warned her against the loneliness and isolation, but she'd been arrogant once again, assuming the children might ease her transition. They had—to a point. Except she'd been naive in assuming they'd make up for true companionship. She'd thrown herself into their care, creating what she hoped was the perfect home for them. They loved her and she loved them, but they didn't fill the lonely void inside her. She'd turned toward the workers to fill the empty space.

Though she'd agreed to a partnership, she'd expected something more from her marriage. Not a grand passion, certainly—she wasn't a complete fool. She'd bullied Shane into the wedding because she'd expected companionship, warmth, the faint stirrings of friendship. Instead she'd got the same monosyllabic replies to her practiced questions.

How was your day?

Fine.

How was your dinner?

Good.

Who could blame her for going a touch batty? Instead of dealing with each other, they showered their attention on Owen and Alyce. The children, the very thing that had brought them together, stood between them as a shield.

She halted in the clearing and planted her hands on her hips. What had she expected? They were strangers. He was a widower. She'd never been a very patient person. If there was a problem, she searched out an answer and didn't quit until she discovered a solution. Maybe if she started asking different questions, he'd give her different answers. What did she have to lose in trying?

Upon reaching the house, she recalled the point of her errand with a sinking feeling in the pit of her stomach. As she doubled back, apprehension snaked down her spine. The potatoes were stored in the root cellar, and she'd put off going into the dank space long enough. She avoided the chore, making the trip last. There was always a part of her that feared pulling a jar off the shelf and discovering a nest full of spiders.

Yanking open the lean-to door, she braced the prop stick into place, then tromped down the stairs. Her boot heel skidded on a patch of ice slicked over the wooden tread. In a sickening flash her feet went out from beneath her.

Pitching backward, she seized the only solid thing available, the prop stick. For a tantalizing moment her hold remained solid. The next instant the stick fractured in two. A vicious blow cracked the back of her head.

Her shoulder slammed into the wall and suddenly she was falling. The door crashed shut, plunging her into darkness. As she plummeted down the remaining distance, a scream tore from her throat.

She sprawled at the base of the stairs, her consciousness ebbing and flowing in nauseating waves. Every part of her body throbbed. She pushed off and yelped at the stinging in her wrist. Agony pulsated behind her eyes. Moaning softly, she slowly reached behind her head and felt the sticky warmth of blood.

Even in the darkness, her world pitched and tumbled, her vision spinning. She closed her eyes, longing for the peaceful numbness of unconsciousness. A thousand hammers beat against her head. The loamy scent of musty earth sent her gagging. There were spiders down here. She felt them already, skittering across her arms.

The children.

How long before someone noticed she was missing? What if they woke and found her gone? She narrowed her thoughts on them, staving off the shadows. Her strength sapped away with sickening speed, and she crawled toward the stairs. Despite her best efforts, darkness swirled around her, sucking her inexorably down. Tears wet her cheeks.

She'd rest for a moment. Gather her strength. Dinner was two hours away. Two hours until Shane returned. Alyce and Owen would never make it that long without going hungry or getting hurt. Children shouldn't be alone. Being alone was frightening.

A thought edged at her consciousness before the comfort of engulfing blackness descended over her. Here she thought the Fulton gang would be the end of her, and she'd been lain low by a sheet of ice.

Shane was going to be so annoyed.

Chapter Thirteen

Shane lingered in the south pasture over an easy repair to the fence line, and yet the answers he sought eluded him. He'd finished all his tasks and even invented more, finding excuses to stay away. He fisted his hand on his leg and stared at the muddy ground. The time had come to face Tessa and apologize.

As he reined his horse around, a rider coming in hot caught his attention.

Wheeler galloped toward him and stopped just short, the horse's hooves kicking up mud clods. Shane caught the animal's bridle, and his nerves thrummed. Wheeler was never rattled, yet raw emotion pinched his face.

"We got a problem." Wheeler spoke without preamble. "Mrs. McCoy is missing."

Shane's heart slammed against his ribs. "What do you mean she's missing?"

"Parker went to drop off some supplies, and the kids were alone. He waited awhile and she never came back. The boys are putting together a search party."

"What do you mean he waited?" A wave of pure

terror swept over Shane. "You should have fetched me sooner."

"Took a while to find you." A note of censure crept into the other man's voice. "You left off without telling anybody where you were going."

A thousand different scenarios crowded Shane's thoughts. Tessa might have left him, he'd given her no reason to remain, but she'd never put the children in danger. "Tessa doesn't ride very well. She must have left on foot."

"She wouldn't leave those kids alone," Wheeler said with a negative motion of his head. "Not unless something bad happened."

Shane caught Wheeler's charged glance and was certain his own expression reflected the same stark fear.

"We'll find her." Wheeler spoke harshly. "She can't have gone far."

Shane marshaled his thoughts. There'd be time for self-recriminations and blame later. "The sooner we get back, the sooner we can start the search."

They took off at a gallop. Shane's horse was the fresher of the pair, and he reached the ranch first. The animal's sides were flecked with foam by the time he arrived. The men were already saddled and mustering in the corral behind the barn.

He swung off and led his horse into the center of the gathering. "What do we know?"

Parker shook his head. "Everything's locked up tight. She's not in the house or the barn. We checked the rest of the outbuildings. She hasn't been around the bunkhouse since this morning."

"No horses missing?"

"Nothing."

"No sign of strangers? Indians?"

Finch stepped forward. "I took a look around the perimeter. There's no fresh tracks leading to or from the road. The last time anyone saw her, she was heading toward the house."

"You checked all the outbuildings?"

"Like I said." Milt paced before the others. "Everything's shut up tight."

A fission of apprehension raised the hair on the back of Shane's neck. Tessa didn't like being alone.

"Let's take another look before we fan out. How long has she been missing?"

"Since four," Wheeler said.

His stomach knotted. She'd disappeared after their argument. "That's over an hour ago."

"About that."

"Probably she took a walk and got turned around," he declared, the words sounding unconvincing to his own ears. Fear threatened to consume him. The thought of her frightened and alone, maybe hurt, sent waves of terror crashing over him. He forced down his panic and fought for concentration. He wouldn't do her any good if he lost focus.

Shane looped the reins around his fist. "The temperature is dropping and the wind is picking up. We don't have much time until dark. Everyone keep your eyes sharp."

If she was injured, she'd never survive the weather overnight. The prairie didn't offer much protection from the frigid chill. Not to mention the search was fraught with challenges. Even in winter, tall grasses reached his waist. If she was down, they'd have to be right on top of her before they'd see her.

"Finch," he called. "You're the best tracker. Take the outer north edge. The rest of us will fan out and work our way in a circle." He glanced around for the missing man. "Is Parker with the kids?"

"He's keeping them busy."

"Good." A part of Shane wanted to gather the people he loved close, assure himself of their safety, yet he couldn't afford to lose any time. "Let's roll out."

The boys set off in opposite directions, but something held him back. Wheeler was right—she wouldn't have gone far. She was fiercely protective of the children. He coiled the reins around the top rail of the corral and set off on foot.

His head bent, he searched the ground. Tracks crisscrossed the area. Each thaw and freeze left a new layer, destroying any chance of singling out a set of footprints. Every door in the place was shut tight. Though it seemed unlikely someone would accidentally close up behind her, he was taking the search methodically.

He crossed to the meat hut and swung up the heavy bar, then heaved open the door. The solitary carcass hung from its hook. Guilt kicked him in the gut. He'd shown her the carcass that first day without thinking how she might react. He'd been raised on a farm, and he often forgot that others weren't as seasoned. Another failure on his part.

Next he set off in the direction of the root cellar. Just as Milt said, the opening hadn't been propped. She'd have never shut the door behind her, and yet he was drawn inexorably forward. As with the meat hut, he wasn't taking any chances. He swung open the door and peered into the darkness. Nothing. He'd almost released the handle when he heard a faint stirring. He threw the door wide and searched for the prop stick that held it open.

The pole was missing.

His heart leaped into his throat and he descended the first few steps. His heel slipped and he caught his balance against the wall. A faint moan snagged his attention. His pulse jerked and he leaped down the remaining stairs. A flash of white petticoat caught a sliver of light.

Tessa wasn't moving.

Emotion clogging his throat, he collapsed beside her. She groaned and her head lolled to one side. Touching her wrist, he felt the weak thread of her pulse beneath his fingers. Her skin was ice-cold and he whipped off his coat, draping the heavy material over her huddled form.

"Tessa, talk to me," he urged. "Where are you hurt?"

She groaned and her eyes fluttered open. "My head."

How long had she been in this dank, musty space? She needed light and warmth, but he was afraid of moving her until he sorted out her injuries lest he harm her further. Gently feeling around her scalp, his hand came away wet. He wiped the blood on his pant legs and gently searched for other wounds. She winced when he touched her left ankle.

He propped her head on his bent knee and brushed the hair from her forehead. "You're going to be all right. The boys are out searching for you. I have to leave you for a moment and holler for help."

The stairs were too narrow to carry her up himself.

She rested a weak hand on his sleeve. "Don't leave me alone."

Murmuring softly, he pressed her cold fingers between his warmer hands. "I won't leave you."

"I don't like it when you leave at night."

Tilting his head, he studied her face in the dim light. Her eyes were glazed, and he had the uneasy sensation she wasn't really seeing him. "I'm calling the boys. This might be loud."

Leaning away from her, he placed two fingers in his mouth and blew out a shrill whistle.

Tessa flinched and recoiled.

"I'm sorry. No more noise. I promise."

He pressed the backs of his fingers against her forehead. "Stay with me."

Her eyes fluttered open. "The children. I left the children."

"They're all right," he soothed. "Parker found them right off. He's with them now."

The tension in her body eased. Voices sounded outside. Finch and Parker arrived first, Red close on their heels.

Shane glanced up at their faces framed in the narrow opening of the door. "Fetch Doc Johnsen. She's hit her head and maybe broken her ankle."

"Right away, boss," Finch replied quickly.

Red motioned with his arm. "Hand her up."

Shane carefully stood and scooped her into his arms. She hissed a breath. "My leg."

"I know. I'm sorry." She was strong, he reminded himself. She'd fight through this. "Don't worry. We'll get you back to the house and warm."

"I'm not c-c-old."

A sure sign of potentially fatal chills. Anxiety sharpened his focus. He braced his foot on the bottom stair and Red reached down. Shane loathed letting her go, even for a moment. With Wheeler's help they lifted her from the root cellar, and he followed close behind, avoiding the ice-covered tread. The moment he stood on solid ground, Red handed her back and he set off for the house.

Tessa clutched his collar. "Why didn't you send a telegram?"

He and Red exchanged a confused glance. "Why would I send a telegram?"

"To show me you care."

"I care, Tessa."

He must have said the right thing, because her fingers loosened.

"Parker can take the kids back to the bunkhouse," Red said. "We'll keep an eye on them until you get things sorted out."

He held open the door and Shane ducked inside. Alyce and Owen dashed toward them, but their faces fell when they saw Tessa's still form. They might be children, but they sensed the gravity of the situation. The two slowed, toddling over, then clutched his pant leg and reached for Tessa.

"Papa, Papa."

"Tess-Tess."

He offered a weak smile. "Tessa isn't feeling well. Finch has gone to fetch the doctor. Doc Johnsen will fix her right up."

Parker and Red took charge of the children, and with

murmured assurances and a promise of sweets, they were bustled away.

Shane rested Tessa on the bed and quickly divested her of her damp coat and tucked the quilt around her. Gathering every blanket he could find, he piled them over her small form. Her teeth chattered and violent trembling racked her body.

Milt hovered in the doorway. "Is there anything I can do?"

"Fire up the stove as hot as you can and put on a pot of coffee. It's going to be a long night."

"Sure thing, boss." He paused. "I looked. Truly, I did. I didn't see her."

"I know. I didn't see her at first either. It's not your fault."

Milt nodded, his throat working, then quietly turned away.

Tessa reached for Shane, her gaze unfocused. "I'm sorry."

"You had an accident. Nothing to be sorry for."

"You'll have to eat supper in the bunkhouse."

"Never mind supper. How's your head?"

He fumbled for a towel and wet it in the basin of water beside the bed. Working his hands through her hair, he discovered an enormous lump behind one ear. Blood darkened her hair and he wiped away as much as he could. She winced at his ministrations.

"I fell down the stairs," she said.

"You hit your head pretty hard."

"Emmett always said I was hardheaded anyway." Her voice quivered. "I miss him."

He still found it odd the way she talked about her

father by his first name, but now wasn't the time for questions.

"Just rest. The doctor will be here soon."

"My leg hurts, too."

"I know." He caught her hand. "Why don't you close your eyes and rest?"

"Will you stay with me? I don't want to be alone." Her words were growing slurred and drowsy. "Keep the light on. I don't like the dark."

Though the setting sun brightened the room, he lit a lamp with a practiced scratch of flint and steel. He adjusted the wick, then replaced the chimney. "I won't leave you."

He pressed her ice-cold fingers between his much warmer hands and she calmed. After kicking off his boots, he perched on the bed beside her. Like a cat, she curled into the warmth of his body.

The quiet lasted only a moment before she began thrashing about. She groaned and clawed at her hair. "I can feel them."

"Feel what?"

"The spiders. The spiders are crawling in my hair."

He threaded his fingers through the silken mass, dislodging the few remaining hairpins. "There are no spiders, see?"

The rhythmic brush of his fingers quieted her, and her eyes drifted shut once more. He ran the pad of his thumb along her closed eyelid, brushing away a spot of dirt. She trembled in his embrace and he tightened his arm around her. She clung to him, her face buried against his chest. Fear and guilt were all mixed together with a fierce desire to protect and comfort her, cherish her.

Though he hadn't admitted the realization to himself, in only a few weeks she'd become a vital part of his existence. His day centered on catching a glimpse of her. She grew more exquisitely beautiful each time he saw her. His footsteps naturally quickened as the evenings approached, his eager anticipation of their time together obvious. Each day he marveled at the good fortune that had dropped her into his path.

After an eternity, the doc arrived, his cheeks chapped from the cold, his bag clutched in his hand. "I heard you had some excitement."

Doc Johnsen was a young Norwegian with straw-colored hair and bright blue eyes. He had an unflappable comportment and astonishing endurance. After the twins were born, he'd stayed the weekend, then visited each day, sometimes twice a day, until they'd thrived. The doc delivered both good and bad news with forthright directness, and Shane appreciated his honesty.

Easing away from her, Shane feathered his touch along her jaw. "She took a bad fall. Bumped her head. She's sprained her wrist and her ankle. Nothing feels broken."

Tessa reached for him and he circled around to the opposite side of the bed. The doc took his place, dipping the mattress as he adjusted his stethoscope over his ears. As the doc examined her, her eyes fluttered open. She mumbled Shane's name and he stroked the back of her hand.

The doc straightened with a frown. "That's a nasty bump you've got, Mrs. McCoy." He lifted each lid and checked her eyes once more, then turned toward Shane. "Has she been lucid since the accident? Speaking?"

"Some. She's talked a little. She didn't always make sense. She thought there were spiders in her hair."

The doc's expression turned grim. "Judging by her eyes, she's got some swelling on the brain. That combined with the cold may bring about some hallucinations."

Shane wasn't a demonstrative man, less so when other folks were around. Heedless of the doctor's presence, he slid his arm beneath Tessa's shoulder and pressed his cheek against hers. She didn't recoil from him, and he relaxed some. Her skin was cool and soft, her body weak. She'd been through a rough time today, and he wanted to infuse her strength with some of his own.

Memories of Abby's illness came rushing back. She'd been laid up so often after the twins' birth, none of them had given much heed when the fever first struck. In a blink everything had changed. The doc's face had taken on that same grim expression. In the final hours, Abby had gone still. Her breathing had turned shallow and uneven and eventually she'd slipped away. The interval between life and death had been sudden and irrevocable. He'd just stood there in mute shock and grief until someone had urged him away.

He didn't think he could survive that kind of pain again.

The doc checked her for other injuries. When he touched her side, she flinched.

"Mrs. McCoy," the doc said. "Does it hurt to breathe?"

She shook her head weakly from side to side, her hair brushing against Shane's jaw.

"Probably just a bruised rib." The doc frowned over her leg where purpling marks circled her ankle. "It's not broken, but it's a bad sprain. She'll be laid up for at least a week or two."

Shane hated the pain she must be enduring. What a punishment she'd taken. He loathed thinking about her lying there, waiting for someone to find her, while he'd been wasting time in the pasture.

The doc wrapped her leg tightly and she struggled away.

Shane held her hand and she squeezed his fingers. "Doc Johnsen is the best. You let him do his work."

Her eyes opened a slit and she flashed him a mutinous glare. "I hurt all over."

"I know you do."

She flashed a weak look of triumph at his admission. "At least we agree about something."

"We're going to be fine, you and me."

For years his only aim had been making the ranch a success. He'd fought against nature and himself, pushing himself and his men until they dropped. Every obstacle in his path had been crushed or removed. If he couldn't fix something, he discarded it in favor of something else. There was no use wasting time on something that didn't fit his plans. He was set in his ways. Because once he'd found something that worked, there was no use changing things.

People were not as easily tamed.

Abby had mostly ignored him. He'd tried creating the life he'd imagined in his youth, and when that hadn't worked, he'd abandoned the effort. With Tessa, he hadn't even tried. He hadn't tried because he assumed the outcome would be the same. Except remaining indifferent to Tessa had proved impossible.

He'd made up his mind about how things were going to be, and Tessa hadn't gone along with his plans. She'd unsettled his rigid control since the moment he'd seen her in Wichita, and all he'd thought about since then was wrestling back that control.

The doc uncapped a bottle of laudanum and measured a dose. "This will help her sleep during the worst of the pain."

"Don't talk about me like I'm not here." Straining halfheartedly away from him, she grimaced. "That smells foul."

Shane tipped the glass to her lips. "Drink. Please."

She flung out her hand and thumped his chest. "Just this once. Because you said 'please.'"

Once she'd taken the dose, he rested her against the pillows, then pulled the covers over her shoulders.

"Close your eyes." He laid his mouth against hers in a gentle pressure, wanting only to offer reassurance. "You need rest."

She breathed a sigh and her fingers unfurled against his chest as she relaxed into sleep. Aware that he needed to reassure the children and check on the men, he reluctantly eased away from her side. Careful not to disturb her, he arranged the counterpane around her shoulders once more and dropped a kiss on her forehead.

The doc stood and motioned for Shane. "We should speak outside."

Milt was pacing the floorboards and his head shot up. "How's she doing? She all right?"

"She's resting now," Shane said grimly. "Will you sit with her while the doc and I talk?"

"Sure thing, boss." Milt hoisted a chair and carried it over the threshold.

Shane lingered as Milt took up vigil, his lips moving in a silent prayer.

The doc laid a heavy hand on Shane's shoulder. "You need some air."

The moment they stepped outside, Shane staggered a few steps away and became violently ill. The doc waited until the worst had passed, then handed over his handkerchief, easing him back and forcing him to sit on one of the risers.

Shane hung his head in his hands. "It's bad, isn't it?"

"Yes," Doc Johnsen replied bluntly. "The bumps and bruises will heal. It's her head I'm worried about. If there's too much swelling or bleeding on the brain, there's not much I can do."

"How will we know? When will we know?"

He couldn't go through this again. But he'd have to. The children needed him to be strong. Tessa needed his strength as well.

The doc removed his stethoscope and coiled the loops in his hand. "Her pupils are uneven, and that's an indication of swelling. I'll stay through the night."

"Why is this happening?"

The two men weren't friends. They barely knew one another. And yet they were inexorably bound by tragedy. Their shared experiences had been both joyful and heartrending.

The doc gripped Shane's shoulder. "This isn't your fault any more than what happened with Abby."

"Everything feels the same."

"No. There's a difference. Tessa is different. I'm a doctor. I know a fighter when I see one."

She'd fight for Owen and Alyce. He pictured the three of them darting around the ranch, the twins trailing after her with rapt attention. She appeared just as fascinated with them, examining each rock and twig they plucked from the ground. She listened to their gibberish and told them silly stories. She was the best thing that had ever happened to him. She deserved some happiness in return.

The doc cleared his throat. "Is there family we should contact? She'll be laid up for a while."

"No. No brothers and sisters. Her parents are gone." He'd taken his own family for granted. Tessa was unbearably alone. She selflessly cared for all of them, with no one to care for her. "She only has us."

"Having the McCoys around is something. She's got more family than she'll ever need by marrying you."

Shane rested his elbows on his bent knees and clutched his head. He'd protected himself and driven her away in the process. Why had he spoken to her that way earlier? He'd been thoughtless and jealous. Ignorant, too.

The doc crouched beside him. "Stop beating yourself up. I've never seen a man quite as bent on being hard on himself. That little lady in there clearly adores you. I have eyes. You deserve someone like that in your life."

"No one deserves anything." Tessa didn't adore him.

She was scared and alone and searching for comfort. He might have been anyone. "What happens now?"

"We wait." The doc pressed a hand into the small of his back and stretched, then blew out a breath. "I think you should send for your family. The next few days aren't going to be easy. You'll need help."

Tessa might be different, but everything about this accident was too familiar. The doc was here and Shane was sending for his family because his wife was ill. Everything was playing out the same as before.

"I'll have one of the boys fetch my aunt Edith," Shane declared.

"She's a good choice."

"She hasn't even met Tessa yet."

The weather had been good enough for a visit. Out of respect for the newlyweds, his aunt and uncle wouldn't come calling until he'd visited first. He'd thought about making the trip, but something had always held him back. Some minor repair or a horse that needed tending. Excuses. All of them. Aunt Edith was too perceptive. He'd feared she'd see his growing affection and call him on his feelings. Feelings he wasn't ready to acknowledge. Instead of facing his fears, he'd avoided the meeting. She'd know soon enough how he felt about Tessa.

The door opened behind him and Milt leaned out. "Mrs. McCoy is asking for you, boss. She's not looking so good."

Shane's stomach folded in two and he followed the doc back into the house. Tessa thrashed about, a sheen of sweat coating her forehead. He perched on the bed and held her hand, murmuring soothing nonsense words. When she finally fell into an exhausted slumber, he stood, wiped his damp palms against his pant legs and backed away. Doc Johnsen had kept vigil as well.

Shane fisted his hand against his mouth and cleared his throat. "I should tend the children. Make sure they're okay."

"I'll check on them." The doc leaned against the door frame, barring his path. "You should stay, Shane. Clearly you're the best medicine for your wife right now."

His wife. At least he finally had something to tell Milt. He knew what made him happy. Seeing Tessa happy made him happy.

Chapter Fourteen

The next few days passed in a murky haze for Tessa. Voices abounded and her head ached. First she was on fire and then she was chilled to the bone. Blankets were fetched, and then ice was packed around her body. She heard the children's voices, but they were beyond her reach. Once she thought Emmett was there. He'd come to take her away. At first she'd wanted to go with him. Then she realized he was taking her to the Hensons and she fought against him.

"Don't leave me here. I hate it here."

A cool hand brushed against her forehead. "I won't leave you."

She grasped Emmett's hand, clinging to him. "I'll be good. I promise. You won't even know I'm there. I promise not to bother you or make a racket. I'll play quiet as a mouse."

"You can make noise," he said. "Little girls should always make lots of noise."

She dozed fitfully, and the next time she woke, Emmett was annoyed. He paced and scowled. "You nearly got us caught."

"It's only a game to you. I don't want to play the game anymore."

"This is how I earn my living, Tessa. Can't you see that?"

At long last a peaceful slumber overtook her, and she was floating on a gentle sea.

A long time later she woke to the scent of frying bacon. People shuffled around the room and she heard a voice speak.

"I appreciate you coming out, Anna," the woman said.

A sense of familiarity teased her senses. The voice belonged to JoBeth, Shane's cousin. Tessa struggled against the lethargy tugging her down. Her throat was dry and her body felt bruised as though she'd been beaten. A curious weakness had invaded her limbs, keeping her paralyzed.

"You should have called me sooner," the second woman said.

What had Jo just called her? Anna. That was her name.

"The whole point of the women's salon is avoiding situations like this," Anna continued.

"They're grown adults," Jo replied. "They'd already made the decision when they came to me."

"You might have at least offered her a different choice."

"You're right," Jo said, resignation in her voice. "I'll admit that you're right. But you weren't here. You didn't see Shane. He was like a man returned from the dead. How could that be bad?"

"But what about this poor woman," Anna grumbled. "Either way, I'm here now. Between the two of us, perhaps we can unravel this tangle."

Tessa made a noise and the speaking ceased. Why were they talking about her as though she wasn't there? A niggling anger brought life back into her limbs. She wasn't "the poor woman." And what tangle needed unraveling?

Forcing open her eyes, Tessa searched the room and found Jo. The second woman approached the bed. Anna was a stunning brunette with brilliant blue eyes dressed in a splendid blue crepe suit. Something about Anna tugged at her memory. Where had she heard that name before?

JoBeth approached the bed, then squeezed her hand before resting her knuckles against Tessa's cheek. "She's awake."

Anna's forehead wrinkled with worry. "How are you feeling?"

"Awful. Thirsty. What happened?"

Jo grasped a pitcher of water from the side table and filled a glass before approaching the bed. "You fell down some stairs and landed a nasty crack on your head."

As Tessa gulped down the water, memories came rushing back. The dank scent of moldy earth, the skitter of tiny rodent feet, the sticky touch of spiderwebs. A shudder racked her body. "I remember now. Shane found me."

The mattress dipped as Anna perched at her side.

"We haven't met yet. My name is Anna McCoy. I'm married to your husband's cousin Caleb."

Tessa finally recalled the name. "You're the mayor."

"Yes, I'm the mayor." Anna touched Jo's sleeve. "She's definitely come around this time. You'd best fetch Shane."

Following Jo's hasty exit from the room, Anna's expression grew somber. "I wasn't here when you arrived in town because of the work I do around the country. I have a charity that helps women who've found themselves in difficult situations. I wonder if you might be in a difficult situation. I gather your marriage was rather hasty. If you're unhappy, if things aren't working out as you supposed, I can help. You don't have to stay here if you don't want to."

"Shane." Tessa pushed upright and winced, cradling her sore wrist in her opposite hand. "Did Shane say something? Does he want me to go?"

"I haven't spoken with Shane." Anna straightened. "I'm speaking with you. I want you to know that marriage isn't the only option."

"But it's too late."

"We can have the marriage annulled."

Tessa glanced away.

"I thought so," Anna replied sagely. "I don't know Shane as well as some of the other McCoys, but the rest of the family speaks highly of him. Whatever the case may be, I want you to know that you have options."

A shiver of panic chased over Tessa's skin. "What if I want to stay here?"

"Is that what you truly want?" Anna's wide blue eyes

shimmered with compassion. "Please know that you may confide in me. There's nothing I haven't heard."

This was all too much. Tessa's head throbbed and her body ached. She wasn't ready for a discussion of her marriage with a stranger. "Thank you for your offer, but I'm quite all right. I don't need to confide anything to anyone."

Her expression unreadable, Anna stood. "I'll go now. Shane will want some time alone with you. It was all we could do to pry him away from your side. He barely slept and ate even less. If you're up for a talk later, I'd enjoy telling you about the women's salon we've opened in town. It's a wonderful way to meet other ladies in the area."

Tessa's hackles lowered. Anna had only been trying to help. "I'd like that."

Shane appeared in the doorway and Tessa's heartbeat tripped ahead. He appeared haggard and almost gaunt. Dark circles showed beneath his eyes, and his hair was badly mussed and shaggy. A dark growth of beard shadowed his chin. Her eyes widened. She'd never seen him disheveled. He was normally meticulous about his grooming.

He exchanged a greeting with Anna as she exited the room.

Catching Tessa's gaze on his hair, he jerked one hand up and smoothed it back into place. "How are you feeling?"

"As awful as you look."

He scrubbed his fingers down the growth of beard on his face. "That bad."

She offered a weak nod. "Gracious, what happened to you?"

"It's been busy around here. You've been ill for three days."

"Three days?" Everything was a flurry of confusion. It seemed as though only hours had passed, not days. Her eyes widened in horror. "Oh no. Alyce and Owen. I left them alone. They were napping."

"They're fine. They didn't even notice you were gone. Parker came by with some fresh eggs just as they were waking and realized you were missing. He sent up the search warning."

Tessa pressed her fingers against her lips. "Something awful might have happened."

"But it didn't."

She sat up and brought her feet around, her legs tangled in the blankets, her hair hanging limply down her back.

Shane was at her side in an instant. "Don't move too quickly."

"It feels good being upright again." She patted a spot beside her. "Will you sit? I think I have a crook in my neck from being in bed too long."

He lowered himself beside her and clasped his hands. "Can I get you anything?"

"I'm fine."

"Jo made bacon this morning."

While she suspected she'd have a raging hunger later, her stomach wasn't quite ready for food just yet. "Maybe in a while."

Feeling sadly fragile, she tipped sideways and rested

the side of her head against his shoulder. "How are Alyce and Owen?"

He wrapped one arm around her shoulders, his touch featherlight. "They're no worse for wear. They're missing you, of course."

A twinge pinched her side but she ignored the pain. She was afraid if she showed any sign of discomfort, he'd move away.

She liked having him near, liked feeling his solid muscles against her cheek. "Can I see them?"

"Finch has taken them for a ride in the wagon. I'll bring them by as soon as he returns."

She swiped at her eyes with the back of her hand, both exhausted and relieved. "I'd like that."

"When you're ready to eat, let me know. Can I get you anything else? Water?"

"Water sounds lovely." She touched her throat. "I'm parched."

He was warm and solid and he moved away far too quickly. While she'd have preferred avoiding a fall down a flight of stairs, she enjoyed the intimacy. She liked seeing this softer side of him. While he was always affectionate with the children, he'd never been the same with her.

He refilled her glass and she drank greedily, feeling as though she'd never be sated.

Sitting beside her once more, he ran his index finger lightly over the bruise behind her ear. His knuckles brushed the nape of her neck, stirring her senses.

"Does it still hurt?"

Behind his raw expression she sensed a tense vulnerability, and she was overwhelmed with the need to absolve him of any guilt. "Not anymore."

She smiled up at him and absently rubbed her cheek against his hand. They stared at each other for a long moment. Then he leaned away, appearing at a loss.

Her hopes faltered a bit at his withdrawal. "I'm glad you found me. I never doubted."

"You took years off my life." He rubbed the back of his neck. "I can't keep track of anything these days. Not the children. Not you."

"Everyone should have someone who minds when they're lost."

"I minded very much. Not to mention I never got my potatoes in the German style," he said, his tone light, his boyish half grin fully in place. "Promise me you'll never disappear again."

"I will do my very best."

Shameless gratitude rushed through her. She believed he was genuinely concerned for her well-being, though she suspected his interest was due to his honorable character rather than any real attachment to her personally. As she'd recently discovered, a casual sort of concern was better than nothing at all.

He rubbed his eyes with a thumb and forefinger. "I'll fetch the children. They'll be anxious to see for themselves that you're well."

Their easy camaraderie had fled just as suddenly as it had arrived. Once again they were two strangers dancing awkwardly around each other.

Her head began to throb once more. "I'd like that. I'd like that very much."

With the children as a buffer between them, there'd be no more awkwardness.

He glanced through the open door, then returned to her side, his hand hovering near her shoulder.

At long last he touched her forehead, soothing the rough pad of his calloused thumb over the scratch at her temple. "I'm glad you're back with us. The house isn't the same without you."

As though embarrassed by his admission, he was gone in a flash. The man had her tied up in knots. A voracious curiosity about his past overtook her. How long would he mourn his first wife? She'd asked a few questions about Abby in the beginning, but his answers had been terse. She'd stopped asking after that.

She considered asking Jo and Anna, then balked. The questions were too revealing of her own insecurity, too personal.

Jo returned with lunch, interrupting Tessa's troubled thoughts, then excused herself when Anna called for assistance with the temperamental cooktop. They promised a batch of bread once they'd mastered the stove, and Tessa was grateful for their thoughtfulness.

She stared at the door for a while before boredom set in. She plucked the worn Bible from her side table and flipped to a random page. The children had discovered the book earlier, and she'd tucked it away for safe-keeping. It looked to be old and well-read at one time, though a fine layer of dust now coated the stiff cover.

The insatiable curiosity had taken root. She wanted every scrap of paper, every clue that might give her insight into what drove Shane. She didn't care if it was snooping. Tiny bits of the puzzle didn't fit. He was open and honest about most things, but shuttered and silent about his late wife. Even a simple comment about the twins' blond coloring had silenced him. Family Bibles often held lists of family members and life events, and she desperately wanted information.

She thumbed through the pages and discovered several daguerreotypes tucked in the back. Lifting the photos revealed a list of important dates in the McCoy family. There were marriages and christenings recorded, along with births and deaths. She traced a path to the last two entries and discovered the date of Shane's marriage to Abby. She recognized his bold script. Below, in the same handwriting, was the date of the children's birth, five months later.

Five months.

Was there a picture of Abby in the stack? Something, anything more? Tessa thumbed through the photos and discovered a young woman with light hair and lively eyes. The woman was looking at someone on her right, though the picture had been cut, leaving only the gentleman's hand visible on the arm of the lady's chair. Squinting, Tessa peered closer. The man in the photo was missing part of his index finger. She read the name scrawled across the back: *Abigail.*

Tessa pictured the children with their blond hair and blue eyes, and the truth knocked the breath from her lungs.

What had Abby's sister said that day? *Abby always did have a way of leaving her problems on someone else's doorstep.*

Owen and Alyce were not Shane's children.

While their coloring might not be irrefutable proof,

she knew Shane. She knew what kind of man he was. If a friend had come to him in trouble, he'd do the honorable thing. That was why he'd married Tessa, after all, a stranger. He'd married a stranger because he was honorable and he thought he'd put her in danger.

Searching her memory, she scrambled for the scraps of information she'd learned about Abby. They were both from town, which meant she and Shane would have known each other as children. Had the father of the babies died? If Abby had been widowed, why hadn't Shane admitted the truth?

Unless he was keeping Abby's secret. Which meant there must be a good reason Abby hadn't wanted anybody to know the real father's identity.

Tessa slammed shut the book and stared at the half-open door. She was keeping this bit of information to herself. Shane was caring for the children and he loved them dearly. As long as he wasn't concerned about their real father, then it was none of her business either.

The depth of his devotion sent her heart aching. How many men would give their hearts that freely? How many would shoulder the burden with such steadfast affection?

Even as she savored the memory of his brief touch, another thought shattered her brief bubble of hope.

Shane had written the date of his mother's death, the date of his marriage to Abby and the date of Alyce and Owen's birth.

Her eyes burned.

He hadn't bothered with their wedding date.

Shane braced his elbows on the porch railing and clasped his hands before him. Anna joined him soon after. She didn't say anything right off. She let him gather his thoughts, and he appreciated her consideration. He liked her, though he didn't know her as well as Jo and Garrett.

Anna had a forthright manner and sharp, crystal-blue eyes. She was a tireless suffragette, and her efforts to gain the vote for women had achieved national attention. She'd even been shot during a rally, arriving in Cimarron Springs to recuperate and eventually marry his cousin.

She was one tough lady—he'd give her that.

Shane pressed his forehead against his knuckles. "Take Tessa back into town. I know you have people, connections. She doesn't belong here. Once she's well enough for travel, I'll send word."

"No."

The single word reverberated like cannon fire.

Shane straightened and gaped at her. "What do you mean? I thought you'd be happy."

"She doesn't want to leave." Anna turned and tucked her hands behind her, holding the railing as she leaned back. "She wants to stay here."

"She can't. Not after what happened. You must see that."

"Her fall was an accident. Accidents can happen in town as well, you know."

"We argued. I was jealous." He stuffed his hands in his pockets and avoided her curious stare. While he might want to hide the truth, she was sharp enough to guess his true feelings. "Tessa was spending too much time with the men."

Anna raised her eyebrows. "You thought she was

stepping out with one of them? Tessa doesn't seem the type."

"Absolutely not. I was…" He was out of his depth. He was terrified of becoming attached to someone who might leave him. "I was jealous of how easily they all got along together. I felt like the outsider."

Anna's expression reflected sympathy. "If I married someone I hardly knew, I'd probably get to know the people around him first. That sounds far safer."

"That doesn't make sense."

How was speaking with Finch or Wheeler safer than speaking with him? They spent every evening together. They talked. She always inquired about his day. She was solicitous and curious.

He shook his head. "I don't follow."

"For a man who's been married, you don't know a lot about women, do you?"

What sort of answers had he given her? Safe answers. Guarded answers.

Shane snorted. "You don't know the half of it. I have a singular talent for landing in impossible situations."

"A trait of all the McCoy men, as far as I can tell." She offered an indulgent grin. "I'm curious. What drew you to Tessa in the first place? You hardly knew each other and yet you married. There must have been something."

"She dealt well with the children. They adore her and she them."

What a liar he was. In truth, he'd noticed her beauty first. He was a man, after all, a man with excellent vision. As maudlin as it sounded, she'd taken his breath away. Even after he'd realized Owen was safe, he'd drawn out the encounter, reluctant to let her go. She was smart and funny and kind. More than anything else, he'd been drawn in by her compassion.

"She likes your children. Very practical," Anna said. "And yet it sounds as though you regret your decision."

"Of course I don't. Except she's miserable out here. I can't make her stay. Especially after what's happened."

"Despite your overzealous feelings of guilt, her accident was not your fault. I gave Tessa every opportunity to confide in me. I offered her my protection. I offered her a way out of the marriage. She declined." Anna cocked her head. "Rather firmly, I might add."

A band of emotion tightened around his chest. "She did?"

"And yet you'd like me to take her away. Rather odd, don't you think?"

"It's not that." He hesitated. The answer was too personal. Too revealing. "I should have given her more time to change her mind."

"From what Jo said, Tessa didn't want that time."

"I should have been stronger, for both of us."

"Hmm." Anna pushed off from the porch railing. "I know this is personal, and you don't have to answer, but have you ever actually courted a girl?"

There was no use denying the obvious. "You and I both know the answer to that question."

She drummed her fingers on the porch rail and studied his face. "I have an intriguing idea for you. Christmas is a few weeks away. Edith has offered to come by each day and help out with the children. Just until Tessa is fully recovered. You'd be wise to take advantage of her assistance and get to know your wife a little better."

Why were women always presenting half of a suggestion and assuming a fellow knew the rest? "I don't follow."

"Spend some time alone with Tessa. Without the children between you. Just the two of you. I have my own little one, you know. I realize how distracting they can be."

Fear pounded like hoof strikes down his back. "I already know her."

"Really? If that were true, then I doubt you'd have been so surprised that Tessa positively panicked when she thought I might insist she leave." Anna crossed her arms. "You'll both benefit from the time together. There's nothing wrong with courting your wife."

His stomach dipped. He'd bore her to death in an instant. All he knew of life was hard work, horses and cattle. He'd traveled plenty, but always for work. He rarely even left the hotel when he visited another city, preferring his solitude.

Nothing in his life had prepared him for courting a woman. He'd humiliate himself if he admitted his ignorance.

Then again, Tessa was worth a little humiliation. "How do you court someone? I don't know the first thing."

Anna didn't laugh or scorn him, and for that he was grateful.

"That is an excellent question, Shane," she said. "Since I'm usually counseling the woman in these matters, I have excellent insight into these sorts of things. It's all very simple. Take Tessa for a walk. Show her around the town. Learn about her likes and dislikes. For example, do you know her favorite color?"

"Why does her favorite color matter?"

"It matters because it's a part of getting to know her. If her favorite color is blue, then buy her a nice blue ribbon the next time you're in town. Get to know each other. I have a feeling you two have more in common than you realize. Women aren't nearly as complicated as men often believe. Everyone wants to know that someone treasures them."

"But what if I buy her the wrong ribbon? What if she doesn't like that particular shade of blue?"

"Don't be difficult. This isn't about ribbons. It's about showing someone that you think of them when you're apart. It's why she mends your socks and cooks your favorite dinner when you've had a bad day. Love is shown in all sorts of ways other than words and gifts."

Love. The word gave him a jolt. "I can't do those things."

"Of course you can. If by Christmas you decide you don't suit, I'll talk with the reverend about an annulment."

He didn't even like thinking about that possibility. Even though letting her go had been his idea, the realization left him hollow. "There'll be a scandal."

"You let me worry about that. I have a few tricks up my sleeve as well, Shane McCoy. Don't underestimate me."

"I wouldn't dare."

The idea terrified him. He'd rather face a pack of hungry wolves than play at being the charming suitor. That was why he'd insisted on a marriage of practicality. Unbidden, he recalled Tessa's ashen face and her cries the evening of the accident. She'd been terrified of being left alone.

Somehow he'd imagined her life much like his, nothing very dramatic. Her desperate ramblings during her illness had hinted at a troubling past. "What if she decides to leave anyway?"

The more time he spent with Tessa, the more he recognized that he could easily fall in love with her. That he was already falling in love with her. What if she never returned his feelings?

Anna shrugged. "If she leaves you, then you're no worse off than you are now." She paused. "Courted by Christmas. That's my idea. Take it or leave it."

Her kind expression belied the harsh edge of her words. She was trying to help. They all were. He simply didn't know if he was the sort of person who could be helped. "I can see why we voted you mayor."

"Thank you."

"Courted by Christmas," he repeated.

Either this was the best idea or the very worst. Only time would tell. At least he finally had an idea where to start.

Chapter Fifteen

"Keep your eyes shut," Shane ordered gently.

A week following her accident, Tessa waited expectantly for Shane's next instruction. The weather had been unseasonably mild and his aunt, Edith McCoy, had been coming by each afternoon, affording Tessa a chance to rest and recuperate.

Her bumps and bruises were healing quickly, and she felt only a slight twinge in her ankle. Her wrist still gave her a jolt now and again, but even that was improving. Doc Johnsen was set to visit that afternoon, and she was certain he'd give her a clean bill of health.

Tessa took a cautious step toward the door, her injured arm crossed over her stomach and held immobile in a sling. "They're closed."

"Wait there," Shane ordered.

"I'm waiting."

Hinges squeaked and a cold breeze ruffled her hair. Something brushed her hand and she leaped, then laughed.

"You scared me," she admonished.

"Sorry." He touched her elbow and his breath whispered against her ear. "I'll lead you a few more steps, but you must keep your eyes closed."

"I will."

"Promise."

"Yes." She sent a playful swat in his direction. "Show me your surprise before I freeze."

He placed her hand in the bend of his elbow and covered her fingers. "Just a few more steps."

Keeping her eyes tightly closed, she trustingly followed his lead. A soft snort sounded and she automatically turned toward the noise.

"Almost there," Shane said.

Hoofbeats sounded and something else as well. The rustle of fabric, the squeak of leather. Anxious now, she fidgeted beneath his hold. "Can I look yet?"

"Almost."

He moved behind her and placed his hands over her eyes. The heat of his body surrounded her along with his distinctive scent—an enticing blend of leather, horse and the outdoors. Turning her head ever so slightly, she inhaled the enticing aroma.

He'd fetched her this afternoon after Edith's arrival, promising a surprise and appearing as giddy as a schoolboy.

His hands fell away.

"You can look now," he said.

She sucked in a fortifying breath and opened her eyes. A man stood at the bottom of the porch stairs holding the reins of a beautiful bay mare.

Tessa turned toward Shane. "I don't understand."

His grin widened at her confusion. "I promised you a horse, remember?"

Tessa's eyes widened and her lips parted. "For me?"

"Yes!" He clasped her hand and gently tugged her forward. "This is John Elder. He lives down the road a piece."

The man holding the reins tipped his hat with a generous smile. He was tall and solidly built with thick dark hair visible beneath the brim of his hat, his eyes shaded from view.

"Pleasure to meet you, Mrs. McCoy."

"Tessa," she replied automatically. "Call me Tessa."

"Come down and meet her." He motioned with one hand. "She's a sweetheart. I trained her myself."

Drawn forward by his easy manner, she cautiously traversed the last few steps with Shane keeping a protective hold on her elbow.

After the last step, he released her and stepped back a pace. She extended her trembling fingers and the beautiful horse nosed her hand. A sprig of holly had been tucked into the mare's bridle. Feeling giddy, she stroked the white stripe on the horse's muzzle.

"She's beautiful," Tessa breathed. "Does she have a name?"

"Bluebell," Mr. Elder replied.

"What a romantic name."

The man flushed beneath her amused gaze. "My daughter, Hazel, names all the animals. She has a rather vivid imagination. You can call her whatever you please."

"I wouldn't change a thing. Bluebell is the perfect name for this lovely animal."

The horse pawed the ground and shook its head up and down. Shane moved beside her and rubbed his hand down the black hair of its mane. "John raises the finest horses in the county."

She playfully elbowed him in the side. "I thought you did."

"John raises the finest riding horses. I raise the finest dray horses. We're not in competition with one another."

"I'm glad to hear that," she replied with a smile.

There was something different about Shane this morning, a lightness in his attitude. He was almost flirtatious and his mood was contagious.

She pressed her forehead against Bluebell's muzzle and rubbed her skin against the soft fur. "You're a pretty lady, aren't you?"

She'd never owned a horse. She'd never owned a pet of any kind. When she was younger, her mother didn't abide animals. Her life with Emmett had been far too nomadic for a pet.

Mr. Elder patted the horse's flank. "She's got a gait like a well-sprung carriage. She's smart, too. I put her through all the paces."

He snapped his fingers and Bluebell's ears pricked in his direction. Tessa trailed her fingers along the animal's side and rubbed her withers. "She's simply beautiful."

"Horse," a small voice called.

Owen toddled outside, Alyce close on his heels. They negotiated the steps, turning backward and crawling feetfirst. They held hands and tipped back their heads, gazing up. They tended to cluster together when they were uncertain.

"This is Bluebell," Tessa explained. "Isn't she beautiful?"

"Horse," Owen stubbornly asserted.

"Bluebell is a bit of a mouthful, I know," she said. "We can call her 'horse' for now."

"Ba-bell," Alyce declared, casting a triumphant look toward her brother.

"Horse." Owen scowled.

Tessa gazed at the animal in wonder. She'd never owned anything this fine, this, well, this expensive. "I don't ride very well. I'm not certain I'll do your excellent training justice, Mr. Elder."

"Call me John. My wife was anxious to meet you, but Moira is a little under the weather."

Tessa frowned. "Nothing serious, I hope."

"Not at all." He grinned from ear to ear. "We're expecting another child come spring."

An aching need inside her unfurled. "Congratulations."

How lucky for Moira. Though challenging, Tessa had discovered she loved children. She adored Alyce and Owen. Hearing John Elder speak about his impending child with such pride in his voice, she realized she wanted more. She wanted a whole houseful of little ones.

John Elder fairly beamed. "Our seventh."

"Oh my."

He must have started his family young to have all those children.

Shane chuckled. "The Elders are a generous family. They've never turned away a lost soul."

"Some of our children come to us as infants," Mr.

Elder said. "And some of them come to us a little older. My wife was an orphan and she's never turned away a child in need. No matter how they come to us, all of them are ours in heart." He squinted at the sky. "Looks like the sun is setting soon. I should be getting back."

Shane slapped him on the shoulder. "Thanks for coming out. You could have sent someone."

"When my closest neighbor asks to buy my best mount, I figure that calls for a personal delivery." Mr. Elder winked at Tessa. "And I got to meet the new bride as well. Welcome to Cimarron Springs. If you need anything, we're just down the road and across the creek."

"You're very kind." Everyone had been so warm and welcoming. Each day the ranch felt more and more like home. With Shane softening toward her as well, she had hope for their future. "Give your wife my regards."

"I will."

Distracted by their conversation, she'd taken her attention off the children. Owen brushed past her legs and toddled directly beneath the horse's hooves. Tessa's heart leaped into her throat and she lunged. John Elder snapped his fingers. Bluebell instantly stilled, standing stiff-legged with only a gentle twitch of her tail.

Tessa reached beneath the horse's belly and hugged the boy against her side with her uninjured arm. "Owen McCoy, you're going to turn my hair gray."

Shane shooed him toward where Alyce sat on the steps, as prim and proper as a porcelain doll.

"Up you go," Shane ordered. "You've frightened Tessa enough for one day."

Alyce scooted away. "Bad."

Owen socked her arm. "You bad."

Alyce sobbed and shoved him back.

Shane quickly intervened and broke up the tussle with a sigh.

Tessa glanced between the two children, their features highlighted in the rosy glow of the setting sun, and her thoughts drifted to the dates written in the Bible. Judging by the picture of Abby, the children's father must have been quite fair as well. She shook away her musing in frustration. Why did the identity of their father matter? Except she'd always had more than her fair share of curiosity.

Edith appeared on the porch, her hands firmly planted on her hips. "Come along, you two. We're making maple syrup crackle."

The idea of candy was far more interesting than the horse, and the twins shoved at each other in their race back inside.

"There was another reason I came in person," John Elder said, jarring her from her musings. "You may have squatters on your land."

Shane's gaze sharpened. "What have you seen?"

"Smoke. Late in the evening. I checked it out this morning and found a carcass. One of your cattle, I presume. The remnants of a fire as well. I followed the footprints. One man for certain, probably more."

"Indians?"

Tessa's breath caught. She'd never considered that danger.

"No," Mr. Elder replied. "These folks wasted a full three-quarters of the beast."

"Nope. That's not Indians." Shane caught her worried gaze and wrapped his arm around her shoulders, giving her a comforting squeeze. "Don't worry. We've never had problems this far north."

If not Indians, then who? *The Fultons*.

Busy with her new life, she'd forgotten all about them. The danger remained. She doubted they'd forgotten about her. Despite Shane's assurances, tiny shards of fear pricked her spine. Her legs shook beneath her, threatening to give way.

Shane tucked her against his side. "Have you informed Garrett?"

Nodding, Mr. Elder said, "I sent someone into town first thing. Garrett isn't there. Called out on a land dispute. Could be a week before he's back. David, his deputy, is taking a look."

"David is good, but I'd prefer the marshal. Tessa and I had a run-in with a man in Wichita. A member of the Fulton Gang." She stiffened and Shane soothed her upper arm in rhythmic circles. "I doubt it's them, but let's not take any chances."

John Elder rubbed his chin. "Can't say that I've heard of that bunch."

"They usually stick around Kansas City. Keep a sharp eye out, just in case."

"I will." Mr. Elder extended the reins to Tessa. "She's all yours."

Shane held out a restraining hand. "Are you certain you're up to it?"

"Indulge me," Tessa implored. "I've never owned anything this beautiful, and I'm not letting go just yet."

"All right. But don't tax yourself."

"Thank you." Even with Mr. Elder looking on, she

stood on her tiptoes and pressed a kiss against his cheek. "She's perfect."

A flush crept up his neck.

His generosity humbled her and her guilt flared. She'd been lulled into a sense of complacency. In truth, nothing had changed. Emmett was missing. The Fultons were a threat. The men John Elder had seen might be beggars or tramps. Or they might not. The horse nudged her hip and she playfully skipped ahead. She enjoyed her new life. She loved the children and she believed she was doing good for them. Shane was coming around.

And yet a deep sense of unease chased away her brief contentment. She gazed at the prairie, the undulating grasses visible above the scattered patches of snow. As long as the Fultons were out there, she'd always be in danger.

If she'd put this family in danger as well, she'd never forgive herself.

For the next few days Shane and the men scoured the fields, searching for any sign of the men who'd slaughtered his cattle. Despite their efforts, their search met with frustration. Shane didn't know whether to be relieved or worried. The unknown nagged at him, and Tessa's lingering fear was more than worrisome. There was something more going on between her and the outlaw, and he needed her trust. Unless she confided in him, he was helpless.

In anticipation of his first evening of officially courting his wife, he'd donned his best coat, and with a fresh shave and a touch of the cologne Wheeler kept in his shaving kit, he nervously approached the door to the ranch house. He'd already made arrangements with Edith, but he'd forgotten to inform Tessa of his plans. Probably he should have done that.

Shane slicked back his hair and lifted his knuckles toward the door. Should he knock? It felt as if he should knock. Yet knocking at his own house seemed odd as well. As he pondered the correct behavior, the door swung open.

Tessa smiled. "I thought I heard something out here."

"I was going to knock," he said dumbly.

"It's your house. I'm your wife. You don't have to knock."

He raked his fingers through his hair again. "I wasn't sure."

"Come inside." She snagged his arm and dragged him off the porch. "You're letting in the cold."

Once inside, she waved him toward the table. He sat and clasped his hands on the table. "How are you feeling?"

She took the chair to his right. "I'm feeling wonderful. Fit as a fiddle. Edith says you're guilty about my accident."

"Edith talks too much."

She covered his hands with her own. "What happened was an accident."

"I said I'd keep you safe."

"Now you're being silly. You can't prevent all the icy patches in the world."

"I—"

She placed two fingers over his lips. "I won't hear another word. We're supposed to be courting. If I don't have something to tell JoBeth when she brings the children around, she'll have my hide."

He splayed his fingers on the table and collapsed forward. "Then you know about the courting? Good. I was going to mention it…"

"Don't worry. Edith filled me in. I hope they didn't browbeat you too much. We can go through the motions, make everyone happy. It'll be our little secret."

"Good. Sure. I have the wagon hitched. How about dinner in town tonight? Just the two of us?"

"That sounds lovely," she replied, and he knew immediately that Edith had also informed her of his plans for the evening. "Let me fetch my coat."

A short time later they were settled on the buckboard of the wagon, two blankets tucked around Tessa's legs and her feet propped on a warm brick. She wore her ridiculous emerald green hat, muffler and mittens, managing to look silly and charming at the same time.

He slapped the reins against the horses' backs and cast her a sidelong glance. "Anna said we should ask each other questions. So, um, what's your favorite color?"

"Peach, I guess. My favorite shade is during the sunset, when the sky turns kind of a peachy pink. How about you? What's your favorite color?"

"Green." He searched for a descriptor. Did he like the green of an evergreen? Or grass? After a moment he said, "Just green."

Not as exciting as a sunset, but it was the best he had.

"When Edith insisted I wear my best dress before she took the children off to her house, I admit I was a little nervous."

"Me, too."

"I've never courted anyone before."

"Me neither." They both grinned and he added, "We're a pair, aren't we?"

The air was crisp and the sky cloudless. He couldn't have picked a better day for their new beginning. Earlier he and the boys had tossed around questions he might ask, and he searched his memory. "This will give us a chance to know each other better. Where were you raised?"

"I was born in Chicago. We lived in an apartment on the third floor of a tenement. I remember my mother hanging laundry between the buildings. My dresses smelled of wood smoke and pipe tobacco."

"But you didn't stay? What happened after your mother died?"

She puffed a breath of warm air into her mittens and warmed her nose. "After my mother died I stayed with some relatives. Some months later, my father, Emmett, took me with him."

Something in her closed expression had him searching for a different question, less personal questions. He'd circle back to her family later.

The next twenty minutes passed in much the same way. With the help of the questions he'd compiled earlier, he pushed and prodded the conversation, cajoling and parrying with her. Yet no matter how carefully he broached the subject of her past and her family, she deftly turned the conversation back on him.

He knew her favorite color, food and time of day, yet frustratingly, infuriatingly, he didn't feel he was any closer to actually knowing the heart of *her*.

"What of your father?" she asked. "What was he like?"

Shane's hands tightened on the reins. "Gone."

She murmured a noncommittal response, and he recalled her previous criticism of his suppertime conversation. He finally understood what she'd meant. He'd been talking, but never really opening up about himself. No wonder she'd been unsatisfied.

Since he'd been pushing her to open up to him, he owed her the same in return. "My father left when I was thirteen. It was just my mother and me after that."

She leaned nearer and hugged his arm. "I'm sorry. That must have been very difficult for both you and your mother."

"We had good times and bad. I heard he died some years back."

He'd always admired Tessa's affection with the children. Recently he'd noticed that affection had been extended to him. She was incredibly demonstrative, touching his bent knee as she scooted past, brushing her fingers along his sleeve, laying a hand on his shoulder as she served him at the dinner table. He'd never considered himself the kind of man who enjoyed that sort of thing. Not anymore. He yearned for her slightest touch.

She straightened once more. "Maybe that's why we're so awkward with each other. Neither of us has ever seen a proper marriage. We have nothing to go by."

"It doesn't have to be that way. There's no reason we can't change things."

"You're uncharacteristically optimistic this evening."

He started. "I didn't realize I was pessimistic."

"Hmm, perhaps not. You're more of a realist, I suppose." She plucked at the red tartan blanket covering her legs. "Have you caught any sight of the men Mr. Elder saw?"

"Nothing," he bit out in frustration. "I'd have liked to settle the thing at least and discover their identities."

As the town appeared in the distance, they lapsed into silence. He hitched the wagon before the hotel and assisted Tessa down, letting his fingers linger around her waist a touch longer than necessary.

They stepped into the warmth of the restaurant, and he surveyed the crowd. Several tables were occupied but there was plenty of seating.

He turned toward Tessa and caught her shocked expression. He followed her gaze toward a dark-haired gentleman rising from his seat.

Tessa abandoned his side and wove through the tables, then launched herself at the gentleman, who caught her against his chest.

"Emmett!' she exclaimed.

Shane's heartbeat thudded against his ribs. This was Tessa's father?

Everything Tessa had said had led him to believe that Emmett Spencer was dead. Yet here he was. Very much alive.

"Emmett!" Tessa squealed again, too shocked to do anything but stare.

Stumbling back, he lifted her off her feet in a bone-crushing hug, then set her away from him. Tall and lean, Emmett's bandit-dark hair had only just started graying at the temples. He kept both his thick hair and beard neatly clipped and his expensive clothes tailored and spotless. Any passerby who didn't know him would think he was a respectable fellow and not a seasoned outlaw who'd spent a lifetime skating in and out of trouble.

"You look as pretty as a peach." His eyes glistened. "I've missed you."

She stepped away and blinked back tears. "Where have you been? I was worried."

She had plenty to say to him but this was not the time or the place. These past weeks had taught her the value of family, and she'd try to remember that when they spoke alone later. He didn't appear any worse for wear, and while she was thankful for his good health, her resentment lingered.

How like Emmett to simply appear unannounced, throwing everything into an uproar.

"I had to go underground. You know that."

Despite her curiosity, there were too many other people around.

Tessa realized they'd drawn the curious stares of the other patrons. She dragged Emmett back through the jumble of tables toward the vestibule. Shane was still standing in the spot where she'd left him, an unreadable expression on his face.

She ducked her head against her own guilt. She'd led him to believe Emmett was dead. No doubt he was curious about her father's sudden reappearance.

"Shane, this is my dad, Emmett Spencer." She sucked in a fortifying breath. "Emmett, this is my husband, Shane McCoy."

"You can't be serious. I'm gone for a few weeks and you up and marry."

"I haven't seen you since last September."

"It can't be that long." He paused, as though mentally gauging the time passed. "Is this why you made all that fuss in Wichita?"

"No. I hadn't even met Shane yet."

Emmett snatched her hand and studied her fingers. "You're not even wearing a ring."

Trust her dad to pick out that one small detail.

Tessa tucked her hands into the folds of her skirt. "It's a long story. We got married rather suddenly. There wasn't time for a ring."

The men exchanged a brief handshake. Both of them wary and eyeing each other like a couple of roosters with their chests puffed out.

Shane hooked his thumbs into his belt loops. "Join us for dinner, Mr. Spencer?"

"Actually, I'd prefer a word alone with my daughter, Mr. McCoy. We haven't seen each other in a while." He looked Shane up and down. "Seems like we have some catching up to do."

Tessa silently pleaded with her husband and he gave an almost imperceptible nod of his head. "I'll wait at the table. There's a parlor in the back for guests. It's usually empty this time of day."

Tessa gripped his hand in a quick, grateful squeeze. He knew something was wrong. How could he not? How was she ever going to explain this?

Together she and Emmett found the tiny parlor with a fire crackling merrily in the hearth and two tufted wingback chairs set before the warmth.

Emmett perched on the edge of one chair and she took the other.

"Who is he…that…that farmer?" Emmett demanded. "Did he take advantage of you?"

"He's a rancher and it's nothing like that. It's a long story." Her chest seized at a sudden thought. "The marshal. The town marshal has met you before. You'd best steer clear of him."

"Have a little faith in your old man. I checked on the local law enforcement before I settled into town. Marshal Cain is resolving a land dispute two towns away. I've got another day or two before he's back. I've been in town for two weeks. I'd given up hope of ever finding you. I nearly fainted when you waltzed in the door."

"You haven't answered my questions properly. Where have you been? Why didn't you answer my telegrams? I've been worried." She chucked him on the arm. "You have some explaining to do."

There was no use scolding Emmett. He was impervious.

"Me?" He rubbed at his arm with an exaggerated grimace. "Why did you leave Wichita? How'd you end up here? This town is filled with nothing but churchgoers and salt-of-the-earth folks." He tugged on his collar. "Makes me nervous. I can't find a poker game to save my hide."

"Thank goodness for that. You leave these people alone. I'm living here now. I can't just pick up and run if you start a ruckus." She stared into the flames. "Is everything squared? Are we safe now?"

He adjusted his trousers over his knees, then clasped his hands before him. "About that. I need your help with a little project."

"No." She shook her head for emphasis. "Absolutely not."

Betrayal shot through her veins. He'd come only because he wanted something from her. Here she'd thought he'd actually discovered his conscious.

"Hear me out. You're the best locksmith west of the Mississippi. You're the best person for this job."

Tessa narrowed her gaze. Charming Emmett was back at his finest. First he'd begin with the flattery. If that didn't work, he'd move to guilt.

"No."

"It's one job," he pleaded. "And it's for a good cause. Me."

"No, no and no."

Emmett's mouth hardened and he stood halfway from his chair. "It's that farmer, isn't it? Has he got some sort of hold over you? I'll take care of him. I know people. Say the word and he'll be on the next steamship bound for the gulf."

"Don't you lay a finger on him. You hear me?" Tessa pressed her hands against his chest and shoved him into his seat once more. "It's nothing like that. I met him in Wichita. He has these two beautiful children. He's a good man. He doesn't know about you. What you do for a living. What *we* did for a living."

"You'll be bored to death in a year with that fellow. People like us don't change."

"I'm not like you. Why can't you see that?"

Emmett's scowl only deepened. "We're back on that again, are we? It's not bad for a man to make a living off his wits. If a fellow can't play a round of poker, then it's not my fault."

"It's not just the poker. You know that."

He crossed his arms over his chest. "Land grabbers don't deserve fair dealings. There's nothing wrong with cheating a cheat. That's the rule."

"It's not a rule. Not everyone thinks like you."

Emmett made a sound of disgust in his throat. "I don't understand. You never had a problem before that preacher got his teeth into you. You want to know the truth? That snake-oil salesman was no better than I am. He's worse, even. You think any of them folks are getting the salvation he promised? At least I'm up-front in my dealings. That preacher has no better chance getting through the pearly gates than me."

She pressed her hands against her cheeks. "I don't want to argue. I had to leave Wichita in a hurry because I spotted Dead Eye. He was looking for me."

That information snagged his attention. "Why didn't you tell me?"

"I tried to. Why haven't you answered my telegrams?"

"Because I can't go near any of my old haunts. Those Fultons have people everywhere." He settled back into his seat and pinched his forehead. "Glad I missed him when I went looking for you. The last place I knew you'd been was Wichita. I picked up the trail there."

"And you came looking for me for a job." She drew her brows together. "You were worried about me, too, right?"

"Sure, sure. Absolutely. But you're smart and capable," Emmett scoffed. "You know how to steer clear of them Fultons. They're not too bright. The delay has put me behind, though. We have to put this plan together lickety-split."

There was no use reasoning with him. Once Emmett got hold of a plan, he was obsessed. Never mind that his only daughter was married and he'd practically growled at her husband. Never mind that an outlaw was on the lookout for her, putting her new family at risk. There was a plan. Time for everyone to drop everything and go along with Emmett.

"Dead Eye Dan had my picture." She spoke through gritted teeth.

"He must have stolen it. I sure didn't give it to him. How can you even think that of your old pa?"

Not even ten minutes into their reunion and already her patience was thinning. "You haven't answered my question. What job are you working this time?"

"You're gonna love this." He held up a hand, silencing her protest. "I found the guy who set me up before. He was working as a teller in a bank in Wichita. Caught him up in Abilene living like a king. Turns out he and Dead Eye Dan had the same particular friend. Dead Eye must have told her about his plan, and she double-crossed him with the teller. They turned us in. That's why there was a posse mustered before we could spit twice. It was a brilliant plan. While I was holed up under the floorboards waiting for dark, that teller was hauling out all the money. Who's gonna believe a bunch of outlaws when they say the money is already gone? Wish I'd have thought of it myself. The law thinks the Fultons have the money. The Fultons think I have the money. And those two got off scot-free. It's brilliant."

Tessa snickered. "Brilliant. Yes. And how do you propose to expose his guilt?"

"I steal the money back from him, give it to the Fultons, then clear my name."

"This teller is living like a king, you said. How much money does he have left? You really think the Fultons will settle for chump change after they'd had a chance at the whole prize?"

"It's better than nothing." Emmett started to rise, then caught himself and paused. "Help out your old man, one last time. If the Fultons put a bullet through my heart, you'll never forgive yourself for not helping."

There it was, the guilt. Right on time. Emmett was nothing if not predictable. "Don't start in on me. I didn't get you into this mess, and there's no way I can get you out."

All at once his face slackened, and he looked older and exhausted. Studying him closer, she realized he was thinner, his cheeks more gaunt than the last time she'd seen him. Guilt gnawed at her gut.

She touched his sleeve. "Pa, you know I can't help you. Especially now. I have a family to think about."

"Don't call me Pa. It's common."

"We are common. Or had you forgotten?"

"We're anything we want to be. I told you that. People believe what they see."

A rock settled in the pit of her stomach. "Things have changed for me."

She loved Emmett. She desperately wanted him safe. And yet having him here terrified her. She'd started over. She liked the person she was becoming. Emmett brought back the past just when she was creating a new future.

Things between her and Shane were finally changing for the better, but their relationship was fragile. She wasn't ready to share her past with him. A sharp pain throbbed in her chest. Emmett was her father. How could she ask him to leave? Especially with the Fultons still after him. He knew her too well. If something happened, she'd never forgive herself.

He wasn't likely to stay long anyway. Especially once the marshal returned. Emmett preferred a fresh audience for his trade, and the marshal was already aware of his proclivities. A little part of her, a hidden part of her, had known that settling in Cimarron Springs had changed their relationship for good. She'd chosen Shane and the future he offered over Emmett, and the decision tore at her.

Making the right decision didn't necessarily make the choice easy.

Emmett tugged on his ear. "What about this husband of yours? You gonna invite me for dinner? You said he had children."

Tessa stood and edged toward the door. How did she introduce Emmett without revealing too much of her past? She didn't want any more lies.

"My husband is a good man." She rested her hand on Emmett's sleeve. "Please don't ruin this for me."

He grinned, smoothing the creases of worry along his forehead into laugh lines. "When have I ever ruined anything?"

Chapter Sixteen

Shane sensed Tessa's unease the moment she stepped into the room. Emmett Spencer was tall and leanly built. He appeared at once affable and charming. His grin was wide and his teeth well cared for. He sported dark hair with a feathering of gray at the temples. Despite the difference in their coloring, there was a definite resemblance between the two.

Though Emmett was at least two decades older than Shane, he imagined Emmett still drew admiring glances from the ladies. Dressed in a deep brown suit, he had the easy, self-confident charm of a man used to getting his own way.

The rest of the dinner passed affably. Emmett regaled them with funny anecdotes from his travels. He assumed the air of a charming host, never letting the conversation lag for long, but never really saying anything personal. By the time the evening ended, Shane had developed a grudging admiration for the man.

Tessa was afraid of something, but her father was not the source of her fears.

All of the proper pleasantries were exchanged. Emmett was dutifully invited for supper on Sunday and Tessa promised she'd visit the following day. A perfectly ordinary meeting between a man and his father-in-law, and yet Shane had an uneasy feeling there was nothing ordinary about Emmett.

Despite the success of the evening, his unease grew. Emmett Spencer was very much alive, though Tessa had led him to believe otherwise.

The ride back in the wagon was far colder and quieter than the ride into town.

Shane stared at the top of Tessa's bent head. "We need to talk."

"I know. Let's wait until we're home and the children are asleep."

"Fair enough."

The rest of the ride passed in silence. The children took their time falling to sleep. Once they'd finally quieted, Tessa sat on the floor and gathered the wooden blocks he'd carved and painted for the children into a wire basket.

He lowered himself onto a chair behind her. "Leave that. I'll clean up later."

Instead of standing, she leaned back against his leg and rested her temple against his bent knee. "I'm sorry I lied about Emmett. I knew you thought he was dead."

His hand hovered above her hair. Some of the pieces had loosened from the neat bun at the nape of her neck and he longed to touch them. To feel the silky tresses. "Why didn't you want me to know about him?"

What are you afraid of? He held his tongue.

He wrapped a tendril of her hair gently around his

finger, marveling at the brilliant color. She didn't flinch or pull away, and her acceptance emboldened him. He let his hand rest on her shoulder.

She rubbed her cheek against the back of his hand. "We all have secrets, don't we?"

"Yes."

"Tell me about Abby," she questioned, her voice soft. "She's the children's mother and I know nothing about her."

Had Tessa guessed about the children? He'd seen her looking between them more than once. Abby had been adamant that no one know he wasn't the children's father. She'd been protecting them against gossip.

He'd clung to the secret as penance for his own guilt. Time had mellowed him. Even if they'd got married that first time, he wouldn't have been able to save her. Abby had always flirted with destruction. She craved excitement. He wasn't going to save her because she couldn't even save herself.

If he let go of her secret, he let go of the idea that the past might have been different.

There was no need to protect them against Tessa. "Abby was already expecting when we married."

"But the children aren't yours."

"I didn't say that."

"You didn't have to." She turned her head and gazed up at him. The lamplight caught her lashes and cast shadows on her cheeks. "I know what kind of man you are."

If she knew what he was feeling now, she might not be as assured. "Abby and I knew each other when we were young."

If he wanted honesty from Tessa, then she deserved something from him. He laid out his story, telling her about his own father and the life he'd lived following his absence. He told her about how Abby had wanted them to marry when they were younger and how he'd refused her. He told Tessa about Abby's return, about how she claimed she'd made a mistake and she'd never stopped loving him. He revealed how he'd foolishly thought they'd go on as they had before.

Tessa listened without interrupting. When he'd finished his story, she was quiet for a moment before asking, "How did you feel about Abby?"

A question he'd avoiding asking himself. "She moved to town when she was eleven. There weren't many children at the schoolhouse, and we were the same age. We studied together, sat together. Seemed inevitable we'd pair up. Just worked out that way. We were friends," he said, recalling those days as though looking through someone else's eyes. It all seemed like a different time and place. "I loved her the way you love someone who's been a part of your life. But I was never in love with her. I didn't know the difference. I assumed we'd go on as we had before, with the same easy friendship. Marriage changed everything. I understood that too late."

Tessa folded her hands on his knee and rested her chin on her knuckles, gazing into the distance. His fingers had tangled deeper into her hair, and he marveled at the springy softness.

"Do you know the identity of their father?" Tessa asked.

"Abby never said."

"But you suspected."

"Yes and no." Tessa was far too perceptive. He'd considered and discarded several possibilities over the years. "Abby had a wild streak. She adored adventure. When we were kids, I'd often catch her too near the train tracks. She'd stand close enough that she felt the wind as they streaked by. She needed danger. She once told me that everything changed when she discovered she was carrying Alyce and Owen. A part of her wanted them safe and secure, but the other part still craved that adventure. She wanted to do the right thing by them, but she was always fighting against herself. Eventually, we all lost."

"She and Emmett would have gotten along well." Tessa sighed. "Her struggles must have been very difficult for you to watch."

"Agony. There's nothing worse than seeing someone you love hurting, helpless against their suffering. I'd have taken her pain if I could have."

While the final days with Abby had been bleak and hopeless, in the beginning there'd been good times. Even after Owen and Alyce had been born, there'd been good days mixed with the bad. He sometimes got caught up in how things had ended and forgot how they'd begun. The further time slipped into the past, the easier it was to forgive. He missed her; he missed who she'd been before time and trouble had blighted the optimistic girl he'd once known.

"We can't change other people," Tessa said sadly.

He'd laid himself open, exposing all his secrets. The time had come for Tessa to answer his questions. "Why did you lie to me about Emmett?"

She braced her hands against his knee and stood, and

he reluctantly withdrew his touch as she moved away. She disappeared into her room and returned again with a distinctive clothbound ledger. He'd seen her studying the book before and vaguely wondered about its contents. He'd assumed it was some sort of diary.

She scraped a chair nearer to his, creating a distance between them. "Are you certain you want to know?"

"I'm tired of secrets and lies, Tessa. They rarely do anyone any good. I'm ready for the truth."

Tessa gripped the book between her hands, her knuckles whitening. Shane had been honest with her. She owed him honesty in return. "Emmett makes his money gambling and swindling land grabbers."

There. She'd said it. Except she didn't feel the relief she'd expected. With the ledger clutched between her hands, the rest of her explanation locked in her throat. She didn't want to leave, and if he knew the whole truth about her past, she feared his reaction.

"Emmett is a good man," she continued. "Truly, he is. Kind and generous. But he and Abby had many traits in common. He enjoys living on the edge of a precipice. Emmett is at his happiest when he's closest to disaster. When I was growing up, he'd win us a fortune, then spend it all in an instant. He always needed a challenge. If there wasn't a challenge readily available, he created one."

Shane crossed his arms over his chest, his jaw tight. She missed the soothing touch of his fingers in her hair, the gentle warmth of his comfort.

"What about you?" he asked. "How did you get along?"

"Fine, really. I know that my childhood sounds terribly unconventional, but after what I'd been through, I didn't mind. When I was very young, all I knew of Emmett were the stories my mother told. He wasn't suited for domestic life. I believe my mother thought having a child might settle him down. Except that didn't work. Eventually, he looked at us as his jailers rather than his family. After my mother passed away, I lived with relatives." She paused, catching her breath. "They did not enjoy having me around. Emmett came for a visit and realized that I was—I was unhappy. He saved me from that miserable fate and I'm eternally grateful to him."

"Was this family called the Hensons?"

Tessa reared back. "How do you know their name?"

"You mentioned them when you were ill." He touched her hand. "I know they were unkind to you."

She tugged her hand from his reach and wrapped her arms around her body. She'd always been ashamed by their treatment. "They had other children. I was the outsider. Emmett saved me from all that. Don't you see? He did his best."

"He was your father, Tessa. It's his job to protect you. You don't owe him anything."

"I know that." She laughed hollowly. "He can't help himself. He tries. I know he tries. We argued last spring. I wanted him to settle down. I was so weary of moving around all the time. I wanted something permanent and lasting."

"Is Emmett mixed up with Dead Eye and the Fultons? Is that why the outlaw was looking for you?"

Her cheeks suffused with color. "It was all a misunderstanding. The Fultons blame him for something he didn't do. He's been trying to fix things, but it's complicated. It's difficult."

"Does your father realize the danger he put you in?"

"Of course! He loves me. Truly, he does. He's just, well, he's just Emmett. He does what he pleases. Everything always turns out right for Emmett."

Shane pushed off from his seat and turned from her. He braced his hands against the kitchen table, leaning forward.

A sudden chill settled over her. "What are you thinking?"

"Why didn't you ask for Emmett's help before? In Wichita."

"I couldn't find him. After his trouble with the Fultons, he disappeared. I wasn't certain if I'd ever see him again."

"Now he's back. In Cimarron Springs. Why?"

"To check on me, I suppose." The answer sounded false even to her own ears. "You must believe that he'd never do anything that might hurt me."

Shane's mood prevented her from saying anything more. She doubted he'd be pleased to hear Emmett had wanted her to help him rob someone.

"Like getting involved with a gang of thugs, then disappearing and sending them after his only daughter?"

She stood and laid a hand against the tense muscles of his back. "Please don't be angry. I thought he'd settle things. Emmett always has a way of slipping out of difficulty. I was certain this time would be the same. I'd have never put your family in danger if I had known he wouldn't resolve this."

"Our family. It's our family, Tessa. Don't you see that?"

She pressed against his back and wrapped her arms around his waist. He didn't understand and she didn't want him to. "Like it or not, Emmett is part of our family as well."

She'd been willing to walk away from Emmett forever all those weeks ago. Realizing she may never see him again had shocked her from her callous indifference. As long as Emmett was alive and near, there were always possibilities.

"He should have been there for you, Tessa."

"Don't be silly. I'm a grown woman. I can take care of myself." Shane didn't call her on the blatant lie, and she appreciated his tact. She'd done a dreadful job looking out for herself and they both knew it. "Please, don't let this stand between us. I know we can work things out."

He turned and they were standing only inches apart. He leaned forward and slid one large hand between her neck and the hair falling over her shoulder, tugged loose by his gentle touch earlier. Her heart began an erratic rhythm. The skin where his fingers touched tingled with the contact.

"If we…if I…" she mumbled, enthralled with the way his thumb stroked the line of her jaw. Fascinated by the rapid pulse beating in the hollow of his neck. His gentle touch set her nerves to attention. Smoothing her hands over his shoulders, she threaded her fingers behind his neck. Feeling emboldened, she raised on tiptoes and his mouth swooped, engaging hers with a swift eagerness. His lips were firm and resolute, yet silken and pleasing.

Long seconds later he lifted his head and studied her face. His eyes held an intense look. Her stomach fluttered. She hugged him close, feeling his rapid breathing. What a fraud she was, what a traitor. She'd happily divulged Emmett's secrets while keeping her own.

The ache of loneliness weighed on her chest. The girls from the Harvey House had welcomed her without reserve, but she'd always held back a part of herself, keeping the full truth hidden.

Her whole life she'd been hiding. As a child, her mother had hidden the truth of her father's activities, keeping up the appearance of respectability. Emmett, on the other hand, had treated each day as a new adventure. He adored the new personas they created and relished starting over again and again. Tessa was weary of starting over. She craved security and permanence.

With Emmett in town, how long before Shane realized the extent of her involvement in his previous schemes? She was not without guilt. Even at eight years old she'd heard enough about Emmett from her mother to understand the choice she was making in leaving with Emmett rather than staying with her relatives.

The words stayed frozen in her throat. Once again she reflected on the precarious nature of their relationship. They were building trust with each other, yet she couldn't bring herself to reveal the truth about herself. She simply wanted to be held and comforted. His arms tightened around her and she imagined, just for a moment, that she was the person he thought her to be.

She'd tell him the truth. Soon. But first she wanted to savor the feeling of being cherished.

There'd be time enough for the truth later.

Chapter Seventeen

The following day, Edith arrived at her usual time. After exchanging pleasantries, the kindly woman shooed Tessa out the door. "Go on, now. I've got everything under control. Enjoy your time with Shane."

A blush tingeing her cheeks, Tessa met him on the porch. He was dressed in his work clothes today and her gaze was drawn to his mouth. She liked kissing him and he seemed to like kissing her as well. Their relationship had changed since last evening. The difference was slight, but encouraging. She glanced down and frowned. Though a bright afternoon, Shane held a kerosene lamp.

Her frown deepened. "Where are we going?"

His expression grew somber. "We need some peaches. Come to the root cellar with me."

Her heart tripped and she dug in her heels, violently shaking her head. "No. I'm not going back down there."

"Sooner or later you have to face your fears."

"No. I don't."

He reached for her hand. "I'll be right there with you the whole time."

As he talked, he drew her inexorably forward. She let him lead her across the clearing even though she had no intention of accompanying him down those awful stairs.

She hadn't gone near the root cellar since the accident. The boys were always willing to fetch her anything she needed, and she repaid them in slices of pie for their trouble. The arrangement was working well for everyone.

Shane squeezed her fingers. "It's just a hole in the hillside with jars of peaches."

"And spiders. And mice. And snakes."

"They're more afraid of you than you are of them."

"Don't be so certain." She returned his good-humored grin with skepticism.

He paused his step, faced her and cupped the back of her neck. "I know you can do this."

Blood rushed in her ears. He was right. It was only a hole in the ground. Nothing to be afraid of.

"Promise me you won't leave." A shiver that had nothing to do with the cold shook through her. "That you'll be with me the whole time."

He reached for her hand once more and tugged her forward. "Absolutely."

As they reached the propped-open door, he faced her once more. "Are you okay? Are you ready for this?"

"Of course I'm not ready for this. I'm terrified." She squared her shoulders. "You go first."

"I'll go first."

Juggling the lantern in one hand, he descended a few steps. Tessa followed him and rested her hand on his shoulder. With his free hand, he crossed his arm over his chest and covered her fingers. The loamy scent of the damp dirt sent her heart racing.

She swayed and Shane paused.

He swiveled in the narrow space and caught her hand. "We can stop here."

She shook her head. "No. I want to go on. I want to go further."

He backed down the next step and she followed. Ever so slowly, they descended the last step. Lunging forward, she wrapped her arms around his middle and pressed her face against his chest. He held her that way for a long time, then crouched and set the lamp on the floor.

She opened her eyes a slit and glanced around.

He didn't say anything, letting her wrestle with her unease. There was nothing to be afraid of down here, and yet the disquiet remained. Memories came rushing back. Emmett often left in the evenings. *The best pickings are after midnight*, he'd say. *That's when the real men come out to play.* He'd douse the lamp and lock the door, thinking her asleep. She'd relight the lamp and stare at the ceiling. She'd listen for every thump, every footstep and every jiggle of the doorknob until he crept back home.

Her whole body trembled and Shane put space between them, gripping her forearms. "We'll go."

"No." She sniffled. "It's not that. I was thinking of something else. I didn't even realize until now how much I feared being left alone. When I was younger, Emmett often worked late into the night. He left me alone. There was no other way. I think…I think that's why being down here bothered me so much."

"Childhood fears don't always end with childhood."

"He told me not to be afraid, but I was." She flashed a watery smile. "You're right, though. I do feel a little better now."

She inhaled a deep breath and searched the brightly lit space. Everything had changed. She didn't enjoy being down here, but she wasn't terrified either. Facing her fear had blunted the force of the effect.

They spent the rest of their time together walking hand in hand along the frozen creek bed. Shane didn't ask about Emmett, and she didn't offer any more information. It was enough that they were together.

They returned to the house and Edith waved them inside. She handed Tessa an envelope.

"Almost forgot," Edith said. "Someone dropped this by the telegraph station for delivery, and I told Jo I'd bring it by."

Tessa recognized Emmett's flamboyant scrawl immediately. She tore open the envelope and scanned the contents.

Dear Tess,
    Please join me at the hotel tomorrow for lunch.
Noon. I have important news for you.
Emmett

She glanced up to where Shane was replacing the lantern on the shelf in the kitchen. "Everything all right?" he asked.

If she went tomorrow, she'd be walking straight into a trap. Emmett never called her Tess. Which meant he was sending her a message: *Don't come.*

Nothing would ever be all right again. "Fine. Emmett wants me to have lunch with him tomorrow."

He was warning her.

Edith tilted her head. "Who is Emmett?"

"My father. He's staying in town."

"Well, land's sake, child. Why didn't you say so? I'll come by earlier tomorrow. There's nothing like family, is there?"

Tessa gave a distracted nod.

She folded the note and scored the seam with her thumb. "Thank you, Edith. I'd appreciate the time with him."

Since John Elder had spotted the abandoned campsite, she'd known things were bound to come to a head. Too many separate pieces were converging. Emmett had arrived and the Fultons were hot on his heels. Or maybe it was the other way around.

This thing had to end, one way or another. If the Fultons had caught up with Emmett, it was just as well. If they were setting a trap for her, that meant they wanted something. If they wanted something, she had leverage.

If they had Emmett, they knew by now he didn't have the money. There was even a chance Emmett had talked them into going after the bank teller. Either way, she'd never know unless she walked into their trap.

Once she'd paid Emmett's debt, they'd finally be free. Then she'd tell Shane the whole truth of her past. If he still wanted her as a wife, she'd put her heart into their family. If he chose to let her go, so be it.

Either way, she had to see this through. She'd already faced one fear this morning. It was high time she faced her other fears as well.

Something was wrong.

Just like the day Tessa had fallen down the stairs, Shane hadn't been able to shake the feeling all morning. John Elder had sent a messenger from his ranch over that morning. Seemed that some of Shane's cattle had wandered onto Elder land. He and the men had been riding the fence line searching for the break.

They'd searched for hours before finally discovering the breach. He knelt before the separated barbed wire and studied the neatly clipped ends.

Milt planted his elbow on his saddle horn and glanced over his shoulder. "What you got there, boss?"

"Someone did this on purpose."

"You think it's them rustlers John Elder saw the other day?"

"Maybe."

His nerves thrummed. "I don't like this. Let's go back to the house."

There was something wrong. All his instincts urged him to return to the house. He mounted his horse once more. "Did Tessa say when she'd be back?"

"According to Edith, she'll be back before suppertime."

Though Shane felt better knowing Red was keeping an eye on things at the ranch, worry gnawed at his gut. There were too many odd events coming together too quickly. First John Elder had spotted poachers on the land, then Tessa's dad had arrived, and now his fence had been cut.

Not to mention Tessa had taken for town, and he didn't entirely trust Emmett Spencer. Being with her father should have been the safest place for Tessa. She'd said he was harmless, and Emmett sure put on a good show. Cimarron Springs had seemed the securest place for the two to meet up. Everyone knew everyone else, and the poker games were tame since the marshal had cleaned up the town. Shane's unease remained. Considering the man's activities, he was a danger.

Even if it meant dealing with Tessa's anger later, Shane needed his own assurances.

He motioned for Milt. "I'm riding in. You okay with that repair?"

"I'll have it fixed in a lick. I'll follow the line, see if there's any more breaks. Check for strays."

"Wheeler will stay and help you finish up."

He kicked his horse into a lope and made it back home in the wag of a dog's tail. He slowed the animal to a walk the last hundred yards, cooling him. Red asked if he could remove the saddle and curry him down.

Shane shook his head in the negative. "I might make another run."

Everything in the house was in order. Edith didn't appear worried about Tessa's errand into town, and the children were distracted with a new set of animals the boys had carved. Restless, Shane crossed the threshold into Tessa's room.

As he turned to leave, Tessa's ledger caught his attention. She'd brought it out the previous evening when she'd told him about Spencer, but she'd never explained why. He hadn't realized the oversight until now.

He flipped open the cover and paused. This was personal. He shouldn't be looking. As he closed the book, the columns of neatly written lists caught his attention. This wasn't a diary; this was a list. A quick skimming revealed the truth of Tessa's ledger. An item caught his attention and he ran his finger beneath the entry on the left across to the entry on the right.

Distracted shop owner while Emmett stole a hat.

In the opposite column she had written, *Returned lost toddler to his father.*

He recalled her coin trick with the children and the way she'd easily overcome the lock at the hotel. Clearly she was atoning for past transgressions.

He flipped to the end of the entries and read the last line.

Married Shane McCoy.

The words blurred and he pinched his eyes with a thumb and forefinger.

He set down the book and left the bedroom. That was what he got for looking.

Edith frowned as he crossed the room. "Is something wrong? You look like you got bad news."

"It's nothing. When Tessa gets back, tell her I'll be busy for the rest of the evening. Someone's been cutting fence and we've got miles of barbed wire to search."

Edith harrumphed. "Cattle rustlers. It's bad enough they gotta take the cattle, but they leave work behind as well."

The children, accustomed to his comings and goings, didn't raise a fuss when he left.

Tessa had married him because he was a charity. He was nothing more than a chance at atonement. At least he finally understood why she'd married a lonely widower with two children. What a sacrifice she'd made.

What had she said all those weeks ago? *I've lived everywhere. I just want to live somewhere.*

He glanced up and realized he was standing in the barn. He sat on a bale of hay and clutched his head in his hands. What was the difference? He'd known she wasn't marrying him out of love or affection.

He liked feeling as though he'd offered safety and shelter. He didn't like thinking she only felt sorry for him. The poor, lonely widower with two children. Compensation for a lifetime of stolen hats and picked locks.

Was he any better? He'd set out as the benevolent protector. He recalled their time together, how she'd kissed him with sweet tenderness. Did she feel anything between them?

Parker came around the corner and paused. "Everything all right, boss?"

"Just thinking."

"About what?"

"Tessa."

Parker chuckled. "I have to admit, the boys and I were a mite worried when you brought home a wife. Never can tell how things are going to turn out, you know? But she's a real find. Things are different around here. In a good way. She's brought new life to the place. I've never seen the little ones so happy."

Shane steadied his hands on his knees. What did it matter why they'd come together? Parker was right. She loved those children. They were the whole reason they'd met, the whole reason the two of them were together. Charity or not, they were married. He wasn't giving up on his marriage.

As Tessa's husband, he was going to have a man-to-man with Emmett. Until Tessa's father cleared things with the Fultons, he was endangering Tessa. As her husband, Shane was putting a stop to that. Emmett was always welcome, he was her father, but not until he'd cleared up his own troubles.

If Tessa's father wasn't going to look out for her, then Shane would take on the task. He pushed off into a stand. "I'm going into town."

He'd have the talk now, with Tessa present. That way she'd understand. Then he'd ask her back home. On the return trip, he'd clear up a few things about her riding off without an escort.

The moment Shane reached town, his cousin JoBeth dashed out of the marshal's office and caught the bridle of Shane's horse.

"You'd best come inside," she said. "The marshal needs to see you."

Shane had known something wasn't right. He should have never left Tessa alone. He glanced down and realized his hands were trembling.

Chapter Eighteen

Tessa stepped into the small parlor where'd she'd spoken with Emmett before. No fire had been lit and the two chairs had been turned toward the entrance. Dead Eye Dan sat in one; Emmett occupied the other.

He caught sight of her and shot out of his chair as though he'd been sprung from a cannon. "Tessa!"

"I got your note," she said easily.

"Then why?" The anguish in his voice gave her pause. "You knew what I meant. Why do this?"

"For you." She steeled her resolve. "It's time this is finished. Everyone else has profited. Why not us?"

Dead Eye chortled. "Your daughter here is the smart one of the two, isn't she?"

Emmett hung his head. "She's here now, Dan. I've made some mistakes in my life, but you're about the worst. We might as well get this over with. Why don't you tell me what you want?"

Dead Eye smacked his lips together. "We're going to rob the bank in town."

"I told you already," Emmett said with a sigh. "The lock on the safe in town is too sophisticated for me."

"I know." Dead Eye rubbed his hands on his pant legs. "Don't worry. I took care of that clerk who messed up the job in Abilene." At Emmett's look of surprise, his grin widened. "You think I didn't know? That fellow was two-timing me with my best sporting girl. She decided they'd rob the bank and pin it on us. Didn't take me long to track her down. Went after that clerk next. Things are all wrapped up on that account—don't you worry."

Emmett shook his head. "Then why come after me? Why come after Tessa?"

"You got it all wrong, fellow. I was never after you. It was always about this little lady here."

Tessa gasped. "Me?"

"Everybody thought Emmett was the lock man. He's good, but you're the real prize, aren't you? Once I got double-crossed, I figured out the flaw in my plan. Too many folks knew ahead of time. I know all about your little talent. Emmett wasn't good for nothing but two-bit gambling after you were gone. Didn't take much to figure out who really had the talent in the family. You're getting us into that bank tonight. Then you're going to open that safe."

Nearly five years before Emmett had befriended a locksmith. Tessa had discovered she had a knack for locks, and she and the locksmith had made a sport out of challenging safe locks. She didn't know if she still had the touch or if the locking mechanisms had changed since that time.

"Tessa." Emmett lifted his pleading gaze. "You've got talent. I know you can do this."

"Yeah," Dead Eye agreed. "You can do this. Because if you don't, I'm gonna kill you."

"What happens after?" she demanded.

As though she had to ask. She'd go the way of the bank teller and the saloon girl.

"You'll get your cut. Do whatever you want after that. I'm not too worried about you turning us in, am I? Because if I go to jail, so do you. No one is going to believe that Emmett Spencer's daughter didn't go along willingly."

"You're just going to let us walk away?" Emmett gave a slight shake of his head. "That'll be the day."

Dan pressed a hand against his chest and assumed an expression of mock outrage. "I'm hurt. After all we've been through together, and you don't trust me. That cuts me to the quick."

Emmett snorted. "What's your plan?"

"It's real simple. The marshal is away, which leaves the deputy. It gets better. The deputy lives on the outskirts of town and has a whole passel of children. We could ride up and down Main Street and fire our weapons and he probably wouldn't notice. Which means the bank is ripe for the picking. This whole town is filled with idiots. We wait until after dark. Tessa here will get us inside and open the safe. After that, we split the money and go our separate ways. Nothing to it. No double crosses. Just the money."

Tessa scrambled for a stall. "I need equipment."

"What do you need?"

"A stethoscope."

Dan snapped his fingers and another man stepped from behind the curtain leading to the back rooms.

"I saw a sign for a doc in town," Dan said. "Why don't you pay him a visit? Real quiet like. We'll be needing his stethoscope."

The man turned and left without offering a reply.

"What else?" Dead Eye demanded.

"I'll need darker clothing. Even if the deputy isn't on duty, someone might see me. I'll pick up something at the mercantile."

"You think I'm an idiot? I'm not letting you out of my sight."

Tessa shrugged. It was worth a try.

"You can come along." She tossed her head. "You don't have to worry about me. I'm ready to get out of this stupid town. Robbing a bank suits me just fine. Right, Emmett?"

Emmett looked between the two and nodded. "Uh, sure. Right. We're up for the job. It's been ages since I ran a good con." He sat up straighter and caught her gaze. "Feels good to have the team back together again."

His smile didn't quite reach his eyes. There was a difference about him. A difference she understood all too well. For the first time in his life, Emmett found himself in a situation he couldn't talk himself out of. Dead Eye wasn't going to be satisfied with glib answers and false promises.

If they were going to outwit the outlaw, Emmett couldn't skate out of making the hard choices. While she'd miss his playful innocence, they all had to grow up sometime.

Dead Eye considered her with a slow nod. "Good."

Tessa exchanged a quick look with Emmett. "It's hours until midnight. As you said before, everyone in this town is stupid. I say we enjoy ourselves. Eat a good meal. Visit the mercantile. Have a little fun before we rob them blind."

She sure hoped her acting skills had improved since Shane had called her out in Wichita.

Shane. Her whole chest ached. He'd hate her once he discovered what she'd done.

How long did she have until he discovered she was missing and sent up the alarm? What happened then? As long as the Fultons believed they were safe, she and Emmett had a chance of escaping. They were dead after they robbed the bank. Dead Eye was only toying with them. Once he had what he wanted, she and Emmett were liabilities.

She'd taken a risk when she'd left. She'd known there might not be any way out. She'd taken the chance at death for a chance at a future. Tessa thought of Shane, then pictured Owen and Alyce, and blinked her eyes rapidly. After tonight, either she'd be dead or she'd be a wanted bank robber. Either way, she'd never see them again.

There was no way to get word to Shane without exposing her plan.

As long as Dead Eye and his gang thought they were merely hiding out in the town, everyone else was safe. No matter what happened, it had to stay that way. She'd take her chances with the gang if it meant keeping Shane and the children safe.

She loved Emmett but he'd known what might happen. The rest of the townspeople were unwilling participants, and she owed them their safety.

She'd take her chances for her family. They were her life. They were worth dying for.

Shane paced the marshal's office. "What do you mean relax? That outlaw has my wife. Why didn't David pick him up right off?"

"I'm sorry, Shane." Garrett shoved his forearm into Shane's chest. "It was my call. I wanted the whole gang. Once Dead Eye settled into the hotel, I knew the others weren't far behind. We have the element of surprise. As long as they think no one is watching them, they'll stay relaxed."

"Then pick them up now."

"If we go in with our guns drawn, who knows what will happen. We're still missing one. If I pick up three out of four, we're asking for trouble. The last one will come back for the others."

Shane punched his palm with his opposite fist. "So you're just going to sit here and do nothing?"

"No. I've got half the town watching out for them. We have to wait until the right moment. We've got bad guys and civilians having dinner together in the hotel. Your wife is right in the middle of that hornet's nest. This isn't the best time to stir things up. We need to separate the Fultons before we make our move."

"I'll stir things up."

Why had he decided to ignore his instincts this time? He'd known Tessa's father was trouble no matter how many times she'd claimed he was harmless.

"Listen, those boys think we're idiots. They're holed

up in that hotel as big as you please. They're not even trying to hide. They think we're all a bunch of yokels. As long as we let them believe no one is watching, they'll keep their guard down. That's how we want them. Relaxed."

A door slammed and David burst into the office from the back. "I waited like you said and I heard everything."

The marshal grinned and slapped Shane on the back. "Just what I was waiting for. It's good having a deputy who grew up in town. He knows all the hiding places."

David brushed a coating of dust from his hair. "There's a grate over the parlor that vents into the room above. My brothers and I used to eavesdrop on the adults when we were supposed to be in bed. Mr. Edwards moved a dresser over the spot when he bought the hotel. Didn't take much to move it out of the way again. Mrs. Edwards has been watching their every move. She picked up a few things as well. She says they're a bunch of slobs with bad table manners."

"I don't exactly care if they used the right fork," the marshal urged. "What did you hear?"

The deputy relayed the plan and the marshal's expression turned grim. "What do you think, Shane?"

"If she robs the safe, there's a good chance they'll send her into the bank alone. We can rescue her then."

"They wanted her all along. I did some asking around. Your wife has quite the reputation as a locksmith. How well do you know her? Can she manage?"

"She'll keep her cool. She's smart. She's got courage." Shane recalled her trick with the coin and the way she'd picked the lock at the hotel. "It's Tessa they wanted. Emmett was the trap. It was always Tessa."

How long had she known they were coming for her? Why hadn't she trusted him?

"Then let's put our own person in the bank. We'll catch them in the act."

David nodded. "Sounds like a plan."

They all had it tied up in a bow, but Shane wasn't playing. "I don't like it. There are too many unknowns. What if they don't send her in alone? They won't let her leave alone, that's for certain. They'll have a plan to get rid of both her and Emmett."

"I'll keep an eye on her," David said. "Mrs. Edwards has the whole staff on duty. They can't sneeze without someone taking note. Those boys think they're invisible. They don't see us as a threat. That gives us the advantage. They're not going to do anything to risk their plan for tonight."

"On one condition." The only person he trusted to keep an eye on Tessa was himself. "Let's get word to her."

"She may not want your help. There's a chance she's right where she wants to be. You know what David heard."

"Not a chance."

"I had to ask. You know her best."

He did know her. There wasn't any doubt in his mind. She was doing her best to keep them all safe. Emmett's arrival had forced her into a Solomon Judgment. Since she couldn't save everyone, she was going to sacrifice herself.

He wasn't going to let her make that sacrifice. "I have an idea."

The marshal reached for his gun belt. "Don't get me wrong—I need your help. Just remember, the last time we had a showdown in town, my wife shot me. Here's hoping things go better for you."

"I'll take the risk."

"I had a feeling you'd say that. Now let's hear this plan of yours. Just keep in mind my wife's family will never forgive me if something happens to either one of you."

The three men made a plan and split up. The marshal was tasked with setting up his part at the bank, David returned to the hotel and resumed his position, and Shane made his way to the mercantile. According to David, Tessa had made arrangements with the outlaws to buy some darker clothing for the evening's escapades.

Not knowing how long he'd have to wait before her arrival, Shane approached the counter and studied the display beneath the glass. Never one to pass up an opportunity for a sale, Mrs. Stuart sauntered over and followed his gaze.

"Hello, Mr. McCoy. What brings you in today? A little something for the missus?"

"Just looking." A glint of silver nestled in a black velvet pillow snagged his attention. "I'll come back later."

She caught the direction of his gaze and lifted a key from the dangling ring at her waist and unlocked the case, then slid out the velvet-lined box. "We've a fine selection of wedding rings, but you put the cart before the horse again this time, didn't you?"

She flashed a sly wink.

She'd always been his biggest critic. Then again, she was everyone's critic. At least he was in good company.

The overhead bell indicated the arrival of a customer. Shane glanced around and caught sight of Tessa's pale face, the outlaw clutching her elbow. His good intentions fled and he took an involuntary step toward her. He halted when he caught a flash of the gun barrel strapped against the outlaw's thigh.

This wasn't the time for playing the hero. Not yet, anyway.

Gritting his teeth, he resumed his task. "Mrs. Stuart, I'll give you the biggest piece of gossip Cimarron Springs has ever heard, but you have to do one thing for me."

Her eyes widened. "I don't gossip."

"Of course not."

"What would you like me to do?"

"For the next ten minutes, act as though you don't know me."

Emotions flitted across her face. She was curious, yet uncertain. Her innate nosiness finally won out. "You better not be fooling me."

"No fooling. You'll have the best story at the quilting bee this Wednesday."

"Then would you like to see a ring, Mr.—?" She flourished her hand with a broad wink.

Shane glanced over his shoulder. The outlaw and Tessa were studying the ready-made clothes near the back of the store.

"Wait." He held up his index finger. "Hand me that whiskey bottle."

Her expression skeptical, Mrs. Stuart reluctantly

reached behind her and retrieved a bottle. After accepting the whiskey, Shane unscrewed the cap and splashed the liquid over his shirt.

"I don't care how good of a story I get out of this stunt." Mrs. Stuart scowled. "That's going on your tab."

"I know." He held his index finger over his lips and hushed her. "Remember what I said."

She jerked her head in a curt nod. "This better beat the time Mabel saw JoBeth shoot her husband."

"Nothing can beat that."

Yanking his hat low over his eyes, he stumbled through the store. As he made his way toward Tessa and the outlaw, he bumped every display he passed, making a point of creating a commotion. Dishes rattled and cans trembled.

As he neared Tessa, he swayed on his feet and knocked into her shoulder. She dropped the shirtwaist she held with a yelp. Her eyes widened in recognition.

He swayed on his feet and grasped her shoulders, as though steadying himself. "Hey there, little mishy," he slurred. "You're jusht the lady I need."

She waved her hand before her face. "I don't think so. Go away, you drunken oaf."

He teetered back then rocked forward. "Aw, please. Jusht for a minute."

She kept her grip on his upper arms, her eyes imploring him to leave.

The outlaw slammed an arm against his chest. "She's with me, mister."

Shane stared into the man's eyes and realized he'd come face-to-face with Dead Eye Dan. One of his eyes was focused sharply on Shane's face; the other was slightly askew.

Shane lifted his hand, his finger waving unsteadily in the air. Then he pressed his index finger against the man's forehead. "You gotta funny eye, mishter."

Dead Eye growled and snatched Shane's lapels.

Tessa threw herself between them and caught Dead Eye's gaze. "Why don't we humor the man? He's obviously drunk. If he causes a brawl, the proprietor will summon the law. We'd hate for anyone to get in trouble, wouldn't we?"

Dead Eye hesitated, then threw Shane off with a hard shove. "What do you want, fool?"

"Rings." Shane snatched Tessa's hand and dragged her toward the counter, the outlaw close behind. Her feet slipped and he instinctively wrapped an arm around her waist and steadied her. She caught his gaze, her eyes wild and frightened. Though she gave a slight shake of her head, she didn't push his hand away.

Upon reaching his destination, he rested his hip against the glass case and made a show of leaning heavily against the counter. He raised her hand until her fingers were an inch away from his eyes. A pulse beat wildly in the base of her neck. If he knew Tessa, she was more worried about his safety than her own.

"Your fingers are about the size of my wif-wif-wife's. Which ring would you like? You know, if you were my wif-wife?"

Tessa strained away. "If this is your usual state, then I would buy her something extremely expensive as an apology."

He studied the case. After making a selection, he slid a gold circle around her ring finger. "Too big."

He yanked off the ring and tossed the circle onto the counter. "There's gotta be something pretty in all this junk."

"Well, I never!" As he pawed through the other selections, Mrs. Stuart glared. "Those are valuable. Do be careful."

He found another ring featuring braided filigree. "Don't you worry about my wife, little missy. She's got the whole town looking after her. The marshal and everything." He slid the ring onto Tessa's finger. "Someone is always watching out for her."

"They shouldn't." Her voice broke. "You should just go home."

"Not until I'm finished." He lurched forward and spoke near her ear. "I'll be near."

He splayed his fingers, giving her a glimpse of the paper in his palm. Her expression flickered.

She shook her head, waving him off, but he wasn't giving her a choice. He slid his hand closer.

Tessa met his unyielding gaze, her eyes registering her reluctant acquiescence. Tears glistened on her lashes. "Your wife sounds like a very fortunate woman."

"I don't care about her past. I only care about her future."

Dead Eye guffawed. "Who'd wanna come home to this drunk?"

Shane stumbled, shielding his hands from the outlaw, and slid the note into her opposite palm. With a deft flick of her wrist, the paper disappeared up her sleeve.

Distracted by the display of liquor bottles, Dead Eye engaged Mrs. Stuart in a haggle over the prices.

Shane lifted Tessa's hand once more. Her fingers were chilled and he chafed them gently.

He should have bought her a ring weeks ago. Her fingers trembled as he slid the gold circle over her knuckles. He rubbed the delicate feathering of veins along her wrist.

Fearful of attracting the attention of the outlaw, he released her. "There, this one fits perfect."

Holding her arm aloft, Tessa admired the ring. "Your wife will like this very much."

"I'll be waiting for her tonight. She'll know where. She's gonna be so happy to see me, she might even give me a kiss."

Tessa smiled a touch sadly. "I bet she will."

Dead Eye shoved him away. "All right already. That's enough. Move along, you old drunk. You've had your fun."

The outlaw caught Tessa around the upper arm and dragged her toward the clothing once more. She glanced over her shoulder and he fisted his hands. He took a step and someone gripped his upper arm. Whipping around, he nearly socked David before he recognized the deputy.

"Everything is going according to plan," David said. "Don't get riled."

"How would you feel if that was your wife?"

"Just like you do. Nothing is going to go wrong."

"It better not."

Shane understood the marshal's reasons for leaving Tessa with the outlaw, but Dead Eye was going to pay for his rough treatment of her. He'd never have agreed except they had Emmett as well. There was no way she was leaving her father alone. If the outlaws wanted Emmett's cooperation, they couldn't harm Tessa. If they wanted Tessa's cooperation, they couldn't harm Emmett. Either way, they had to bide their time.

Mrs. Stuart grunted. "All right, I did my part. You owe me for the whiskey and the ring. She was still wearing it when she left."

Shane smiled grimly. "I know."

She belonged to him, and she'd wear his ring. Now and forever.

Chapter Nineteen

Emmett paced the locked room while Tessa stared at the ring on her finger. He knew. Shane knew. The marshal knew. They were all watching out for her.

Muttering beneath his breath, Emmett yanked on the window, but it held firm. One of the Fultons had nailed it shut. "As soon as we're out in the open, I want you to run. I'll distract the rest of the gang."

She motioned him over and spoke near his ear. "The marshal knows the plan. He'll be waiting for us in the bank."

Emmett blinked. "How does he know?"

"He just does. I'm fairly certain everyone in town is in on the plan."

"You're joshing me?"

"I'm not."

The door flew open and Dead Eye's brother Randall stood on the threshold. "As long as you two don't give us any trouble, we're eating in the dining room."

Tessa raised her eyebrows. "Very civilized."

"Well, we're all just a bunch of friends here, aren't

we? Wouldn't want these folks getting suspicious or anything." He glared. "Just remember, one wrong move, and I put a hole in your daughter. Got that, Mr. Spencer?"

Tessa smirked. They weren't all that concerned about her getting away. Excellent.

Emmett waved his arms with a flourish and she preceded him through the door. They made their way to the dining room and Tessa paused.

Over half of the tables were filled, and she immediately recognized most of the patrons. The entire dining room was filled with McCoys. She spotted Edith and Eli McCoy sitting with Jo and another boy she didn't recognize.

Cheerful lengths of evergreen looped from the arches, and a sprig of holly dangled from the center.

The Reverend Miller occupied a table with a younger, dark-haired man. She didn't see the marshal, Garrett, but she figured he wasn't far away considering all the others. As she searched the room, her gaze landed on a very familiar hat.

Shane sat alone.

Her heart swelled. He wasn't letting her out of his sight. None of them were. Even though she was surrounded by outlaws and preparing to rob a bank, she'd never felt safer.

She took her seat and Randall and Dead Eye sat opposite her and Emmett. Mrs. Edwards took their order and Tessa complimented her on her bright yellow crocheted collar.

"Thank you." Mrs. Edwards touched the edge. "I

sell all sorts of pieces over at the mercantile. Hats and scarves and mittens. For gentlemen, too," she added.

Emmett flashed his most charming grin. "If they're as pretty as you are, I just might take a look."

Mrs. Edwards giggled.

Randall glowered. "Shut it. We're here to eat."

"How rude." Mrs. Edwards huffed, then turned and flounced toward the kitchen.

The conversation ground to a halt after that. When Mrs. Edwards finally returned, Tessa reached for a plate, but the proprietress held the meal out of reach.

She set it before Randall with more force than necessary. "Enjoy your meal, sir."

The second dish she slid gently before Tessa. "This one is yours, ma'am," Mrs. Edwards said with wink.

Tessa suppressed a grin. She didn't know what Mrs. Edwards had done to Randall's food, and she didn't want to find out.

The rest of the meal passed in silence and they returned to their room once more.

Randall peered in. "We leave at midnight. Be ready."

The door shut and the key turned.

Tessa snorted. "Bold as brass, aren't they? Eating in the dining room, staying at the hotel. Where do you suppose the other two are hiding? There's four of them, aren't there?"

"They're doing this on purpose," Emmett declared with a huff. "Don't you see? They want us to be seen with them. One way or another, they're going to pin that bank robbery on you and me. We'll be hanging from a tree before the weekend, mark my words."

Tessa pictured all the familiar faces in the dining room. "I told you, we're fine."

"We'll see," Emmett muttered.

With nothing else to occupy the time, she rested on top of the duvet, dozing off and on. Despite her precarious situation, she sensed Shane was near.

Emmett shook her awake a few hours later. She stretched and yawned, then stumbled behind the screen and changed into her dark clothing.

Once they'd unlocked the door, she stepped into the corridor and met with Randall and Dead Eye. Dead Eye took her by the arm and Randall planted his hand in the center of Emmett's chest.

"You're staying," Randall declared.

"No!" Tessa spun around. "I need his, uh, I need his help."

"Nope." Randall muffled Emmett's protests with a gag. He unfurled a rope and secured Emmett's hands, then shoved him onto a chair. "Your pa is our insurance. Just in case you get any ideas."

Tessa's heart wrenched. "I'm not leaving him."

With languid ease, Randall took his gun from his holster, cocked the trigger and aimed the barrel at Emmett's temple. "Go. Or I kill him."

"I'm going."

He didn't have to tell her twice.

Tessa scurried after Dead Eye. She crept through the corridor and slid into the chilled evening air. Keeping a sharp eye on her, Dead Eye led her behind the row of buildings. Everything was silent. Not even a whisper of wind stirred the air. A sliver of moon illuminated the remaining snow and lent enough light to traverse the streets.

They reached the bank's service entrance and Dead Eye scouted the perimeter. "All's clear."

Tessa removed her hairpin and carefully worked the lock. Her fingers grew stiff with the cold. Beside her, Dead Eye fidgeted and held his hands to his nose, puffing cold air onto his fingers.

Tessa smirked. "Maybe you should have gotten some of Mrs. Edwards's mittens."

"Shut up." He smacked the side of her head. "Stop dawdling."

Tessa worked the lock, breathing a sigh of relief when the mechanism sprang free. "It's open."

She turned the knob and stepped inside. The outlaw shut the door behind him. "Dumbest town I ever seen."

Once inside, she approached the cage surrounding the teller area leading to the back where the safe was kept. She quickly worked the much easier lock and swung open the barred door.

She cast a furtive glance over her shoulder, searching for the marshal. Once they reached the vault, Dan slid his hand into his coat and revealed a stethoscope.

She wiped her damp palms against her dark skirts. Where was the law? Had something happened? She was certain she'd read Shane's clues correctly. His note had said only that he'd be here.

With no other option, she knelt and donned the earpieces, then pressed the diaphragm against the cold metal. She spun the combination dial right and left, listening for the telltale click.

Dan shoved her shoulder. "Hurry up."

She brushed him aside. "Be quiet. This takes time."

Despite the cold air, a fine bead of sweat formed on her brow. She got the first number, then the second. Her brow knit in concentration, she heard the third number spring free. Holding her breath, she reached for the handle.

Dan leaned close, his hot breath stirring the hair on her neck.

Tessa twisted the handle.

The outlaw shrieked. Someone slammed against her. Though it was dark, she caught Shane's distinctive scent. He urged her behind the safe and shielded her with his body. The scuffle continued behind them.

"We got him," Garrett called. "It's safe."

Shane stood and lifted her upright. He sheltered her against his side and led her into the lobby, then lowered her onto a chair and knelt before her. "Are you all right?"

"Emmett. They've got Emmett."

"Don't worry. They won't get out of the hotel. The boys have the place surrounded."

Another man approached with a lantern. He held the light near her face. "I'm Caleb McCoy, ma'am. That's a nasty bruise on the side of your face."

She unconsciously touched the mark.

Shane made a sound like a growl. "Did Dead Eye do that?"

She smoothed her fingers across his forehead. "It doesn't hurt, I promise."

"Tessa, I—"

She pressed two fingers against his lips, preventing

his answer. "No words. Before you read me the riot act, I need to know Emmett is safe."

The marshal stepped into the lobby, Dead Eye handcuffed beside him.

The next few moments passed in a blur. Dead Eye shoved against the marshal. Garrett lost his grip. Shane straightened. His arm swung around and his fist made contact with the man's jaw. A sickening crack sounded. Dead Eye crumpled.

Shane leaned over his prone body. "That's for hitting my wife."

As Tessa gaped, absorbing the sudden violence, Shane knelt before her once more and smoothed the hair away from her face.

Behind him, Garrett chuckled. "Well, Shane, you made my work a little harder. How am I supposed to get him back to the jail?"

Shane clasped her hands and drew her to her feet. "That's your problem."

They stepped outside and Tessa started toward the hotel, but Shane held her back. "I'm not letting you out of my sight until we know it's safe. A man can only handle so much."

Main Street was lit up and crowded with people. Tessa stared. "Where did they all come from?"

"Word spread fast that we had a gang of bank robbers in town."

Someone broke through the crowd and dashed toward them. Emmett held out his hands. "Tessa!"

He caught her in his embrace and her insides melted.

After crushing her against him, he held her at arm's length. "You'll never guess what happened. Randall took one step out the door and Mrs. Edwards beaned him with a frying pan. Caught him right across the temple. He's out cold. I don't envy Mr. Edwards."

"Mrs. Edwards is a widow."

Emmett scratched his temple. "You don't say."

Main Street had taken on the feel of a winter fete. People milled around and an enterprising worker from the restaurant had set up a table where he was peddling hot coffee. The two outlaws captured near the livery were delivered to the deputy holding Randall. Garrett and Dead Eye came around and joined the group. All four outlaws were paraded down Main Street with much applause for the lawmen leading them away.

Navigating the festivities, Shane led her back to the hotel. As they wove their way through the crowds of people lining the boardwalk, Mrs. Stuart appeared from the mercantile.

"You owe me, Shane McCoy," she declared.

Tessa looked between the two.

Mrs. Stuart shrugged. "Never mind. Bring your little ones around soon. I've got some peppermint candy for them."

Shane's eyes widened. "Will do."

Tessa tugged on her ring. "I almost forgot. You'll be wanting this back, Mrs. Stuart."

Shaking her head, Mrs. Stuart grinned. "Oh no. That's all yours. Bought and paid for. Your husband has good taste, Mrs. McCoy."

"You'd best call me Tessa. There's too many Mrs. McCoys around here."

"Ain't that the truth?" She laughed. "Ain't that the truth."

They arrived back at the hotel where Doc Johnsen had been roused. He inspected her bruise and prescribed a compress of raw meat, which Tessa politely declined.

As he turned to leave, she called out, "I've got your stethoscope."

He rubbed the back of his neck. "I wondered why someone broke a window for that. Why do a bunch of outlaws need doctor's equipment?"

"To crack a safe."

"I had no idea." The doc shrugged. "All's well that ends well, I guess. Try and stay out of trouble, Mrs. McCoy. I don't think your husband's nerves can stand another incident."

Left alone with Shane, Tessa grew shy. "Thank you for looking out for me."

His expression was stern. "The doc is right. You're gonna be the death of me. Promise you'll never put yourself in danger like that again." He heaved one of his great, gusty sighs, and this time she didn't even mind.

Shane grasped her hand. "Why did you marry me?"

The marshal had urged honesty in the marriage, and it was high time she found her courage. "I noticed two things about you that day in Wichita. The second thing was how much your children loved you and how much you loved them. I knew right then I wanted to be a part of that love."

"What was the first thing you noticed?"

"I noticed how handsome you were. Alyce had mussed your jacket, your trouser leg was caught on your boot and your hat was set at an odd angle. I'd never seen a finer-looking gentleman in all my life. So there you have it, Shane. I married you for your striking good looks. Now you know the truth."

"And because you felt sorry for me. I saw your book, Tessa."

Her stomach dipped. "Then you know everything?"

"Yes."

She ducked her head. "I had this idea that if I made up for all the things I'd done, I'd be worthy of love from someone like you. But it doesn't work that way, does it? Now the whole town knows I can pick a lock and open a safe."

"That's where you're wrong. I love you. I love everything about you. Your past, your present and your future."

Her whole world burst into color. "Truly?"

"Truly." He squeezed her hands. "The hardest thing a person can do is change. You're the bravest person I know, Tessa."

"I love you." Her voice caught and she tugged her hands free. "I love you, but I was afraid to tell you. I was afraid if you knew who I was and what I'd done, you'd hate me."

He reached for her but she strained away. "I endangered your life and the life of the children."

"You walked right into a trap for us." His eyes shimmered with emotion. "If that's not love, I don't know what is."

"I had to do something. As long as Emmett owed the Fultons, they'd never let us live in peace."

"You put your life in danger for us. For Emmett. Even though you knew you'd expose your secret?"

"Yes."

"That sounds like a very honorable thing to do. I love you, Tessa, and I don't love dishonorable people."

"But the children," she implored. "Who wants a former outlaw for a mother?"

"Outlaws make the best parents. You'll always know what they're up to. They'll be the most popular kids at school."

"And your family? What about the McCoys?"

"Did you see that restaurant this evening? Once word spread about what was happening, the whole town turned out."

"For you," she said.

"For us."

Someone knocked on the door frame and Jo peered around. "Now that the excitement is over, I thought you might want a little company. Edith has had her hands full with these two. They must have sensed something was wrong, because they wouldn't go to sleep."

Alyce and Owen toddled into the room in their pajamas. Tessa knelt on the floor and gathered them close, kissing each one in turn. She glanced up and caught sight of Emmett.

Tessa waved him forward. "Come and meet your grandchildren."

For the second time in her whole life, she caught the sheen of tears in Emmett's eyes. "And who is this little princess." He crooked his finger toward Alyce, who grinned in return. "Why, you're as pretty as a new penny."

"Aw-ice," she replied.

"Alyce," Shane corrected her.

Owen toddled nearer Tessa, who knelt by his side and smoothed his hair. "This is Owen."

Emmett stared at the boy, his expression faltering. He stooped and tilted his head, then scratched behind his ear. "Hello there, little Owen. You are the spitting image of a fellow I knew some years back."

"Don't be silly," Tessa scoffed. "He's a child."

Emmett tugged on his ear. "Oh, well. You're probably right. It's the coloring and the name. The other fellow's name was Owen, too, and he had the same eyes. That blond hair really stands out. You're nothing like that rascal, are you, little fellow? That other Owen was a real outlaw. Got himself hanged a couple years back." Emmett caught himself and grew solemn, crossing one arm across his chest. "Sorry. That's not fit talk around the children."

Shane had stilled, his expression frozen.

Emmett rubbed his chin. "Strangest outlaw I ever saw. He lost his trigger finger in an accident. Had to learn to shoot left-handed. He was never very good after that. Probably how he got himself caught."

Tessa gripped Shane's arm. He'd gone ashen.

There was little chance Emmett's observations were a coincidence. "I'm so sorry."

Shane sat back on his heels. Everything fell into place. Abby had always loved danger. She'd run off and disappeared. She'd never revealed the identity of the children's father. The one photo he had of her, the one he'd saved for the children, she'd cut out the man standing beside her.

The hand resting on the arm of the chair had been distinctive...

Tessa touched his shoulder. "If Abby had wanted them to know, she'd have given you the information. She had every opportunity."

"I think in the end she was trying to protect me."

"We'll never know for certain if he really was their father."

"No. Everyone who knew the truth is gone."

"It's strange, isn't it?" Tessa tilted her head. "How everything came together for us? What are the chances of us meeting on that platform?"

"What are you saying?"

"Maybe God was looking out for you all along." Tessa cupped his cheeks. "For you, for the children. Even for me."

"I'd like to think that," he replied.

Of all the people in Wichita, Owen had approached Tessa. What were the chances?

"Abby chose you," Tessa said. "You're their father in every way that counts."

"And you're their mother."

"No." She pressed a kiss against his cheek. "I'm their stepmother. Abby will always be their mother. She loved them. She did her best. I'll do my best as well."

"She was more troubled than I knew."

"She's at peace now. What about you, Shane? Are you at peace?"

He captured her lips and kissed her until she was breathless and sagging in his arms. "I'm moving back to the main house."

"You better. You know I don't like to be alone at night."

He nuzzled the sensitive skin at the nape of her neck. "Then I'll have to make sure you always have company."

Owen pushed his way between them and held up his arms. "Up. Up."

Tessa giggled. "I think someone is jealous."

Shane rolled his eyes. "I told myself I'd stay away from you until Christmas. I promised myself I'd give you the space to get used to me. To see if you liked me."

Tessa made a strangled sound in her throat. "I gave myself until Christmas to convince you that we suited. It's a wonder we had such trouble. We were working at cross-purposes."

"No more." He folded her in his embrace once again. "You're my wife."

"And you're my husband. You're the only man for me." Tessa drew the children in and they all hugged. "And we're a family."

Unheeding of who heard, Shane let out a whoop. He was finally the right man.

Epilogue

The top of the fir tree appeared in the door first. With much muttering and shuffling of feet, the rest of the enormous tree emerged into the ranch house. Emmett held the front and Shane anchored his arms around the cut trunk.

Tessa gasped. "I hadn't expected anything quite this, um, large."

Shane grimaced beneath the heavy weight. "An ice jam upstream changed the course of the creek. The roots were already rotted. Figured I might as well take something that was going to die anyway."

"All right." She waved him inside. "But I have no idea where you're going to put that thing."

The two men wrested the tree into place and adjusted the base around a device Wheeler and Finch had designed.

Tessa grinned at Emmett. "I was at the ladies' salon yesterday and Mrs. Edwards was asking about you."

His cheeks pinkened. "Probably wondering about the sale of the hotel."

The reward money for capturing the outlaws had been spread all over town. Tessa and Shane had refused their portion. Emmett had approached Mrs. Edwards about buying the hotel with his cut. Since her husband's passing, managing the restaurant and the hotel while keeping up with her knitting had proved too difficult.

Tessa studied her father's blush. "I heard her telling JoBeth that the new owner of the hotel was quite handsome."

Her father puffed up. "She did, did she?"

Emmett was still Emmett. The disaster with the Fultons had changed him, but she didn't know if the change was permanent. He was here now, and Tessa was going to enjoy his company and pray for the best.

"She did."

Shane caught her around the waist. "It's not a bad place to start. Tessa married me for my good looks."

"It's true," she replied. "That and some other stuff as well."

"Other stuff," he repeated with a grin.

While Tessa and Shane strung loops of berries and popcorn around the tree, Emmett sat on the floor and played with the children. He was even better with a coin than Tessa, and Alyce and Owen were delighted.

Since she'd been feeling more exhausted than usual lately, Tessa joined them. Owen toddled over and grasped the locket around Tessa's neck. She released the clasp and revealed the two tiny oval pictures.

She pointed at each one in turn. "That's my mama, and that's my dada."

Owen reverently touched each of the pictures. He

pointed to Shane and said, "Dada." Without hesitating, he pointed to Tessa and said, "Mama."

The confusion was natural. She started to protest but Shane interrupted her reply. "Yes, Owen. Mama and Dada."

Touching Shane's cheek, Tessa smiled tenderly. "Abby is always with us."

Shane covered her hand with his. "Yes. Always."

Owen held out his chubby hand. "Ball."

Tessa glanced upward. "Thank You."

She didn't know why they'd been brought together all those months ago, but she was eternally grateful.

She stood and strung another length of popcorn around the tree. "This is the first tree I've ever deco-rated. I'm glad it's such a fine one."

Shane knelt at her feet.

Tessa laughed. "What are you doing?"

He took her hand, his gaze solemn. "Tessa Spencer McCoy, I have officially asked your father for your hand in marriage."

Emmett glanced up and winked. "He did."

Shane beamed. "Emmett Spencer has enthusiasti-cally agreed to my suit."

Her father grunted. "I don't know if *enthusiastic* is the word I'd use."

"With Emmett's *enthusiastic* permission," Shane continued, "I officially ask for your hand in marriage. To love and to honor, to laugh with, to cry with, to hold and to cherish. I promise that I will always build forts with you and help you hide from our children."

Her eyes misted. "We're already married."

His expression grew serious. "Someone once asked

me what made me happy. I didn't have an answer. Now I know. You make me happy. I love your sharp wit, your ability to cook potatoes in the German style and your eccentric family."

Emmett grunted again.

Shane's throat worked. "I love that you brought joy into our house and peace into my soul."

Tessa knelt before him and cupped his face. "Merry Christmas, my darling. I love you more than Owen loves his ball."

"Merry Christmas."

She indicated the snow falling gently beyond the window. "If this weather keeps up, we may be snowed in after Emmett leaves."

Shane dropped a kiss on her forehead. "The weather has always been good to me where you're concerned."

In deference to the falling snow, Emmett left an hour later. The twins were exhausted from all the attention and collapsed into slumber soon after.

Shane took a chair before the Christmas tree. Tessa perched on his knee and gazed out the window.

He rested a hand on her hip. "Are you hungry? Thirsty? There's some spiced cider left."

Tessa wrinkled her nose. "No, thank you."

His grip tightened on her waist. "Are you feeling all right?" His voice vibrated with concern. "You didn't eat much dinner."

"My stomach has been bothering me lately."

Shane grew still. "Should we call Doc Johnsen?"

Tessa shook her head. "No. I feel fine otherwise. Just a little tired. And my stomach usually only bothers me in the morning."

Their gazes locked.

Shane's expression filled with wonder. "Do you think?"

"It's too soon." Tessa touched her stomach. "Far too soon."

Shane smiled. "I guess we'll know in the fall."

Filled with wonder and hope for the future, she leaned back and tucked her head into the crook of his neck. "Wouldn't that be wonderful?"

"Yes." Shane pressed his lips against her temple. "You know what would be even better?"

Tessa frowned. "No."

"Another set of twins."

She groaned. "Be careful what you hope for, Shane McCoy."

He kissed her then, long and sweet. "I hope we're snowed in for a week."

"Merry Christmas, my love," Tessa whispered.

"Merry Christmas, my love," he replied quietly.

Outside the window, moonlight sparked off the snow, and one star twinkled brighter than all the rest.

* * * * *